SOLD
WARWICKSHIRE
COUNTY LIBRARY.

THE SNOW BEES

by the same author

NOBLE LORD
(published under the name Peter Lauder)

ALL RISKS MORTALITY

THE SNOW BEES

•

Peter Cunningham

MICHAEL JOSEPH
LONDON

MICHAEL JOSEPH LTD
Published by the Penguin Group
27 Wrights Lane, London W8 5TZ, England
Viking Penguin Inc., 40 West 23rd Street, New York, New York 10010, USA
Penguin Books Australia Ltd, Ringwood, Victoria, Australia
Penguin Books Canada Ltd, 2801 John Street, Markham, Ontario, Canada L3R 1B4
Penguin Books (NZ) Ltd, 182–190 Wairau Road, Auckland 10, New Zealand

Penguin Books Ltd, Registered Offices: Harmondsworth, Middlesex, England

First published in Great Britain 1988
Reprinted before publication

Copyright © Peter Cunningham 1988

All rights reserved. Without limiting the rights under copyright reserved
above, no part of this publication may be reproduced, stored
in or introduced into a retrieval system, or transmitted, in any form
or by any means (electronic, mechanical, photocopying,
recording or otherwise), without the prior written permission of both
the copyright owner and the above publisher of this book

Typeset in 11/13pt Baskerville by Cambrian Typesetters, Frimley, Surrey
Printed and bound in Great Britain by
Butler & Tanner Ltd, Frome and London

ISBN 0 7181 2931 8

The epigraph quote is from *Station Island* by Seamus Heaney,
reproduced by kind permission of Faber and Faber Ltd.

For
Peter Frederick,
William Stephenson
and
Benjamin Lauder

'And there I was incredible to myself, among people far too eager to believe me and my story, even if it happened to be true.'

Seamus Heaney
Sweeney Redivivus

PROLOGUE

The dark-haired man stood in the arrivals building, not seeing anything, not hearing the bedlam around him. The dead body lay before him, face down. Beside it the baggage carousels went around and around.

'We found this on him,' the smaller man said. 'Mean anything to you?'

He took the papers. They were tattered, clipped together. There were pages from a copybook, written in a sloping, childlike hand and, alternately, faded yellowing newspaper cuttings.

He read the first handwritten page.

Who says that we forgot?

There is no forgetting. Through this wall of ice, the shadow goes on towards the distance, without the flame of passion, I know, but still distinct, in focus, unmistakable.

There is a war, but it has hardly touched Guernica. Except for the dead brought home that we bury and the shortage of food, the war is a far-off thing.

It is market day in Guernica. I am in bed with a *fiebre*. Papa and Mama are downstairs with my baby sister; I can hear their voices. This minute, if I listen hard, I can hear them.

I get out of bed to go to the window and see the faces of the men in the street below; interesting, different faces from the outlying areas, some who have come from as far as the coast. I can see the beauty of the evening, the clear sky; I can smell the pine woods outside Guernica, their scent rich after the earlier rain.

Then I stare, straight up into the sky. I can see the dark shape, swelling with every second. I can see it. Then I can hear it. Turning, I begin to shout for Papa.

He turned the page. He fingered the old newspaper, almost brittle.

At 4.30 p.m. on Monday 26 April 1937, a single Heinkel 111 bomber from the German Condor Legion stationed in Burgos flew over the Spanish Basque town of Guernica and discharged half a dozen shrapnel bombs.

On the next page the writing resumed.

One moment I feel the timber of the stairs beneath my feet, the next I am standing, looking out into the dust-filled sky through the gable wall that is no longer there. There are cries, moans, the coughing of people and beasts. Above these, suddenly, there is the sound of the church bell. I cannot see the evening sun through the dust cloud. My way is blocked by rubble.

The church bell has stopped.

A voice calls: 'Marcellino! Marcellino!'

I cry: 'Papa!'

Then there is another voice: '¡A los refugios!' it shouts, 'to the shelters!'

Then Papa is beside me. 'Marcellino.' He kisses me. He looks at me, smiling that I haven't a scrape. He holds me and we approach the edge, hanging over the street.

'¡A los refugios!'

I can see now whose voice it is. The priest is standing there, looking up. Papa hands me down.

'They will be back!' the *padre* is saying.

I cannot speak. I am staring. I am staring at a woman. I am staring at my mother, her back to me, on her knees, tearing with her hands at the mound of rubble that was our house. Her breath comes so quick.

'Take the child,' says my father quietly to the priest.

Then he drops down beside Mama.

'Come, child.'

I am led. I walk, led by the hand, walking backwards. Briefly, from his kneeling position Papa looks back at me, but then he turns to resume his clawing.

Suddenly there is the droning of minutes ago, except tenfold.

'Run!' screams the priest.

At 4.45 p.m. a squadron of twelve Heinkel 111 bombers flew over Guernica, dropping bombs. At 5.05 p.m. the Luftwaffe's Heinkel 51 fighter squadron out of Vitoria flew over the town using machine-guns and grenades.

We are running. The cellar we hid in was collapsing, the dust choking, so we scrambled out. Now we are running out of Guernica. It is like going from night into day. All around, in the open fields, clear of the killing smoke and dust, people are on their knees, drinking in the clear air like water. I see men choking, men and women running, nuns, animals, children from the hospital, their bedclothes wrapped around them.

We are in open ground. There is a new sound in the air, higher pitched. The *padre* throws himself headlong, bringing me with him. There is a rattling sound, then dull thumps. Looking up I can clearly see the faces of the pilots.

'Get down!'

I look to see who the priest shouts at. It is Dionisio, the church sexton, attempting to run on for the trees.

'Dionisio!'

It's not real. It can't happen. A man, a person, a human being like you or me can't burst open, disintegrate.

The overhead engines recede.

'The woods, *Padre*,' I say, standing up.

The final newspaper cutting was almost worn away.

Beginning at 5.15 p.m. and continuing in twenty-minute relays for two and a half hours, three squadrons of Junkers 52 bombers out of Burgos carpet-bombed Guernica. Their loads were made up of small and medium bombs, as well as 500kg bombs, anti-personnel twenty pounders, and incendiaries.

The final, torn page swam before his eyes.

There is no forgetting.

We are in the trees, looking back at Guernica, into which bright glinting tubes are falling like snow. I am wearing the priest's coat, sitting on a tree stump, building a mound of pine cones. I see him stare out, his face suddenly afraid. I follow his gaze. Out of the smoke charges a crazed form, bucking, crashing from side to side, its mouth soundlessly open, its body blazing with thermite and white phosphorous. It is a cow. It runs straight at us, then, ten metres short, plunges to the ground, still ablaze.

Can heat make ice?

In my core that creature's end made something cold as death.

'Is it the devil who has done this to us, *Padre*?'

His arm goes around me.

'No, Marcellino. This was done to us by men.'

PART ONE
The Bordeaux Job

CHAPTER ONE

'Hit him, Pat! Hit him!'

The gym was filled beyond its 300-seat capacity, the crowd jammed against the wooden side walls, peering in through the heavy, smoky atmosphere to the ring at the centre. The noise was intense.

Two fighters circled and jabbed, their heads tucked tight. One was low-sized, flat-nosed, butt-headed. He had large biceps which, with thick forearms, relentlessly drove questing, pummelling fists.

His opponent weaved and ducked. He had dark eyes, dark hair and skin: not Levant-dark, more southern Italy, or Spain, the dark complexion of the *torero*. The likeness to a bull-fighter was apt: his shoulders were broad, his waist slim, his face long, with a generous mouth and a proud nose. Sweat glistened on his body as he danced, his long reach scoring on the other's bruised face and his own upper lip testimony to the cutting edge of a bludgeoning glove.

The crowd roared them on. In under a minute the bell ending the third round would go and the result was still too close to call. The lighter man now backed, springing, to a neutral corner, leading his adversary. The thick-set man went for it, head down, attacking with a heavy body-punch. At the last moment the dark-haired boxer jinked right. His stocky opponent, committed to the target, desperately tried to stop and turn. For a millisecond his left-handed guard dropped a fraction below the level of his stubbled chin. It was enough. An iron fist which might have come from the other side of town slammed him square and he slowly folded.

The crowd became delirious. The referee pushed the dark fighter away, then ceremoniously counted the floored man out. The ring was invaded.

'The winner of the Accountancy Boxing Tournament by a knock-out,' bawled the MC to deafening cheers, 'from the London office of Abelson Dunwoody' – he held the winner's arm high – 'Patrick Drake!'

In a barrage of noise Patrick Drake was lifted shoulder-high and, after several circuits of the ring, borne away.

Five minutes later in a small changing-room, Patrick sipped from a mug of champagne as best as his upper lip would allow. A girl with blonde hair bent to apply a cold compress to the red marks on his body. Every so often she paused to kiss his cheek.

'My warrior,' she murmured.

Patrick sat, a great desire to sleep rapidly replacing jubilation. Black hair fell across his forehead as he leaned forward. The tiny room was crammed with supporters, all of whom wanted to congratulate him.

'You and I,' said a man, swaying happily and attempting to pour more champagne into Patrick's already brimming mug, 'you and I are going to go out on the town after this. I had two months salary on you, you bloody Irishman!'

The decisive knock-out was being analysed in detail. In a corner a group burst into 'We Shall Overcome' and the walls of the clapboard gymnasium vibrated in harmony.

'Don't go to sleep, Rocky!' said a man in a dinner jacket.

'My poor Patrick,' purred the girl, applying the ice-pack to Patrick's chest where angry marks lurked, waiting their chance to blossom into haematoma.

Patrick nuzzled his face into her sweet-smelling hair. 'Let's go home, Georgie,' he said faintly. 'I want to sleep for a week.'

'That sounds nice,' she whispered. She had very large hazel eyes.

A youngish man had pushed through.

'Patrick,' he shouted. 'Telephone. It's Mitchell.'

'Oh shit, I don't believe it,' mumbled Patrick. 'What does he want?'

'Wants to speak to you urgently, says it's important,' said the messenger.

'Darling, he probably wants to congratulate you,' said Georgie.

Patrick got to his feet and allowed Georgie to help him into a towelling robe.

'Like hell he does,' he said, making his way from the changing-room.

The telephone was in a small booth outside the door.

'Yes, Sammy.'

'Patrick, I'm sorry to intrude on your fun and games.'

Patrick sighed. 'But . . .'

'Yes. But,' said Sammy Mitchell, 'you're needed down here.'

'When?'

'Now.'

'Oh go to hell, Sammy. It's ten o'clock. I've just fought the inter-office final.'

'I wouldn't have rung if I didn't need you.'

'It will have to wait until tomorrow. I'm dead-beat right now.'

'Listen, Patrick,' said Mitchell, 'the reason you're wanted is that Abelson himself wants to see you. Now. This instant. He's sitting up in his office at this moment waiting for me to tell him when you'll be here.'

'Shit,' Patrick said. 'What the hell does he want me for?'

'I can't talk over the phone.'

'All right, Sammy,' Patrick sighed, 'I'll be there in half an hour.'

'Don't be late,' came the voice on the other end. 'This could be an opportunity for you.' The tone changed. 'By the way, Pat, well done. I understand you pole-axed Denver's man. Congrats. My money was on you.'

'Oh piss-off, Sammy,' said Patrick Drake.

Moonlight reflected on the housing of the entrance barrier as Patrick used a coded pass-card to raise it and then drove in. He pulled up before the main doors of a forty-storey building – Abelson House – which looked out over its own fountain and plaza, Dunwoody Plaza, on the City of London. A security guard opened aluminium doors. Patrick signed a book, stepped into a lift and pressed the thirty-first floor. In the mirror he examined himself: his left eye was puffed, his upper lip a balloon.

The lift doors hummed open directly on to rows of desks

stretching the length of the dim building. Filing cabinets and steel presses made up one side of a long corridor, its other side the doors of offices. Halfway down light flooded out. Patrick knocked.

'Christ, look at his face!'

'I told you,' Patrick said.

'You didn't tell me you'd gone through the windscreen of a bus,' said Sammy Mitchell.

Sammy was short, bespectacled, dark-suited, about fifty-five; he had a round birdlike face, thin hair of uncertain colour pasted from one ear to the other and quick eyes. When he spoke he cocked his head to one side, which Patrick always thought made him look like a blackbird. Now Sammy jerked his head, picked up a telephone and punched four numbers.

'He's arrived,' he said. 'Yes,' he nodded, 'right away.' He stood up. 'Come on then,' he said, 'we're to ascend to the mount.' He gathered some files.

'What's going on, Sammy?' Patrick asked.

'God almighty will explain,' said Sammy as he headed for the door, 'but we have a problem on a job in France.'

Patrick frowned. 'France? I didn't think we had any big jobs over there.'

'We haven't.' Sammy shook his head. His short legs propelled him down the corridor. 'There's a Mickey Mouse outfit we audit down there called Churchtels,' he said. 'It used to be part of the shipping group, Church Lines,' he said. 'Before your time.'

Patrick stopped dead. Five yards ahead Sammy also stopped and was turning. Patrick. Shoulders back. That's the good boy. Right back so that you're standing on your tiptoes. Good boy. Now two deep breaths, that's it: in, out, in, out, deep as you can go.

'What's the matter with you?' Sammy's voice. 'You look as if you've seen a ghost.'

'Did you say "Church Lines"?'

'Yes, Church Lines, Church Lines,' Sammy said. 'Come on, lad, this boxing is loosening up your brains. Church Lines went bust, but Churchtels, their hotel subsidiary, was sold – we were the liquidator.' They had reached a lift and Sammy stabbed at the button. 'They own hotels over there,' he said: 'brothels most likely by the sound of them, amusement parks and a wine château which by all accounts produces gut-rot.' They stepped into the lift. 'Don't ask me why,' Sammy said, 'but it's a job that Abelson takes a close personal interest in.' Sammy closed his eyes. Then he handed Patrick his files and began to make adjustments to his tie. 'Up to this morning I thought the job had been finalised,' he said grimly, his small hands straightening and tightening. 'Then I get a call from Bordeaux to say that something has cropped up, something so bloody serious that we can't even discuss it on the telephone, and would I please come down right away. Me, go to Bordeaux? I've fifteen deadlines coming up the end of September, every one of them ten times more important than bloody Churchtels.'

There's a grassy slope. There are elder trees. There is gravel and warm stone steps. Papa's socks have a bright, criss-cross pattern and Patrick can smell the fresh polish from his shoes. Far off, behind, there is the noise of the sea.

'Who's in charge down there?' Patrick asked as Sammy took back his files.

'Alan Ridgeway,' said Sammy, throwing his head to heaven.

'Alan Ridgeway?' Patrick's mouth opened in disbelief.

'Christ, it's little Sir Echo again! Alan Ridgeway, Alan Ridgeway, Patrick,' Sammy cried. 'You want to sharpen up, lad. We're going to see the boss, you know.'

'Sorry,' Patrick mumbled.

'I was wondering what to do when my phone went again,' Sammy resumed, his nose pointing towards the ceiling. 'Like a madman. He's heard what's going on by some other route. Of course he's been away, swanning around the world and he's forgotten all about this job, although why he needs to be kept informed about it Christ alone knows.'

'Abelson knows that Alan has a problem?'

'So it seems.' Sammy looked up fearfully at the ascending floor numbers on the overhead console. 'He wants someone down there straight away to sort it out. I came up with your name.'

'You know I'm just about to take a week off,' Patrick said.

'Take ten days after this,' said Sammy as the doors opened.

The lobby into which they stepped was different from the thirty-nine below it. It rose the height of nearly two storeys, a great vault, glazed along one side with vivid stained glass and along the other with dark, wooden panelling. A visitor might believe that he had arrived in the atrium of a miniature cathedral.

'Ever been up here?' asked Sammy out of the side of his mouth.

Patrick shook his head.

A middle-aged woman with blue hair and chromed glasses, whose upper frames mimicked the eyebrows of Dr Spock in *Star Trek*, was approaching.

She smiled thinly to the senior partner, then stippled Patrick's face with her needle-point eyes. 'This way, please,' she said and resolutely strode ahead, pushing through a door.

They entered a room in which the lights were recessed and muted and the floor was covered by a pink carpet of deep pile. Two walls were made of uninterrupted floor-to-ceiling glass, revealing the clear September night and the City of London twinkling and sparkling above and below. The feeling was of being suspended in air at great height.

The outline of a man sat motionless at a central desk. Sammy murmured an appropriate greeting and seated himself deferentially on the edge of a deep, leather chair, indicating that Patrick should do the same. The lights were arranged in such a way that whilst their host sat in a pool of shade the head and shoulders of his guests were picked out with clarity. The small group sat in silence. Patrick could discern a sharp face, restless eyes and hands resting on the arm-tips of the chair.

'Quite a sight, I agree.'

The voice of John Abelson was almost disembodied.

'I have often sat here at nights and calculated that, with the exception of St Paul's, every building I can see, every one of them has at least some connection with Abelson Dunwoody. They have all been built or designed by, or are owned or rented by someone we audit or advise.'

The two men before the desk admired the vista anew. John Abelson made it sound as if London had been built with him in mind.

'This is Patrick Drake, Mr Abelson,' Sammy said.

Abelson appeared not to hear. From where he sat Patrick could see him reach forward. There was the soft hum of motors, and from the point where the glass walls met the ceiling, curtains slowly began to unroll downwards. They were more like sections of a tapestry than curtains, each with scenes of medieval knights on horseback and marching foot-warriors, all depicted in sensitively woven colours. Abelson pressed another switch and the lighting in the room brightened uniformly, allowing the warm shades of the tapestry and the carpet to unite.

'Modelled on the tapestry at Bayeux,' Abelson said. 'It depicts William the Conqueror on his way to the Battle of Hastings.' He turned his eyes, now blue and clear, on Patrick. 'An event I understand not entirely unrelated to your evening's activities, Mr Drake,' he said.

'Patrick has just won the inter –' began Sammy.

'I know, Sammy,' interrupted Abelson, 'I know. By a knock-out in the last minute of the third round. Abelson Dunwoody keep the inter-office trophy. My congratulations, Mr Drake. Let us hope,' he added smoothly, 'that you have the same clout in the matter which we are here to discuss.'

A hand smoothed snow-white hair; the eyes were unwavering blue ice.

Patrick shifted and coughed. 'I'll try my best, sir,' he said.

Abelson had fitted half-rimmed, tortoise-shell spectacles and was studying a file.

'Churchtels, Mr Drake,' he said as if thinking aloud. 'Mean anything to you?'

Patrick is so small. Through the white bars he looks out at Papa who has just come home. Papa is smiling. When he laughs he throws his head back and his teeth sparkle. Patrick wants to be like Papa – big, strong, laughing.

'Mr Drake?'

Patrick leaned slightly forward.

Abelson was looking at him sharply. 'I asked if Churchtels meant anything to you, Mr Drake.'

Patrick felt himself redden. 'Not a lot, sir,' he said, 'just what Mr Mitchell has told me in the last five minutes.'

Abelson's eyes grew in wonderment. He threw down his glasses. 'So Mr Mitchell actually knows something about Churchtels,' he said. He allowed his eyes to strafe the audit partner. Sammy Mitchell swallowed. Abelson rose and began to pace the length of his rooftop office. He was sparse and clean-shaven and dressed in a dark suit.

'Churchtels, Mr Drake,' Abelson began, 'is the name of a

modest company in the leisure business, based in south-west France. They own one hotel in Biarritz and another in Bordeaux. They own an amusement park and a company which franchises video games. They also own a wine château in Loupiac, outside Bordeaux.' He spoke in a clipped, hard voice. He was at the far end of the room and swivelled. 'Five years ago, Mr Drake, we were appointed liquidator to a shipping company called Church Lines. Churchtels was their subsidiary. In the course of the liquidation I was lucky enough to sell Churchtels as a going concern to a company called Panworld, an investment company based in Lichtenstein.' Abelson had stopped with his back to William the Conqueror. 'The deal was the difference between the Church Lines creditors getting something or nothing at all,' he said. He set his jaw. 'Churchtels,' said Abelson, 'appointed Abelson Dunwoody their auditor, Mr Drake, and I have kept a close eye on the job ever since.'

Filling his lungs noisily and at length through his nostrils John Abelson very slowly lowered himself behind his desk. 'So why are we all sitting up here on a Thursday night?' he asked. He looked at each man. His jaw popped ominously. 'Twenty-two years ago,' he said, 'when I joined this firm, there were less than ten people in all, and we worked out of third-floor offices near Moorgate.' There was silence. 'We are where we are because we deliver on time. Companies like Churchtels are where they are because they have worked hard to establish other people's confidence. Success, Mr Drake, is the business of maintaining confidence: the confidence of people, financial people such as banks, creditors, all creatures of habit, people who like constancy.' He held the last word, his lips drawn back from his teeth. 'Confidence, Mr Drake, is what keeps banks solvent, the stock of great companies high and the world afloat.' Abelson picked up a pencil and held it between the thumb and forefinger of each hand. Again he rose. 'I have been away,' he began. 'I arrived back this morning. Among the messages waiting for me was one from the owners of Churchtels.' Abelson made a sharp laugh which sounded more like a cough. '*They* told me – not anyone here, mind you – these people told me, that their accounts are going to be delayed because the man in charge of the audit of the vineyard in Bordeaux seems incapable of finalising it.' Abelson looked at them, flabbergasted by the sheer crassness of what he had said. 'An important set of accounts are being delayed because of a pissarse vineyard in Bordeaux.'

There was a loud snap as the pencil was halved.

Sammy Mitchell closed his eyes. 'Alan Ridgeway is in charge down there,' he said. 'He's very meticulous.'

'Meticulous?' Abelson snarled. 'He's a socialist. He's tried to turn this firm into a trade-union branch.'

Sammy nodded weakly, his eyes still closed. 'Ridgeway claims he has unresolved queries in Bordeaux,' he said. 'He wants me to go down there.'

'Look here, Mitchell,' Abelson said, 'this is a farce. And it's not the first time. As I understand it Ridgeway has not even explained what his problem is.'

Sammy gulped as, slowly, Abelson turned his attention to Patrick.

'I asked for the best manager to put this job to bed,' Abelson said. 'I was told to look no further, Mr Drake.'

Sammy's eyes remained closed.

'Get over there right away,' Abelson said crisply. 'Ridgeway has been told that you are in charge now and he has been ordered to remain in place to help you. I want a signed-off set of accounts by Monday morning at the very latest – do I make myself clear?'

Patrick nodded. 'Yes, sir,' he said.

Slowly John Abelson moved around to the front of his desk where he rested himself against it, opposite Patrick.

'I understand that you won't be a thousand miles from home,' he said, his tone softening.

'Patrick's half-Spanish . . .' Sammy began.

'I know, Sammy, I know,' said Abelson. 'A Spanish Drake had not escaped my attention.' A smile tugged at his thin mouth and he crossed his thin, tailored legs so that one toe nudged Patrick.

'We've never met before, Patrick, have we?' he asked.

'No, sir,' Patrick replied.

'I like people who deliver,' Abelson said smoothly. 'I see to it that their star rises.'

Then he uncrossed his legs and returned behind his desk, the unsaid antithesis hanging in the room like London smog. 'Remember, Monday morning,' he said, without looking up, as

Patrick and Sammy made their way from the room, murmuring their goodnights.

Slowly he released the brass handle. With great care he slid along the carpet, feeling his way. The fingers of his left hand touched wall, then a chest of drawers, guiding him forward in the blackness. He ran his hand up, searching. His forearm brushed: there was a crash. 'Shit,' he swore as the room was flooded with light.

'What are you doing?'

Patrick shook his head. 'I was trying not to wake you.'

Georgie blinked and peered at the bedside clock. 'It's nearly one,' she said, then she stared. 'My God, look at those bruises. That's what you get for rushing away.' She slid out of bed. Her body was gold, all over. Her hair was also gold; cut in a fringe across her forehead it came to her shoulders. She moved towards him and gently probed the marks on his abdomen and chest, working her way to his face. 'You're a complete mess,' she murmured. 'I prescribe a week in bed with around-the-clock nursing.'

'Thank you, Nurse Ridgeway,' said Patrick, bending to her ear and kissing it. 'But do you think that a week will be enough?'

'I may have to revise,' she said as his arm went around her. 'In the case as currently presented, probably not.'

'I've got one of those very rare diseases,' he whispered, his mouth seeking hers.

'Oh?' She snapped out the light.

'Yes.' He felt her arch. 'I've got to be seduced every three hours, or else I regress.'

'That's no problem,' she whispered, 'no problem . . . at all.'

The bedside clock showed 1.30 a.m. as Georgie kicked the door shut and placed the tray on the bed. Patrick attacked the thick sandwich.

'Hmm, that's good,' he said.

She smiled. 'I am here to cater for all your needs.'

Patrick chuckled and took a gulp of hot, sweet cocoa.

'Well, come on,' she said, snuggling in beside him, 'let's have it. What happened?'

'I met Abelson,' he said, munching.

'I know that, Patrick. What did he want?'

'There's a problem on a job,' he said, reaching for the cocoa. 'He wants me to sort it out.'

Georgie made a face that she was impressed. She drew her knees to her chin.

'What's he like?' she asked. 'According to Alan he's a slippery merchant.'

'Oh, I don't know.' Patrick picked up another sandwich and looked away. 'He's one of those people who is on rocket fuel the whole time. You should see his office – it must have cost an absolute fortune. You think you're up in a plane hovering over London.' Patrick licked a crumb away from his lip and laughed. 'You should have heard the way Abelson treated poor old Sammy.'

Georgie was leaning on one elbow, staring at him.

'When is this sorting-out to take place?' she asked, suddenly quiet.

'Pretty much straight away,' Patrick mumbled.

She caught his wrist before it got to the cocoa. 'Patrick?'

He took a deep breath. 'Immediately. I've got to go to France in the morning.'

She drew back, her mouth set. 'Just like that,' she said, snapping her fingers. 'France in the morning. Sod everything else. And everyone.'

Patrick opened his mouth, but Georgie was not to be diverted.

'All this heady stuff consorting with the gods probably means that you haven't bothered to remember the other minor plans which have been made for tomorrow.'

Patrick closed his eyes.

Georgie said, 'Forget completely the fact that I have taken a week off from the library: that's irrelevant, I know, to you and that creep Abelson, but consider, if you can pause for an instant from your headlong dash to promotion and riches, the feelings of a nice, old man, who just happens to be my father and who has very generously made his house in Scotland available to us for a week when he doesn't really want to come to London at all and at bottom disapproves of his only daughter living with a man she's not married to.'

Large, crystal tears had emerged to sit on the ledge of each marvellous eye. Patrick pushed back the tray and leaned over.

'Georgie,' he murmured, catching her gently. 'Please listen.'

'I'm just disappointed,' she said, the tears now in flood. 'Why the hell couldn't you say no? They've got thousands of people working in there.'

'Georgie, there's a problem. Alan's involved.'

'Alan?'

He nodded, his mouth tight.

'How?' She wiped each side of her face with her upper arm.

'It's hard to say,' Patrick said. 'He's on a job in Bordeaux and hasn't signed off. Abelson's out for his guts.'

'I thought Alan only got piddling little jobs,' Georgie sniffed, 'ever since he and Abelson crossed swords.'

'That's all he does get,' Patrick said. 'He's sent to the cat's arse of every job there is. But there's been a mistake: he's been sent to one that Abelson takes a special interest in.'

Georgie crossed her legs beneath her, placed a heavy glass ashtray on the sheet in her lap and lighted up a long cigarette. She blew smoke at the ceiling. 'Do they know the connection?' she asked.

'You and me?' Patrick smiled and shook his head. 'Who would ever think that Alan Ridgeway could have a gorgeous sister like you?'

Georgie drew deeply on her cigarette and wrapped her arms around her knees.

'You look fantastic when you do that,' Patrick said.

'Alan is so obstinate,' Georgie said. 'Do you remember all the fuss on that job he was on up north somewhere?

Patrick nodded. 'He questioned valuations by some of the most senior men in the profession.'

'Father says that Alan was always too stubborn,' Georgie said, 'even when he was young.'

'He's got Abelson's back up on this one,' Patrick said.

Georgie looked at him, her hair like honey against the sweep of her neck. 'He'll find it very difficult to get another job, you know,' she said. 'He's over forty.'

'I know,' Patrick replied. 'That's why I didn't object to going down there.'

'God, I hope he's all right,' Georgie said. 'I worry all the time about him. He's an innocent. Everything is black or white and fits in a box. He's never learned to . . . deal with the world. He'll never get married now. He'll never get promoted in a company like Abelson Dunwoody. I expect all he wants is to be left alone.'

'Well, he's not being left alone now,' Patrick said, yawning. 'He's gone and landed himself in it up to his elbows.'

'What will happen to him?' Georgie asked.

'Don't worry,' Patrick said, 'I'll sort him out.'

Georgie smiled. She leaned over and rubbed Patrick's cheek with the back of her hand. 'I know you will,' she said. 'I told you earlier tonight. You're my hero.' She kissed him. 'Sorry about being silly,' she said.

Patrick smiled, kissed her nose, then lay back and closed his eyes.

'What's the company in Bordeaux?' Georgie asked. 'Patrick?'

Patrick is standing, his hands down by his sides. He sees Papa's big, brown face burst into a smile and hears his laugh fill the room. Come here to me, darling. Come here, come here. Patrick runs and is collected in the big arms. Now he is held, but flying through the air. He is hugged close and smells the strong, man's smell that has ever since meant comfort to him. Patrick knows that never before has he been as happy as he is this minute.

'Patrick?' Georgie put out the light as beside her his regular breathing continued, undisturbed. Outside in the darkness a police car or ambulance rushed through Battersea.

'Look after Alan for me,' she whispered.

Then she curled up so that her head was at his chest and went to sleep.

CHAPTER TWO

Shadows crept from the mass of the overpass. Two blocks away the noise from the playground drifted out. The playground ran back for a hundred yards; it was fenced in front with high wire-mesh and on either side by the gables of ten-storey apartment blocks. At the back there was an eight-foot wall, red-bricked and topped with broken bottles.

Touching the metal in his hip holster, Sergeant Joseph Vendetti began to walk, head down, across the playground. He was a strong man of thirty with blond, untidy hair, a straggling moustache and an open face with wide-set blue eyes. He wore faded jeans, a threadbare, red pullover and scuffed running shoes. He worked his way through the playing children, doing his junkie-walk, head down, twitching a shoulder, scanning for trouble. His eyes were on a small group ten yards from the rear wall. They were youths, two kids and an older one astride a bicycle. Joe tried not to look at them as he approached. He was within twenty yards of the bicycle, thirty of the back wall. Suddenly one of the two kids turned and stared straight at him. He was a handsome, clean-limbed Hispanic, no more than thirteen. His eyes opened wide.

'*¡Bahonda!*' he said.

The result was electrifying. The older youth sprang away from the bike. In less than a second he measured his position.

Joe saw wild eyes, a tall, well-built frame.

'Police!' Joe shouted. He reached inside his pullover for his police shield, suspended around his neck on a silver chain. The youth sprinted straight at the red-bricked wall and sprang. It was a spectacular jump which brought the tips of his elbows to rest on the sloping brick lip. He levered himself, his hands grasping at the jagged glass for purchase. Joe jumped and grabbed a foot. There was a scream. Joe tugged, hard. The free leg kicked with frenzy. Another figure had appeared beside Joe. The youth on the wall screamed again. The two policemen pulled and all three of them fell backwards into the playground.

Joe was first up. He freed his .38 and, double-handed, pointed it at the dark face.

'He's cut himself badly, boss,' panted Detective Hughie Cruzero.

Joe Vendetti nodded, his chest heaving. 'Call an ambulance,' he said. Then, 'Jesus Christ!'

A bottle had fragmented on the asphalt two feet away.

'Grab him and get out of range!' Joe cried.

Each of them caught the injured youth and ran back into the middle of the playground. There was a whizzing and another bottle exploded in the spot which they had just left. Joe looked up at the high-rise apartments. He could see dark eyes at several balconies.

'Get away from those windows!' he yelled up, waving his gun.

'¡Camorones!' came the shouted reply.

He holstered the gun, then walked to the bicycle and wheeled it nearer the road. He opened the saddle-bag. Inside was a sweat-shirt, a cheap magazine and a brown paper bag. Joe felt the smooth, tubular shapes through the paper. He put in his hand and took out a fistful of shining glassiness. Hughie was speaking into a hand-held radio.

'Crack?'

Joe nodded. 'Hold these,' he said, handing Hughie the transparent vials. He narrowed his eyes, then made his way back towards the brick wall. He walked along it, to the very far corner of the playground, towards a semicircle of unused drainage pipes. He reached them, then, on the balls of his feet, vaulted up. He drew in his breath. Below him, in the shadow made by the pipes and the wall, were three bodies. Two were of Hispanic boys, fourteen years old: their blue-jeaned legs were stuck straight out; one of them lay, his head back, his eyes bulging and unseeing; the other was concentrating his whole being on sucking from the end of a narrow, glass pipe whilst he held the flame of a lighter to its end. The third body was that of a chocolate-skinned girl, roughly the same age. She lay face down, the dress of her school uniform at her thighs, a pool of vomit around her head. Joe jumped in. He grabbed the girl's hair and jerked her up. Her mouth sagged soundlessly. He stuck his fingers into her throat and she spasmed and retched. Then she sagged backwards, moaning. Joe stepped back, then he bent again and took the thin pipe from the youth's hands. There was a feeble protest; Joe crushed the hot glass in his hand, dropped it and ground it into fragments under his heel. Gulping for air he climbed out.

Hughie Cruzero was standing there.

'We'll need that ambulance over here when it comes,' Joe said. He leaned his hands on his knees and rested back against the grey pipes which were warm from the sun.

'It's like a plague,' Hughie said. 'It's like trying to empty the Potomac with a teacup.'

Joe nodded silently.

'We're out of our fuckin' minds if we think we beat these guys – whoever they are,' Hughie said.

Joe looked at him. 'We'll beat them.'

'You think so, Joe?'

Joe tilted his head back and closed his eyes, savouring the sunlight. 'We've got to get to the top,' he said quietly. 'You cut the head off and everything else dies.'

There was a siren wail and a streak of red and white as an ambulance flashed by the perimeter fence.

'By the way,' Hughie said suddenly, 'your brother, the one you often talk about . . .'

'Frank.'

'Yeah, Frank.' Hughie's eyes were concerned. 'Is he still away?'

Joe still drank in the sun. He nodded fractionally.

'He's OK, isn't he, Joe?' Hughie asked. 'I know you're close.'

Joe's eyes remained closed.

'I think he's OK,' he said.

Joe Vendetti checked the shine on his shoes as he walked across Franklin Park. Some dirty Washington pigeons hopped out of his way as he stepped off the kerb at Thirteenth and I Street. As he pushed open the chrome doors of the ugly building on the corner he felt spots of rain.

'Joe.'

'Captain Izaguirre.'

'Joe, I'm glad you got here.'

Mike Izaguirre came barely to Joe's shoulder. Despite being in his middle fifties, he had jet-black, closely cropped hair. His face was uniformly sallow, his mouth a straight, stern line.

'Joe.' Izaguirre took Joe's elbow and steered him to one side, away from the guard in the central glass cubicle. The police captain's dark eyes fixed Joe's. 'Joe, this all happened so quick. They called me first: you were out on a job. I thought the best thing was to come and meet you here.'

Joe felt dizzy. 'Captain?'

Izaguirre said, 'Joe, the news is not good.'

Joe fought to control himself. 'I guessed,' he managed to say, aware that his mouth juices were gone. 'When you called I guessed.'

Captain Izaguirre's face was grim. 'You want a few minutes alone?'

Joe shook his head. He allowed Izaguirre to walk him past the guard. A woman had appeared in front of an open elevator. For some reason she smiled.

'Mr Kahan himself is up there,' Captain Izaguirre said grimly.

The tightness in Joe's chest was constrictive. 'I need some water,' he said.

They had reached the eleventh floor; Joe was dimly aware of a large reception area, a wall full of gold shields, a girl at a desk. The woman handed Joe a glass; then they were walking through another room, between the desks of two secretaries and into the office of the man who administered the drug enforcement apparatus of the United States. Joe saw bright windows, dark wood panelling and a circular table. Two men stood up. Captain Izaguirre shook the men's hands and murmured something. He turned. 'Joe, this is Mr Marshall Kahan, Administrator of the Drug Enforcement Administration. Mr Kahan, this is Sergeant Vendetti.'

A man with wavy, snow-white hair and a high complexion

came around the table. He was as large as Joe; he took Joe's hand in both of his.

'Sergeant.' The voice was deep. 'I am very sorry.'

'Joe.' Izaguirre's firm hand was guiding Joe to a chair.

Kahan was saying something. 'This is Special Agent Waters. He was a colleague of your brother's.'

Dimly Joe saw a tall, younger man with straight, blond hair, parted centre. Joe took his outstretched hand. It was cold.

'I have been directly in touch, Sergeant,' said Marshall Kahan softly, 'with the President. Like all of us, he is very upset. He feels shaken by what has happened.'

Joe closed his eyes to try and stop the room spinning.

'What has happened?'

The administrator of the DEA inclined his head indicating that the question was reasonable. 'You know,' he said deeply, 'that we've been gravely worried for nearly two weeks now.'

Joe's vision kept coming and going.

'You know your brother Frank was working undercover – you may not know where.'

Marshall Kahan was breathing heavily. Joe wanted to scream.

'He was in Spain, Sergeant.'

Rain beat against the window in a steady pattern.

'Spain,' Kahan said, 'as far as drugs go, is maverick territory. The people there have very close ties with Latin America and drugs dealing – the whole art of *narcotráfico* and *contrabandista* is second nature to them. In Madrid they have recently substituted crack in place of cocaine. We thought that there might be a link to South America, to the root of our problem. We decided to send someone.'

'Frank,' Joe said, knowing he sounded stupid.

The DEA administrator produced a white handkerchief to dab his forehead.

'He managed to get us one report,' Kahan said. 'He failed to make any subsequent contact.'

There was silence in the room. Joe glanced around: on every wall there were small flags, plaques, framed scrolls and photographs.

'I sent Special Agent Waters to Spain,' Marshall Kahan was saying. 'He got back yesterday morning. Bob?'

Special Agent Waters rose. Joe dug his fingernails into his palms.

'Thank you, sir,' said Waters quietly. Beside Kahan he appeared cool, fit. 'I got to Spain last weekend,' he said. 'I set up operations in Pamplona, centre of the Basque country. The so-called country of the Basques extends to both sides of the Pyrenees. With men from our Paris and Madrid offices I initiated an extensive check of each city and large town in the area, contacting hospitals and police. When this did not yield I went to the smaller towns.' The agent's blue eyes took in the police sergeant. 'No success.'

He's enjoying himself, thought Joe.

'On Sunday night *gendarmes* in the French Pyrenean village of St-Etienne-de-Baigorry received a tip-off and contacted us.' Waters had produced a map. 'The next morning I drove with two agents, from Pamplona, across the border to Baigorry. The *gendarmes* brought us up into the mountains, until we came to a twenty-foot high, metal-on-concrete incinerator just off the roadway. It is in twenty-four-hour use, dealing with all the garbage in the area.'

It took all the strength at Joe's command to remain seated. Waters's voice seemed miles away.

'It took twelve hours, first to shut it down, then to clean it out,' Waters paused. 'There are photographs,' he said, tapping a brown envelope. He sat down.

There was silence.

'How was, uh, identity established?' asked Captain Izaguirre, clearing his throat.

'There is no doubt, Captain,' said Marshall Kahan quietly. 'Some points of identification were still possible, but the dental-chart match-up we got last night confirms it beyond question.'

Joe closed his eyes.

'The remains are being shipped home through Paris,' Kahan was saying. 'The French are cooperating.'

Three faces in attitudes of sympathy stared.

Izaguirre said, 'We will understand, Joe, if you wish to leave.'

Administrator Kahan nodded and made to push back his chair. Joe's head buzzed. The faces swam in and out of his vision. He was breathing as if he had just run the length of a street.

'I'd like to hear more.'

'Joe?' Izaguirre's face was concerned.

'I'd like to hear more,' said Joe, hearing his own voice in an echo-chamber. 'I know that the work of the DEA is classified, but Mr Kahan knows I'm on the sharp end, out there on the street, I see what the drugs do. I'd like to hear more.' Joe's heart thumped mightily. He saw Kahan's eyes narrow.

'More about what, exactly, Sergeant?'

'More about this investigation that my brother was on. I'd like to know if he actually achieved anything or if he died for nothing. I'd like to know why he died and what went wrong. I'd like to know what happens now and how you are going to nail the bastards who murdered him and then burned his body in a garbage incinerator.'

Administrator Kahan exchanged glances with Captain Izaguirre.

'I can't cross the line any more on this one, Captain,' he said. He turned back to Joe. 'This has been not only a tragedy but a severe setback, Sergeant,' he said. 'Everything must now be reviewed.'

Joe felt he was drowning. 'How long will a review take?'

The DEA chief replied, 'Probably some months.'

'And is there a murder investigation taking place?' Joe asked.

'The French police are active,' said Special Agent Waters.

'The French police,' Joe heard himself echo. 'Jesus Christ, a man has been murdered and all you're going to do is review procedures? Now is when action is needed, now, when the trail is still warm. You need to put another man in Frank's place right away, Mr Kahan.'

'There are other ways, Sergeant,' Kahan replied. 'The net will close slowly but surely. No one wants it more than I. Your contribution, in the street, is invaluable. It's just a matter of time.'

'But in the meantime,' Joe's voice was hoarse, 'kids all around this country are blowing their brains out.'

Marshall Kahan bristled. 'Sergeant, it's not just like replacing a cop on the street. Your brother was chosen because he was a skilful agent who was completely unknown to the people he was infiltrating.'

'Or so he thought,' Joe said.

Marshall Kahan's face-blood drained. The most powerful man in US Drug Enforcement looked straight at Izaguirre, his lower lip working. 'Captain, there are certain limits . . .'

'Sergeant.' Izaguirre's voice was harsh, his dark eyes clouded with anger.

Joe stood up. 'Thank you, gentlemen,' he said. He could see Kahan still looking, white-faced, across the table, and Special Agent Waters, his eyes once frank, now flint, drilling.

'You want to wait for me outside?' said Izaguirre, still very angry.

'Nah, I'll go on home,' said Joe. 'It's been quite a day.'

The men nodded as the big police sergeant made his way from the room.

The church was dimly lighted. Candles flickered behind him and up on the altar two men were hanging speakers and arranging microphones. Joe sat in the back row, almost under the organ gallery, its carved, Gothic figures suspended between the high roof and the marble-tiled floor. If he looked to the right, he could see, through a glass door, jagged, upright headstones, fenced around by an iron railing.

He had been sitting for nearly an hour. Now he looked again at the papers in his hands: the creased envelope and the scrawled scrap which it had contained. He looked at the flap, sealed by the juice of a living tongue.

It was peaceful in the church. Peace and eventual peace. He felt a sharp pain and suddenly remembered that he had not eaten for six hours. He returned the bit of paper to the envelope, the envelope to his jacket. At the door he glanced back once.

There was a payphone on the next block. Washington had emptied out; a wind was blowing trash along the street.

'Hughie?'

'Yeah? Hey, Joe, yeah. Listen.' Joe could see the detective's concerned face. 'Joe, I heard the news. Jesus, I'm sorry.'

'Thanks, Hughie.'

'We were all hoping, just hoping, you know?'

'I know, Hughie.'

'Joe, you want to come over or anythin'? I'll get Jeannie to cook somethin' up.'

'I'm not hungry, Hughie, but thanks anyway.'

'Anythin' I can do?'

'Just one thing. I don't want to bother the lieutenant at home, you understand?'

'Sure.'

'In the morning just tell him I'm takin' a few days off. OK? I'm due some time. Mahoney can fill in fine.'

'Sure thing, Joe, I'll tell him. Where are you goin' to go?'

'I'm going to stay with my sister, she lives in Seattle.'

'You try and relax, Joe. And listen, if you need anythin' . . .'

A newspaper blew under the payphone and wrapped itself around his legs as he hung up. He bent down, balled it and tossed it into a trash-can. Then he shivered as he hunched into the wind and began to walk.

CHAPTER THREE

The girl stretched back her tanned arm to a board where keys hung from hooks, smiled and handed a set to Patrick Drake. It was 5.30, Friday evening, Bordeaux.

An hour later Patrick was in a one-way system, on a boulevard along the river. He passed a bridge, crowned with lanterns, then another which curved up and out over the wide Garonne. Daylight was waning but looking back he could see the elegant quays of the ancient city of burghers.

He had spoken to Georgie from the airport in Paris. 'Did you call your father?'

'Sure,' she said, 'you know Dad, there's no problem.'

'What did he say?' he asked.

There was a small laugh. 'He wanted to know when we are getting married,' Georgie had replied.

Patrick drove south through countryside. The white bluffs of cliffs towered upwards from the wet flatlands. He stopped and walked down a sandy bank; savouring the balmy evening and the noise of the last few crickets, he relieved himself into the muddy river.

After Cadillac Patrick turned off the main road and climbed through hills covered with mile after mile of neat vines, visible under a pale moon rising. He passed clusters of houses where life seemed to be suspended. On a plateau he stopped at a lighted door where a buxom, aproned woman held an infant to her breast.

'Château Diane?' She shouted instructions in voluble French, her right hand straight and cupped by turn, her left supporting the rooting child.

Patrick followed the road winding through the vine fields. He passed some idle tractors and a trailer, then rounded a sharp bend.

Somehow in his mind's eye he imagined that all châteaux would be like Versailles. He had turned down a bumpy, dirt avenue, where untrimmed hedges on either side scraped at the car's doors. After two hundred yards there was a right-angled bend and suddenly Château Diane appeared, stark in the moonlight like a cardboard cut-out. Patrick could see a hotch-potch of towers and turrets. Beneath them, great Gothic windows, big enough to drive a coach through, almost reached the ground, and high above, much smaller windows were set in towers of slender elegance. Battlements for men with longbows ran between the turrets, and at each lofty corner grinning stone dogs leaped out to defend their fortress.

Patrick drove slowly across a forecourt and parked by a creeper-clad wall. He got out. He could hear the hum of machinery. He took a step towards the outline of an arched foot entrance. In the moonlight his eye caught a shadow of movement: high in Château Diane, in the dark window of a turret, a figure moved away from the glazed bars of the narrow aperture.

'*Monsieur?*'

Patrick whirled. His eyes strained. The voice had no form. Then he saw white: a man in a white dustcoat came slowly from the shadows. Patrick saw deepset eyes, ginger hair, a drooping ginger moustache and a long, thin mouth on a head like a pole.

'*Monsieur?*'

Patrick let his breath out. 'I'm looking for Mr Ridgeway from London,' he said in French. He held the stare. Then the man turned, looking back over his shoulder to indicate that Patrick should follow.

They passed under the arch to an enclosed, cobblestoned courtyard. There were pallets of empty bottles, ten high, and high stacks of crated, gas cylinders with signs warning smokers to keep away. Patrick smelled stale wine. They went by a building, its doors swinging plastic flaps; Patrick could see a bright interior, tiled like a dairy, and windowed vats. There was hissing and throbbing and the sound of bottles being crated. They passed parked cars and skirted a series of pits where recessed, steel screws gleamed. At a long, two-storey building a single, upstairs light shone out. The guide pointed.

'*Merci*,' Patrick said.

'*A votre service.*'

Patrick knocked. There was a rattle as the overhead window was opened.

'*Oui?*'

'What do you mean, *oui?*' he laughed. 'Let me in.'

'Oh, Pat, it's you.'

The head disappeared and there was the rattle of feet on a stair. The door opened.

'Pat, I'm glad you're here,' Alan Ridgeway said warmly. 'Come on up. How did you get here?' Alan had a small, alert face and wore thick, horn-rimmed glasses over tiny, black eyes which lurked like bullets.

'I hired a car in Bordeaux.' Patrick said. 'It's out front.'

'I couldn't believe it when I heard who they were sending,' said Alan, leading the way. 'Was the trip OK?'

They entered a room where files, stacks of papers and a calculator stood on a table. Alan smiled and blinked in the room's neon lights. 'Welcome to the wine centre of the universe,' he said. 'Would you like a drink?'

'That sounds like an excellent suggestion,' Patrick said. 'No need to ask what's on offer, I suppose?'

'You must be joking,' Alan replied. He went to a filing cabinet and took out a bottle of Glenfiddich and two glasses. 'Three weeks of the house poison in this place is enough for anyone.' He poured them each a good three fingers, then sat at the table, pushing Patrick's glass across. 'Cheers,' he said as they both drank. Alan leaned back, savouring the hit of the whisky and lighted himself a cigarette. 'How's Georgie?'

'She's fine,' Patrick said. 'She sends her love.'

In the corner a one-bar electric fire glowed. Alan Ridgeway's small eyes were scanning. 'As a matter of interest,' he asked, 'who hit you?'

Patrick rubbed his eye and smiled. 'It was the inter-office final. Denvers put up Jim Burns.'

'Did you win?'

Patrick nodded.

'Congratulations,' Alan said. 'We should be in Bordeaux

celebrating instead of burning the oil in this dive.' His nose twitched. 'Do you smell?'

'Yes,' Patrick said. 'It's like the morning after a good bash.'

'It's the grape-skins that come out of the vats when they've been pressed or fermented or whatever they do with them,' Alan said. 'In the daytime you'll see mounds of them waiting to be taken away as fertiliser.'

There was a screech of tyres. Patrick turned to look out and saw a yellow forklift driven by his guide of five minutes ago trundling through the factory doors with a crate of gas cylinders.

'Who's the man who showed me here?' Patrick asked. 'Narrow head, suspicious eyes.'

'Probably the relief foreman,' Alan said. 'He got here yesterday – the regular one is on leave.'

Out of the window Patrick could see over the courtyard in the direction of the château.

'What's your brief?' Alan asked quietly.

'To get the hell out of here,' answered Patrick.

'Is there a stink?'

'Sort of.'

'How high?'

'As high as you can go.'

Alan crossed his legs showing his pointed knees. 'All right,' he said, 'I'd better fill you in. First some background. Château Diane, which you saw on your way in here, was bought ten years ago by a company called Churchtels, the expanding leisure arm of the then thriving Church Lines. They spun this place off into a separate subsidiary, modernised the plant and put it on a viable footing. Everything went well until five years ago when Church Lines went bust. Abelson Dunwoody was appointed liquidator and Abelson sold Churchtels to an outfit called Panworld, in Lichtenstein. Are you with me?'

I want you to close your eyes, Patrick. No cheating, now, close them. Patrick is led, his eyes screwed closed, his heart belting like the heart of the big fish they landed on the strand at Ballynanty. Now, Patrick, open your eyes.

'Château Diane is run by a manager,' Alan said. 'There's a woman who looks after the office, a plant foreman and about half a dozen women who work in the bottling plant.' Alan got up, walked to the window and opened it. 'But there's something going on here, Pat,' he said. 'My eyes have been opened.'

Patrick opens his eyes. At first he cannot see anything distinct, just flashes and sparks and faces. Then, as the Christmas wind whistles in under the door with all the ferocity of the Atlantic behind it, Patrick sees the new, red bicycle.

'All the wine is shipped out of here by container,' Alan said and leaned forward. 'But for security purposes there is also a brand new automatic weighbridge. The weighbridge dockets have never formed part of the audit procedure, that is, until last Friday.'

Patrick could hear the trundling noise of the forklift-truck in the courtyard below them.

'Last Friday,' Alan said, 'I came across this.'

He took out an elongated strip of paper.

'What is it?' Patrick asked.

'It's a weighbridge record showing that on 19 August of last year a container of wine left these premises,' Alan replied.

'I can see that,' Patrick said. He looked up quizzically.

'19 August is my birthday,' Alan said. 'Last year it was on a Sunday. This place doesn't work on a Sunday.'

Patrick looked at him. 'So this is a concealed sale?'

'On 19 August last year this container of wine left Château Diane,' Alan said. 'Its laden weight shows that it is a full container – eight hundred cases. I went to the Goods Outwards book. There was no mention of the container in question. Then I had an idea. I went to the stocks of bottles either side of 19 August and tried to reconcile them with the officially recorded sales. There is a discrepancy of nearly eight hundred cases,' he said.

'What did you do?' Patrick asked.

'I couldn't go to anyone in here,' Alan said. 'Obviously any one of them could be ripping the place off. I traced the container to a shipping firm in Bordeaux. They were able to tell me that the container was collected on 19 August by a haulage company called Transportation Pyrenean with an address in Pamplona, Spain. I went back over the records, but could not find any previous dealings with this Transportation Pyrenean. I went right back, to when Château Diane was taken over, five years ago. I had nearly given up when something caught my eye, an entry made barely four months after the takeover: it was a payment for 550,000 French francs, and the entry is to "TP".'

Patrick watched the smoke curl from the ashtray where Alan's cigarette glowed.

'It's the same outfit,' Alan said quietly. 'There's an old invoice on the file, unexplained, but passed in the very first audit by none other than Sammy Mitchell.' Alan produced a square piece of paper. 'Here is the invoice,' he said. 'You'll notice something interesting from the company details, I think.'

Patrick studied the voice. 'Transportation Pyrenean is a company incorporated in Lichtenstein,' he said.

'Precisely,' Alan said.

Patrick took a deep breath. 'Are you saying that Sammy . . . ?'

Alan was holding up his hand. 'On Tuesday the shipping company called again. They had traced the destination of the wine.' Alan went to the file and like a conjuror, produced another document. 'It went to Ireland,' he said, 'to a company called Golden Grape Imports Ltd which has an address in somewhere called Mullingar.'

The moon was shining straight into the office and bounced brightly from Alan's glasses.

'I called our Dublin office and asked a friend of mine, Tim Shaw, to have a look at Golden Grape imports. He came back to me the next day. Golden Grape are simply a nameplate on the office door of a manufacturing outfit called International Hydraulics Limited. Golden Grape Imports is just a postbox.'

Patrick watched Alan's face.

'Tim had also looked up both companies in the Dublin Companies Office,' Alan was saying. He nodded slowly. 'Yes, both are wholly owned subsidiaries of companies registered in Lichtenstein. In the case of International Hydraulics, they set up in Ireland three years ago with the help of a substantial cash grant from Ireland's Industrial Development Authority.'

Outside the window only the throb of the plant could be heard. 'To get a grant like that,' Alan said, almost wearily, 'there is a considerable application procedure. Tim Shaw knows people in the Industrial Development Authority. He asked them to look up the details on International Hydraulics to see who had negotiated the grant for the company.'

Patrick stared. Even before Alan said anything, Patrick knew what was coming.

'The grant was negotiated by John Abelson, Pat,' said Alan.

In the cobblestoned courtyard beneath high stacks of pallets Patrick leaned against a car and listened to the hum of the bottling plant in action. Alan appeared, locking the door of the office behind him.

'I've tabulated everything on one sheet of paper,' Alan said. 'Here's a copy. It shows everything from the payment nearly five years ago. I've also done a reconciliation for the last two years, bottles used versus sales of wine. It's crazy. In each year Château Diane buys about fifty thousand more bottles than it uses.'

'That's what – about five containers?' Patrick asked.

'Yes,' Alan said. 'It amounts to about fifty thousand pounds in value of wine sales.'

Patrick folded the photostat and waited as Alan opened the car boot and tossed his briefcase in.

'When I went back to the shipping company in Bordeaux,' Alan said, lighting up a cigarette regardless of the sign on the pallets behind him, 'the clerk who had previously helped me was no longer available – I wanted the information in writing, but now all I got was a stone wall. At this stage you probably won't be surprised to hear that Tim Shaw isn't returning my calls any more. And as you know, Sammy Mitchell and now Abelson are going berserk in London.'

They made their way out under the arch.

'You wanted some fresh air,' Alan said. 'There's a river not far from here. It reminds me of Scotland.'

On the avenue Patrick looked back: the cold, leaded turrets of Château Diane winked at him in the light of the moon. 'Who lives in the castle?' Patrick asked.

'No one,' Alan replied. 'It's been uninhabited for seventy years. Why?'

'I just wondered,' Patrick said.

They reached a gate and turned right, down a sharply descending track which wound through the spreading hectares of vines, each perfect row silhouetted in the clear night. The track levelled off and joined a broader cutting, deeply indented with the marks of tractor wheels. Alan hunched along, his head bent as if looking for pennies in the dark earth. There was the noise of water dancing over stones.

'The river,' Alan said.

Patrick saw a low, stone bridge, its courses of masonry visible in the brightness. Alan sat on the bridge and lighted one of his cigarettes, throwing the spent match down into the water. The spiced night smells of Sauternes mingled with those of tobacco. About twenty yards upstream stood the outline of a ruined byre where bats chased each other in and out of blind windows.

'The thing that astounds me more than anything,' said Alan quietly, 'is the payment made by this company barely four months after its takeover – the £50,000, or its equivalent, which was paid to Transportation Pyrenean. It's quite clear from the records, that Château Diane could not, under any circumstances, have owed that sort of money to a transport company – the company was only trading for five months. What wine transport had been done? Yet the accounts were passed by Sammy Mitchell.' Alan looked at Patrick. 'Do you remember the Church Lines liquidation?' he asked.

Patrick remembers.

Although it is windy they are out in the long field behind the house. It must be a Sunday because Papa is wearing his dark suit. Mama is there too, wrapped in a big coat with the collar turned up. She often wraps Patrick inside her coat with her. Now her face is glowing. Try again, Patrick, Papa says. I can't, I'll fall like the last time and hurt myself. Try again. I can't. Patrick, this time I'll hold the back of the saddle and see you don't fall.

'You probably don't remember,' Alan was saying, 'but it caused one hell of a stink at the time. Church Lines went bust for four or five million quid, which was a lot of money then. John Abelson was appointed liquidator of Church Lines and very shortly afterwards announced the sale of Churchtels to an investment company from Lichtenstein. There was an uproar. Several other companies who had been in the wings publicly said that they would have given much more for Churchtels had they had a chance to do so. But Abelson was the liquidator and his decision stood. The unsecured creditors only got something token at the end of the day.'

Patrick remembers.

He is pedalling. His legs are minutely too short and on each down pedal he loses contact. The pedal flies up and sometimes catches him on the shin. He is also careering, continuously, to the right, always on the verge of his balance.

'It looks to me,' Alan said very quietly, 'like Abelson sold Churchtels for a rob and probably got himself a fat backhander.'

Patrick stood up and leaned on the stone parapet, watching the dark water race beneath.

'If I'm right,' Alan said, 'you can understand why Abelson was frothing at the mouth last night up in his fancy office. If I'm right he must be shitting himself wondering what I have found.'

Patrick took a deep breath. 'If you're right,' he said evenly. 'But let's look at each of these transactions on their own, beginning with the payment five years ago. Abelson may have been quite within his rights to sell to the people from Lichtenstein. The quality of whoever else was waiting in the wings may not have been high – they had not bid and might never have bid. Abelson would have failed in his primary function as a liquidator: to get as much money as he could for the creditors.'

'And the payment?' asked Alan quietly. 'Why was 550,000 francs put through the books – and certified by Abelson Dunwoody incidentally – as a haulage payment to a company now involved in a rip-off, a haulage company also registered in Lichtenstein, with connections in Ireland who also employ John Abelson?'

Patrick hit the stone ledge with his hand. 'Jesus, Alan, it was five years ago. You're making huge assumptions.'

'Even a very amateur statistician could give you the odds against what I've found out being pure coincidence,' Alan said drily.

'All right, I accept that,' Patrick said. 'But whatever happened happened five years ago. You were sent down here to audit last year's accounts, not to go off into the past and conduct an investigation on behalf of the one-time creditors of Church Lines. It is outside your terms of reference, Alan. It's got nothing to do with this job.'

Alan's chin stuck out defiantly. 'Very well,' he said. 'Then take the year I am auditing. The company is being ripped off. Is that to be ignored? Abelson is now somehow tied up with companies in Ireland and Lichtenstein, companies who are getting wine from Château Diane that's not going through the books. Is that to be ignored as well?'

Patrick spoke precisely. 'If it is proved that there is a misappropriation,' he said, 'then you must qualify your report accordingly and it will be up to the directors of the company to take any action they see fit. If someone is stealing their money, then they will undoubtedly want to get it back.' He looked into the water.

'You amaze me.' Alan sat quietly, outlined by the moonlight.

'What you have told me amounts to misappropriated wine, not a case against John Abelson,' Patrick said. 'But just for a moment let's say that I agreed that Abelson was involved. What on earth would you propose to do?'

'I've thought about that,' Alan said. 'Normally I would go to the owners of the company. But in this case, that's no good – if they got the company on the cheap then they're not going to do anything about Abelson. The other option would be to approach Abelson Dunwoody, but clearly that's impossible.' Alan took off his glasses and rubbed his eyes. 'I think I should send a report on this whole business to the Council of the Institute of Chartered Accountants in London and let them decide what to do.'

Patrick looked at Alan in disbelief. 'Abelson's the bloody president,' Patrick said. 'You're out of your mind.'

Alan put his glasses back on and sat in silence for a moment. 'All right, Pat,' he said, 'let's be practical. The decision is not mine any more. Sammy made it quite clear on the phone that you were coming down as the person in charge. So it's over to you. What are you going to do?'

Patrick did not immediately reply. 'Business is dirty, problematical and no place for the good, you know that,' he said eventually. 'We're turning the blind eye five days a week. The new word is "commercial". Auditors make "commercial" decisions. The textbook is really something to put under your mug of hot coffee.'

'So is that what you are now, a commercial accountant? Is that the sort of discussion you had in London last night, a commercial discussion?'

Patrick shook his head in exasperation. 'I'm only trying to get on in life,' he said. 'I want to get married and buy a house and go on holidays and send my kids to good schools.'

'If you signed these accounts,' Alan said quietly, 'would you feel good about them, knowing what we know?'

'To feel good about something is not always the best or only criterion,' Patrick replied. He held up his hand and sighed. 'What I suppose I'm trying to say is that in the upper echelons of business, things are going on the whole time which would astonish the proverbial man in the street. What you've shown me, the records you've put together, the conclusions you've reached . . .' Patrick looked at Alan. 'I'm trying to say, qualify your report, then go home and forget about it.'

'I never thought I would hear you say that,' Alan said.

Patrick is falling. He knows he is going to fall. He is pedalling as hard as he can, but he has gone too far over and now he is falling. It is only on to grass, but he falls, sideways to the right, and the bike comes down on top of him. Painfully. It hurts his leg. His shin is hurt. Patrick is crying.

Patrick closed his eyes and took a deep breath. 'Alan,' he said, his voice hard, 'we're businessmen dealing with businessmen, not a bunch of starry-eyed idealists going over the tea-break records of the church choir.'

'A highly questionable payment was made to a company which is now involved in another scam with another company set up by John Abelson,' Alan said. He shivered and stood up. 'It's getting cold here.'

They began to make their way slowly back uphill.

'To go on with an unproven case like you have shown me,' Patrick said, 'means not only the end of the road with Abelson Dunwoody but virtually guarantees that no one else in London will offer you a job. You would be gambling the rest of your career on a principle.'

Alan made no reply. The edifice of the hotch-potch castle appeared briefly through the trees. They left the broader track and walked steeply up between the vines in shadow.

Against the gatepost of the avenue, Alan leaned. 'When I heard that you were to take over here,' he said, 'I made two decisions. I resolved that whatever you decided, then that would be it. I would accept it.' He nodded. 'You will hear no more from me on the subject of Château Diane.'

Their eyes met.

'I'm also leaving Abelson Dunwoody.'

Perhaps it was a trick of the light, but Alan's face and the light behind it had a warm glow.

'Oh Jesus,' Patrick said, 'the place is on fire.'

They sprinted, Alan panting at Patrick's shoulder.

'It's not the castle,' Alan said, 'it must be the plant.'

They could now see flames licking into the sky over the wall of the courtyard, orange, sharp-tipped licks, strangely beautiful against the night. They ran through the arch. The whole courtyard appeared warm and full of light. They stopped.

'The office!' Alan cried.

At the far side of the courtyard, the building which they had recently left was blazing, both floors, like a torch.

Patrick stared. Women were running from the bottling plant, bringing aprons to their mouths in awe. A bell was ringing. At the blaze, two men and a woman had formed a pathetic bucket brigade and were flinging water through the bottom window into the inferno. To his right Patrick saw the foreman, standing, looking at them; then the man hurried out through the arch, the flames illuminating his exit.

All at once the office roof took. In a great explosion of heat it disintegrated upwards in balls of spinning fire. People ran back. Then someone remembered the crated cylinders of gas, mid-courtyard, with every second coming into greater danger. As one, the gathering turned and ran, wild-eyed, for the arch. Patrick heard a familiar sound: at the far side of the central stacks someone on the forklift was attempting to shift the gas pellets.

'Let's get out!' Patrick shouted. 'This whole place could go.'

He and Alan made for the arch.

Then Alan stopped, his eyes drawn irresistibly back towards the office, now a furnace. 'The briefcase,' he said. 'It's in the car.'

'Forget it!'

Before Patrick could do anything to stop him, Alan was running back over the yard to where his car and several others were parked.

'Leave it, Alan!' Patrick cried.

Alan was at the car. He was fumbling with his keys. There was a crashing sound. Incredulously Patrick stared. Stacked gas cylinders were toppling over in slow-motion horror.

'Alan!' he screamed.

Alan had made two strides when the first of the cylinders hit the car roof and went through it like a jack-hammer. In horrified fascination Patrick saw Alan, his small eyes wide, slip and half fall.

'Alan!' Patrick rushed forward.

There was the deafening crash of heavy metal. In a blur, one cigar-shaped cylinder bounced from another embedded in the car, made a soaring parabola and caught the scrambling accountant square in the back. Patrick heard the sharp cough as Alan Ridgeway's life was expelled from his chest. He ran to the crumpled body, now ridiculously frail on the dancing, polished stones. He turned him over. Men were babbling in French. Together, they lifted Alan and ran with him, out through the arch, into the gravelled forecourt. Someone spread a coat. His eyes streaming, Patrick dropped down and clamped his mouth over the thin white face; with all the strength he ever had, he began to pump. He held the head between his hands and sucked and blew in great regular gulps, willing something to happen within the body on his lap. After five minutes he stopped, exhausted, and as he did so his own breath seeped out of Alan's mouth in a slow, moaning gurgle. Then there was a mighty explosion which shook the ground and the people and the castle itself. Trembling, Patrick leaped to his feet.

'Out of my way!' he shouted at the circle of gaping faces.

He dashed through the arch: the whole courtyard was a shimmering cremation at whose centre the blazing shapes of cars could be seen. Insanely Patrick drove himself towards them, blindly, savagely gritting his teeth against the intense heat. His vision went. He felt strong arms grasp him and pull him back. Devastated, he sank down, crashing his clenched fists to the warm ground again and again.

'Jesus Christ,' he wept as the significance of his disbelief overwhelmed him.

In the far distance of the surrounding night and the outside world, the siren of a fire brigade became clearer, winding up through the manicured vine fields of Loupiac.

PART TWO

Buenos Aires, Argentina

CHAPTER FOUR

1961

'¡*Abajo Kennedy! Abajo Kennedy!*'

The rag-tag band swarmed past the dark window, on down the Avenida Córdoba. From the table inside the four people could see them: shouting, marching youths with upraised fists. A large effigy suddenly appeared in the mob with a photograph pinned to it and a sign, crudely scrawled, which said 'Stevenson'. There was smoke and the doll-like figure began to burn brightly as the chanting procession went its way.

'*Porteñitos*,' said one of the men at the table. Disdainfully he turned his eyes from the window. 'Children. They need their arses spanked.' He looked across the floor of the nightclub to the pianist who had suspended playing as the march went past; immediately the man resumed. The two women and the man smiled at their host. As always Marcellino commanded events around him. Now he sat, the centre, a man in his mid-thirties, his hair black, slicked back, his face the colour of cured hide, his powerful torso clothed in a spotless white tuxedo. A waiter placed another bottle of Argentine champagne in an ice-bucket, bowed respectfully and withdrew.

'They are not children when they have you in a corner,' said the other man. He was an American, in his early twenties, with an open, handsome face, a large forehead and closely cropped, smooth brown hair. He smiled at the woman. 'If it were not for Marcellino,' he said in passable Spanish, 'they might be burning me out there right now, not Adlai Stevenson.'

Marcellino snorted. 'I detest people with the manners of pigs,' he said. 'You are a visitor, Cherry. How could I have passed what I saw?' He looked around. '*¡Camarero!*' He was clicking his fingers. '*Un cuchillo para trinchar la carne*,' he commanded. 'A carving knife.'

The woman at Marcellino's right hand opened her mouth in a smile. She was a beauty in full bloom, an olive-skinned, dramatically handsome woman with hair of ink swept up and back from a face of clean, unflawed lines, a wide, laughing mouth and almond eyes of sparkling green. Marcellino called her Esmeralda. Her shoulders were bare, two perfect and irresistible sweeps of bone and flesh, gathering between them the rise of her breasts. Cherry could not keep his eyes from her.

Marcellino took the bottle from its bucket and placed it on the table. The other girl, a plump pudding named Rosa, drew in her breath. The waiter returned with a long, smooth-edged knife which he presented handle first to Marcellino; then the waiter picked up the empty ice-bucket in both hands and withdrew to stand two yards from the table.

Cherry looked on in fascination. People from other tables had risen to watch. Marcellino took the heavy knife in his right hand; in a movement too quick for the eye he swept the blade through the air and sliced the top from the bottle at the point where the wire secured the cork. As the cleanly severed top landed in the bucket, Marcellino caught the foaming wine in his glass. He smiled at the applause.

'The instrument you use,' he said, 'must be an extension of yourself. That, together with the resolve of your mind, and you can achieve anything.'

They drank.

'In my country,' Marcellino said, 'there is a dance: it is performed by the Zamalzain, a traditional horseman. He concludes by leaping three, maybe four feet in the air, then landing on an upright, full wine-glass. He will keep his balance – and not spill the wine.'

Cherry shook his head. 'Can you do it?' he asked.

'No,' replied Marcellino, 'I left before I was old enough to learn. But I have seen it done, here in Argentina.' He squeezed his woman. 'One day I will bring my flower Esmeralda with me to see the Zamalzain in the old country,' he smiled. 'We will go in July and she can see me run the bulls in Irunea.'

The man at the piano began to sing 'Mona Lisa', the new Nat King Cole number. Marcellino drained his glass, nodded to the other girl, Rosa, then walked out on to the dance floor on the balls of his feet.

Cherry looked to La Esmeralda. Her eyes had followed Marcellino to the dance floor; now she turned and looked openly at Cherry.

'He likes your company,' she said. 'As I do.' She raised her arm and shook golden bracelets down to her elbow.

Cherry felt his blood surge under her gaze.

'He will never really be accepted here in Buenos Aires,' she said. 'He is a *forastero*, an outsider, to them.' She turned down the corners of her mouth. 'Most of them are dirt,' she said. 'But you are different.'

'He speaks of "my country",' Cherry said, sipping champagne. He looked across at the dance floor. 'He has spent most of his life in Argentina. Is this not his country?'

La Esmeralda shook her head. 'For him, never.'

'I guess he still wants to go back to Spain.'

'Not to Spain.'

Cherry frowned.

'To Euskadi,' La Esmeralda said. 'The country of us Basques.'

'But that is part of Spain.'

'You say that to Marcellino,' La Esmeralda said. She had perfectly even, white teeth; she brought out the tip of her tongue and rubbed it over them. Cherry found himself staring. She caught his eye and smiled.

'He will go back,' La Esmeralda said softly. 'Some day he will go back.' She crossed her legs and leaned forward so that Cherry could see the swell of her breasts gathered just inside the line of her dress. 'And you, Cherry,' she said, 'what of you? Do you have a wife in *el norte*, in America? And a family of little children, perhaps, for whom you send home an envelope full of money every month?' She laughed lightly and Cherry felt himself colouring before her assurance.

'I am not married,' he said.

'But nearly married, perhaps.'

'Not even nearly.'

La Esmeralda's eyes danced. 'And in Argentina, here in Buenos Aires,' she said, 'you have met girls?'

Cherry shook his head. 'Regrettably, no.'

'And you have been here how long? Three months?'

Slowly a smile like bright sunshine spread over La Esmeralda's face as the music from the dance floor ceased.

The nightclub staff lined up at the door to receive their *propiñas*, hundred-peso bills which Marcellino peeled from a thick roll. '*Padrino*,' they whispered. Outside, a new Chrysler coupé was running, a uniformed doorman holding open its doors. Suddenly there was a flash. Marcellino froze. A smiling pavement-photographer came out from the shadows, scribbling a ticket.

'*¡Cabrón!*' Marcellino stepped towards him.

'*Con calma*,' said La Esmeralda, taking the ticket from the suddenly frightened man.

Scowling, Marcellino turned back to the car. 'Sit in the back, Cherry,' he commanded, 'with Esmeralda.'

They drove west on Diaz Velez, Marcellino slowing at each intersection to flash his lights. He drove expertly, running the car through its gears, passing slower vehicles fast and close.

'Where are we going?' Cherry asked when they reached the Avenida San Martin.

'For a nightcap,' Marcellino said. 'To Esmeralda's.'

Cherry saw the girl open her mouth and laugh softly. His heart thumped. He felt her arm with its bracelets on his leg and then her long fingers as they cupped and squeezed him. Cherry kept his eyes to the fore, his hands on the seat, his rampant human need tempered only by his cold fear of the man in front.

La Esmeralda's apartment overlooked a courtyard. Marcellino led them up two flights of steps. Inside, he led the way directly to a wide bedroom, threw off his jacket and began to unbutton his shirt. Cherry watched as the women also undressed. Marcellino's torso was powerful, the build of a wrestler, his chest and back covered by dense mats of hair. Cherry caught his breath. La Esmeralda had climbed on to the bed, her body in the soft lights flawless and fluid-moving. In her hand she held a bottle and as Cherry watched, she uncorked it and spread sweet-smelling body oil over Marcellino's back. As La Esmeralda kneaded the oil into the long muscles running along his shoulders, Rosa went to a wardrobe and returned with a small box of polished wood which she handed to the Basque. He opened it, and removed a square of glass and a vial. With care he tapped out two lines of white powder on to the glass. He took a tube from the box and handed it to Cherry.

'First our guest,' Marcellino said.

'What is it?'

The women laughed and Marcellino looked at Cherry in disbelief. 'It is candy,' he answered, smiling, 'cocaine, the powder of the gods.'

Cherry shook his head in bewilderment. From the corner of his eye he could see La Esmeralda smiling.

'Show Cherry,' Marcellino ordered.

Obediently La Esmeralda came around and sat cross-legged. Holding one end of the tube to the powder and the other to her nose, she sniffed powerfully once, then again, up the other nostril. She winced, then jerked sharply, her nose pointing to the ceiling. Then she sat, inhaling deeply, her shoulders back.

Marcellino inclined his head to Cherry. The American, still in his shorts, took the flat glass and watched as the Basque tapped out two lines. Beside him La Esmeralda's eyes were closed, her head thrown back in pleasure.

Cherry snorted both lines. He sat there. For some seconds nothing appeared to happen. Then he felt a pleasing numbness rush first into his nose, then into his upper front gums. Fires ignited, millions of them, all over his body. Slowly he saw La Esmeralda rise, slow-motion-like, and come around to kneel directly behind him. He could feel her fingers at his shoulders, and her breasts and softness begin to rub him, back and forth. Cherry's fear of earlier fell away. In its place he now felt euphoria, power and an amazing ability that felt totally natural. Rosa had moved across to stroke Marcellino's chest. Cherry turned; he was tingling all over. La Esmeralda lowered her head so that her lips brushed his chest. She caught Cherry's hand and guided it down. Cherry slipped from his shorts and unmindful of anything but the awesome power which was surging in him, he lifted her, bodily, and spread her out on the bed. He had the strength of ten men and a total clarity of vision and understanding.

Cherry felt himself being guided in; he looked down at La Esmeralda who was lying open-mouthed, gasping, and for a moment he wondered if there was a danger that he might actually go right through, kill her.

But what Cherry remembered most was not the magnificent creature beneath him whom he was now part of, but Marcellino, sitting there like a frog, his tongue occasionally darting, his hands joined together in the body-hair of his lap and within them his useless manhood, small and flaccid, smaller than a child's finger, unmoving, dead.

That was what Cherry remembered best of the first night on which he snorted *perica*.

CHAPTER FIVE

They sat on the floor, their backs to the bed, their bodies luxuriating in the morning sun which streamed through the open french window. La Esmeralda raised her hand and with closed eyes she brushed away a wisp of black hair from her face.

'This is beautiful,' she murmured.

'You are beautiful,' Cherry said. 'Men would go to war for a woman like you.'

She smiled and tilted back her head, breathing deeply in the lovely morning. She had a perfect body: wide shoulders, full, firm breasts, a slim, collected waist flowing out again to the gleam of her hips and her long, shapely legs.

'I feel so lazy,' she said.

Cherry's bedroom overlooked someone's back garden, an oasis of quiet in the heart of Buenos Aires.

'I want to stay here for ever,' La Esmeralda said.

Cherry ran his eyes over her, savouring every second. In such moments time for him became infinitely expandable at both ends and lost all meaning. Eventually the desire became too much. He knelt and went to her, starting with his tongue at her throat and with stealth, working his way downwards, circling in her navel, then plunging until he found her essence. He lay, chest down, his feet at the windows. He could feel the firm press of her thighs against his ears.

'*Maravilloso, maravilloso,*' she kept saying as her fingers grasped his head and pressed him even more. She drew up her knees and sat straight. Cherry felt the movement of her body, pulsing up and down, and her cries, unmindful of the nearby garden. At last she shouted out so loud that he kicked the windows shut behind him. When she was still he brought his head up and laid it on her stomach and they both lay, their bodies shining, the happiness of their release spreading over them in a glow. They slept.

'Where do you come from?' Cherry asked.

The sun had moved and they with it, across the window.

'A tiny village called Veronica,' La Esmeralda replied. 'It's about a hundred kilometres from here.'

She snuggled closer. 'My father was the station master. We were poor, but not as poor as some. My mother was first generation Basque, she had a little money which her father had given her on her wedding day and she used it to send me, her only daughter, to a convent here in Buenos Aires. It was a brave decision. She wanted me to have more than she had – a two-bedroomed house on a railway platform on the way to nowhere.'

'It was brave.'

'I never went back.' La Esmeralda turned and lay on her stomach, her fingers playing with a thread of the rug. 'The money ran out, after the first year I think.' She smiled. 'My mother was very simple – she would not have been able to work it out beyond that. The nuns took me over. They kept some girls on the whole year round; we earned our keep working in the laundry, ironing, sewing.'

'Very often girls like that become nuns,' Cherry said, amused. 'Why not you?'

La Esmeralda laughed and held up the middle finger of her right hand. 'I discovered men,' she said.

Cherry kissed her. 'Tell me about you and Marcellino,' she said.

La Esmeralda adjusted her head so that her cheek lay on his belly. 'Marcellino,' she sighed, her eyes lidded. 'I would walk on my bare feet to Tierra del Fuego if I thought it would please him.'

Cherry felt a pluck of jealousy. 'He means that much to you?'

'He means *todo*, everything to me,' La Esmeralda said. 'He is not just an ordinary man. He is a man apart, a man in whom God has reposed great designs, a messiah. A saint.' She opened her eyes and their colours immediately began to change. 'To me,' she said, 'he is a saint.'

'I have never met anyone like him,' Cherry agreed. 'He

commands with his very presence. If you stand in a crowded room with your back to the door you will know it the instant he has entered.'

La Esmeralda smiled. 'But . . .?'

Cherry frowned. 'But, nothing.'

'But,' she persisted, 'the tone of your voice said "but".'

'It didn't.'

'What you want to say,' La Esmeralda said, 'is, how can I feel so much for a man like Marcellino when I know that physically he can do so little for me when you can do so much?'

Cherry remained silent.

'You see it is not a question of his failing me,' La Esmeralda said, 'because he has never tried. He can't. You saw that yourself. There, as in every other aspect, he is different to other men. That does not stop me being his woman or his being proud of me. Nor does it stop me living my life to the full.' She rubbed the muscles on Cherry's chest. 'I am a healthy woman. Marcellino knows that and he encourages me.'

'Is that why he . . . befriended me?'

'Perhaps initially.'

'Because I was an outsider? Someone not known? Because I was someone who wouldn't let out the secret?'

La Esmeralda nodded. 'Perhaps, I think you could say that.' She smiled warmly. 'But now he really likes you, Cherry, for yourself, I really mean that.'

Cherry turned his head away. 'It's like being a gigolo,' he said.

La Esmeralda slapped his chest softly with her palm. '*No seas mimado,*' she said, 'don't be spoiled.'

'Look,' Cherry said, 'you are the most beautiful woman I have ever seen, let alone met, anywhere, in movies, magazines, anywhere. You are full-blooded, loving, you have . . . needs. How can a man who omits those parts of you say he truly loves you?'

La Esmeralda shrugged.

'It's like he's your father, or your older brother,' Cherry said. 'But not your man.' He caught her head in his hands and turned her face up to him. 'I want to be that,' he whispered fiercely, 'I want to be your man.'

Her eyes as ever gave him her reply. The green rushed out to the boundary of the irises, driven by a spreading, golden yellow, whilst the centres telescoped into tiny points.

Cherry filled his lungs with air. 'That sounds as if I'm kicking Marcellino,' he said, 'and I don't mean to. I can't help it, but I want you so much.'

La Esmeralda rose and put on one of Cherry's shirts which lay on a chair. She went to the small kitchen and Cherry could hear her pouring water into a pot.

'Why is he like that?' he called, shifting further into the sun.

'He suffered a huge shock as a child,' she answered him. 'He was there when they bombed Guernica, it's the religious capital of the Basque country, near the northern coast. Franco wanted to wipe them out.'

'Marcellino saw it happen?'

'He has never really discussed it with me. I just know what happened from spending time with him. The experience has shaped his whole life and provides him with the driving motivation for everything he does.'

La Esmeralda arrived with a jug of black coffee and two cups. 'Our breakfast,' she laughed. 'I am a bad housekeeper, I'm afraid.'

'What does Marcellino want?' Cherry asked.

La Esmeralda sat. 'To free his people,' she said quietly, 'our people.'

They sat in silence, sipping the thick coffee.

'On the first night I went with him,' La Esmeralda said, 'I got a shock. He's such a physically strong man, I thought he would be . . .' She looked out the window. 'He saw me looking down at him. He said: "I was a child in Guernica." No more. It is his explanation.'

Cherry caressed her neck.

'He likes you,' La Esmeralda said. She leaned back and kissed him. 'He also likes it that you are with me.'

Cherry stroked her hair with the back of his hand. 'He's a drugs dealer, isn't he?' he said quietly.

The girl's shoulders shrugged.

'Isn't he?'

'I don't care what he is,' the girl answered softly. 'Whatever he is doing, it is for a purpose.'

'Let's hope he doesn't get caught,' Cherry said.

The sun warmed only a small patch of carpet now, a space big enough for one person. Cherry sat in it with La Esmeralda between his outstretched legs. He could scent her. He licked her all along the base of her neck, tasting the oil of her skin.

'*Hazlo otra vez*, do that again.'

He put his cup down and peeled the shirt collar back so that the ripple of her shoulders was exposed. 'You're driving me insane,' he murmured.

La Esmeralda was in his lap.

'Jesus Christ!' Cherry gasped.

He drove upwards with all his strength, bringing La Esmeralda with him, up off the floor so that she went right over, Cherry on top of her, both on all fours in the sunny window. He finished it, a huge beast straddling its thing of beauty, and as he did she cried out.

'Marcellino,' she cried to the warm morning, '*Dios mío*, Marcellino.'

CHAPTER SIX

Extract from *The Times*, March 1962

PERONISTS KEEP ARGENTINA ON THE BOIL

From our correspondent
BUENOS AIRES, 20 MARCH

A fog of chaos continues to envelop the Argentine political scene. Government-appointed commissioners have assumed direction of the affairs of provinces where Peronists won electoral victories last Sunday.

This afternoon the newspapers were ready to go to press with news of the resignation of President Frondizi, but had to change over when it was learned that he had not resigned. Tonight there were again strong rumours of the President's impending resignation.

The value of the peso slumped from the normal 83 to the dollar to 110 during yesterday's short operations of the exchanges. The banks and stock exchange remained close again today.

BUENOS AIRES, 20 MARCH. A group thought to be neo-Peronists attacked a police patrol in the Villa Crespo area of Buenos Aires last evening and captured a police officer. The officer's body was later found in the Plaza de Mayo, the traditional centre of the city. He had been shot through the head. Police are questioning suspects.

Reuter

'It is time to get out of Argentina.'

Cherry looked at Marcellino. The Basque had put down the *Critica* and was looking out at the street, his leathery face impassive, his shirt buttons open halfway down his chest. The time was six in the evening, the temperature in the seventies. Nearby, Cherry could hear the delighted shrieks of *porteñitos*, slum children of Buenos Aires, as they dived from the street into the sluggish waters of the Riachuelo.

'Frondizi is a tired old woman playing in a game of men,' Marcellino said. 'He will finish his days in the prison on Martín Garcia. Even Peron from his exile in Madrid now has more power in Argentina than Frondizi.'

'Frondizi has the support of President Kennedy,' Cherry said. 'Argentina gets much aid from the US and Kennedy is a powerful ally.'

'Kennedy, Kennedy,' said Marcellino dismissively. 'No offence, but the Yankees need us more than we need them. They are terrified of communism in South America and they will do anything, deal with anyone to stop it. Frondizi?' Marcellino made a crude stab with his finger. 'That is what the Yankees will do with Frondizi.'

Cherry pointed to the newspaper. 'The peso is collapsing,' he said. 'They say that the banks will not open tomorrow. Today I got 95 to the dollar – on the black market I imagine the rate is well over 100.'

'I told you,' the Basque said softly. 'Give your dollars to me. Today I could have got you 120. It is my business.'

The American smiled and shook his head briefly. 'Thanks, but no thanks,' Cherry said. He looked out at the evening crowds strolling without concern through La Boca. 'It's hard to imagine that there's a crisis,' he said. He indicated with his head. 'They don't seem too worried.' A group of half-naked children, dripping wet and laughing, ran past. 'What is a crisis?' Cherry asked. 'Very often I think it's something created by a rumour or a newspaper. The crisis in Buenos Aires may be much more real in the imagination of men in London or New York than it is here on the banks of the Plata.'

Marcellino looked at him. 'You were not here in '56,' he said. 'Then it was not imagination. The military took over then as they will do now. I myself saw a truck with over twenty bodies on the outskirts of San Isidro, all Peronists, never reported. Ask their mothers: their children never came home. Was that imagination?' Marcellino snorted contemptuously. 'The military will move in again,' he said. 'Mark my words, it will be a surprise if Buenos Aires is not a heap of rubble within seven days.'

Cherry considered the coiled power of the man. 'You sympathise with the Peronists?' he asked.

Marcellino made a face. 'To me,' he said, '*me da iqual*, there is no difference. I told you. It is time to get out of Argentina.'

A girl arrived from the back of the café and placed a plate of ham and fried eggs in front of Marcellino. The Basque began to eat, rapidly, cutting all the meat into thin strips and bloodying the plate with the yolks of the eggs. He ate like a dog, forking the food into his mouth in a series of jerks until the plate was clear. Then he sat back.

'*Ona da*,' he said with pleasure.

Cherry sipped a coffee. 'Basque?' he asked.

Marcellino nodded. 'The oldest language in the world,' he said. 'It was spoken in the ark.'

Cherry laughed outright and felt the dark eyes on him.

'I am not joking, my friend,' the Basque said quietly. 'Our tongue is connected with no other. This *porquería*, this Spanish rubbish that we speak is a mongrel; its father is a monkey from the jungles of India, its mother a bitch from the back streets of Rome.' Marcellino belched loudly. 'But Eskuara,' he said, 'is the purest language in the world.'

The girl placed a *café negro* in front of Marcellino.

'You love your country above everything else, don't you?' Cherry said.

A faraway look had entered the Basque's eyes. 'Above all else,' he agreed simply.

Cherry looked admiringly at the powerful figure, the residue of such natural authority. 'We spoke of Peron earlier on,' Cherry said with respect. 'In a way you are like Peron, aren't you, Marcellino? You are both men exiled. Vast oceans separate you from the country you love where events happen which you cannot control. You are the Basque Peron.'

Marcellino smiled and shrugged as if the statement did not take him by surprise. 'There is one difference,' he said without emotion. 'Peron will never return to Argentina.'

* * *

An hour later they mingled with the busy street crowds of La Boca, stopping at open doors or windows to listen to American transistors as newsreaders hurried out the latest on the political situation. Some men nodded and smiled, others inclined in a bow as the Basque passed them.

'There is something I must tell you,' Cherry said. 'I guess my delaying telling you means that I really don't want it to happen.'

Marcellino raised his eyebrows.

'I am leaving,' Cherry said quietly. 'I got the news this morning. I am to be posted home in two weeks.'

They stopped by an arched doorway. Marcellino placed his hand on Cherry's shoulder. 'I like you, Cherry,' he said. 'You have been a friend.'

'And you have shown me a Buenos Aires a stranger could never know,' Cherry replied. 'I will never forget you.'

The eyes in the dark head darted like fireflies.

'We will have *una fiesta!*' Marcellino said. 'We will have a party tonight!' He took the American's arm and steered him back down the crowded street the way they had come. 'It is just what we need,' Marcellino said, 'an excuse for a party! Why should our lives become dark and empty because an old, constipated man in the Presidential palace won't resign and the Navy is lining up in the Plata to bomb the shit out of us? Why should we care?'

Cherry laughed at the infectious enthusiasm.

'I will call Esmeralda,' the Basque was saying, stepping into a café as men stood aside. 'It will be the best party of all time, a *fiesta* for my friend Cherry who is leaving our midst to become a Yankee again. The most beautiful women in all of Argentina will be there, and we shall party all day and all night, until either we fall down or the bombardment is over and no stones remain standing in Buenos Aires.'

The party was in Villa Crespo, a residential area ten minutes north of downtown Buenos Aires. The house had been modelled many years before on a Florentine villa; it had a long, narrow garden behind it which ran back to a lane. Like other parties which Cherry had been to with Marcellino no one seemed to know, or particularly care, who owned the house – which was always different – or who the host was for the occasion. People came and went, danced to records on an old gramophone, drank, had endless discussions and created a gradually descending cloud of marijuana smoke which crept into every corner of the villa and out of the opened windows into the night.

It was after midnight, Cherry would remember, because a sweet-smelling very Spanish girl with deeply tinted, flaxen hair and enormous eyes had asked him for a light for the joint between her lips, then requested the time before walking towards the garden, her hips rolling, leaving a deliciously confusing amalgam of smells in her wake.

Marcellino stood in the dining-room, just inside the garden doors. La Esmeralda stood attentively; as usual Cherry could not keep his eyes off her: she was in a sweeping dress with a cut-away back which revealed her deep, brown vertebrae. La Esmeralda listened as Marcellino spoke quietly to the men around him; occasionally she brought him a cold Quilmes, the local beer, or lighted a flame for his *cigarro*. The old gramophone in the hall beat out a tango; couples danced, others drifted casually up and down a carved wooden staircase, to and from the accommodation above. There were front rooms left and right and, off the rear dining-room where Marcellino stood, a kitchen in which half a dozen *mujeres*, girlfriends or wives, were preparing platters of *cosas para picar* and *tapas*, and brewing the ubiquitous *café negro*. There were over a hundred people in the house, dancing, talking in groups, passing around joints, or snorting precious white mounds of *perica*.

In the years that followed Cherry would regularly reconstruct the night in an endless attempt at comprehension. Nearly five years later, lying on his own in his bedroom, it abruptly came to him. Marcellino had had about him that night a restlessness which belied the subdued power, the controlled hegemony with which the Basque normally dominated his immediate surroundings. That night Marcellino was ill at ease, inattentive to La Esmeralda, listening with only one ear to the men around him . . . waiting. Marcellino had been waiting!

'A great party, Marcellino,' Cherry said.

The Basque turned. Out of the corner of his eye Cherry could see La Esmeralda leave the hall and begin to mount the stairs. If he noticed her Marcellino did not show it. Instead his eyes were on the garden, on the hall and fleetingly on the gold watch on his thick, brown wrist.

'Marcellino,' Cherry said, 'we spoke today of Euskadi. You left it when you were a child. How can you love a country you cannot really know?'

A slow smile spread on Marcellino's face, the smile of the possessor of a special secret. He turned and tapped a finger to his chest. 'In here,' he said, '*el corazón*, the heart, it knows.'

'Tell me what it knows.'

Marcellino turned around. A very slight, youngish man stood there whom Cherry had not noticed before. His face was pale, his eyes bright blue behind steel-rimmed spectacles. He wore an ill-fitting white jacket; this, combined with tousled fair hair gave him the appearance of a youthful, if tired, schoolmaster. Marcellino put his arm around the thin shoulders.

'This is my friend Sainz Perez,' Marcellino said to Cherry, 'my young friend who will give Euskadi her freedom – am I right?'

The man called Sainz Perez nodded without affectation. 'With your help I will,' he said, 'with your help.'

'Ask him about the heart,' Marcellino said to Cherry. 'Ask Sainz Perez what his heart knows.'

'What does your heart tell you, *Señor?*' Cherry asked.

Sainz Perez sighed. 'Euskadi is an island,' he said. 'We are a people who from the dawn of history have always been apart. Spain is the warm cunt of Europe who for all millenniums has been ravaged, by Celts, by Romans, by the savages from the north and by the filth of Africa. But Euskadi, the land of the Basques, has never submitted to an external authority. Although we have been conquerors, never have we been conquered.'

From the garden, rich with the smells of the late summer night, a thin-faced, hook-nosed man materialised. Cherry could still see him. He had a thick, drooping moustache. His eyes met Marcellino's, then he slipped into the kitchen.

'*Señor*,' Cherry said, still addressing Sainz Perez, 'today Marcellino told me that it is time to get out of Argentina. Do you agree? Will you go back to your Euskadi?'

Sainz Perez looked at Cherry as if he had not heard. Cherry looked to Marcellino.

'Euskadi?' said Marcellino. 'No, *todavía no*, not yet, not yet.'
Then the hall door burst in.

Cherry's first impression was that an exuberant party-goer had been unable to gain access and had just put his shoulder to it. With the eye-level smoke it was difficult to see. The door crashed back, then all at once the hall was full of uniformed men holding guns. A woman screamed.

'*¡Ertzaina! ¡Ertzaina!*' someone shouted. There was chaos. As one the crowd surged into the dining-room and towards the garden. Cherry felt himself carried along. He saw a man break free, rush into the kitchen and empty something down the sink. The crowd stopped. There were frenzied shouts: in the garden more uniforms had appeared. Cherry looked back to the hall and saw a blue flashing in the front, behind silhouetted police caps. Now the crowd became divided in its intentions: people fought their way in both directions. There was a deafening thunder-clap as a gun discharged into the ceiling.

'*¡Alto!*' The voice came from a megaphone near the door. '*¡Este es el Departamento de Narcóticos de Buenos Aires!* Everybody here is under arrest!'

All the lights died.

The surging crowd whom the gun-shot had frozen began to scramble again. Only the flashing outside the hall door provided any illumination.

'Halt!' boomed the megaphone. 'This is an arrest!'

Cherry felt terror. His arm was caught by a strong hand; he drew back in the darkness, but he remained held and felt himself led. He could see nothing, just feel the panic-stricken press around him. He bumped a wall, then allowed himself to be impelled along in the blackness. Reassurance flowed from the warm hand. They were pushing against the tide of bodies. There were shouts and cries as people fell; a torch had begun to probe from the door, but it disappeared and Cherry realised that he had entered another room. He felt the outline of a window-ledge.

'Climb out, follow me,' whispered Marcellino.

Cherry tried to come to terms with the inky night: where were the street lights? He realised that the black-out must have affected the whole neighbourhood. They were outside the house, at the side, and visibility was only slightly better than within.

Marcellino was flattened against a high, wooden fence, the boundary of the property, separating it from the garden next door. Inside the house there was another gun-shot.

'Over!' Marcellino commanded. He leaped and caught the dim top of the fence, then jackknifed upwards. Cherry saw his outline steady, then a hand came down. Cherry caught it and felt himself powered aloft. The fence quivered with their weight.

'Come on!' Marcellino hissed and launched himself into the darkness. There was a crash of breaking. '*Se aluia!*' Cherry heard the Basque grunt. He leaped himself, hit soft ground and rolled. He scrambled up and could make out Marcellino as he began to run, limping heavily, down the garden parallel to where the party was taking place. Cherry could hear breath fighting in the powerful chest. Cherry's eyes had become more functional and the end wall of the garden appeared with a small door inset. Marcellino's face was creased in pain.

'What have you done?' Cherry panted.

'Broke my fucking ankle, I think,' the Basque replied.

Quietly they opened the wall door.

'Which way?' asked Cherry.

'*Izquierda*,' said Marcellino, 'left. And walk slowly, for Christ's sake.'

They had made ten metres, past the house of the party and up the empty lane. As suddenly as they had failed, lights everywhere were abruptly restored. Cherry could not prevent his head from turning. Behind them, at the very other end of the lane, two Buenos Aires police squad cars, dark blue with pale blue tops, were blocking the way, two armed officers sitting on their bonnets, smoking.

'Don't turn!' Marcellino rasped.

But they had been seen.

'Hey, you! Hey you two! Stop!'

'Shit!' swore Marcellino. They had nearly made it to the top of the narrow way, to the comparative safety of a street where they could mingle with traffic and the pedestrians of Villa Crespo. The running leather soles behind them echoed in the lane.

'¡*Alto!* Stop!'

'I can't run!' swore the Basque.

The police were a hundred yards behind.

'You go!' Marcellino hissed.

Cherry slipped his arm under the powerful shoulders; together they stumbled towards the bright street.

'*¡En nombre de la ley!* In the name of the law!'

Cherry and Marcellino rounded the corner of the lane and stopped, gasping. Parked in front of them, its near wheels up on the kerb, was a Ford Falcon from the Buenos Aires Police Department. In the driver's seat sat a smooth-cheeked, hatless young officer, his eyes to the fore, glued to the front gate of the party house which he had been told to watch.

Marcellino shook himself free of the American. The policemen behind them were closing. Cherry stood rooted as the Basque's arm snaked back, then flashed steel as he crouched and approached the squad car.

'Jesus Christ . . .' Cherry began.

The Basque used his left hand to fling open the car door; then the same hand dived in, grabbed a fistful of hair, wrenched the alarmed face around and held it until it touched the rock-steady tip of the stiletto.

'Get his gun, fast!' panted the Basque.

The pursuing police were so near that their uniforms could be seen through the hedge of the nearby garden.

'Get it – before they see who I am!' cried Marcellino.

Cherry dragged a pistol out from its leather holster. He heard shouts.

'Take him in!' shouted Marcellino.

Shoving the officer's pistol up under the line of his jawbone, Cherry pushed the man across the seat. There was a lurch as the car was brought to life and driven blindly out into the road and away.

There was gunfire behind. They crossed one intersection, then another.

'*No me mata, no me mata.*'

As the pounding washed relentlessly over Cherry's eardrums, he became aware that the policeman was whispering something.

'*No me mata.*'

'What's he saying?' Cherry gasped.

'He's saying "don't shoot me",' Marcellino replied.

They had half a minute's head start. Marcellino gunned the Ford through block after block, its siren wailing. He swore savagely, hitting all the switches on the dash in turn before he finally killed the noise. Beside him Cherry kept the pistol stuck rigidly into the young officer's gullet; the youth's eyes were wide with terror, his head jammed tight against the car door.

'This is madness,' Cherry cried. 'We've got to ditch the car and disappear.'

'What do you think I'm trying to do?' Marcellino snarled. He swerved violently as they overtook a truck with no tail lights. 'I can't fucking run – I've got to get into La Boca.'

'What about him?' Cherry cried, the gun a ton weight in his hand.

'*No he visto nada, lo juro,*' the youth whispered, 'I swear to you, I've seen nothing.'

At a broad intersection a car to their left almost stood on its nose to avoid the squad car as it roared through.

'We've got to get off the main avenue,' Marcellino swore. Then, 'Shit!'

'What is it?'

'Look behind!'

Cherry shoved the pistol an inch deeper and glanced back. At the limit of vision flashing lights could be seen, growing every instant.

'Jesus!' Cherry cried out.

They were doing eighty, heading directly east, downtown, on Avenida Córdoba. They flashed past the Hospital Escuela, the biggest in Buenos Aires, then the Gran Deposito Córdoba, a huge, black block of shadow. Overhead the bright, summer night could be seen through a maze of tram wires. Cherry felt uncontrollable fear flood through him. The flashing lights at their rear had now multiplied and were closing.

'Stop!' he shouted. 'Stop, for God's sake! This is insane. We must stop and surrender.'

Although they were travelling at three times the speed of the other vehicles in a street which was getting busier with each block that flicked by, Marcellino took the time to give Cherry a long, dispassionate stare.

'An Eskualdunak,' he said with cold contempt, 'never surrenders.'

'Watch out!' screamed the American.

A darkened bus was crossing Córdoba, northwards up

Montevideo. The Basque swung the Ford right. The car careened for the hoardings of a building site, swerved left, right again in a crazy lurch, then righted itself as Marcellino regained control.

'*¡Hijo de puta!*' he swore.

They could now hear the police sirens behind. Cherry watched in horror as they powered ever deeper into the heart of Buenos Aires, his finger frozen on the trigger of the pistol. He could hear the broken breath of the young policeman and sense his appalling fear. Cherry's eyes went to the back window; then he looked forward again and nearly vomited: half a block in front a line of figures with hand-held lights and cars parked lengthways were blocking the width of Avenida Córdoba.

Marcellino's reactions were electric. Without hesitation he swung the Ford right and jumped it at seventy on to the broad empty pavement outside the Jewish synagogue. There were shouts; Cherry could see policemen run towards them brandishing guns, but not firing. With a loud crash and a scrape they hit the road again. The car suddenly swerved blindly, its spinning front wheel caught temporarily in tram-tracks, then with a roar they jumped free and were heading south on the Avenida 9 de Julio. It was practically deserted. They sped past the massively squat jewel of the Teatro Colón.

'We'll head for the river,' Marcellino said through clenched teeth. 'When we get into La Boca, you jump first. I'll lead them on for a few more blocks, then I'll ditch this.'

Cherry's chest was pumping for breath. Behind, the unrelenting lights were in view again. 'What will I do with him?' he cried. The young policeman's breath stank with fear.

'Knock him on the head,' Marcellino said, speaking in broken English. 'Turn his head away from you, then when he cannot see you club him with the gun butt as hard as you can.'

The Obelisk of Buenos Aires towered before them.

'Jesus, I can't do that,' cried Cherry, 'this is a policeman!'

'What do you want?' snarled the Basque. 'To spend the next twenty years in an Argentine jail?' He spun the wheel of the car and launched them into an expertly judged, left-hand drift, around the massive Obelisk at the head of the Avenida 9 de Julio. They were now pointing due east again, in the direction of the Rio de la Plata.

'Knock him out, fuck you!' hissed the Basque. 'What are you? A woman's soft underbelly?'

'I can't do this,' Cherry groaned, 'I can't.'

They were passing the Comega Club. White-aproned waiters stacking chairs upsidedown on tables paused to stare at the police car as it tore past.

'I'm doing this for you, damn you!' urged Marcellino. 'This I can handle, this is my life. But you – you will be finished.'

Tears coursed down Cherry's face. With his free hand he caught the boy's smooth face and turned it towards the window.

'*¡Vuelve la cabeza!*' he commanded. 'Look away!'

The youth began to babble incoherently. There was a foul stink as he lost control of himself.

'Do it, damn you!' shouted the Basque.

In horror Cherry saw that they had swung, almost overturning, into Plaza de Mayo. To their left was the Catiedro de San Martin, to their right the Cabildo, the birthplace of free Argentina. Without warning, lights blazed to life opposite them, and then the police car which had been parked outside the City Hotel began to pull across their bows. With amazing strength Marcellino swung the Ford's wheel all the way left. Two things happened simultaneously: the passenger door flew open and the gun in Cherry's hand went off. He screamed as he saw the road coming up to meet him. He felt himself being grabbed, then levered up. In disbelief he saw bright, wet blood dripping from his gun hand and spattered on the window of the swinging door. They were rounding the lower end of Plaza de Mayo, right-handed, and the door crashed shut. Cherry was numb. He stared at the gun in his hand.

'Get rid of it!'

Shaking, his mouth a rictus, Cherry jerked the window down and flung the gun as hard as he could in the direction of shrubbery. They veered left again, then right on the Paseo Colón.

'In two blocks,' said Marcellino, his breath coming in gasps, but his voice assured, 'I'm turning right, then stopping, on the Avenida Martin Gracia.'

The American was staring unseeingly into the night.

'Do you hear me?'

Dumbly Cherry nodded.

'You will get out,' Marcellino was saying, 'run left, down into La Boca. Go to *tío Vicente*, you know where I mean?'

Cherry nodded. They were turning.

'Tell them Marcellino sent you. Wash yourself, tell them to change your clothes, rest. When you are sure it is safe, but not until then, return home. You understand?'

The car rammed the kerb as it stopped. Cherry jumped.

'What about you . . . ?' he tried to say, but already the Ford was halfway down Avenida Martin Gracia. Cherry could hear sirens. He ran flat out, across the *avenida* and headlong into the maze of tiny streets that are La Boca.

Without knowing what he did, Cherry followed Marcellino's instructions, waiting shivering in a small, upstairs bedroom of the tiny café, trying to warm himself with the steady flow of *cafés negros* brought up the stairs by an old woman whose face told absolutely nothing. The sirens came and went for hours. Twice in the night foot patrols came to the door to question the bleary-eyed owner.

'*Han matado a un policía,*' Cherry could hear the muted voices. 'A policeman has been murdered. Someone will have to pay.' At nine the following morning Cherry left the café, terror still clinging to him like a leech, but his clothes were cleaned and pressed, his shoes were shining, his face shaven. As he left them, the old man and his wife looked at him curiously.

Like a man in a trance Cherry walked the twenty-five blocks directly to his office on the Avenida Cerrito, avoiding the curious crowds and the police barriers in the distant Plaza de Mayo. It was an exceptional day, full of warmth and good smells. Traffic streamed in both directions, horns hooting. Newspapers could speak of nothing except the Presidential crisis.

Three days later Cherry went home.

PART THREE

Inverary

CHAPTER SEVEN

'. . . and may the Lord have mercy on his soul.'

Georgie huddled close underneath Patrick's umbrella. The four ruddy-faced, big-handed men steadied themselves; a fifth pulled away the two cross-planks; slowly they began to feed out the canvas ropes and lower the coffin out of sight.

Patrick looked around. There was only themselves and two neighbours and a distant cousin of Georgie's father, a retired dentist from Penrith. Most of them were over sixty, blank-faced like the local canon, kindly but inured, essentially unaffected. It was all meaningless. The funeral from Glasgow to Dumbarton, up the Firth of Clyde in sheeting rain, down into Inverary – meaningless. The service in the unheated church, the burial he was now seeing, Alan going down beside his mother, her headstone adroitly engraved to accommodate her husband, such circumspection now wrecked by Alan – meaningless. Just as meaningless as the endless afternoon and evening which would follow, when Mr Ridgeway and the dentist would reminisce at length, and various kind neighbours would call to mark their sympathy for the pale boy whom most of them no longer remembered; numerous cups of tea and drams would be poured and served and people would eat cake and brack and sit; and every now and again someone would pipe up to say that life must go on.

'Patrick.' Georgie was holding the telephone.

'I'll take it in the bedroom,' Patrick said. He walked down the hall of the cottage. Through the large, picture window he could see clouds of mist tumbling down the mountain, isolating them into a world alone. He picked up the telephone.

'Yes.'

Patrick frowned, then began to shake his head in frustration as the man on the other end spoke.

'When did you discover this, Mr Enright?' he asked. He sat down on the bed.

'This morning at eight o'clock, Mr Drake,' said the London caretaker. 'I tried to call you earlier, but there was no reply.'

'That's all right, we were out,' Patrick said. 'Please go over what the police said again.'

'Just that it seemed a professional job,' Mr Enright said. 'Although there were a lot of things thrown around, nothing seems to have been taken, but of course no one but you and Miss Ridgeway can say that for certain.'

'Of course,' Patrick said. 'And they actually opened the filing cabinet?'

'Broke it open, Mr Drake,' came the caretaker's voice. 'Wrecked it, I'm afraid. All your files were stacked beside it on the floor. Naturally I can't say if any are missing, but when the police are finished I'll put them back best I can.'

'Thank you, Mr Enright,' Patrick said.

'Don't forget to notify your insurance,' said Mr Enright.

Patrick sat and stared out into the blackness. So much had taken place in the days just gone by, so much had been demanded, that his mind had run flat-out without the back-up of reflection.

There had been a series of harrowing telephone calls: to Georgie, to the British Consul in Bordeaux, to undertakers, and to Abelson Dunwoody. A warrant for the arrest of the forklift driver was issued, but the man had disappeared. Patrick persuaded Georgie not to come to Bordeaux, a post mortem took place at the Institute Medico-Legal, and Sammy Mitchell arrived.

'What in Christ's name happened?' Sammy asked.

Patrick told him.

'Mother of God,' Sammy said. 'Poor bugger. He was killed outright?'

Patrick nodded.

'Well, at least that's something.' Sammy loosened his tie. 'It looks as if the place has been totally gutted.'

'It has.' Patrick watched his round, pasty face. 'The bottling plant is gone, plus the office buildings, plus of course every record that ever existed.'

Sammy wasn't slow. 'What about Alan's working papers?' he asked, his head cocked like a bird.

'They were in the car,' Patrick said. 'Alan was trying to get them out when he was killed.'

Sammy licked his lips. 'So let's have it,' he said grimly. 'What did he say he had found?'

Again Patrick told him, factually. He could hear Sammy's breath shorten.

'Have you mentioned this to the police?'

'I thought I'd speak to you first.'

'Well, thank God for that.' Sammy sucked air. 'I've never heard such madness.'

'What are you going to do?' Patrick asked.

'I'm going to do you a big favour,' Sammy replied, 'I'm not going to mention it to anyone.'

'What Alan showed me seemed sane enough,' Patrick replied carefully.

Sammy gathered himself. 'You know about Alan and Abelson, of course?'

Patrick looked blankly at the tilted head. 'You mean that Alan was able to stand up to him?'

Sammy made an ugly shape with his mouth. 'Listen.' He sat forward. 'The Abelson thing had become an obsession – Alan Ridgeway had gone totally over the edge.' Sammy glanced behind him. 'We're beginning to hear stories,' he said grimly, 'and they're not very pretty.'

'What kind of stories?' asked Patrick, his colour rising.

Sammy shrugged sadly. 'Things he said about the firm on jobs, the standard of his work, his drinking. It's all coming out, I'm afraid.'

'For Christ's sake!' Patrick stood up and walked to the window in disgust. 'He's hardly cold.'

'You didn't tell me you were living with his sister.'

'What's that got to do with it?' Patrick asked, rounding savagely.

'Is she in the pudding business, then?'

'Fuck you!' Patrick said, stepping forward.

'You were given a position of trust,' Sammy hissed, standing up. 'You should either have declined it or else revealed your interest before you took it on.'

'That's a load of bullshit and you know it,' Patrick shouted. 'My relationship with Georgie Ridgeway has no bearing whatsoever on my approach to this or any job.'

'I'm simply telling you the view which is being taken,' Sammy said. 'It's being seen as a conflict of interest.'

Patrick's fists were clenched. He said, 'I would say that anyone wishing to study conflicts of interest should probably start here in Château Diane with John Abelson's name on the top of the list followed by your own.'

The images crowded. Sammy went back to London. Patrick spent a fitful night. The next morning there were only the two of them in the Pompes Funèbres, himself and Alan. Alan looked up from white, frilly taffeta, his partially joined fingers resembling thick strips of candle grease.

Patrick had helped the French undertakers screw the coffin bolts home.

The last of the visitors – the dentist – was helped into his coat and left. Patrick sat with Georgie and her father for an hour, a small group on the side of a Scottish mountain, staring disconsolately into the fire.

'You saw his will?' Mr Ridgeway said.

Patrick nodded. 'Georgie told me this morning.'

Mr Ridgeway puffed pipe smoke in a cloud around himself. 'I didn't make a will until your poor mother died,' he said, looking at Georgie distantly. 'Still, that was Alan.'

Georgie's face was set in a sad smile.

'It will come to nearly a hundred thousand pounds,' her father said, puffing earnestly. 'I never knew he was worth so much.'

'He had been working for over twenty years, father,' Georgie said gently.

'What's that?' Mr Ridgeway tapped his hearing aid.

Georgie bent over and kissed him.

'It's a lot of money,' Mr Ridgeway resumed. 'I'm glad you're getting it.'

When her father at last went to bed, Georgie came and sat by

Patrick's feet. He closed his eyes, made the decision, then with his hands on her shoulders, he told her. As he went on she turned and stared into his face, her own twisted in consternation as she tried to take in what she was hearing.

'I need a drink,' said Georgie in a whisper. Patrick poured whisky into two tumblers and sat down beside her at the fire. Georgie had to use both hands; she drank it down in one and then began to shake. Great sobs convulsed her body as the tears she had tried to contain burst from her eyes. 'The bastards,' she wept over and over.

'What I've told you is what I think may have happened,' Patrick said quietly. 'But there is no proof, nothing to back it up whatsoever. Alan is dead. All that exists is a photostat, a tabulation of figures in his own handwriting which could refer to anything.' Patrick spread his hands. 'That all adds up to nothing,' he said.

Georgie shook her head hopelessly. 'What are we going to do?' she whispered.

Patrick sat still. 'After the weekend, I'm going to go back to work. From the inside I'll see what I can find. I'm going to start where Alan started – at the Church Lines liquidation five years ago.'

'What happened five years ago?' Georgie asked. 'Patrick?'

Patrick cannot speak. He is on his feet. He has fallen from his new bicycle. There are tears in his eyes. He has cut his lip. Ah, darling boy, come here to me.

'Patrick?'

Wind roared in the chimney.

'I honestly don't know what happened five years ago,' Patrick replied.

Georgie shivered. 'I'm afraid,' she said, 'I don't understand what's going on. And now the flat in London has been broken into – that's never happened before.' She swallowed, her face creased in concern. 'What's happening?' she said and began to cry again.

Patrick put his arms around her and kissed her. He bit his lip as he recalled the turrets of Château Diane. 'Don't worry,' he said. 'You stay here for a couple of weeks with your father. Give me time to try and work it out.'

The cottage shook as a powerful gust hit it.

'Hold me,' Georgie said.

She trembled and he covered her small hands with his; despite the fire they were cold.

'I can't live without you,' Georgie said in a small voice.

Darling boy, come here to your Papa.

'You won't have to,' Patrick promised.

Patrick took the overnight sleeper from Glasgow and a taxi from Euston directly to the office. He walked across Dunwoody Plaza, suitcase in hand. As soon as the uniformed commissionaire stepped out of his office in the foyer, Patrick knew there was trouble.

'Just a moment, sir.'

Patrick turned, frowning. 'Good morning, Bill,' he said.

'Would you please just step this way a moment, sir.'

Patrick followed the commissionaire into his room. 'What is it?' he asked.

'Would you please ring Mr Mitchell, sir.'

Patrick put down his case. 'Ring him? Where is he?'

'In his office, sir.'

Patrick shook his head. 'Then I'll see him in the next three minutes, won't I?' he said and bent to pick up his suitcase again. But the commissionaire had moved to the door. 'Please do it, sir,' he said.

Patrick took a deep breath and picked up the telephone. He got Sammy Mitchell's secretary. There was a long delay.

'Patrick!'

'Yes, Sammy, I'm ringing you from the lobby. What is – ?'

'Did you get my letter, Patrick?'

'What letter?'

'Have you not received a letter from me?' Patrick could hear Sammy Mitchell cover the phone with his hand and speak to someone. 'It was sent three days ago to your London address,' Sammy said.

'I've just arrived straight from Scotland,' Patrick said, a weight plunging inside him. 'What's the letter about, Sammy?'

'I think you should go to your flat and read it,' Sammy said quietly.

'What does it say?' Patrick cried.

'Just read it,' Sammy said.

'Sammy!' Patrick shouted into the phone, but the connection had been cut. Fighting for his breath Patrick replaced the instrument and picked up his bag.

'Goodbye, sir,' said the commissionaire as Patrick walked slowly out of the building.

The letter contained one paragraph and a severance cheque. Patrick stared at it in disbelief, then grabbed the telephone and dialled the familiar number.

'I'm sorry, but Mr Mitchell is tied up at a meeting. Can I take your number and I'll give him your message.'

'Sheila, this is Patrick Drake,' Patrick said to the woman who worked as Sammy Mitchell's secretary and whom he saw every day of the week. 'I want to talk to him.'

'I'm sorry but he's tied up, Mr Drake. I'll give him your message.'

'He's never so tied up that he can't take an important call.'

'I'm sorry.'

Patrick took off his shirt and tie, put on a pullover and went outside. He walked for an hour, down to and along the Thames, past a park and a children's playground and gangs of men painting barges. He looked across the water to the City, to its clusters of office blocks filled with working men and women. He looked around as children from the playground shrieked and felt a knife of panic go through him. He returned to the flat.

'I'm sorry but he's still tied up.'

Patrick crashed the phone back. Then he composed himself and dialled again.

'A personal call,' he said, changing his voice.

'Yes?' Sammy Mitchell sounded apprehensive.

'Sammy, I want to meet you.'

'Patrick?'

'I want to meet you, Sammy.'

'I'm afraid that's not possible.'

'Sammy, you just can't . . . Sammy?'

Trembling, Patrick stood up and went to the window of the flat. If he looked hard, through stacks of chimneys and forests of television aerials, he could just make out part of the green dome of St Paul's.

Mervyn Lang was a family friend who had run his own

solicitor's practice for thirty years. He finished reading the five-page, handwritten report and removed his glasses.

'Potent stuff,' he said.

'I still can't believe it,' Patrick said. 'To the whole world, here you have an ultra-respectable, very large firm of multinational accountants.' Patrick clenched his fists. 'People look up to Abelson Dunwoody, Mervyn,' he said, 'we ... they issue recommendations about things which then become standards for the profession. But I'm saying that at the top of this whole structure is a man who I now believe is somehow responsible for Alan Ridgeway's death.'

Mervyn Lang shook his head. 'I don't envy you what you've been through,' he said.

'I worked for them for six years,' Patrick said. 'I worked nights, weekends to deliver jobs on time. All right, I got well paid, but all the time I genuinely believed they were beyond reproach.' He gritted his teeth. 'I feel soiled and I feel heartbroken for Georgie and I feel very, very angry.'

'I've never met Abelson,' Mervyn said. 'But he's got a high reputation in the City.' The solicitor fingered the handwritten report. 'This might prove slightly ... ah ... difficult to get anyone to believe,' he said cautiously.

'I don't care,' Patrick said. 'They're not going to get away with it, Mervyn. I want your advice as to the best course of action.'

Mervyn Lang looked sympathetically over his spectacles. 'You and I, Patrick, are professional men,' he said. 'We both know what circumstantial evidence means.'

'Mervyn!' Patrick cried. 'I'm saying this could amount to murder!'

Mervyn Lang looked across the desk in slight admonishment. 'Patrick,' he said gently, 'I understand how you feel. But what do you want me to say? I know you well enough to accept that you believe everything you've told me to be true, or should I say, everything that you were told by poor Ridgeway.'

Patrick's face glowed red. 'What about the police?' he asked.

Mervyn Lang put his elbows on his desk. 'They'll listen to you politely, find out that you've been sacked, and then laugh behind your back,' he said. 'People who've got the sack are in the same category as a woman scorned.'

Patrick sighed deeply. He got to his feet and walked to the window of the office. It was a dull, grey London day; traffic clogged the street below. Patrick suddenly felt exhausted.

'I've been sacked without any reason,' he said, sitting heavily down. 'Can't we get them on that?'

'I suppose you could try having a go under wrongful dismissal,' the solicitor said, 'but . . .' he shook his head, 'in your position I wouldn't advise it. I mean, let's face it, no matter what happens, you're not going back to Abelson Dunwoody, are you?'

Patrick sighed.

'They may not be too difficult about a reference,' Lang said. 'My advice to you is, draw up a fresh curriculum vitae as fast as you can and get back out there into the market.'

Patrick looked at him. 'And what about that?' he asked, pointing to the report on the desk. 'Could we at least not refer it to the Director of Public Prosecutions?'

'As an auditor you will be more aware than most of the difficulty in proving what is in there,' Mervyn Lang said quietly.

'You think I'm off my head, don't you?' Patrick said.

'I've known you since you were a small boy,' Lang said kindly. 'I've followed your career and greatly admired you for everything you've achieved. This is an unfortunate interruption, but knowing your reserves of character, I have no doubt that you'll get over it.'

Patrick looked at him. 'That's a nice way of telling me to stop playing the fool and to get back to work.'

'I think you're behaving normally. You have a very clear-cut view of what is just.'

'This may sound pompous,' Patrick said, 'but I want to find out the truth.'

'The truth is very often elusive,' Mervyn Lang said. 'When you eventually find it, it's often not a crock of gold at all, but something made of uncertain shades of grey.'

They walked to the door together.

'I think I'll take your advice,' Patrick said. 'I'll go back to Scotland.' The two men shook hands. 'If nothing else it will give me time to work on my curriculum vitae.'

'That's the most constructive thing you've said all morning,' smiled the solicitor as Patrick walked down the stairs.

* * *

Sweat poured from Patrick's face as he pressed upwards. He lengthened his stride against the hill road and squinted into the September sun, its orbit in the late afternoon close to the horizon. Left, the rising lowlands were a thatch of browns and greens fractured by flashing bands of mountain water, and far below was Loch Fyne, rippling as a breeze swept its grey face and rattled the shopkeepers' signs in Inverary.

The road curved up and left; a red telephone kiosk appeared where a rough track was cut into the heather. Patrick took it, attacking the sharper gradient, his thick-rubbered soles sure on the mountain, driving him almost vertically up into the silence.

Dead ahead something erupted. In mid-stride Patrick tried to throw himself left. There was a blur of white, then he was on his back and the ewe with her lamb scampered in panic up the mountain.

Heather formed a luxurious bed. Each springy plant with its flower-tips of multicoloured tweed sprang from a bed of snow-white lichen. Patrick leaned to examine the bright growth; each was a masterpiece, tiny as a pinhead, perfect in its formation. He became aware of a little stream near him, working its way busily down the mountain. He rolled over and cupped water to his mouth. The brackish taste was good. Then he lay back, staring straight up into the totally empty sky, and thought of the neat photocopied sheaves, laid out on a table in the cottage, waiting to be stapled.

Age: 33. Place of birth: Galway, Ireland. The Atlantic was such a different sea, full of towering rage and indignation. There had been an uncle with a tiny cottage in Clifden, fifty miles from Galway, and they had visited him each summer for the month of August. There was the cottage with its thatch of oaten straw and the backyard full of ducks and hens and tottering calves which were hand-fed from an aluminium bucket. The sea was down a lane and over green fields; they went there every day and his mother rolled her dress up her long brown legs and lay on the warm sand as he played in the rock pools where a million shrimps had been left by the outgoing tide.

'When I was girl,' his mother said, speaking in Spanish, 'we were brought down to the beach in Noja on the first Monday in May and we never left it until the last day of August.'

'Where is Noja, Mama?'

'Noja.' His mother said the name fondly and leaned back to allow the weaker Irish sun to bathe her face. 'It is where the north coast of Spain meets the sea. You will go there one day, when Papa has made lots of money. We will all go to Noja and stay there until the summer ends.'

'Are there shrimps?'

'Of course.' She laughed and watched him. 'We will stay by the sea all day, except for the days when our friend Señor Sarasola gives us his donkey and trap. Those days we will explore inland and take a picnic with us: you, Papa and me.'

'Where will we go?'

His mother narrowed her eyes and looked out over the Atlantic where the sea swelled smooth like the shell of an egg. 'We will go to Isla,' she said quietly. 'There is an old church there and years ago my Papa took me to it. All around the church are the resting places of those from the district who were killed in our Civil War. It is a happy place: warm, friendly, a good place to picnic. But what I remember most about it is the bees.'

'I hate bees.'

'These are nice bees,' she said, smiling. 'My father explained to me that they had been there for as long as anyone could remember. There were so many of them that they did not have to be afraid of man. Instead they went about their lives, collecting the pollen from the flowers in Isla and bringing it back to their church to make honey. No one ever collected the honey – it was impossible to get at, too high up in the old church's walls.' His mother had nudged the sand with her toes. 'I'm sure they are still there, those bees of Isla,' she had said.

Patrick felt the beginnings of chill begin to creep as the sun started its slip behind the shoulder of mountain. He got to his feet and began the long, horizontal traverse, jumping lightly over ledges of shingle and clumps of gorse and heather, the breeze now in his face, the body of the loch stretching out and away below him. He came to a plain and pushed himself flat out, as fast as his legs would pump, so that when he slackened off and stopped he stood, his hands resting on his knees and his breath coming in deprived gasps. He walked in a small circle, where he could see the red kiosk, now above and to his right, and the smoke from the Ridgeways' chimney beneath it, a grey line drawn on the blue evening. He sucked in air, tilting his head back. He felt the last rays of sun in his eyes and saw ewes high on a mountain ridge, not far from the peak, and beside them the blue track-suit of a jogger like himself, making its way from left to right, away from Inverary.

Turning, he began to jog slowly home where Georgie would be waiting.

CHAPTER EIGHT

The butterfly had a wing-span of three inches. It danced along the surface of the river, its wings vivid orange, spread up and out behind it like a parachute. At the other side of the river, amidst yellow-flowering eucalyptus trees, the glossy black head of a tucon flashed.

La Esmeralda turned her head away from the garden and looked at him, sitting across from her at the open windows. Twenty-five years, she thought. Half a lifetime. A smile played on her lips. She had been just a girl in Buenos Aires, Marcellino already a man in his late thirties. Now she saw him with pride. The years had thickened an already formidable frame, but not slowed it; with the passage of time his face had become more like dark leather; the brows over his eyes denser; the eyes themselves deeper; the hair on his body and his head still full and coal black. But he had grown. From the days in Buenos Aires to the years in Bolivia to the first, hesitant start in Medellin he had soared. Now he straddled Colombia, as the *número uno*, the one everyone feared and answered to, the *padrino* of all *padrinos*, the indisputable king. La Esmeralda looked at Marcellino. Anyone would have said that with his wealth he might have also achieved happiness.

'What are you thinking of?' she asked quietly.

'Of how difficult it is,' he answered. 'Of how little time remains. Of how much money is needed to do what has to be done.'

'You are giving them a lot,' she said.

'I am giving them everything,' he replied.

La Esmeralda went behind him. She emptied fragrant oil into

her hand from a bottle and peeling back his shirt began to work it into the muscles of his neck.

'You will make the money back,' she murmured, 'all of it and more.'

They fell silent, she working to make him relax, to yield. As if in a theatre, the light outside suddenly began to fade. The colours in the gardens and in the trees vanished, and where seconds before the butterfly had made its way, there was the silver glint of a trout.

'I hate it when you go away,' he said abruptly.

La Esmeralda made no reply.

'Although it is I who am sending you,' he said, 'I hate it when you go.'

'Must I go to Spain?' She was kneeling beside him.

He closed his eyes. 'Yes. There is so much at stake. I cannot go, but I want you there as my envoy, to show to Sainz Perez and the others that I am not an outsider but part of them. So I am sending something that is not just money but more precious to me than even Euskadi.'

La Esmeralda and Marcellino sat either side; between them, his back to the jungle night, the tall man with the white hair sat, sweat popping on his face despite the revolving ceiling fan. He wore a correctly starched and buttoned white shirt, and a lightweight but still too warm pinstriped suit.

Marcellino took a cigar from his lips. 'Mister,' he said in heavily accented English, 'I am disappointed.'

The Englishman swallowed.

'I do not allow people in my organisation to be so out of my control,' Marcellino said. 'Otherwise I do not think I would succeed.'

'It was most unfortunate,' the Englishman said. 'However, I am making enquiries and already I think we may have found another vineyard in France.'

La Esmeralda understood nothing of the conversation, but she watched the Englishman. He sweats too much, she thought. Also he is vain; he thinks of himself, of his own body, not of others.

Marcellino pulled deeply on his cigar. 'What of the other man?'

His guest blinked. 'Other man?'

Marcellino narrowed his eyes.

'Oh,' said the Englishman, sweating profusely. 'He's no problem, we've got rid of him.'

Marcellino leaned forward in genuine interest, a slow smile on his leatherish face. 'What was your method, mister?' he asked.

The Englishman took a deep breath. 'What I mean is,' he said, 'that we terminated his employment.'

Marcellino sat back. His large mouth curved down, lizard-like in its disapproval. 'So, mister,' he said slowly, 'you open the cage and let the bird go, so.' He sprang open the tips of his fingers. 'Instead of keeping the bird in the cage, feed him extra, make him happy, you let him go, to talk to his friends, to think his thoughts about you, about his dead friend for sure. What you know the dead man tell him? How much? About me? About my business? Eh?' Marcellino shook his head. 'How can a man like you who has made much money be such a fool?'

The Englishman opened his mouth, but no words came.

Marcellino looked at the starry sky. 'This gives me a bad feeling,' he said, 'in here.' He tapped his chest. 'I know men. I know no one can be trusted. I know a mistake, and this is a mistake.'

'I'll . . . we'll find him,' the other man said.

'Find him, mister,' Marcellino said, 'and find him quick.' He inhaled smoke and closed his eyes, indicating that the subject was closed. There was silence, broken for a moment by the screech of a *guacharo*, the night bird of Colombia.

'I have almost one hundred million dollars in cash in various places,' Marcellino said.

La Esmeralda saw the Englishman blink.

'I have friends,' Marcellino said, his face impassive, 'good friends, mister, who live in Spain. The north. Near the border. I want to give them this money.' Marcellino sat back as if what he had said explained everything.

'You want to give them . . .'

'A hundred million is a lot of money,' Marcellino went on, looking towards the invisible river. 'To transport it, three or four trucks, to store it, a warehouse like Fort Knox.'

'Arrange for it to be transferred,' his guest said. 'Use an offshore account.'

'My friends do not have bank accounts,' said Marcellino icily. 'In their own country they cannot even speak their own language – how then can they have bank accounts?'

La Esmeralda watched the Englishman's eyes: blue eyes, cold, quick with fear.

'I'm sorry,' he said. 'You're . . . talking about . . .'

'Friends,' Marcellino repeated, 'friends who wish to liberate their homeland.'

The Englishman swallowed. 'My use to you,' he said, 'is probably very limited. I'm a financial man.'

'These people are alone,' Marcellino said softly, 'hunted on every side like animals, derided by humanity as *terroristas*, unfriended. When they make their bid for freedom, like a baby just born, they will need help to take their first step in the cold world, and then their second. They will need money, worth, something they can use to buy food, arms, their independence.' He turned his face to the other man. 'How do I give them this help, mister?'

The Englishman considered the question. 'What about treasury bonds, bearer bonds, in a number of different accounts for delivery somewhere in Europe, say Geneva?' He looked to Marcellino for approval.

'I do not trust such things.'

'They're bearer certificates, guaranteed instruments of US government debt: they can't be violated.'

Marcellino turned down the corners of his mouth. 'They are pieces of paper,' he said. 'Issued by a government who can pass laws with the stroke of a pen.' He tapped his chest. 'Purchased by money which they consider unclean.' He shook his head. 'Not bonds, mister.'

La Esmeralda could see the Englishman's mind race.

'Gold?'

Marcellino was unimpressed. 'Too much weight, too bulky, too difficult to transport in a hurry.' He rose and slowly walked to La Esmeralda. He reached and cupped the point of her chin with his hand and turned it towards his guest. 'What do you see here, mister?' he asked.

The Englishman began to colour, a creeping tinge beneath white skin. 'A . . . a very lovely lady,' he said.

'Ah-hah! OK,' said Marcellino, 'but look, mister, look here, what do you see?' Marcellino had brought his other hand, the cigar in its fingers, to La Esmeralda's eyes.

The other man blinked. 'Amazing,' he said. 'They're . . . they're like . . . diamonds.'

Again La Esmeralda saw the Englishman's fear, as Marcellino released her and went back to his chair.

'A hundred million,' Marcellino was saying. 'They will fit into a bag, so.' He held an imaginary case. 'They can be sold, one by one, if need be. They cannot be cancelled, or outlawed, or made worthless. Money can be borrowed against them. They are worth.'

The white-faced man listened, mesmerised.

'But where can I get them?' Marcellino asked. 'Where is the centre?' He nodded his big head. 'London, mister, London. Your city. All the diamonds in the world, they go through London.'

The Englishman shook his head and gave a short laugh. 'I'm afraid you've got the wrong man,' he said. 'I know nothing at all about diamonds, nothing at all.'

'Mister, why do you think you are here? You must learn.'

The Englishman opened his mouth, closed it, reached for a glass of water.

'You must go back to London and learn,' Marcellino said. 'But quickly. In one month at the most delivery must be made.'

Momentarily the fear of what lay ahead superseded the other man's fear of the man at the table. 'Are you asking,' he swallowed, 'that I deliver diamonds worth a hundred million dollars down to . . . to Basque terrorists in the Pyrenees?'

Marcellino's smile was that of a huge cat. 'I have not asked you, mister,' he said. 'Just buy them for me. Someone with *cojones* will make the delivery.'

To herself, La Esmeralda smiled. The Englishman's pallor was that of death. His *cojones*, she thought, if he has them, are this moment the size of little peas.

La Esmeralda awoke, just before the call came through. It was an hour after midnight. She could tell from the unused bed that Marcellino had sat up; she could also tell by his expression that he had been using *perica*. He held the phone to his ear with his left hand whilst his right hand travelled the circuit of his bare chest. La Esmeralda turned on her side towards him, imagining the face of his caller, 3,000 miles north.

Marcellino was speaking. 'Cherry, there is something you should know. Recently I have had dreams, bad dreams. I dreamt that there is something moving against me, out there, out of my control. We are one, Cherry, you understand that? Anything which destroys me, destroys you. More than ever we must now work together, be vigilant, exchange information. It is our common interest. Like all those years ago when we helped each other. Except now the stakes are bigger. We are survivors, Cherry, you and me, but we survive as one. You will always keep my secrets, and until the day I die, no one will ever know the things we did together on the banks of the Rio de la Plata. But Cherry, the time is soon coming when I am going to be asking you for something much bigger than you have ever given before. It will be the last time, Cherry, and I will not ask for it unless I need it desperately. But we both understand what it is to be desperate, Cherry, don't we? I know you will understand.'

La Esmeralda saw Marcellino break the connection, then reach for the tube and bowl and inhale sharply. She closed her eyes. The only sound was the sighing of the wind; even the scavenging *guacharos* had settled down.

La Esmeralda slept.

CHAPTER NINE

'I'm taking father to his cousins in Penrith,' Georgie said. 'I should be home by seven.'

'Try and get me last Saturday's *Financial Times*, the one with the appointments page,' Patrick said.

Patrick typed out four letters. It was after five as he slammed the cottage door and walked to the post-box outside the village.

He decided to take the long way home, cutting vertically upwards, leaving the loch and Inverary to his left, the Ridgeway cottage behind the hill to his right. It was a dull evening with a hint of approaching rain which pared minutes from the daylight that remained. He met a track which took him in a slow, curving descent, over a stream which cut through a small plateau; he jumped the water and stood for a moment, the mountains behind him and at his feet, the cottage, the valley and the body of the lake. He stood and he stared. Below him, microscopically, but quite clearly, a figure in blue was leaving the back door of the Ridgeway cottage.

'Hey!'

Patrick began to descend in leaping bounds. The wind whipped his eyes as the cottage came nearer. He gritted his teeth as he saw the figure begin to run away from the cottage and across the mountain.

'Hey, you! Stop!'

A boulder as big as a truck blocked Patrick's view; he emerged from behind it and saw that the runner was a good two hundred yards into the hills. Patrick was still above the cottage, but near enough to it to see the pane of broken glass in the kitchen window. Patrick felt a rush of anger. He began a steady, horizontal tack, right-handed, in pursuit of the figure who was still below him, but vanishing fast in the fading light.

Patrick was on a track, the line of least resistance, but one which tended to bring him nearer the other man. It was, now, clearly a man, a big man whose strides carried him along without effort, his knee action unusually high, like a rugby winger. Something about him, something about his head and shoulders shape disturbed a memory ember. Patrick settled into a rhythm. The man vanished as he crossed a shoulder of mountain; Patrick came to the lip and saw him pumping at twice the speed along the floor of the narrow dell which had been hidden by the darkening folds of lowland. Patrick propelled himself down as the other was ending his climb of the far ridge. The covered head turned once, then disappeared. Patrick attacked the rising ground, grasping clumps of heather to hasten his ascent.

At the top Patrick paused, still breathing easily; they had now entered a glen at the back of the mountain, away from the cottage and Inverary. Light was failing rapidly but still he could see a movement of blue, in the lee of the hill, at a distance impossible to define. Patrick drew a breath and resumed, jumping over small boulders, slipping occasionally on the shingle of this new gradient. He decided to gain height in order to find better going. He scrambled upwards. All around him were boulders, jagged promontories and outcroppings of rock silhouetted against the stalking dark. He stumbled, recovered, then clawed on up; the terrain, tricky by day, in the sudden night was treacherous. He came to a winding deer-path and took it, brushing through the gorse, but on ground that was firm, above the shingle. Behind him Inverary could no longer be seen, just its glow, pulsing out around the corner like a distant glimmer of hope.

The decision to come up the mountain had been the right one. Below, the contour swept into a crevice which meant that the traversable ground headed into a bottleneck. Patrick parted harsh gorse, his eyes straining and beginning to water as the air in the night turned to dew. He stopped as if a mallet had struck his chest. Six yards, vertically below him, the blue-headed form began to turn.

Patrick leaped.

At first he thought he had landed on rock. He cried out in pain, then sprang to his feet. Something rigid began to choke him from behind. His eyes popping, Patrick pummelled with elbows and heels into hard bone. The grip slackened. Patrick could smell strong sweat, could feel hot breath. Crossing his arms he slammed upwards with his elbows. A hand grasped for his hair. Patrick turned and swung a hard, connecting left, then followed unerringly with a right hook that jerked the hooded head up and back. He felt himself being caught, then they were falling, rolling steeply in the blackness, like two dogs locked together, painfully, on hard stone and shingle, each trying for the advantage as they revolved downwards. The body on top of Patrick led over and then abruptly stopped as they hit a boulder. He felt the grip loosen a fraction as the other man took the impact. Patrick sprang, one knee forward and into the throat, the other pinioning the heavy shoulders. The village lights had more influence down here and he could see blue eyes glinting. The angle of the man's head meant that he could offer no resistance for risk of his neck being snapped. The chest beneath Patrick was heaving, as was his own. He adjusted minutely, then felt his hand brush metal. He felt again and back, then closed his fingers over the unmistakable butt of a gun. Gingerly he transferred it to his right hand, felt for the safety catch, then pressed the pistol into the throat beside his knee.

'You know what this is,' he panted.

Gradually he released the pressure of his knee; keeping the pistol stuck to the other man's gullet he climbed off, then warily drew back, steadying the weapon with his two hands.

As his breath returned Patrick surveyed his captive, now revealed by the village lights, his mouth open, leaning against the rock which had stopped their fall. He was a very big man, about thirty, with a shock of blond curls and a moustache.

'We're going to go very quietly down the mountain,' Patrick panted, 'all the way into Inverary.' The gun was steady in his hands. 'I'm sure they will be very interested in the police station to meet an armed burglar.'

The man closed his eyes.

'Up,' Patrick ordered.

There was a long sigh. 'You know they torched Château Diane?'

Patrick blinked. The accent was American, the statement made as a fact.

'After you and Ridgeway left the foreman guy went into the office with two jerry-cans and sent it up.'

Patrick stared. His hands felt numb.

'What did you say?'

'I said, he burned the place to the ground. I saw him do it.'

Patrick looked at the head and shoulders silhouetted against the glow that was Inverary; the earlier irritation in his mind found its niche: the person who had observed his arrival from the high window of Château Diane was in front of him.

'I was in the castle, up in a high room,' the man was saying. 'I had a complete overview of the courtyard. You and Ridgeway came running back when you saw the fire. The foreman guy left the courtyard and came into the castle – he stood in another window, at right angles to where I was, same level.'

Patrick's ears hurt.

'He could see everything just the same as me,' the big man said. 'There was chaos down there, but when Ridgeway went back to his car to get his briefcase, the foreman actually signalled the driver on the forklift to push the pallets on top of him.'

'Who are you?' Patrick asked.

The blue eyes closed. 'I'm a cop, my name is Joe Vendetti. That's a .38 police-special you're pointing at me.'

Patrick's mind raced. 'Why are you here?'

'I saw Ridgeway hand you a sheet of paper in Château Diane. I wanted to see what it said. I discovered who you were and where you lived in London. Then followed you here.' The big shoulders shrugged. 'I'm sorry about your apartment.'

A moon had come out. Patrick's breathing was even as he looked at the big figure. 'How can I tell if there's a grain of truth in what you're saying?' he asked.

Joe Vendetti answered quietly, 'Because the gun you're pointing at me is empty.'

They walked together, back towards Inverary. The threatened rain arrived, blowing strongly across the lake and uphill in squalls. Where flat stones had been laid across boulders as a crude, sheep shelter they sat, crouched.

'I'm a cop with the Metropolitan Police Narcotics Squad

working out of Washington DC,' Joe Vendetti said. 'Washington is also the headquarters of the DEA – that's the Drug Enforcement Administration, the premier organisation in our country in the fight against drugs.'

Rain began to drip down from the roof of their shelter.

'Today,' Joe said, 'the main drugs problem is cocaine and its derivative, crack. Heroin isn't what it used to be since the AIDS scare; cocaine has taken its place as the number-one drug entering the United States. Cocaine today is causing the DEA most of their problems.'

The cop shook his blond head.

'They've made little progress. The word is that up to three DEA agents, undercovers, have had their cover blown and been murdered in the past eighteen months: one each in Colombia and Mexico and one right in the middle of New York City. Then three months ago, customs in Red Hook, New York, caught a ship's captain, a Colombian, coming in with five kilos of cocaine. Faced with a twenty-year stretch he began to talk: he said that if they really wanted to find the source of most of the cocaine coming States-side, the place they should start looking was Madrid. This tied up with a couple of other straws in the wind, so the DEA decided to initiate a deep-cover mission to Madrid. Because of the other agents having their covers blown it was decided to use an agent who would report directly to Marshall Kahan who is the Administrator of the DEA.'

Patrick watched as Joe ran his hands through his hair.

'I had a brother,' Joe said. 'His name was Frank, he was six years older than me. Up to eighteen months ago he worked with the DEA out of San Francisco.' Joe smiled faintly. 'He didn't look like me. He was very dark, handsome in a Latino way, and spoke fluent Spanish.' Joe looked at the earth between his feet. 'They picked him,' he said quietly.

Patrick said nothing. He could see the man compose himself.

'That was eight weeks ago,' he said. 'Two weeks ago my sister in Seattle got this letter for me enclosed in another addressed to her.'

Joe reached into the pocket of his track-suit. 'He must have thought they'd be watching me,' Joe said. 'No one would ever think of Sis.'

Patrick watched as he withdrew a long scrap of paper.

'Frank is in Madrid. He has met a girl, an American girl

named Shirley, who has connections to minor figures in a huge cartel. This cartel's chief business is controlling the cocaine which pours into Spain from South America, and running it north again into France. From there it finds its way into all of northern Europe and is shipped back across the Atlantic into the United States.'

Patrick stared, fascinated.

'This whole cocaine business is controlled from South America,' Joe continued, his eyes on the flimsy letter. 'And the man in control in South America lives in Colombia and is called Marcellino.'

A gust of wind hit their shelter.

'Marcellino Epalza Adarraga. He's a Basque. He's the top *padrino* of the Medellin cartel and that makes him the *numero uno* of the whole South America drugs trade. No one knows where he lives or what he looks like,' Joe said. 'In 1966 a man of the same name was arrested in Bolivia and got sentenced to ten years for drugs trafficking. He spent two weeks in prison. All records of his arrest and trial have disappeared. There are no photographs. But the DEA think this is the same man.'

Patrick sat quietly.

'All the cocaine going north from Spain crosses the Pyrenees, safeguarded by a Basque separatist organisation,' Joe continued. 'These guys are as familiar with the mountains as with the barrel of an Armalite. It's a sort of cocaine junction up there: all the drugs are shepherded over the border and then go onwards to their different destinations. In return, Marcellino gives the Basques financial support for their cause and kids all over the United States are liquidising their minds with crack. Frank reasoned that if he could get a handle on this operation he would then have the key; he'd find out how the cocaine was crossing the border, where exactly it was destined for in Europe and how it was then shipped into the States. He was going to bust the whole thing wide open.'

Joe's face was grim.

'Frank learns of a consignment,' Joe said. 'Somehow he hears that its destination is a wine château in Bordeaux called Château Diane.'

'My God,' said Patrick softly.

'Frank leaves his apartment in Madrid to go north,' Joe said.

'He has just walked down the steps to the street when he sees a car drive by with two men in it. Frank stares: he has seen the car for only a second, but he is sure that the man on the near side is a DEA agent named Bob Waters, a guy who acts as sort of personal assistant to Kahan, the Administrator of the DEA. Frank can't believe his eyes: remember that three agents have been wasted in the last eighteen months on just this kind of mission; he's meant to be strictly deep cover; so what's Waters doing in Madrid – and outside his apartment with some other guy? Who is this other guy? What's going on? Frank contacts Kahan in Washington. Kahan assures him that he is mistaken, that Waters is in the United States, in Chicago in fact on some assignment, that no one, absolutely no one except Kahan and a couple of other key people at the top of the DEA, knows that Frank is in Madrid.'

Joe shook his head.

'He decided to keep going,' he said. 'But he also tried to take out some insurance.' The big man's eyes met Patrick's. 'He wrote to me.'

Patrick watched as Joe Vendetti held the paper up to the faint light.

' "I hope this is all middle-aged jitters",' Joe read, ' "and that we can joke about it over a beer. I'm going over the Pyrenees, because that's where the answer is. But if something happens to me, if I don't come back, it's because someone in the DEA has given my head on a plate to Marcellino and I was a dead man before ever I left home. It all makes sense: I'm the fourth in a row. We've all had good cover – why has it been blown? I know this sounds crazy, but I think the man is Kahan." ' Joe looked up. 'It's signed "your loving brother, Frank",' he said, a tremor in his voice. 'They burned his body in a garbage incinerator.'

Neither of them spoke. Only the dripping rain, the wind and the occasional cry of an owl broke the silence.

'How could someone get into Kahan's position and be a crook?' Patrick asked eventually.

'It's a political appointment,' Joe said. 'I've met the guy and he wouldn't look me in the eye. He's the man.'

'But you've no proof.'

'None other than what my brother told me.' Joe's head was bowed. 'Château Diane must be just one scam of many,' he said quietly. 'I saw how it's done there: they dissolve cocaine into the wine, bottle it, export it to Ireland, then presumably distil it off and send it on to the States – how I don't know.'

'Jesus, I don't believe this,' Patrick said.

'It's true,' said Joe.

Patrick let his breath out in a long whistle. 'Let me tell you,' he said eventually, 'about a man whose name is John Abelson.'

After ten minutes Joe leaned back. 'Tell this to the police here,' he said, 'and they'll go straight to the FBI in Washington. What are the FBI going to do? The DEA report to them, for Christ's sake.' He clenched his fist. 'I asked Kahan when I met him in his office, I asked him, what's being done now that my brother's dead? Who's being put in his place? Do you know what he told me? He said no one's replacing Frank because they're holding a review. A review! Jesus, he must have been laughing to himself over that one. How many tons of cocaine is a review good for? Ten? Twenty? How many tens of millions of dollars?' Joe gave a bitter laugh.

Patrick looked at the big cop; in the faint glow his blond hair might have been a halo.

'I've thought of going to Madrid myself,' Joe continued, 'trying to take up the trail, of using Frank's contacts, of seeing what I could find.' He shook his head. 'I'd get as far as the airport and every *narcotráfico* in Spain would know that I'd arrived. Jesus, look at me: do I look like a wop?' He paused. 'The only person who could go down there,' he said, 'would be someone from outside the system, a person who, as far as the intelligence apparatus of the United States is concerned, does not exist, someone who has never had their prints taken, either as a criminal or a member of a law-enforcement body, if you like, someone created, a man without a past. Anyone else is dead. Unfortunately,' he said quietly, 'I don't think that person exists.'

Joe looked up and the two men's eyes met. In the confines of the stone shelter Patrick felt what seemed like a series of electric shocks shoot up and down the length of his spine. He could see a face in front of him and it was not Joe Vendetti's. The face he could see was that of his own father, big and trusting, ravaged by pain and bewilderment. Patrick stood up, shakily.

'Let's go down to the cottage and drink something hot,' he said.

CHAPTER TEN

Washington DC

Mel Krupin's restaurant on Connecticut Avenue was, as usual, crowded. At the back wall, seated at a corner table, Captain Mike Izaguirre of Washington's Metropolitan Police put a match to a cigarette and wondered for the hundredth time why the man opposite him had invited him to lunch. They had discussed everything, from football, to the dollar, to the price of property in Maryland and Virginia, to Star Wars. There's no bite yet, thought Izaguirre, no bite. He looked at the younger man, early thirties, cool and fit, blond hair with the centre parting. Come on, son, thought Izaguirre, I've got to get back to work.

'Waiter!'

Robert Waters, Bob to his friends, DEA special agent and assistant to Administrator Kahan, raised his hand. He made a squiggle in the air for the bill, then turned smiling to the cop.

'I enjoyed this, Mike,' he said.

'Me too,' said Izaguirre.

'It's been my pleasure,' Waters said. 'I don't get to talk to people on the ground here in DC as much as I used to.'

'Thanks for inviting me,' responded Izaguirre.

'Power lunches are what it's all about, isn't that right?' Waters laughed.

Beneath it all you're as cold as charity, thought Izaguirre.

'I don't get time for lunch most days,' Izaguirre said, 'certainly not in places like this.' He watched as the bill arrived and Waters signed it. Never checked it, Izaguirre thought, and no plastic involved. So the DEA have an account here; so what, who is this kid trying to impress anyway?

'I spent two years in New York,' Waters was saying, 'setting up deals with guys who you'd swear were as legitimate as an archbishop. For the first few times they'd never agree to a location until five, ten minutes beforehand. Often I'd arrive in a place for lunch, there'd be a call and I'd have to go to another restaurant, maybe twenty blocks away. These guys were paranoid about electronic surveillance, but it meant I did get to a lot of good places to eat.'

They stood and began to make their way towards the stairs which would bring them up to street level.

'I've got to tell you, Mike,' said Waters, his hand lightly catching the older man's arm, 'I've got to tell you that Mr Kahan was most impressed with that man of yours we saw some time back, Sergeant Vendetti.'

'Joe Vendetti impressed him?' Izaguirre responded. 'Joe's a good man.'

'His brother was also a fine man,' Waters nodded. 'The whole business was most unpalatable.'

Mike Izaguirre stopped at the top of the stairs. 'You reckon?'

'Mr Kahan was upset,' Waters was saying. 'The meeting was kind of strained – understandable, of course, due to Sergeant Vendetti's state of mind.' Waters took a plastic number from his pocket and handed it in to the hat-check. 'Mr Kahan asked me to try and get in touch with Sergeant Vendetti, to see if anything further could be done – purely on a goodwill basis, you understand.'

'Of course,' Izaguirre nodded, putting on his coat. 'I think that gesture would probably be very much appreciated.'

'Good,' Waters said, 'I'm glad you agree.' Then he frowned. 'Trouble is,' he said, 'I've been trying to get in touch with the guy for nearly three weeks, but' – Waters laughed – 'I'm damned if anyone can tell me where to find him. I was hoping that you could help me.'

'Son,' said Captain Izaguirre, 'if you'd asked me this two hours ago, I could have told you and saved you sixty-five dollars.'

'Oh?' The baby-blue eyes were ice-cubes. 'So where is he, Mike?'

'You may not believe this,' said Izaguirre, 'but as far as we're concerned, Joe Vendetti has gone like a puff of smoke.'

CHAPTER ELEVEN

The light flicked on and Georgie sat upright in the bed, her eyes wide.

'Repeat what you've just said to me,' she said incredulously. Patrick repeated it.

Georgie shook her head from side to side as if trying to clear her ears of water. 'I'm not really hearing this,' she said to herself, 'I'm dreaming, tell me I'm dreaming.'

Patrick moved to put his arm around her, but she drew back, rigid. 'Don't come near me!' she cried. 'Please God, help me, I'm living with a raving lunatic!'

Patrick sighed and looked away. 'I half expected you to say that,' he said.

With shaking hands Georgie lighted a cigarette; the first deep draught of smoke seemed to steady her. She swallowed hard as she fought back the tears. 'Why?'

'I'm the obvious person,' Patrick said. 'I'm half-Spanish, I look the part, and no one knows me.'

Georgie closed her eyes. 'Patrick,' she said slowly, 'I was there last night when Joe Vendetti told us what they did to his brother. His brother was a professional and he didn't stand a chance. Are you so stupid to think that you are going to succeed where he failed?'

'Joe's going to teach me everything he knows,' Patrick replied.

'Dear God, let me wake up somewhere other than in this place for the insane,' Georgie whispered.

'Georgie,' Patrick had caught her free hand.

Georgie drew her hand away. 'You're not just talking about hardened criminals,' she cried, 'you're talking about terrorists!

These people have already killed my brother. They'll kill you.'

'I've got a much better chance than Frank Vendetti,' Patrick said. 'I'm not known, and I know more than he did: the link to Abelson.'

'Frank Vendetti,' Georgie said, 'Joe Vendetti. Suddenly these people have taken over our lives. Who are they, anyway? Joe Vendetti is someone who broke into this house and who you chased up the mountain. He could be anyone.'

'You've met him,' Patrick said quietly. 'Do you think he is anyone other than who he claims?'

Georgie put out her cigarette. 'At the time he seemed OK,' she said, 'but that was before I knew that he had talked you into doing his dirty work in Madrid.'

'Let's settle that right away,' Patrick said. 'This is my idea. When I mentioned it to Joe he refused to take me seriously; it was I who insisted. He never suggested anything.'

'But why?' Georgie cried, her voice breaking. She looked uncomprehending at Patrick's profile, light years away. 'Why?'

The days of shrimping and of warm sand, of swimming with Mama and waiting for Papa to come back from Galway are all over. Now everything revolves around tube trains and bus timetables. Mama is frowning. Where are you going, Patrick? Have you finished your homework? No? Well then, sit down and finish it. Anything you start you must always finish. Always. Do you hear me, Patrick?

'Why, Patrick?' Georgie repeated.

'Because I let Alan Ridgeway down,' Patrick replied softly. 'I didn't believe him.'

'Alan wasn't the sort to hold a grudge,' Georgie said. 'Do you think he would approve of an insane mission like you're suggesting?' Georgie shuddered. 'At the start we were talking about John Abelson being involved. The thought that he's a criminal was bad enough. Now we're talking about someone in Colombia called Marcellino, a drugs baron, and about you taking off like James Bond. I think I'm going mad.'

'Georgie, listen to me,' Patrick said. 'All right, it has escalated into something far bigger than either of us could have ever imagined. But these people killed Alan – I saw him die. Suddenly everything Joe Vendetti says makes sense, everything

Alan discovered fits. Take the relief foreman: he was a hit man sent in specially to get rid of Alan – everything fits, Georgie, everything!'

Georgie closed her eyes. 'That's all the more reason for you not to go,' she said despairingly.

'Maybe so,' Patrick sighed. 'But it doesn't alter the way I feel.'

'You'd risk your life because of the way you feel?' Georgie cried. 'Doesn't that tell me something about the way you feel for me?'

Patrick caught her other hand and brought both of them to his lips. 'The way I feel about you is simple,' he said. 'If I was told that I would never see another person but you for the rest of my life, I would nearly be a happy man.'

'Nearly?'

'Nearly, because it wouldn't be completely true. I would have to look at myself at least once a day, and that's something I'm not sure I could do.'

'Forget about me,' Georgie said, her eyes pleading with him. 'Have you no fear for yourself, for what they might do to you?'

Patrick held her hands tightly.

'Patrick,' Georgie said, 'is there something else? Is there something you're not telling me? Patrick! Answer me!'

I read your school report, Patrick. Papa is smiling. Proud. I showed it to my clerk of works and d'you know what he said? He said that lad should be an accountant, it's the coming thing. An accountant. Think of the help you'll be to me! Think of what we'll do together. Drake and Son. Papa is laughing he's so happy. Drake and Son, Patrick. They'll all have to make way for Drake and Son.

'Answer me!'

Slowly Patrick turned his head.

'There's nothing else,' he said, drained. 'But I'm going to do it.'

Georgie shivered and came to him. Patrick scooped her into his arms and held her tightly.

'Tell me what you're going to do,' she said in a small voice, 'and how I can help you.'

'Joe is going to teach me,' Patrick said.

'He can move in here,' Georgie said. 'How long will it take?'

'I should learn a lot in ten days,' Patrick said.

'Then what?'

'I go Madrid. I infiltrate where Frank Vendetti left off. Frank gave Joe the name of a girl he'd met, someone with connections to the cartel. I find her, learn how the cartel operates, discover who's who.'

'What can I do?' asked Georgie.

'After I've gone,' Patrick said, 'try and help Joe find out if this man Kahan is really working for Marcellino.'

A blast of rain hit the bedroom window and Georgie ducked her head under the covers, pulling Patrick with her. In their cavern she came to him urgently, her fingers pinching the muscles of his shoulders.

'You're not to worry about me,' he said when it was over. 'I'm depending on you.'

'How can I not worry?' she asked.

'I'll only be a couple of hours from London,' he said.

'Right. From the top. What is it called?'

'*Neive, perica, cocaina, la mercancia,* coke, snow, candy, toot, every place has its own favourite word.'

Joe Vendetti nodded his head. 'In its natural state, what does it look like?'

'It's a small, bright-green leaf.'

'And what is it?'

Patrick rubbed the dark stubble of his five-day-old beard. 'Botanically it's the plant *Erythroxylon coca*. Geographically it's found along the entire eastern spine of the Andes – in other words from southern Chile right up into Colombia.'

They were walking up a steep track of mountain.

'Where and how is cocaine made?' Joe quizzed.

'The cycle starts in countries such as Peru and Bolivia. The coca leaves are picked and dried, then put into steel drums. They are crushed in a solution of kerosene, potash and sulphuric acid. The result is what the *campesionos* call *pasta*. We call it cocaine sulphate and it can fetch up to two thousand dollars a kilo.'

Joe inclined his head.

'The *pasta* goes north, into private labs, mainly in the jungle territories of southern Colombia,' Patrick continued. 'The labs are owned by the big Colombian drug syndicates and they employ the best cooks in the business. A good cook can turn that two thousand dollars into nine, ten grand. He turns the *pasta* into cocaine hydrochloric, or simply, cocaine.'

They had reached a ridge. A great, inland bowl swept before them, distant saucers of water shimmering behind curtains of waving, brown reeds.

'So you're a buyer,' Joe said, 'you want to score a little coke.'

'For a start,' Patrick answered, 'there's no chance that what you buy on Forty-Second Street is going to be pure cocaine. It will have been cut, probably a number of different times.'

'Cut?'

'Dealers make their money by diluting or cutting cocaine,' Patrick explained. 'The ten grand kilo in Colombia becomes a hundred grand in New York. The New York dealer can cut that hundred grand up into half a million bucks.'

'How?'

'Shaving it into powder, then mixing it with substances of similar appearance. Using sugar cuts by mixing dextrose, or salt cuts mixing quinine. Boric acid is used, even talcum powder. Sometimes what you buy may actually contain no cocaine.'

'How can you tell?' asked Joe.

Patrick sat. 'Taste it,' he replied. 'Dab your finger in it: the flavour should resemble that of a lemon. If the cocaine has been cut the taste will be perceptibly altered.'

Joe was nodding.

'Cuts also reduce the cocaine's anaesthetic effects,' Patrick added. 'Rub some on your gums and see what happens.'

'Not very scientific,' Joe said.

'You can be more scientific if you're faced with buying larger amounts. Then you can use the burn test.'

Joe's blue eyes were hard. 'Which is?' he asked.

'Get some aluminium foil,' Patrick said. 'Place a small amount of cocaine on it and hold it over a low flame. Refined cocaine leaves a dark red stain on the foil and a very small amount of residue. The larger the amount of residue, the larger the cut. You'll also smell a sugar cut burning and it leaves a black stain.'

A smile appeared on Joe Vendetti's large face. 'Not bad,' he said.

They both rose and attacked a steep wall of rock, using clumps of grass and indentations for footholds. Atop the next rise they stopped, breathing deeply, and looked south to Loch Fyne and out over Cowal.

'It's so beautiful up here,' Joe said. 'What's that peak over there?'

'That's Beinn Bheula,' Patrick replied. 'On a clear day if you stand on top of Beinn Bheula you can see the Clyde.'

They sat.

'You're Irish?' Joe asked.

'My mother was Spanish,' Patrick replied. He brushed his hair back from his forehead. 'She was from San Sebastian, the Basque country. She met my father when she was a student at university in Galway, that's in the west of Ireland.'

'So what does that make you?' Joe asked.

'Sort of an Irish-Spanish-Brit,' Patrick said. 'The old man moved over to London to work in the building trade when I was a child.' He tilted back his head and inhaled the clean air. 'I haven't been to Ireland for years,' he said. 'I'd forgotten how much I missed it until I met Georgie and we started coming up here.' He looked at the cop. 'Who knows you're over here?' he asked.

'No one,' Joe Vendetti replied. 'No one. That's the one thing I regret: I couldn't risk telling anyone I was coming, and that meant not telling my captain, Mike Izaguirre, the best goddam policeman anywhere in the world. The fact that I've just disappeared into thin air will be hard on him.' Joe shook his head. 'Izaguirre used to say to us, "Boys, you can bet your life on me as long as I can bet my life on you".'

'It's hard to imagine it, isn't it?' Patrick asked. 'What we've been talking about is a different planet to this one: Marcellino, cocaine, crack, Marshall Kahan betraying everything he's meant to stand for.' Patrick looked away and out over the timeless scene. 'Thank God they're not part of this,' he said quietly.

'You don't have to do it,' Joe said. 'This is your world – these mountains, the heather, your lovely girl in her cottage. You're right – mine is a lousy, dirty world. I swear I'll disappear and you'll never see or hear of me again.'

Finish it, Patrick. This time finish it. No matter what it takes, no matter how hard it is, this time seal the tomb so that he can rest in peace.

'Patrick?'

Patrick smiled faintly. 'You could go, but Alan Ridgeway and John Abelson and someone else you've never heard of would still be in here,' he said, tapping his head.

They began to descend the far side of the rise. 'Try me again,' Patrick said.

'What's crack?' Joe asked, as they began to run.

'Crack is what you get when you mix cocaine and water with baking soda, heat the mixture, and then when it cools, strain it through a coffee filter. The filter catches small, chunky crystals – these are crack. You put one in the end of a pipe and hold your lighter under the pipe-bowl. Wham! You're on the moon in five seconds flat.'

Joe stopped and caught Patrick's arm. 'That's good,' he panted. 'But listen well: whatever else you may come across – and I'm including heroin – if it comes to crack, pass.'

Patrick's eyes were unwavering.

'It's suicide,' Joe said. 'Believe me, I've seen it. Crack can lead to clinical dependency in one afternoon.' He paused. 'That,' he said, 'is why it's a marketing dream come true.'

'There was a funny call today,' Georgie said. 'Long distance, I think. Asked me our number, then hung up.'

Patrick looked at Joe. 'No one knows you're here?' he said.

Joe shook his head. 'Could it be your friends in London?' he asked.

'They couldn't get rid of me fast enough,' said Patrick.

'Maybe they've changed their minds,' Joe said.

Georgie came over with a steaming mug and a plate with buttered brack. Patrick and Joe's chairs were turned towards the fire.

'We've only a few more days,' Joe said. 'I want to tell you some things about the smuggling business.' He sank his teeth into the golden brack. 'This is good,' he said.

Patrick put his arm around Georgie.

'First of all, it is primarily a business,' Joe began. 'Like every business it's got its fat cats and its little guys. The little guys are called mules.' The cop joined the fingers of his hands. 'These mules will often try a one-off, desperate attempt to get some capital together. The mule psyches himself or herself up, gets on a plane in Bogotá and then, via another Latin American country, flies to Miami or Madrid. Maybe the snow will just be in a handbag, or the false compartment of a suitcase, or worn in a padded girdle. Maybe, but unlikely. Cocaine can be soaked into fabrics, the clothes you are wearing, and extracted at the other end. It can be dissolved in liquor as we know, or shampoo or aftershave, and got out afterwards. You can sew it into the ribs of your bra or wear it in your hair.' He nodded. 'These numbers all work – but they're cumbersome and the actual rewards are small; you can't traffic a significant volume of cocaine the way I've described.'

Patrick threw some peat on the fire.

Joe continued: 'Your sophisticated *contrabandista* will try and lay his kilos on an innocent at an airport – an urgent package that's missed the mail – or in a plane – excess duty-free, could you help me bring it in? But more and more the trend is towards bodypacking.'

Patrick raised his eyebrows.

'You get a gram of cocaine,' Joe explained, 'and you put it in a rubber, an ordinary condom. You tie the top and then either secrete it' – he looked at Georgie – 'you'll excuse me, but if you're a woman then obviously you have two options, or you swallow it.' He nodded. 'Swallowing is by far the most effective; you can actually ingest over a hundred of these *uvas*, grapes as they're called in the trade, and pass them at your leisure when you check into your hotel in New York or Miami.'

'It sounds foolproof,' Patrick said.

'It isn't,' Joe replied. 'The customs get to know the types – they put them on a pot and wait. X-rays show them up as well. But if a planeload comes in from Cartagena, you can't put every man, woman and child in a room and give them enemas.'

'The mind boggles,' Georgie said.

'I know,' Joe said, 'but bodypacking is one of the most dangerous procedures known. You've a hundred of these little white balls in your guts – a belly full of potential bombs. You're sitting in your plane seat, looking down at the deep, blue sea and suddenly a few grams of refined cocaine take a walk inside you. It's like swallowing a gallon of gasoline and then a lighted match.'

Patrick drank some tea.

'Why do people do it?' asked Georgie.

'Lack of money, lack of education.' Joe shrugged. 'Lack of fear. When you're young your own death is the last thing you're prepared to consider. And if there's fifty grand at the other end – then why not?'

Patrick swung his feet over the side of the armchair.

'Marcellino uses armies of the people I've just described,' Joe said, 'worker ants, totally disposable. He uses them the whole time to dribble cocaine into the States, Europe and Australia. But they're just the canteen end of the operation: the volume they shift could never satisfy the demand. He has to go for the bulk runs.'

'I suppose that means cargo,' Patrick said.

Joe nodded. 'Cargo directly into New York or any other US port, maybe from South America or in a transhipment from Europe, hidden somewhere in one container, itself one of 2,500 such units on a ship.'

'And air cargo?' Georgie asked.

'Private jets,' Joe replied. 'Flying consignments directly up from South America and landing in places in the Mid-West that you've never heard of. Sometimes they catch them. But what DEA actually seize represents at most around 10 per cent of the total. Last year was their best ever: four and a half tons.'

Patrick calculated. 'At a hundred dollars a gram, that's worth nearly half a billion dollars,' he said. 'What do the DEA do with it?'

'They mainly destroy it,' Joe said, 'that's as soon as they get court orders allowing them to do so. But there's always a backlog and, depending on the frequencies of busts, a lot of it sits in DEA vaults around the country.'

'If I were Marcellino,' Patrick said, 'that's what I'd try and get my hands on.'

He could tell she was awake beside him. The bedroom window rattled as it was struck by gusts. He stretched his arm out and she caught it and pressed it to her.

'Can't you sleep?' Patrick asked.

'No,' Georgie murmured. Then, 'It's a bad night.' She came to him, wrapping her arms around his neck. 'Two weeks?'

'At the outside,' he replied. 'That's a promise. In two weeks I'll be home.'

'It will seem like two hundred years,' Georgie said. She shivered and tucked closer. 'What am I going to do for two weeks?' she whispered.

His mouth was at her ear. 'What about me?' he murmured, his hands all over her.'

'You'll find some sultry, Spanish beauty to look after you,' Georgie said.

Patrick crushed his mouth on top of hers. 'There will never be anyone but you,' he whispered, 'you give me everything.'

'I love you so much,' Georgie said.

It was the last day. They were in the north valley, having left Inverary far behind. They had run for nearly five miles and now sat fighting for breath on the side of the mountain.

'Again,' said Joe after some minutes, 'who are you?'

'*Me llamo Curro Cano*,' Patrick answered.

'In English,' said the cop. 'Where do you come from, Cano?'

'Córdoba,' Patrick replied.

'What did your father do?'

'I don't know for sure – he was in and out of jail. I think he was probably a pimp. He left my mother when I was six or seven. He may have gone to Madrid.'

'That's good, the vagueness is good. Now your mother.'

'She told me she was a singer in a club in Córdoba. When I was ten I discovered she was a whore.'

Joe Vendetti nodded his approval.

'Didn't you go to school?'

'Only long enough to learn to read and write.'

'After school?'

'I got a job in a restaurant washing plates and dishes.'

'Where?'

'Córdoba.'

'How old were you?'

'Fourteen.'

'And then?'

'I went to Barcelona where I got a job in a café; then I crossed the border into France and went to work for a guy who ran a truck service out of Narbonne. One day in Marseilles I saw an ad for a cabin-boy on a steamer. I got the job.'

'Name of the ship?'

'*The Marieke Mia.*'
'Flag?'
'Greek.'
'Cargo?'
'Dry.'
'You liked life at sea?'
'It was rough.'
'How, rough?'
'Everyone tried to fuck me except the ship's cat.'
The two men laughed until their sides hurt.
'I wonder who Curro Cano really is,' Patrick asked at last.
'God knows,' Joe said. 'Probably a respectable schoolteacher someplace.'
'How come you have his passport?' Patrick asked.
'A pedestrian found it outside the National Air and Space Museum in Washington six years ago,' Joe said, 'and handed it to the first rookie cop who came along. The cop forgot all about it, never reported it, and then when he did discover it among his things, decided not to say anything about it.'
Patrick smiled. 'You never reported it?'
'Never. No one, the cops, the FBI, no one knows about Curro Cano. I even checked the Interpol computer on the chance that he might have a criminal record in some other country. He doesn't exist.'
They began the long walk down the mountain.
'When did you get into the drugs business?' Joe asked casually.
Patrick blinked. 'After about a year at sea,' he responded. 'I realised I was the only one not doing it.'
'Horse?'
'Sure, horse, smack, heroin, call it what you like. In Spain it's called *caballo*. Back in Marseilles they just walked off the ship with it in their bags, half-kilo, kilo, no problem.'
'That's good,' Joe said, 'keep it simple, that's the way it's done.' They breasted a little hill. 'So you stayed with this ship?'
'For two years,' Patrick replied. 'One day I jumped ship in Bangkok. I heard the real action was in the north of Thailand, in Chiang Mai.'
'The Golden Crescent?'

'The Golden Triangle. The Golden Crescent is between Iran and Afghanistan.'

'Go on.'

'In Chiang Mai money buys anything. You can buy smack openly on the street, but I wanted to get to the source. After waiting three weeks I eventually got to a man called Jantong Lee.'

'A smuggler?'

'A trader. He bought refined heroin from the jungle labs in Burma and Laos and sold it on.'

'Quality?'

'Number Four, Star and Crescent, 707. Lee could sell you brown sugar as well.'

'Go on.'

'I assembled a small consignment of the best smack Lee could offer, six kilos. I put it in a rucksack, got a bus down to Bangkok and joined a rice shipment back to Europe.'

'How much did you make?'

'Twenty thousand dollars.'

'You did this often?'

'For nearly seven years.'

'Until last year?'

'That's right.'

Patrick stopped, then dropped to drink from a small stream.

Joe looked down at the dark, bearded figure.

'You know as much as I do now,' he said. 'Your education is almost complete.'

Patrick squinted up at him, his eyes narrowed against the evening sun. 'Almost?'

'That's right,' Joe said. 'You're good. Now there's only one step left.'

'What's that?' Patrick asked, getting to his feet.

'Let's go back to the cottage,' Joe Vendetti said.

'Do you remember your first beer? Do you remember how goddam awful it tasted?'

Patrick nodded. Georgie had gone to shop in Inverary and they were both sitting in the bright kitchen.

'It's the same with this stuff,' Joe said. 'The first time people snort snow they frequently show alarm because it's such a completely new sensation. They burn and their eyes water.'

Joe had produced a package the size of a small fist, wrapped around with greaseproof paper.

'It's only a suggestion,' he said, 'and it may never arise, but we can't have you crying like a baby when you're meant to be a *narcotráfico*.'

Joe had taken a mirror and emptied a small mound of white powder on its surface. Patrick stared.

'Before you ask the question,' Joe said, 'let me give you the answer: I came across it in my official capacity.' With the edge of an English ten-pound note he was arranging the cocaine into two neat lines. Then he rolled the note from its end. He sat back.

'You want to taste it?' he said.

Patrick looked at the cop, then slowly he wet his index finger and prodded the end of one line. He rubbed his upper gum, then sucked his finger. His tongue tasted bitter, his gum felt as if it had been blasted with Novocaine.

'Shit!' Patrick grimaced.

He took the mirror, shoved the smooth note-end into his left nostril, held it to the powder and inhaled as hard as he could. He repeated it with the right, fascinated as the white powder was sucked up and disappeared.

Nothing happened. A slight burning inside his nose gradually ebbed away. He looked at Joe Vendetti. 'Are you sure this is the real thing?' he asked. Then, involuntarily, he stood up. A catherine wheel was going off somewhere near the core of his head, somewhere he hadn't been before. He filled his chest with air and felt the potency of his limbs. Waves of pleasure engulfed him. He ran his hands through his hair.

'Jesus,' he said. He dropped lightly to the floor and began to knife up and down in press-ups. He was experiencing complete elation; his arms drove his body effortlessly; he was humming along in top gear; his body was weightless. He laughed continuously as he crossed the hundred mark. Or the thousand – anything was possible, no barriers existed any more.

Patrick felt an arm on his shoulder. His arms still pumping, he turned.

'Let me get you a coffee,' Joe Vendetti said.

* * *

The three of them sat by the fire sipping a celebratory, 25-year-old malt.

'Let's hope I don't get caught entering Spain with a quarter kilo of your best *neive*,' Patrick said. 'It would be a lousy start.'

'You won't,' Joe said. 'Do it the way I've taught you and you won't.'

Patrick smiled. 'Here's to our reunion,' he said. 'Two weeks' time in London.'

Joe's face was sombre. 'There's just one thing,' he said.

They both looked at him.

Joe sighed. 'No one knows we're sitting here,' he said. 'But right now I'd bet every cent I have that someone is looking for me.' He held up his hands. 'I'm not trying to be spooky,' he said, 'but I thought I should say it. These are dangerous people we're up against, people who don't like the idea of a maverick cop playing sheriff and ending all the fun. They're powerful as well: a man like Marshall Kahan can command the security network of the United States and use it against me.'

Patrick shook himself. 'You're making me nervous,' he said. He reached to an inside pocket and took out the photograph. 'Kahan doesn't even look like a crook,' he said. 'He looks too respectable.'

'He's a crook,' Joe said quietly. 'I only wish I knew why.'

Patrick reached for the bottle and topped their glasses. 'What time are you two going to London?' he asked.

'As soon as father gets back,' Georgie said. 'That will be tomorrow after lunch.'

'And every night at nine,' said Patrick, 'one of you will always be in the flat; at that time the phone will always be free.'

'Affirmative,' Joe said.

Patrick stretched. 'I've got an early start,' he said. 'I'm going to take some fresh air, then turn in.'

Joe stood up and poured a dram into their glasses. 'A toast,' he said quietly. 'For my brother, thank you.'

Georgie raised her glass. 'And for my brother,' she said.

Patrick walked up into the mountains. Wind whipped at his hair and brought moisture to his eyes. All his life had suddenly rushed into a single point, caused by a man he had never met, although Patrick felt they now knew each other intimately.

For there had been no Drake and Son. Laughter and warm days near Clifden had gone. They had been replaced by enthusiasm and some initial prosperity in London – the enthusiasm of an eager, simple man – and then even that had gone. With it went everything of the old order, a sea-change which even now he could not bring himself to talk about to Georgie. Like a time bomb it had waited for him, unavoidably.

Finish it.

He kept to the path he knew, pressing into the strengthening gale until he came to a bluff which, by day, would give unforgettable views of the loch. As he stood there, out from him, over Inverary, the wind blew patches of night cloud apart so that for brief instants the light of the moon flashed on to the serrated surface of the lake. Patrick gazed. His moist eyes began to play tricks: the erratically illuminated lake began to take on a shape, the round solid shape of a man's head, the eyes deep black caverns, the mouth a great, distinct scar. Patrick stared and as he did so his mouth became dry.

'Marcellino!' he shouted from the mountainside, and then more strongly, '*Marcellino!*'

But clouds blocked the moon and Patrick's words were whipped by the wind and lost in the eternity between himself and Inverary.

PART FOUR
Elizondo

CHAPTER TWELVE

Pyrenees
Present-day

The room was a low-ceilinged *etcholak*, a shepherd's hut with irregular, overhead beams running out from a rock face to join a crude stone wall. Beside the rock on a hearth of round stones, a fire smouldered, its smoke curling up and out through a hole in the roof. A chain hung from the roof, suspending a black, open pot over the fire. There were no windows.

'The wind is up,' said a small man with a red beard. 'It will have a good blow tonight.'

In one corner of the hut there was movement; sacking was pulled back and two men – one middle-aged, one a youth – entered.

'Castor, Teodoro, *kaixo*!' greeted the men at the fire.

'*Kaixo!*'

Castor Arocena was massively built with a deeply creased, weatherbeaten face and black, curly hair without a speck of grey. His son, Teodoro, was built like his father, if anything taller, but his hair was the colour of oaten straw.

'It's turning into a real bitch out there,' Castor said, shaking the rain from himself. 'Are we late, Mattin?'

The red-bearded man shook his head. '*Ez*,' he said. He nodded to another corner where the dark mouth of an opening into the rock could be seen. 'Geraldo has been in there for over half an hour.'

'Who is here?' Castor added.

'Colonel Sainz Perez,' Mattin replied.

'Sainz Perez?' Castor's mouth was open. 'Surely you jest?'

'I do not jest,' Mattin said. 'Sainz Perez has come to visit our command.'

Teodoro listened to the talk and felt his scalp contract with excitement. At the feet of the men around the fire he could make out the dull barrel-glint and the oil-smell of automatic weapons.

'Sainz Perez has come a long way,' Castor was saying. 'Something must be going to happen.'

'It is a time of action,' Mattin said. He bent to the floor and picked up an Armalite rifle. 'We are told to have these oiled and ready.'

'Action?' snorted a man with a flowing black beard. He took a briar pipe from his mouth. 'What sort of action? Action like we get now, night after night, playing nursemaids to thugs from Madrid with their cargos of vile filth?'

'Ssh, Xalbador,' said Mattin. 'You will be heard.'

'Why should I care?' Xalbador said. 'What I say is true. Tell them, Caro.'

Caro was a young man, very large and plump, who despite the lateness of the evening wore a cotton T-shirt revealing arms of massive proportions.

'It is true,' he said. 'The cargoes increase with every week. Geraldo says it puts us all in danger.'

Xalbador shook his head. 'It cannot go on,' he said.

Mattin cleared his throat. 'I have been in there,' he said. 'Sainz Perez said to me, "Mattin," he said, "are you ready to die for Euskadi?" I said to him, "Colonel, I have made my peace with God." '

Mattin sat back, once again the centre of attention.

Beside his father, Teodoro watched their faces; he became aware that he was being observed, by a pair of eyes at the extremity of the group, across the fire and beside the rock face. The eyes were deep and large and their owner wore rough clothes and a cap like a man. Teodoro had been so absorbed that he had not seen her: she was Paulina, the sister of Geraldo, a trainee nurse of eighteen or nineteen who had recently begun to travel with her brother to the meetings. She had a pale, intense face, ending in a point at her chin. She wore her jacket open and Teodoro could see the clover-leaf emblem of the Basques, a swastika shape in burnished copper, hanging from a silver chain around her bare throat. Teodoro smiled at her slightly and she returned it, then lowered her eyes.

'Our greatest danger,' Castor said, 'may be from the north.

Gone are the days when the border was our guarantee of escape. Gone are the days of safe houses in Franzia. The Common Market has destroyed everything.' He spat. 'Now we are on our own.'

'I prefer it so,' Xalbador said.

Castor nodded. 'We wish to be apart,' he said. 'We might as well become accustomed to being on our own.'

A man ducked out through from the cave mouth. He was groomed compared to the mountain men, smoother. His flaxen hair went back from a high forehead over quick, intelligent eyes. He was clean shaven. He wore blue denims tied by a thick belt and a clean, pressed shirt under a leather jacket. He nodded to Castor and smiled.

'*Kaixo.*'

'*Kaixo*, Geraldo!' Castor had got to his feet and held the younger man's hands in both of his. '*Kaixo*, Teodoro and I are here and ready.'

Teodoro also stood up and shook Geraldo's hand.

'You are rested after your journey?' Geraldo asked.

'A journey only begins when you have walked to Zaragoza,' Castor said, 'and then it is time to walk home again.'

The men laughed.

'Very well,' said Geraldo, slapping Castor's arm, 'we had better go in.'

Castor and Teodoro followed Geraldo back through the opening. It marked the mouth of a natural, winding tunnel, cut into the rock, low and damp, causing them to stoop as they walked. In front grew a warm glow. Teodoro was the last to be able to straighten himself as they reached the cave. He blinked. It was a high, hollow dome lighted by the single flame of a storm lamp. Towering shadows were thrown up the walls and as Teodoro stared he could discern the white outlines of animals engraved all about them.

'Castor Arocena Gomez and his son Teodoro,' Geraldo said. He turned to the two men. 'Colonel Sainz Perez from the High Command of the Government of 27 April,' he said.

Castor nodded and stood awkwardly in the middle of the cave, his big hands clasped before him. Teodoro stood at his side. Seated before them, behind a table, was a slight man: bareheaded, silver-haired, his long face drawn and pale, his eyes a very bright blue behind steel-framed glasses. Teodoro stared. The famed Sainz Perez of whom it was said that never had he given an order twice; the probable future prime minister of a free Euskadi, frail almost, in a thick, city overcoat, its collar turned up to his neck, his fingers constantly revolving a pencil.

'You are the explosives man,' he said to Castor in a very quiet, nearly tired voice.

'*Bai*,' said Castor, shifting his feet, 'yes, sir.'

Sainz Perez nodded. 'You have done time for it before, I think,' he said.

Castor swallowed. 'Yes, sir. Two years in Santina in the sixties.'

'And you are not afraid of going back there?' Sainz Perez said. 'Maybe for ten years? Maybe for the rest of your life?'

Castor's face was creased in concern. '*Ez*,' he replied, 'no, sir.'

'You are certain?'

'I am certain, sir.'

'Why?' Sainz Perez said in a voice which Castor had to strain in order to hear. 'Do you like the view of the sea?'

Castor stood open-mouthed, unable to comprehend. Geraldo was smiling to himself. Sainz Perez laughed quietly. 'Very well, Arocena,' he said. He looked from father to son and his face became set in a mask. 'Very shortly the hour will come. Right across the face of Spain, at exactly the same hour of the same day, the birth roars of the new Euskadi will be heard. You are a man of the hills, Arocena – you understand how all birth is accompanied by blood?'

Castor felt his excitement surge. 'Yes, sir.'

'You understand how the centre must be finally made to realise that there is a powerful, new force in Euskadi, a body which they will be forced to recognise?'

'Yes, sir.'

'Military precision,' Sainz Perez said in his flat voice. 'It is crucial that when you are told the final time everything then proceeds with military precision. Do you understand?'

'My son and I are ready, sir,' Castor gulped.

Sainz Perez's gaze held them for a moment, then flickered down to a book in front of him. 'Arocena,' he said, 'your mission is particularly important.'

Teodoro looked at his father's chest, thrust massively out, and at Geraldo, absorbing every word spoken by his commander-in-chief.

'The target for your explosives will be the nuclear plant at Lemoniz.'

Teodoro looked at his father but Castor never flinched.

'You won't get within a rifle-shot of it, of course,' Sainz Perez said drily, 'but an explosion beside a nuclear installation – carried out as part of a nationwide, coordinated strike – that will attract attention all over the world.'

Castor's back was rigid. 'It will be done, sir,' he said.

'*Ona da*,' Sainz Perez said. He looked at the big, mountain man and his son, both of them huge in the shadows of the cave. '*Ona da*, Geraldo will give you your orders. And don't forget – military precision.' He turned his face back to the book in front of him, indicating that the meeting was over.

'*Gora Euskadi!*' Castor blurted out.

Sainz Perez looked up over the top of his glasses, his blue eyes cold and unemotional. '*Gora Euskadi*,' he said. '*Euskurrik asko*. You may go now.'

Sainz Perez waited until the two big men had left the cave.

Geraldo made to follow them.

'Wait,' Sainz Perez said. He took off his glasses and rubbed his hand over his eyes and his colourless face. 'I have received word from Madrid today,' he said. 'The number of crossings is to be increased, doubled in fact in the next three weeks.'

'Doubled?' Geraldo's face was creased with apprehension.

Sainz Perez nodded. He replaced his spectacles. 'It appears they have had a problem,' he said, 'in France. Stock is short. They must increase crossings.'

'*Madre de Dios*,' Geraldo said in frustration. 'Already we are at the limit to provide them with cover for the traffic that exists. There's a war on against drugs. Last week the French had five hundred soldiers in the Basque area alone. We risk our own cause, our own organisation by being involved at all. The French and the Spanish aren't going to turn a blind eye if when they're looking for drugs they discover some of our commands, or the caches of weapons or ammunition which have taken us years to build up. This thing is going to ruin us.'

Sainz Perez spread his hands briefly. 'What can we do?' he

said. 'A revolution cannot run on hopes and thin air. We must help our benefactor.'

'At the beginning it was just some crossings, not often, just two or three of our men to lend a hand,' Geraldo said. 'Now the position is that every night we are asked to help. Men who should be training, preparing, they are now working for Marcellino Adarraga!'

'There is no choice,' said Sainz Perez.

'Can you not see?' Geraldo said. 'We have become the European crossroads for cocaine. From us it goes to Bordeaux, Rotterdam, Antwerp, Hamburg, every night of the week. Can you not see?'

'We have no choice,' Sainz Perez repeated.

'I beg you!' Geraldo cried. 'This thing will tear us apart.'

'Captain Olaso,' said Sainz Perez, his voice like a razor in the damp cave. 'I have spoken.'

Castor sat by the fire, his eyes shining. Teodoro had gone to sit beside Paulina. The red-bearded Mattin was passing around a dark bottle.

'*Izarra*,' Mattin said.

Castor put the bottle on his head and slugged the sweet liqueur down. He smacked his lips, belched, then looked at Teodoro who was watching expectantly. Castor handed the bottle back to Mattin.

Teodoro smiled at Paulina. 'Old enough to die, but not to drink,' he said.

'Sainz Perez exhausts himself,' said Mattin from across the fire. 'Every night he sleeps in a different house, every day is spent planning for the hour.'

Castor stood up. 'Come,' he said to Teodoro. 'We must go home to mother.'

'Ssh!' Paulina held up her hand for quiet as she pressed her ear to a small transistor radio. '*El tiempo*,' she said.

Castor watched anxiously as Paulina listened.

'It's a storm,' she said, 'coming from the west to the east over the Pyrenees. They are advising people not to travel before morning.'

Castor's face dropped. 'We must get home,' he cried. 'Mati's time has come, she is on her own.'

'What was that?' Geraldo had emerged with Xalbador. Paulina repeated the forecast.

'Damn,' Geraldo said. 'I must get the colonel down. We have a car and a driver at the bottom. Others are waiting.'

'Castor's Mati is due tonight,' Paulina said to her brother.

'I have asked a neighbour to spend the night with her,' Castor said, 'but it is me she will want.'

'Why not go down with Colonel Sainz Perez?' Xalbador suggested. 'When he has reached his destination he can have you driven around to Aldudes. It will take over two hours by road, but at least you will be able to get home.'

'It is not possible,' Geraldo said. 'Including the colonel's guards there are six of us already in the car. There is no room for Castor and Teodoro.'

Castor's concerned face looked at Teodoro. 'It is I who am needed,' he said, turning back to Geraldo. 'If the colonel will take me, Teodoro can wait here and come home himself when the storm is finished.'

'That's still too many,' Geraldo said.

'I don't have to go,' Paulina said. 'I am not on duty in the hospital until tomorrow afternoon. I can come down in the morning and meet you then.'

There was a cough and all the men stood up as Sainz Perez appeared. Geraldo explained the position. Sainz Perez looked at Castor, then shrugged. 'So, let us not waste time,' he said, buttoning up his collar as far as it would go and covering his head with a flopping, black beret.

'*Eskerrik*,' Castor said gratefully, '*eskerrik asko*.' He nodded to Teodoro. 'Do not follow until it is safe,' he said.

Mattin dimmed the light as the men left by the outer door, its sacking blown violently inwards by the gathering storm.

Caro placed dry sticks criss-cross over the glowing hearth. Soon a healthy flame leaped for the roof hole. Paulina brought a saucepan of water to the boil and poured it over coffee in an open jug. Mattin took out the *izarra* again and everyone served themselves tin mugs of coffee.

'I did not know your mother was near her term,' Xalbador said to Teodoro as they sat back. 'But then I have not seen her for nearly a year.'

'She says it will be tonight,' Teodoro replied. He paused. 'She did not want my father to come here.'

'Ah, *emakume*,' Xalbador said with the weight of years, 'women.' He puffed ponderously on his pipe. 'They are all the same, women. They are beautiful creatures, but they do not think like us men: their world is more confined, their pleasures simple. What does a woman want? A warm house, a child to raise, a man to cook for and a bed to sleep in. Isn't that so, Mattin?' Xalbador's face was deadly serious, but his eyes twinkled with mischief. Teodoro saw Paulina sit forward, her eyes wide in disbelief.

'That is so,' Mattin agreed gravely. 'They are simple creatures, like hens. They want food and water and eggs to sit on when they are broody.'

'Such nonsense I can scarcely believe!' Paulina's normally pale face was scarlet and her eyes blazed. 'If women are hens, then what are men, I ask you? Braying asses who rush after the first ginnit that shows its stupid head over the wall!'

Xalbador puffed impassively. 'Don't upset yourself, child,' he said.

'I'm not a child!' Paulina's body was taut. 'I'm a woman! You speak of women like a species that you might see in a zoo. Such rubbish!'

'I know you are sincere,' Xalbador puffed, 'but –'

'Your attitude is that of your grandfather!' Paulina cried. 'I ask you! The new Euskadi? Your minds are as stale and twice as slow as the milk from last year's goat. Nowadays a woman can do anything a man can!'

Mattin had to cover his mouth with his hand, but Xalbador puffed away seriously. Teodoro saw the enormous Caro stare in wonderment at Paulina; she sat like a female hawk, upright and bristling, its cliff nest attacked.

'Anything?' Xalbador asked with great import.

'Anything,' Paulina flared, 'anything and more!'

'Women are born,' Xalbador puffed, 'in need of man's protection. It was so in the jungle, it is still so.'

Paulina's fists were clenched. 'That is simply nonsense! A woman trained can do anything a man can.'

Xalbador's smile was patronising. 'Of course,' he purred, smoke licking from his mouth, 'of course.'

'You are pigs!' Paulina cried as the other men tried to hide their laughter. 'Tell me something here and now that you can do but that I cannot! Tell me!'

She stared defiantly across the fire at Xalbador, her nostrils dilated. Teodoro felt himself stir: her neck was thrust out, a graceful, rigid neck, its clover-leafed, copper mascot swinging against her small breasts.

Xalbador considered the question. Slowly he took the pipe from his mouth and composed his face in its patient mode. 'I would not be so unfair,' he said.

'Tell me!'

'I could not live with the ignominy –'

'You cannot!' Paulina cried triumphantly, her anger masking her alertness for the trap. 'You cannot! You are beaten, the woman has yet again won!'

She sat back, her arms crossed, her face smiling defiantly at all of them. Teodoro stared in admiration. Caro licked his lips. Then their eyes went to Xalbador; he had risen and slowly went to a corner of the hut where loose straw was piled to the ceiling.

'I used to be a shepherd in my young days,' Xalbador said, pocketing his pipe. 'In every *etcholak* such as this, somewhere you would find the stones.' He rooted in the straw, then turned smilingly to Paulina. 'Things have not changed,' Xalbador said.

Against the wall of the cabin, beneath the straw, the four men and the girl could see four round stone balls, the smallest twice the size of a man's head, the largest an enormous water melon. With his foot Xalbador rolled the smallest ball to the middle of the floor. Standing, he bent and with one hand scooped the ball, first to his knee where he worked his palm under it, then to his chest and finally, effortlessly, up and over his head. He replaced the ball slowly to the floor. 'Do that using both hands,' Xalbador said to Paulina and sat down.

Paulina had become pale. She went to the middle of the floor, took off her jacket, then tucked the sweater beneath it into the belt of her trousers. She rolled her sleeves up, showing white, thin arms, then licking her lips she stooped and caught the ball between her hands. She grunted incredulously as she found herself bent over, stuck as it were to the ball. Teodoro felt his colour rise.

'Use your legs,' he whispered.

'No help, now,' Xalbador said, his hairy face split in a grin.

'Use your legs!' Teodoro persisted.

'How, my legs?' the girl asked in exasperation, her face broken out in sweat.

'Squat down and bring it up with you,' Teodoro said.

'Whose side are you on, Teodoro?' Xalbador asked, good-humouredly.

Teodoro had gone out beside Paulina and was demonstrating what she should do. Paulina squatted as he showed her, grasped the sphere and with difficulty, straightened up. She stood there swaying slightly, the weight held between her upraised palms. The giant Caro sat mute, a trickle of unattended sweat running down his face.

'Now, flex again, just before you raise your arms,' Teodoro said. 'Flex, ready, then up in one big push.'

Paulina's face was ravaged by the effort. Teodoro could hear her breath coming in gasps.

'Flex and press!' he urged her. 'Now! Before it becomes too heavy!'

Gathering all her concentration Paulina prepared. Biting her lip she began to bend her legs, but the weight took over and she began to totter backwards, the heavy ball impelling her. She cried out. With one arm Teodoro saved her, with the other hand he caught the falling ball.

'All right,' he said, 'I have you.'

'An excellent attempt,' said Xalbador, rising and bowing with great courtesy. 'And if I may say so, I retract everything I said before.' He looked at the faces around him. 'These women of Euskadi,' he said, 'they are true tigers, the match of any man.' He sat down and the men clapped.

With his hand still around her, Teodoro helped Paulina to her stool.

'Thank you,' she gasped and smiled at him.

Teodoro poured from the bottle into a mug and handed it to her. Paulina drank the *izarra* and sat, her chest heaving.

Caro was smiling sheepishly. 'But the competition is not yet over,' he said.

Teodoro looked at Caro, who was sitting there like a massive child, his eyes continually darting to Paulina's heaving chest.

'Very well,' Teodoro said slowly, 'it is not.' He glanced down at the girl. 'But our team captain has retired and she sends out her *lugarteniente.*'

Paulina squeezed his arm and Teodoro felt himself tingle all over. He covered Paulina's hand briefly with his own, then went to the floor.

'The *gizon,*' Caro beamed. 'The grandfather.'

Teodoro shrugged.

'To the count of five?' Caro asked.

'To the count of five,' Teodoro agreed.

The very largest of the spheres was trundled out to the centre of the floor. They faced each other over the granite bowl and formally shook hands; beside Caro Teodoro looked scrawny. Paulina sat by the fire, her knees drawn under her chin, her eyes wide.

Caro lifted his head until it brushed the roof, then taking air through his nostrils he swelled himself up to the limit, then emptied himself out, letting his shoulders slump forward. He repeated the action half a dozen times, filling and emptying. Then suddenly he squatted, grasped the *gizon* and, his eyes swollen large, straightened. Staggering under the great weight Caro went back two steps. He steadied himself and with a loud, painful groan brought the *gizon* to his chest. The others could see the muscles in his arms standing out. Caro's face was puce. His cheeks were puffed fully out and his eyes fixed inwardly on the ball. As if in great pain he readied for the final effort; he jerked down to get below the ball and then, bringing every pocket of strength in his body into play, he willed his trembling arms aloft. Agonisingly, as his legs and back straightened out, so his arms rose. His audience watched in wonder. Both Caro's arms were rigid over his head, swaying.

'One, two . . .' Xalbador began.

Caro began to totter backwards.

'. . . three . . .'

With a great roar Caro lost control and the granite orb went crashing out behind him, hitting the floor of the hut with a deafening smack. Caro himself ended spread out, face up in the straw. Teodoro was quickly over. 'Are you all right?'

Caro winced and shook his head as he grabbed Teodoro's hand. 'I couldn't hold it,' he gasped, his face now white, 'I couldn't hold it.'

'Here,' Mattin was at his side. 'Drink some of this.'

Caro took the bottle and slugged from it.

'Aaaah!' he exclaimed as the alcohol coursed into him.

'Look,' Mattin said. He was pointing at the floor: where the *gizon* had struck the stone a deep fissure had appeared.

'It cannot be lifted,' Caro said as he sank down by the fire.

With his foot Teodoro rolled the giant stone back to the floor's centre. He pulled the knitted pullover he was wearing over his head and then unbuttoned his check shirt and threw it to one side. Beneath it he wore a sleeveless singlet, through which his physique could be seen. The audience held its breath. Teodoro squatted and reached for the *gizon*. He caught it, grimaced, then jerked up to a standing position. He felt the ball drag every fibre in his body towards it. Shifting his hands Teodoro widened his feet, flexed and pushed.

'Aaagh!'

With a great cry Teodoro brought the *gizon* to his chin. The three men and the girl sat wide-eyed, each one of them feeling the weight with Teodoro. They saw him catch his breath and brace against the *gizon* as it tried to push him back. Teodoro fought against it.

'Quick!' Xalbador hissed. 'He must do it quick!'

Teodoro flexed. His legs seemed to swell out as they took the weight. He pushed. Up. The ball rose, inexorably. First to his nose. Then his eye. Then past his forehead. His mouth was open in soundless agony, his chest now unbreathing as the lungs were asked for the ultimate. Inch by inch his body straightened, his face a scar of pain. The *gizon* swayed over the room. It was aloft.

'One, two . . .'

Teodoro felt the *gizon* take him back, like it had Caro. He managed to get a foot behind.

'. . . three . . .'

Inhuman pain in his arms. Xalbador's voice in a cave a hundred miles away.

'. . . four . . .'

Teodoro couldn't hold it. He had to . . . He was falling.

'. . . five . . . !'

Teodoro brought the rock to his chest, his waist and then the floor. The others were on their feet. Paulina ran to him and threw her arms around his pounding neck. Teodoro felt Caro's handshake and saw the big youth nod.

The small hut was perfectly weatherproofed, keeping its occupants out of sight and sound of the storm. By the hearth Caro slept peacefully, an old coat thrown under him. Mattin sat propped against a stool, his snores whistling out. Teodoro saw Xalbador shake himself like a dog and then lie down.

Slowly Teodoro sat up, gritting his teeth as the straw beneath him crinkled. In his stockinged feet he crept on cold stone to the cave mouth. He could see only ink. Pressing against rock Teodoro left the shadows of the hut behind him. His hands touched damp. The rock curved, once his head bumped, then he found that he could stand. His feet touched straw underfoot, the same straw that he had brought in an hour before.

'Who is that?' Her voice was a whisper.

'It is Teodoro.'

'Come and sit here,' Paulina said.

Teodoro felt for the straw and his hand brushed against the sacking under which she lay. 'I could not sleep,' he said.

'Nor I,' Paulina said.

'What were you thinking of?' Teodoro gulped.

'Of my brother, Geraldo,' Paulina answered. 'He is worried, I can tell. He dislikes running drugs when he is meant to be fighting for our freedom.'

'Colonel Sainz Perez knows what is best,' Teodoro said.

'Maybe he does, maybe not,' said Paulina quietly.

Teodoro's head was throbbing with the intensity of this situation. He felt his helplessness rise. Then he heard the girl laughing quietly.

'Paulina,' he gulped, 'this evening ... ever since I first saw you in the hut ...'

'Ssssh!' she said. 'The others!'

Teodoro closed his eyes, then trembling he reached his hand out until it touched her head. 'I ... you ... I ...' he stammered.

He felt her move. He felt her head rise, bringing the feel of warm skin under his fingers, and then the long, nobbled length of her back. His head was on fire. He thought he would burst.

'I –' he began.

'Sssh,' she said again, but more softly.

Teodoro felt fingers at his lips. 'I . . . love you,' he gasped.

He felt her hands at the buttons of his shirt. 'Let me do it,' she said as he tried to assist her. She laughed. 'And slowly,' she said as his urgent hands suddenly raced all over her.

'This is my first . . .' Teodoro gasped.

'I know,' Paulina said, 'I know.' She reached for him. 'Come to me, my soldier of Euskadi,' she murmured gently, 'and I will teach you.'

CHAPTER THIRTEEN

A whirlwind. A wind so strong that you are picked up, sucked into the greater force, hurtled without choice in totally new directions. Patrick Drake scratched his beard. So it was: everything now part of a greater force, changed. No longer a safe job, responsibility, prospects; suddenly a last-minute ticket on a Gatwick charter to Málaga. Through Spanish immigration, where his new identity received only the briefest of glances from a yawning official, and then customs, watching his shoulder bag ahead of him entering Spain on the luggage trolley of a tipsy man with children. A series of trains, northwards, inches at a time, through the mountains and into the great plain of Castille, until at last the mighty Tajo was crossed and he was at the gates of Madrid.

Inexorable movement. To where? A tiny, grimy, sixth-floor hotel, Hotel Nevada, wedged into the corner of a building overlooking a dirty lane off the Gran Vía. The Gran Vía. Swirl. Turmoil. Patrick Drake's new hinterland. A night world where the owls had human faces. Whores in the same doorways. Wrinkled old women on every corner, crouched over suitcases of cigarettes. The roar of the traffic; the smells, of garlic, smoked ham and high-octane gasoline; and the beats of the *camello*, the pushers, working the bars and cafés, the public toilets, the street underpasses, their whispers, *'chocolate, chocolate,'* their faces woven through the overall texture like a crochet, trawling the night with efficient deliberation, rebutting time and time again the laughable proposition that there is no advantage in human misery.

Patrick looked in the bar mirror. Black hair, bristling black beard, brown eyes and skin. Man of Spain. Name of Curro Cano. And where was Drake? In London? Or in Scotland? Or still a small child in the west of Ireland? Was Patrick Drake at last mercifully entombed, along with his passport, in the safe-deposit box which he had hired that morning off the Paseo de la Castellana? Would this finally finish it?

An hour ago the telephone call he had made was a blessed relief.

'Georgie?'

'Patrick! Are you all right?'

Patrick bit his tongue as the loneliness in him surged. 'I couldn't be better. I'm just checking in.'

'How is it going?' Georgie asked.

'I've made contact with our American friend,' Patrick said softly. 'I hope to get further tonight.'

'For God's sake be careful,' Georgie said. 'Are you feeding yourself?'

'Of course.'

'Patrick, there was a letter here for you when Joe and I got to London,' Georgie said. 'I opened it. It's from Abelson Dunwoody, very official, they want you to get in touch to hear, I quote, "something to your advantage".'

'Screw them,' Patrick said.

'Joe said you should know that there have been two of those funny phone calls as well,' Georgie said.

'Any idea who it is?'

'No idea at all. Patrick . . .' Georgie hesitated, 'this may sound silly, but I think someone followed me home from the library this evening.'

'Followed you?'

'Yes.'

'Georgie, you're to keep in touch at all times with Joe, do you understand me? He's to know where you are every minute of the day. Is that clear?'

'Yes, darling.'

'You promise?'

'I promise.'

Patrick looked in the mirror. The bearded man looked blankly back. There were two worlds: Georgie's world in London, where he belonged; and the world he thought he now stood in, where, outside, children shrieked, kicking a ball in the dusty Plaza de Santa Ana.

He looked at his watch. He had been sure she would come.

'Shirley! *Una llamada para Shirley!*'

Two nights ago. The barman had held up the phone. Patrick saw her in the mirror, a strong face with a wide mouth, even teeth, eyes that half hid under sleepy lids. Their eyes met. He had been watching her watching him for an hour. Slightly detached from her group. And then the telephone call. American Shirley.

Last night she was there again. Same time. Mirror encounter, but this time a slight smile. She left her group, a graceful walk. Her hair came halfway down her back.

Patrick found her on a bench out in the square.

'*Hola.*'

She looked at him with frank interest. 'Too stuffy,' she said in Spanish. '*Mucho humo.*'

Patrick smiled. '*Soy Cano,*' he said.

'Shirley.'

She produced two cigarette papers which she licked and welded lengthways. From a leather pouch she tapped out the dark green, chopped marijuana, up-turned the pouch until every last fragment of dust had been emptied. She jostled and firmed the joint between thumbs and forefingers, then ran her tongue along its edge before sealing the rice-paper on itself.

Patrick lay back on the bench and took in the variety of odours: he passed the joint back to her: it was as if his senses had been heightened: he had the ability to isolate each scent and savour it on its own, or to shake them all up together into an olfactory cocktail. He smelled the grass, the night, the *tapas* in the surrounding bars and the body smell of the girl. He switched from his nose to his ears: individual sounds, of his breathing, the girl's breathing, of the wafting cries of children, of their mothers, theirs occasional and sharper, high-pitched scolds, of the traffic somewhere far off and of her fingers as they wandered through his beard. He jerked upright just as he began to slide into a time-warp. The *chocolate* was dynamite.

She caught his hand. 'I know where we can get some *neive*,' she murmured. 'Do you like cocaine?'

'*Claro*,' he said, 'sure I do. When?'

'Tomorrow night,' she replied. 'Here at nine tomorrow night. I'll come alone.'

Patrick's head swam. His mind had only barely registered the fact that that was why he was there.

He was certain she would show. The distant bells of many churches peeled out ten over night-time Madrid. Then he saw her, walking over the Plaza de Santa Ana, a cigarette between her fingers. Patrick drained his glass and went out.

'*Buenas noches*,' she said.

'Hi,' he said.

'You didn't think I'd turn up, did you?'

'I knew you would.'

Patrick looked at her. She had the sort of half-awake, dishevelled, warm look of someone who had just got up.

They walked out of the Plaza de Santa Ana, across the Calle de la Cruz, up to the Puerto del Sol.

'I know this guy in Tetuán,' Shirley said. 'I've heard he's got some grams in.'

They descended into the busy depths of the Puerto del Sol.

'I've scored some really good *neive* here before,' said Shirley.

In the dirty, steel carriage Patrick sat opposite her. Her face had a tightness that had been absent the previous night; he looked at her fingers twisting a tissue in her lap.

'What's this guy's name?' Patrick asked.

'What's a name?' Shirley asked. 'He's just a guy I know.'

They left the train and surfaced in a residential area of shuttered windows and parked cars. They left the main *calle* and walked past a row of sleeping houses, then down a curving, left-hand laneway which led to steep steps cut between walls of stone. Somewhere a dog barked.

Suddenly Shirley froze and flattened herself against the wall. Patrick did the same. They crouched in the shadow. They were at an arch, the pedestrian entrance to a terrace of houses which could be approached by road from the other side. Now Patrick could hear the voices which had alerted her. Very slowly he looked around the corner. A car stood in the centre of the terrace, its lights on. Men stood at an open doorway, and on his own, pacing up and down, his hands behind his back, another man observed the proceedings, his longish hair tied at his neck with a ribbon.

'Anguila!' Shirley whispered.

Patrick looked at the scene fifty yards away. He could see faces peering out the upstairs windows of adjoining houses. There were shouts, then, from the open doorway, three men rushed out dragging a figure with them. Shirley's hands went to her mouth. The men propelled their captive into the terrace and slammed him across the bonnet of the car.

'The scum!' Shirley hissed.

Patrick watched Anguila. They were too far to hear, but Patrick could see Anguila approach the prostrate figure, bend to say something, then clearly run his hand in a caress across the man's buttocks. The figure on the car turned his face and spat into Anguila's face. Shirley caught her breath. Anguila was stepping back. Another man grabbed the prone figure's hair and slammed his head powerfully downwards on to the metal.

'Come on,' Shirley said.

They retraced their way back up the steps.

'Where to now?' Patrick asked.

'To my place, I suppose,' Shirley said.

Shirley's place was a room at the top of a run-down, turn-of-the-century building which formed the bottom of a dead-end and where plaster had fallen away in chunks to reveal timber beams and courses of red brick.

'My father thinks I live in a smart apartment near the university,' Shirley said. She laughed drily. 'It's a drag. I have to go over there to collect my mail.'

There was a tiny kitchen, a bedroom, a single window, and outside the door a room with a shower and a hole in the ground between two enamel footplates. They removed their shoes and sat cross-legged on the bed. Patrick looked at her as she broke open a cigarette and mixed tobacco and marijuana together.

'It's a pity about tonight,' she said, 'I really wanted a good snort.'

'I feel sorry for your friend,' Patrick said.

Shirley sniffed. 'He's a fool,' she said. 'Anyone who thinks he can take on the cartel in this town and win is a fool. Anguila has eyes everywhere.'

She reached under the bed. From a matchbox she began to pinch tiny white granules into the line of tobacco and marijuana.

'Any port in a storm,' she said.

Patrick blinked. 'Crack?'

Shirley nodded. 'This aircraft leaves this miserable, shitty little planet in thirty seconds,' she murmured and closed the joint.

Patrick watched as she placed the cigarette on the bed, then scooped her pullover over her head. Kneeling, she unclipped her skirt, flung it to one side, wriggled from her panties, then resuming her cross-legged position, lighted up.

Shirley sucked hard. The effort made her throw her shoulders back and arch so that her breasts stood out. Open-mouthed, her teeth bared and her neck sinews rigid, she took the smoke down as far as it would go. Patrick took the joint and watched her. There was a metamorphosis. Shirley sat, her eyes closed, a smile of total triumph spreading over her. Where before there had been tension and concern now there was smoothness and relish. She shivered with ecstasy and reached again for the joint. She drew it deeply. Her face appeared lighted from within, innocent and delicious. All over her, rollers of euphoria, breakers of total pleasantness swept and washed, surging into pores and crevices that had been dry and dusty.

'Oh Jesus,' she kept saying. She opened her eyes. She had not noticed that he had not smoked. 'Such music,' she whispered, 'such amazing music.'

She rubbed her hands up and over her breasts, circling them, then reached into the air as if she might elevate. She opened her eyes and took the joint. 'Come on,' she said, smiling but impatient, 'come on.'

Patrick went to her. The joint was just a butt now. It glowed near her fingers, nearly burning them. Patrick took it and doused it.

'Just touch me,' she said in English, 'now, touch me now when I'm climbing.'

She took his hand. She began to shudder, then jump. In the rush of her exhilaration her face had attained a quality of delinquent beauty.

'There's such music up here,' she said. 'Oh my God,' she cried out, 'oh my God, now you own me.'

They walked together up the north side of the Gran Vía and entered a brightly lit bar. The high walls and ceilings overlapped or were hung with the smoked legs of ten thousand hams. They ordered beers and stood drinking them, one foot on the bar-rail, looking at themselves in the zig-zagging mirror. Behind them a little hunchback played a one-armed bandit: occasionally he won and the first bars of the 'Harry Lime Theme' blared out.

Patrick looked at Shirley's reflection. After three days he was becoming tuned into each part of her cycle: she was now beginning her descent, a section marked by irritability and tension. The night before she had free-based for two hours whilst he had sat by. In the mirror, she caught his glance.

'I'm just going through a phase,' she said abruptly. 'I don't intend to spend the rest of my life doing dope.' She lighted a cigarette.

Patrick looked at her as she dragged the smoke down. Because she oscillated constantly between the two poles of chemical emotion, it was difficult to speculate on what she might have been. Her life was a switchback where the vigorous, healthy Shirley of the stratospheric high alternated with a despairing psychopath.

'Where do you come from?' Patrick asked her.

'Chicago.'

'That's a long way from Madrid.'

Shirley gulped down smoke and air. 'It's a long story,' she said, as if the ability to explain it was beyond her. 'It involves ambitious parents, a precocious only daughter, an absurd belief that only in Europe is anything really worthwhile, a superficial nouveau-riche approach to art – you name it, it involves it; I am Middle American thought incarnate.'

Patrick watched her suck at her cigarette so hard that it lost its uniform rotundity.

'My father makes a fortune altering the way people look,' Shirley said. 'He's one of the best plastic surgeons in the business. He and my mother believe recreation means that on a Friday evening when the last breast lift has been done, you get dead drunk and don't sober up again until Monday morning.

Their life consists of work and this frantic attempt to annihilate themselves.'

'What are they trying to forget?' Patrick asked.

'Shit, how do I know?' Shirley replied. 'Themselves? Each other? The fact that when they die their house will be sold and two months later no one will be able to remember who it was who lived there? I don't know, what are any of us trying to forget?'

A man in his mid-twenties came in. He had shoulder-length chestnut hair, pale skin, dark darting eyes. He saw Shirley, flicked his eyes over Patrick, around the bar, back to Patrick. He wore black trousers, a shimmering black silk shirt and an expensive-looking white jacket with a quilted surface. Shirley muttered something and went to him.

Patrick watched the man put his arm around Shirley and guide her towards the slot-machine. The hunchback greeted him familiarly. Patrick saw Shirley make fists of her hands in emphasis; her new friend shrugged, glanced at Patrick; Shirley shook her head, smiled, reached over and kissed him. The man stepped back out on to the Gran Vía, his hair bobbing at his neck, and Shirley came back to the bar.

'Jackpot,' she said, her face radiating victory.

Patrick looked at her inquiringly.

'That, Cano, was Tomás,' Shirley said, her humour totally changed. 'Jesus, I must like you, Cano,' she smiled. She caught his head behind and pulled it down to her mouth. 'You screw like a jack-rabbit and I adore you,' she said. 'That must be why I have just told one of the few people in Madrid who can get genuine cocaine that you're one of us, a 100-per-cent, safe proposition.' She hit her hand on the counter and laughed out loud. 'You're lucky for me, Cano, lucky!' she cried.

'Who is he?' Patrick asked.

'Tomás? He's just someone who knows his way around, know what I mean?' She paused. 'You're a 100-per-cent, safe proposition, aren't you, Cano? I mean you're not some sort of a weasel, are you?'

Patrick met her eyes. 'What do you think?'

Shirley lighted another cigarette.

'I've been unlucky before,' she said, 'but you, I think you're lucky for me, Cano.' Then she was smiling again, any suspicion she might have had washed away by her good fortune.

A car horn hooted outside. Tomás was sitting there, a tipped cigarillo in his mouth, the roof of the Golf Cabriolet off, its engine running. Patrick followed Shirley out.

'This is Cano,' she said.

Patrick saw cool, intelligent eyes.

'Jump in, Cano,' Tomás said.

They roared off in the direction of the Plaza España.

'Where are you from, Cano?' Tomás shouted, the wind whipping his long hair out behind him.

'*Soy del norte*, I'm from the north,' Patrick said.

'Where, north?'

They had stopped momentarily at lights.

'San Sebastián.'

'Ah, Euskadi!' Tomás cried as they tore downhill again. '*Goro Euskadi!*'

Patrick smiled. 'I don't speak Basque.'

Tomás looked at him in horror, nearly lost the car as the road swerved uphill, then corrected again. 'A Basque who can't speak Basque!' he cried, as they all laughed.

'What brings you to Madrid, Cano?'

'Money, work,' Patrick said.

'How long have you known my little Shirley?'

'Three days.'

Tomás considered the reply. 'In Madrid,' he said, 'three days is often a lifetime.'

They passed the Torre de Madrid with its galaxy of flashing signs; Tomás was doing seventy on the wide Calle de la Princesa. They entered a maze of back streets, swinging left and right before stopping sharply at the side entrance of a house. Tomás led them through wrought-iron gates and up steps.

'Shirley and I have been friends for many years,' Tomás said as he opened the door.

Tomás's *apartamento* was furnished with expensive taste. On the walls were hangings with an oriental flavour, on the polished floor Kurdish rugs. The furniture was real leather, the light fittings real brass.

'You like it?'

'Tomás, darling, it's stupendous,' Shirley said. 'You've done so much.'

Tomás turned to Patrick. 'I like nice things,' he said, briefly fluttering his eyelids to show another part of his personality. 'Now, please be seated. A little wine?' He opened a cupboard and found a bottle of Rioja. 'Some glasses.' He made his way to another room. 'And a little something special for Shirley and her new friend,' he called.

Shirley smiled like the little girl who deserves to go to the top of the class.

'One of the perks of knowing the right people in this town,' said Tomás, sitting down, 'is a supply of vintage crack.'

Patrick felt sick. Tomás had shredded two cigarettes and was thumbing their tobacco into the bowl of a briar pipe.

'This stuff doesn't hit the street,' Tomás continued. 'It's pure rocket juice, as you'll soon see. Man, this is where you forget all your troubles and your cares.'

Tomás produced a brown tablet bottle. He uncapped it and shook out four small chunky crystals into the palm of his hand. With all his will Patrick summoned up the dead face of Alan Ridgeway.

'Pure rocket juice,' said Tomás, pressing the rocks into the tobacco. He snapped a lighter aflame, put the pipe into his mouth and with a couple of deep, practised sucks brought the contents of the pipe-bowl to a glowing red.

'I'm from Cadiz myself,' he said with a smile. 'But I've met quite a few Basques in my time.' He leaned his head back and sucked the pipe again. 'I believe in their right to self-determination,' he said, sitting up and handing the pipe to Patrick, 'but I don't see the sense in blowing everyone to smithereens. Don't give a shit what you do to each other, but frankly, it's lousy for business.'

Patrick placed the pipe-stem between his lips. He wondered if the other two could hear the screaming in his ears.

'Gone are the days,' Tomás was saying, 'when an innocent camel with three kilos of *neive* up his arse could wander across the Pyrenees. Your mad Basques have seen to that.'

Patrick knew they were watching him. He sucked smoke from the pipe and drew it into his lungs. The tobacco was sickly sweet.

'The border is alive with pigs,' Tomás was saying. 'Pigs, military, choppers in the air, day and night.'

Patrick sucked again, this time keeping the smoke down until his heart drummed, then let it out and passed the pipe to Shirley.

He sat there. He saw Shirley put the pipe in her mouth and Tomás take it from her before she inhaled. He frowned. His whole system was braced on alert for the effect he knew must follow. He had reasoned that if he could try to concentrate on a fixed point then the effect might somehow be minimised. Instead all he felt was a slight dizziness.

'That's pure piss,' he heard himself say.

Tomás was lying back in the chair, laughing. 'You're right, Cano,' he said, 'and you pass!'

'Pass?' Patrick felt himself tingle all over.

'You pass,' Tomás laughed. Even Shirley was smiling. 'How do I know who you are, Cano?' Tomás asked. 'Someone in my position can't be too careful. However, now one thing I do know is that you're not a cop. No cop would ever smoke crack,' Tomás said. 'I'm sorry, my friend,' he said, extending his hand. 'They were sugar crystals. I don't use crack myself, it's pure suicide. But I had to be sure.'

Patrick took the outstretched hand.

'You forgive my joke?' Tomás asked.

Patrick nodded. '*Claro*,' he said quietly.

'Very well,' Tomás said, taking from his pocket a small pouch. 'Now, especially for Shirley, some white joy.'

It was eight, the *hora de tapas*. The bar was filling rapidly. Half a dozen barmen presided over brimming dishes on a glass-fronted counter, served the *tapas* out on small plates and chalked up the running totals on the wall.

'Tomás's OK,' said Shirley, licking her fingers. 'He's a good guy. I shared an apartment with him for six months – that was two years ago.' She lighted a cigarette. 'The answer to the question which you probably want to ask is, he likes it both ways, you know what I mean? Tomás also likes to spend money. He's got in with the cartel, done some jobs for them. Anguila, as you saw the other night, he likes to have his way with boys, you understand? Tomás's a chicken; he wants to please. He wants money so he'll play anybody's game.'

They left the bar and walked towards the subway station on Alcalá.

'Tomás's father is a lawyer in Cadiz,' Shirley said, 'a good family. They think Tomás's working indentures up here.' She laughed. 'If only they knew.'

They stood on the platform, looking at their faceless counterparts on the other side. 'He called me this morning,' Shirley said, looking at Patrick's profile. 'He thinks he may be able to use you. You are looking for work, right?'

'Right.'

The train was preceded by a blast of hot air.

'Be careful,' Shirley said, as they sat down. 'Tomás's become a bit of an entrepreneur as well.'

'How?'

'He said to bring you tonight. You'll see for yourself.'

The house was detached with its own front gates and garden. Tomás and another youth sat on a bare floor of sandalwood. There was an eye-level cloud of marijuana. As Patrick and Shirley entered, a chocolate-coloured poodle began to bark, then shut up as Tomás rose, smiling to Patrick, kissing Shirley on the cheek.

'This is Luís,' Tomás said, indicating his companion.

Luís, a serious-looking youth, nodded.

At that moment a door opened and a plump girl with a pretty face appeared. She stood there, her face in a drowsy smile. Tomás caught her hand and they left the room together.

'*Qué pasa*, any problems?' asked Shirley.

Luís rocked his hand to say 'could be'.

Patrick looked at him questioningly.

'That was Consuela,' Luís said. 'She's at fifty thousand feet right now. That's the way she does it. She gets up before a journey, then stays up for the whole trip.'

Patrick looked towards the door. 'She's bodypacking?'

'She's an unmarried mother with two small children,' Luís said. 'She reckons if she does two or three more of these trips she'll be able to hold on to the kids. She's meant to deliver first to the cartel, but we have been investing a little of our own capital in her trips.'

The door opened and Tomás joined them.

'OK?' Shirley asked.

Tomás shook his head. 'She's blocked solid,' he said. 'She hasn't moved for a couple of days. She's terrified of coming down,' he said. 'Her nerves are in pieces.'

'What will she do?' Patrick asked.

'She's swallowing speed tablets in there like lumps of sugar,' Tomás said.

'It's very unsatisfactory,' Luís said. 'Every extra moment with those things inside her increases the danger.'

'Luís is a medical student,' Shirley whispered. 'This is the house he rents.'

'It's her nerves,' Luís said. 'It has happened to her before on long trips. She came in today direct from Bogotá.'

'What did she score?'

'A hundred and fifty.'

'Christ,' Shirley said.

Luís shook his head grimly. 'She's been worried before about her bowels moving too soon,' he said. 'Now the opposite has happened.'

'What is the danger?' Shirley asked.

'Your stomach is like an acid pit,' Luís said. 'It's continually breaking down the food you eat and passing the result into your intestine for onward excretion. The longer anything stays in there, the more saturated it becomes by the acid. Although she is blocked the chemical process keeps working, putting something like rubber at risk.'

'And she's packed full of rubber,' Tomás said.

'Why not give her a laxative?' Patrick said.

'I don't want to suggest it yet,' Luís said. 'An enema to someone in her position is a very high risk. It would make her move very violently and that is the last thing we want. If just one part of one of those rubbers has been eaten into by her natural acids, then any violent purgative might easily –'

They all turned their heads to the door which had opened. Consuela stood there, against the doorframe, her eyes unfocused. In her hand she held an opaque, green bottle, its top downwards. Luís was first to his feet.

'¿*Tomaste esto*? Did you take this?' he cried, grabbing the bottle.

The fat girl looked at him uncomprehendingly. She swayed.

'¡*Dios mío*!' Luís shouted. He lowered her to the floor and then opened her mouth and smelled. '¡*Dios mío*!' he repeated. 'She's taken the whole bottle!'

Tomás stared. 'What is it?' he asked.

'It's a hospital laxative, only meant to be taken in very small doses under prescription,' Luís cried. 'Here, help me quick! Get her kneeling.'

Consuela's face had a benign smile. Patrick caught her under one shoulder and together he and Tomás brought her to her knees. Luís opened Consuela's mouth and stuck his two fingers down her throat.

'Oh my God!' Shirley said.

Consuela gagged. Luís drove down further and although the girl produced an involuntary, dry retch, she again slumped. She tried to say something.

'Lie her down,' Luís said.

Patrick and Tomás did as they were told. Then Patrick saw Luís bring both his hands up to his mouth. He followed the medical student's stare. Consuela's dress had worked up over her hips revealing her belly, wide folds of white girth. As if something within them was suddenly trying to get out, they had begun to churn.

'Oh dear God,' cried Luís, tears now running down his face.

'Get towels and water,' Patrick said to Shirley.

On the floor Consuela's breath was coming in gasps. Tomás held her hand and was shaking his head back and forth in helpless concern. 'Look at her,' he whispered, 'just look at her.'

Consuela's stomach was heaving with a life of its own. In the now silent room the sound of the turmoil taking place inside her was quite audible.

All at once Consuela sat upright and open-mouthed began to look around her, her eyes wide as saucers.

'It's OK,' Tomás said to her, 'just be still and it will be OK.'

'*Me voy a morir*,' the girl began to whimper, 'I'm going to die.'

'We are here, you are OK,' Tomás said.

Consuela began to scream. 'I'm going to die!' she screamed. 'I've got two little girls and I'm going to die!'

Luís was babbling to himself as the small group stared helplessly at the girl's hopping stomach.

Consuela continued to scream and Tomás continued to try and calm her. Shirley came back into the room with the basin. Abruptly, Consuela stopped, then turned to Tomás.

'The girls will be safe, won't they?' she asked very calmly. Her belly writhed massively.

'Of course,' Tomás soothed, 'of –'

'Oh!' Consuela drew in her breath in a gesture of complete surprise. Her mouth opened in a soundless gape, then as if a valve had been turned, her face haemorrhaged vivid scarlet and she collapsed backwards.

Luís tried to pump her chest with his hands. After five minutes he gave up.

Shirley was weeping, holding the dead girl's hand. Ashen-faced they sat, motionless, staring.

In the silence of the room the poodle began to whine.

Patrick sat on the limestone steps, in the Parque del Oeste, the gardens near the University of Madrid. It was afternoon. The lawns around him had been mowed that morning and the scent of fresh-cut grass was strong. White statues, some defaced by paint aerosols, broke the sweeping expanse of green lawns and correct hedges. Late the night before he had checked in with Georgie; her cheerful voice in London had somehow made Consuela's death seem unreal.

'You'll be home in a week,' Georgie had said.

Patrick turned: he could see Shirley approaching with Tomás.

'*Qué desastre*,' said Tomás sitting down. 'I had five thousand dollars invested in Consuela's last trip. I've lost everything.'

'The word is getting out,' Shirley said. 'The cartel will find out where Consuela died and then guess that Luís was freelancing her. They'll make an example.'

'Of Luís,' Patrick said, 'but not of Tomás.'

Tomás looked up, his face grey. 'The problem,' he said, 'is that I owe the cartel money. I'm due to make a repayment tomorrow. I've never let them down before. If I don't come up with the money, they'll connect the two events, go to Luís, make him squeal, then . . .'

'Why don't you borrow?' Patrick asked.

'I'm already up to here,' said Tomás, touching his chin. 'I've sold everything in the apartment, even the chairs. It's still not enough.' He shook his head. 'I'm going to have to sell the car,' he said, tears brimming into his eyes.

'How much do you owe them?' Patrick asked.

'Five thousand dollars,' Tomás replied. 'It's hopeless.'

Patrick looked at him for a long moment. 'What would you say if I said I could produce ten grams of pure Colombian cocaine?' he said at last.

Slowly they both turned their eyes on Patrick as if they were seeing him for the first time.

Patrick unwound the top of the cellophane package. Tomás dipped his finger in it, tasted it, then rubbed it on his upper gums.

'Tastes OK,' he said. 'Where did you get it?'

'Let's just say I have a source,' Patrick said.

They sat, shoes off, on Shirley's bed. 'You're a deep one,' she said. 'And I had you down for a *bebé*, a baby.'

Tomás asked, 'What's the deal?'

'Take the coke, step on it, do whatever you like with it,' Patrick said.

'You trust me?' Tomás asked.

Patrick shrugged. 'You trusted me,' he said. 'You need to make five grand by tomorrow. Give me your number and I will contact you.'

Tomás smiled. 'No other conditions?' he asked.

'Just keep me out of it,' Patrick said. 'No mention of my name to anyone, *comprendes?*'

'*Comprendo*,' Tomás said. He wrote out a number on the page of a notebook and handed it over, then he looked at the package. 'Mind if I try it?'

'Be my guest,' Patrick said.

Tomás left the bed and went to a small table. He returned with the transparent shell of an old biro. Without preamble he opened the package, stuck the plastic in and took two snorts, straight up. Shirley sat there, expectantly, her tongue constantly lubricating the length of her upper lip. A smile of serenity was slowly spreading across Tomás's face as he shook his head from side to side.

'*Exquisito*,' he murmured as he grinned. '*Exquisito.*'

They were walking through the tree-shaded Paseo del Pintor. Shirley had just slept for five hours; now she was in a dawn zone, still buoyed by the sleep, not yet in the drag of withdrawal. She puffed a cigarette and watched some children playing in fallen leaves. 'It's a filthy business,' she said. 'All I have to do is think of Consuela to remind myself how filthy it is.'

She squatted down, sorting leaves with her hand, then squinted up at Patrick. 'But you don't fit in, Cano,' she said slowly. 'I've been trying to figure it, but there is no way that you fit. It sounds silly,' she said, 'but you're a combination of too hard and too soft.'

'Tell me about the people Tomás's connected with.'

'Now you're far from soft.'

'Tell me about them.'

'I don't know.' She stood up and looked away. 'I hear names occasionally.'

'What name do you hear most in Madrid?' Patrick asked. He caught her eye. 'Who does Tomás mention?'

'He . . .' She stopped, fighting with herself.

'Go on.'

'I'm crashing,' she said. 'I need a snort.'

'The name.'

'Ask Tomás, not me,' she shouted. 'Now I'm crashing, damn it, I want to go home.'

Slowly Patrick got up and kicked back a ball to two little girls playing under the trees under the watchful eye of a white-haired woman.

An hour later Shirley's face was beatified in a glorious smile.

'This is pure heaven,' she said. 'This is worth everything.' She looked at Patrick, all her valves wide open, her eyes clear and bright, high-octane blood jet-spraying into her. 'How come you didn't snort?' she asked him, her elbow on the pillows. Then, 'Where do you get this stuff? What's your source? Who are you anyway, for Christ's sake?' She lay back, pulled the sheets up to her waist, then began to laugh uproariously, her whole body shaking. At last she had to sit up, her breasts swinging, holding her sides.

'What's so funny?' Patrick asked.

Shirley shook her head. 'The look on that weasel Luga's face,' she gasped. 'That was worth a gram of your *neive*.'

'Luga?'

Patrick felt goose-pimples spread over him like a chill.

'Luga,' the girl panted, 'he's a little pusher who sells crack.' She threw her head back and started to laugh again.

'Does he know about me?' asked Patrick quietly.

'He must do. He told someone this morning that he's dropped his price by nearly half' – she caught his arm as the laughter shook her – 'by nearly half,' she managed to get out, 'and he still can't sell any crack.' She shrieked as she lay back. 'Tomás's fucking up his market with your cocaine,' she cried.

An hour later Shirley's eyes had lost their sparkle. 'I need a snort,' she said. 'I'm coming down, fast and bad.'

'I haven't got any more,' Patrick said.

'You bastard,' the girl cried, 'I don't believe you.'

'I'm out, I swear.'

'I don't believe you.'

'Who is Luga?'

Shirley rounded on him. 'You bastard! Now I've got to give you more information, do I? Go fuck yourself, I want a snort.'

'I don't have any here,' Patrick repeated. 'Who's Luga?' he asked again.

Shirley shook her head fretfully from side to side. 'I told you, he's a little weasel, he's a pusher like you.'

Patrick's ears buzzed. 'Where does his *neive* come from?' he asked her.

Shirley had begun to cry. 'Jesus, please give me a snort, Cano,' she pleaded. 'I'm hitting the bottom, it stinks down here, please God, please understand.'

Patrick took a deep breath as he watched her disintegrate. 'I told you, I don't have any here, but I'll get some,' he said quietly. 'Tell me first about Luga.'

'He's a rat, Cano, he's got white skin, teeth like a rat.' She shivered. 'He's . . . obscene.'

'What did you tell him about me?'

The girl's eyes were moist, but clever. 'About you? Nothing, I told him nothing, you weren't mentioned, I swear it, I was only fooling, Luga's never heard of you, your *neive*, nothing, believe me, it's the truth.' She laughed at him expectantly.

'You're lying, Shirley.'

She began to wail. 'I'm not . . .'

'I want the truth. Who is he?'

'His name is Luga Pintor,' she sobbed, 'he works the

university by day, around the Plaza de España by night.' Her body jumped.

'What did you tell him about me?'

Shirley's head shook. 'Nothing,' she wailed, 'nothing.'

Patrick looked at her swollen eyes. 'Does Anguila run Luga?' he asked her.

'Yes,' she whispered. 'He's run by Anguila.'

'Is it true that the cartel uses *terroristas* to smuggle cocaine north?'

'Jesus!' Shirley gasped. 'You're a cop!'

'I swear to you I'm not.'

'Then why do you ask these questions?'

'Before I go to work for someone I want to know all there is to know about them,' Patrick said. 'Now, is what I'm saying true?'

'Yes,' Shirley whispered. 'What you say is true.'

Outside there were footsteps in the narrow street; a dog barked as a car pulled away. Shirley tried to dry her eyes.

'Now can I have a snort?' she asked. 'What do I have to do? Do you want me to crawl? To lick your arse? Just give me a snort, I swear I won't need another.'

Patrick shook his head. 'I want to hear exactly what you told Luga about me,' he said.

Shirley tore at a fingernail and then threw all caution out of the window. 'Everyone hates Luga,' she panted, 'he's a weasel, a rat, you understand?' She lowered her head. 'I was only trying to give him back one.' Now she sobbed, out of control. 'I told him his crack was the dregs, that he was out of business, that he would have to go back to Anguila and tell him that he had lost one of his best pitches. I told him that you were moving in.'

Patrick swallowed. 'And what did Luga say?'

Her head came up. 'He said . . . he said that within a week . . .' She buried her head.

'Go on.'

'. . . that within a week you will be *criando peces*,' she said, almost inaudibly. She looked into the brown eyes. 'Do you know what that means?' she whispered.

Patrick nodded. It meant food for fish.

Shirley reached out and caught his hand. She brought it to her lips. 'I wanted you as soon as I saw you in the Plaza de Santa Ana,' she said. She looked at him, every vestige of her self-respect gone. 'I'm hooked, Cano, I know I'm hooked.' She hecked. 'I wanted you, that's the truth, but' – she opened her mouth as if the words wouldn't come; Patrick thought she was going to retch – 'but Luga treated me like a whore.'

She had descended into the belly of the pit. Patrick left the bed and began to dress. Shirley was lying, shivering, her knees up to her chin, her teeth clenched in the clutches of clinical withdrawal.

'I've no money,' she cried softly. 'Luga's a rat. I wanted to show him how things had changed. I wanted to show him I had you.' Her face came up, unrecognisable from the face of an hour ago. 'I was so proud of you,' she said. 'I would have done anything for you.'

Patrick pulled on his boots.

'Get out of this town before they get you,' the girl was saying, 'go back to wherever you came from.' She met his eyes.

Patrick took a step towards the door. He looked back. Shirley had kicked off all the bed sheets and made a ball of her body. In the abyss of her prostration she had allowed herself to wet the bed in which she lay.

'Promise me you'll be back with the *neive*,' came her voice. 'Promise me. If you don't come back I'm going to kill myself. Cano, promise me?'

'*Te lo prometo*,' said Patrick quietly as he closed the door and made his way down the stone stairs. 'I promise.'

CHAPTER FOURTEEN

The flashing neon projected the stark outline of scaffolding over the bed. Patrick Drake swung his legs to the floor, then went to the corner basin where he splashed his face, trying to wash away the torpor. He squinted out of the small window.

Hotel Nevada was the sixth floor of an old building, covered whilst repairs took place in a framework of steel. Between buildings, if he craned hard, Patrick could glimpse crowds milling on the Gran Vía. The hotel had fifteen rooms and enjoyed occupancy levels of several hundred percentiles as the working girls of Madrid hummed up and down with their clients from the street. The hotel reception was a wall-hatch manned by a small, sour man and an Alsatian dog.

Patrick used the winding, stone stairs, the centre of each step worn thin and white from the days and nights before lifts. In the forty-eight hours since he had left Shirley, Patrick had not risked going near the neighbourhood of the university and Chamberi. He had risen late, hung around the cafés of the Centro, gone for long walks in the Parque del Retiro, returning to doze, rise, eat and sleep again. He had rung the number which Tomás had given him, but each time there was the long, dull whine of a disconnection. He had tried to retrace the drive with Tomás to his apartment but without success. Once on Alcalá Patrick thought he had spotted him in the distance; he had sprinted through the milling, morning crowds but by the time he reached the point there had only been a sea of faces, the beating sun and the blare of traffic.

He had continued down Alcalá, towards the Plaza de la Cibeles and stopped for a shoeshine. The shoe-black was chattering about a soccer score when Patrick glanced across the busy street: the driver of the red Seat parked opposite abruptly brought his hand up to cover his face before driving away. And the next day, yesterday, at an open-air café near the Plaza de Colón, Patrick could have sworn that the Seat which drove slowly past on the far side of the avenue was the same, although the way the sun was shining it obscured the driver's face, and in a city of ten thousand red Seats, who could tell?

He had returned to the small hotel. It was hopeless. Shirley, his only contact, was now too dangerous. What was the point of going on? What chance had he against a huge cartel? Against a man in South America who used fanatical terrorists for his own personal gain? Against a man in London who was among the most respected in his profession?

Patrick sat on the bed, staring at the wall. Loneliness began to creep all over him, together with a feeling not unlike panic. Driven by himself, by his own guilt, he now found himself alone. Alone. No one to talk to. No one to whom he could explain. He could have explained to Georgie, but that opportunity was now missed, perhaps forever.

Despair became part of him, always there. To end it should be simple: buy a ticket, return to London, forget the game he had forced himself to play. He sat on the side of the bed, staring at the neon reflection, flashing through the closed curtain. Why this game? Because of Alan Ridgeway? Or Abelson? Or someone called Marcellino?

In his hotel for whores in Madrid Patrick was clearly able to see the big, trusting face, suddenly all its brightness gone, the same way it had when Mama died. They can't do it to me, Patrick, they can't and they won't. But they did. Pulled the plug when every cent that Papa had was in to meet cheques that the bank would never pay. To Patrick the roar of Madrid outside was now the roar of removal vans on a dark November evening; when other folk were letting off fireworks, the retreat of Drake and Son was taking place under cover of night. Just until we fight them, Patrick. We're going to fight them and win, then we'll be back and show them all the way. Come here to me. Patrick felt the embrace odd, out of place, even though there were only the two of them. We'll fight them and win, Patrick, because that's what we're made of.

A good left and right will put most men away. The left which powered into Papa's unprepared chest was the court throwing out his case against the bank: no case to answer. The right, square to his jaw, was Church Lines, the company whose demise had ruined him; he had been building its headquarters in Felixstowe when they went under, and the company's subsidiary, Churchtels, was sold by the liquidator for what everyone said was a fraction of its value. Patrick, do you see this? Patrick had seen it. What am I to do? If the papers are right, any hope I might ever have had is gone. This man has given away Church Line's only valuable asset – given it away for nothing, Patrick. Patrick doesn't know what to say. He is preparing to leave home, if that's what the one-bedroomed bedsit in Willesden Junction is, near the meat factory to which, at 7.30 each morning, the man who once made Mama laugh makes his way in dull, brown overalls, with sandwiches and a flask wrapped in a shopping bag.

You're all right, Patrick, your accountancy is the thing, isn't it?

Patrick hears people talking. On his own he goes down to Dunwoody Plaza. His first instinct is to run away and hide. Only three months have passed since they've met, but the change is amazing. Where before there was great strength and vitality, now there is just a shell, a stooping, shuffling husk, inadequately wrapped against the cold, two big hands grasping the pole. Patrick turns, pale-faced, and collides with Jeavins, a manager in the tax department. Coming out to see the fun, Pat? I understand this old spacer has lots of goodies about God Almighty written up on his placard.

Then there is a wall of sirens as the welcoming party arrives.

It couldn't have happened, Papa, believe me. They robbed me, Patrick. Papa, walking up and down with a placard, isn't going to get any money back. What have I left, Patrick? They'll put you away, Papa. They robbed me, Patrick, they robbed your Papa. Papa, I know these people, I work for them. The barely comprehending eyes rise. You work . . .? Yes, Papa, in that building you were picketing today. I work for Abelson Dunwoody. They're above reproach. I know you feel you were swindled, but you are wrong. I want you to stop.

And now, Patrick, all these years later, sitting on your own in

Madrid, knowing what you know, can you even now begin to understand why your father cried?

Patrick made fists of both hands and held them to his head. If he pressed hard enough the image was replaced by physical pain. He stood up, slipped on his boots and reached for his room key. He needed sanity. He needed to talk. He needed to talk to Georgie.

Patrick dodged lightly through the night-time traffic on the Gran Vía. It was just after ten, nine o'clock in London.

The Plaza Santo Domingo was quiet compared to the main drag. There were a few cafés doing business, the inevitable children playing, the window shutters over street level mainly closed and barred. At the far side of the Plaza was a stand of phones, a quiet spot which Patrick had noted, away from the blare of traffic and people. The booths were at head-and-shoulders level. He lifted the receiver, stacked his coins, then began to feed them in. There was a shadow.

'Cano.'

Patrick jumped around. American Shirley, her face in its down-mode, was standing there.

'Shirley . . .' Patrick swept the coins off the box and dropped the phone. 'I was going to . . .'

'Cano.' The girl was weeping. 'Cano, I'm sorry, I have to have the shit, I'm sorry.'

Patrick stared at her. Then he saw the men.

At times descriptions of someone are so accurate that when one at last comes face to face recognition is immediate and complete. In this case there was no doubt that the low-sized man with parrot-mouth and small, fixed eyes was Luga. Luga stood, his body tensely crouched, his right arm straight down by his side. The girl still stood between them. Patrick's eyes flicked behind Luga: he saw a broad figure, sleeves rolled to the elbow, the dirty, curling blues and reds of tattoos, and the outline of someone else at the back.

Suddenly Shirley sank down on the kerb. 'Luga made me do it,' she began to wail.

'¡Cállate!' The parrot-mouth curled as Luga stepped forward. Patrick felt his whole body come on charge. Luga's teeth were bared like a rat's and as he brought his right hand up steel flashed in the street lights. It was a carpet-cutter, held rigid, at half-arm's length, defying Patrick to escape the confines of the booth. With a hiss Luga's arm swept up and in. Patrick dropped. He felt the painful impact as his shoulder hit the kerb's edge, then he rolled at speed for the centre of the road. He saw blinding lights and heard a car's horn. The taxi missed him so narrowly that he could feel the heat of its exhaust on his face. Luga's voice was swearing. Patrick jackknifed to his feet and ran blindly, looking back once to see the three men within half a dozen strides of him. There was an alleyway between houses, and he took it, his soles slipping as he rounded the sharp corner. He heard Luga cry out something from behind; Patrick ran, into the darkness. He cursed as the running feet behind him grew nearer. He was in a dead-end, a site where a house had been demolished leaving a cut in the Plaza as in a round of cheese. Wooden hoardings blocked the end.

'¡Cógelo y no le deja escapar!' Luga's voice shouted. 'Catch him and hold him!'

Patrick's eyes strained in the dark. He sensed rather than saw a shape behind him. On springing feet he turned and powered out a crisp one-two to the point where the rib-cage should end. There was a gasping grunt and the outline of a descending jaw. Patrick whipped an upper-cut and connected with a crack to the point of a chin. He felt his hair grabbed.

'¡Lo he cogido! Aqui! I've got him! Here!'

It must have been the tattoo man. The hair-grip was excruciating; an arm throttled him.

'¡No le deja escapar! Hold on to him!' came Luga's voice, desperately near.

Before his eyes Patrick saw the glint of the carpet-cutter in the arc of its downward sweep. For the second time in minutes he hit the ground, bringing the man behind him with him. Patrick prayed that the tattoo man had no weapon. He felt the larger man scramble for the advantage, kicking with powerful legs, panting, grasping with powerful hands. Patrick was being forced over on his back. He struck upwards, hard, and felt his fist connect with bone.

'¡Mierda!'

'Where is he?' screamed Luga.

Patrick felt the other man's impetus check; he drove upwards again this time with his knee. There was a soft, yielding crunch, and a scream, surprisingly high-pitched, as the tattoo man arched up and off.

'¡Ladrón! You thief!'

Patrick saw the steel and did the only thing possible: still supine he swivelled with all his strength on his backside, bringing his outstretched legs in an arc to sweep Luga off his feet. The little pusher went backwards, flailing. Patrick felt a red-hot poker in the calf of his leg.

'You bastard!' he shouted.

He jumped up. In the darkness he could see Luga near him on all-fours, reaching for his weapon which lay shining. With the concentration and purpose needed for a penalty in the last minute of a cup final, Patrick steadied, judged, then delivered his booted foot at the presented head. Luga's whole body left the ground before sprawling backwards, soundlessly, beside the groaning tattoo man.

Patrick ran headlong, back for the lights of the Plaza Santo Domingo. There were distant police sirens. Shirley was standing forlornly in the centre of the wide road, her hands by her sides. 'I called the police,' she said hopelessly, 'I didn't know what to do.' Then, 'Thank God you're all right.' She looked at him, her face ragged. 'Take me with you, Cano, I'll look after you.' She tried to catch him. 'Take me with you.'

The sirens were closer. Patrick ran for the other side of the square, limping as his leg began to stiffen. He could feel his trousers sticking and wondered dimly if Luga had nicked an artery.

'What am I going to do?' screamed the girl in English, her voice following him. 'Cano, what am I going to do?'

At the top of the Plaza Santo Domingo Patrick stopped to look back at Shirley. He could see the police car, flashing half a block away.

'Go to a hospital!' he shouted back to her in reply.

Then as the squad car appeared behind her back he sprinted and within fifteen seconds was lost in the crowds of the Gran Vía.

Gingerly Patrick put his leg up on the seat of the chair in front of him and folded the *ABC*. The afternoon sun still made it a pleasant sixty degrees on the Plaza de la Cibeles. Pigeons hopped about under the trees on the central island of the Paseo del Prado; in the distance the early evening traffic swirled around the fountain of the Plaza Canovas del Castillo; and beyond that, through the leaves which still clung to the stands of oak, the grey roof of the Prado itself could be seen.

A woman in her mid-forties was standing there, a scarf wound tightly around her head. She carried a basket.

'*Para niñas anormales, Señor,*' she said, 'please, for handicapped children.'

Two tables away a group of dark-suited businessmen laughed and looked in Patrick's direction. '*¡Cómprelo!*' one of them called and waved the calendar he had just purchased from the woman. 'Go ahead! It's for a good cause.'

'*Por favor, Señor.*' She smiled at Patrick and handed him a plastic card with her credentials.

Patrick took it, then handed it back with a *cien* peseta note. He shook his head as she handed him a calendar.

'*Gracias, Señor,*' she said and went on to the next table.

Patrick got stiffly to his feet, left money on the table and made his way up Alcalá. It was nearly seven. Halfway down the Calle de Hortaliza he stopped at a cheap restaurant and ate a plate of chips and two fat sausages which had been made from the meat of a horse. It was dark as he belched his way back on to the Gran Vía. He saw a sharp-faced man slip by, his eyes gimlets; that afternoon he had been just one of the pushers to whom Patrick had sold cocaine for 30,000 pesetas a gram.

The traffic noise was intense, a blanket of sound. He walked down the crowded *calle*, over the Redonda de San Luís, walking six blocks west until he stopped to sit at a café in the Plaza Callao. He sipped a coffee and watched Madrid go by. A girl from the Nevada, an enormous blonde painted like a tart in a nightmare, came and sat at the next table. She winked at him like an old pal, then crossed her fishnetted legs high up and lighted a very long cigarette, immediately turning its filter tip red.

Patrick continued west on the south side of the Gran Vía. The doors of a cinema opened and hundreds more people were added to the massing street. He sat on a wooden street-bench beside a boy of no more than eighteen, a gaunt derelict with staring eyes and a pitted face.

In the shining bar the hunchback stood as always at the slot machine. As Patrick entered he hit a win and the 'Harry Lime

Theme' blasted out. The hunchback smiled at Patrick pleasantly and played on. The smell of smoked ham hung pervasively over the busy bar, the floor of which was already half an inch deep with cigarette butts and *servilletas*, the ubiquitous paper napkins of Madrid. Patrick had a beer, then another. He ordered ham and ate it, wiping his fingers with the mini-napkins and letting them fall crumpled to the floor. His confused emotions, his loneliness, the pain of his memories and his envy had all been replaced by an ice-cold determination and anger. The night before they had been playing for keeps – the same way as they had with Alan.

A man and an attractive woman came in. A group of kids with motorbike helmets took a table. Patrick ordered a third beer as the bar began to fill up. The barman placed the glass on the stainless steel of the counter, together with the cash-register slip; as he did so he leaned forward and murmured something. Patrick looked at him.

'*Mira la ventana*,' the barman repeated. He jerked his head towards the street window. 'Look at the window.'

Patrick turned and stared. The hunchback was standing there looking at him through the clear glass. As their eyes met the hunchback bowed slightly then slowly began to walk uphill.

Patrick put a *cien* note beside his untouched beer and walked to the door. Ten yards up the street the hunchback waited patiently. When he saw Patrick he turned and led on, unhurriedly, uphill for twenty yards, past a wooden bench, a pile of black garbage bags and a bus-stop. Four telephones, two each side stood in a cluster. As they reached them, one on Patrick's side began to ring. His misshapen guide looked at him, then executing a courtly bow, he strolled away.

Patrick looked at the ringing phone. The traffic on the Gran Vía seemed all at once to have been blotted out. Patrick looked around the far side, to the other two phones: a man and a woman continued their conversations. The phone still rang. Patrick picked it up.

'*Si?*' he said, dry-mouthed.

'Señor Cano.' It was a man's voice.

'*Si*,' Patrick said.

There was a long sigh from the other end. 'Señor Cano,' said the voice, 'I am probably known to you as Anguila.'

CHAPTER FIFTEEN

Colombia

The helicopter had cleared the northern industrial suburbs of Medellin when the financial secretary plucked up the courage to speak.

'*Padrino*.'

Marcellino half turned. Sitting in the front, beside the pilot, his bulk measured that of two men. The secretary sat behind with papers on his knees and an opened briefcase on the seat beside him.

'*Padrino*,' the man said again, and cleared his throat. He raised his voice so that he could be heard over the engine: 'I have been making calculations, following your direction to transfer dollars from the US to Zurich.'

The leather which was Marcellino's face remained impassive. 'So?'

'The total amount comes to over 105 million dollars,' the man said. He closed his eyes briefly as they hit open country; he hated travelling by helicopter, but it was the only chance to secure the meeting which he had been requesting now for five days.

Marcellino looked at the man curiously.

'*Padrino*, if I go ahead with the transfer, then the cash position in the United States will be *nada*, nothing.' The man wished he was a thousand miles away. 'We have, as you know, substantial cash needs, every week, just to support the organisation up there – the payments which must be made to people in customs, in airports, on the docks, in the police, payments to the families of our own people who are imprisoned.'

'Always,' said Marcellino slowly, 'always I have left such matters to you.'

'*Si, Padrino, si,*' the secretary said uncomfortably, 'and we have always had enough to cover our needs. But never before have you asked me this.' The man made a despairing gesture.

'I have money here, in Colombia,' Marcellino said. 'Use it.'

'It is not enough,' the secretary persisted, as Marcellino tried to turn away. 'You know the way your business works: the worth is earned in *el norte*.'

'So what do you suggest?' asked Marcellino, his face clouded.

'Defer the transfer,' the secretary suggested, 'or reduce it.'

Marcellino did not reply at once. They had begun to fly over the red roofs and coffee plantations of Antioquia. Marcellino's eyes had taken on a faraway look. 'You see, *amigo*,' he said slowly, 'I am trapped by the flesh and blood of my promises.' He shook his head. 'How long now have you worked for me – ten years?'

'Eighteen,' said the man earnestly.

Marcellino smiled distantly. 'Eighteen years.' He looked at the man almost tenderly, in a way which the secretary had not ever seen before. 'When you see me,' Marcellino said, 'you see your *padrino*, you see me, but when I look at myself I see a boy playing with pine cones.' He spread a wide hand. 'I see him here, struggling with his books, here in the house of the priest, here hurrying along a dark road, passed from hand to hand, under a bright moon by men whose eyes are white with fear.'

Although they were barely skimming the trees of woodland, the secretary did not notice.

'In this adopted land of mine,' said Marcellino, 'what do I see? When I sit in the evening, do I see jungle, the moon upside-down, dancing fireflies?' He shook his great head. '*Amigo*, I see hills clothed in oak and birch and succulent chestnut. In a valley I see the spire of a church, the mist of evening, and behind, patchwork rising fields of pastel greens, speckled with their flocks of sheep. The air I breathe is fresh and cool. The church bell is carried up to me from the valley, a leaf of sound on the evening breeze. There is the dull clanging of churns as the evening milking gets under way. Then the darkness begins to rush and I hear a cry of "Marcellino! Marcellino!" Slowly I descend the mountain, cross the sheepfold and stand outside as the smell of ham curls out to meet the dusk.'

Open-mouthed the secretary could see a film of moisture on the Basque's eyes.

'Send the money,' said Marcellino, turning his face forward.

'*Si, Padrino,*' whispered the man, as the helicopter began its descent.

CHAPTER SIXTEEN

The farmhouse was just below the tree line. From the front door everywhere appeared downhill, miles of valleys which flashed with running water, and fold after fold of mountain.

A woman, beating flour from her hands on to her apron, came out. She was small, in her late thirties, fair-haired and blue-eyed. She walked across the farmyard, through picking hens and ducks in a water puddle who, on seeing her, got up and waddled towards her. Her blonde hair was tied in a scarf and she walked like one of the ducks, rolling from side to side, her belly out before her in a point, her legs apart with the discomfort of her pregnancy. She entered an old hayshed where a tractor sat up on blocks and the heads of calves peered out from makeshift corrals. As they saw her they bawled.

'¡*Callate!*' she said to them. 'Shut up!'

Above the calves was loose hay in a loft, smelling sweetly of early summer and packed tightly in. From another pen came the pungent smell of a sow. As the woman passed by, the pen's occupant ran to her, its pink belly touching the straw bedding. 'You've been fed,' the woman chided.

At the back of the shed more hay was piled from ground to roof.

'Castor!' the woman called.

'What is it?' The voice came from behind the hay.

'Your dinner is on the table. It is getting cold.'

'We're coming.'

There was some noise, then at chest level the hay began to move. A section was lifted outwards and Castor's head appeared. He stooped through and straightened.

'Leave that,' he called back through the hole. 'Come on, Teodoro, your mother is waiting.'

'I worry about you in there,' the woman said as they walked out through the shed. 'One mistake and we are all dead.'

'Don't worry, mother,' Teodoro said. 'There is no danger.'

'What do you know, Teodoro?' she said, rounding on him. 'You haven't even started to shave. What do you know of anything, let alone explosives?'

The youth bowed his head.

'He has to learn some time,' Castor said.

'He should be down there,' the woman said pointing to the valley, 'learning a proper trade instead of up here with you, tinkering with your lives in the back of that shed.'

'Mati, Mati.' Castor put his big arm around her. 'This is our land,' he said softly. 'Just look at it today, look at its beauty. It has always been ours.' He turned to their son. 'This is what I want him to have long after we are gone: his land, his country – but free.'

Mati shrugged herself from his grasp and went into the house before them. Two plates of thickly carved ham lay on the table. Silently the men sat. Mati went to a squat stove on which a black pan simmered. She served them scoops of fried potatoes and four bright-yoked eggs each, flicking the last egg on to Teodoro's plate from a height of over a foot causing grease to splash on him. Castor cut white bread in wads from a loaf and they ate.

'I am sick of these children's games,' Mati said from the stove. 'What games do you see me play? For me it is work, work, whilst you men pretend to be children.' She plunged the pan into a basin of water and attacked it with vigour. 'The time for the *terrorista* is over,' she raged. 'Now that the police in *Franzia* hand back our people to the *gobierno central*, of what use are your beloved mountains? What are we to achieve anyway? What is freedom? Can you tell me how our lives will be different in any way if we get this great freedom? Can you?' Mati slammed down the pan on a draining table and began on pots. 'You men live in a dream world of the clouds. You are selfish, always thinking of yourselves and this marvellous country of Euskadi. You leave us women here alone, worrying, whilst you go off and for your selfish dream risk your lives.' She hit her stomach. 'What

163

happens to this if you are killed, eh? Answer that. Who will feed this new citizen of Euskadi?' She wiped her forehead. 'What more do we want? Holy God, we already have a government in Vitoria, we have our own police, we collect our own taxes, we speak our own language, what more do we want?'

Castor belched resonantly. 'Our freedom,' he replied. '*Gastanmera.*'

'You and your selfish freedom.' Mati slammed a bowl full of *gastanmera*, sweet, thickened milk preserve, down on the table. 'One week ago you left me here to have my child whilst you went off about your Euskadi.' She tapped her belly. 'It has heard about the home it is coming into,' she said, 'and it does not want to come out. You think you are both heroes, you and this smooth-faced baby. You are nothing.' Mati's anger was rampant. 'You are nothing,' she repeated, 'you and your Euskadi, you are nothing.'

'Be quiet, woman,' Castor growled as he spooned white preserve into his mouth. He ate in silence as his wife went about her kitchen. Teodoro sat back, his legs stretched, and looked distantly out of the window and over the expanse of mountain-tops and valleys. Wood hissed in the stove.

'Listen!'

It was Castor who had heard it first. Teodoro jumped to his feet; even Mati paused in her work. A car had driven into the yard.

'Did you replace the panel properly?' Castor asked savagely.

'Of course,' Teodoro nodded.

Castor looked out, then exhaled in relief. 'It is Mattin,' he said, going to the door. 'Mattin, *egunon*,' he called, 'greetings.'

Mattin came over from his car. He shook hands with Castor and Teodoro, nodded politely to Mati who stood there, pregnant, glowering.

'Will you come in?' Castor asked.

Mattin shook his head. 'Thank you,' he said, 'but I must hurry. I have a message from Sainz Perez. You know that Geraldo is away?'

Teodoro and his father looked at each other and shook their heads.

'Away, gone to *el norte*,' said Mattin, pleased with his

knowledge. He lowered his voice. 'Gone to return with a treasure which will allow Euskadi its own existence.'

'Treasure?' Castor's mouth hung open.

'I can say no more,' Mattin said. 'I must spread a message through all the stations of this command.' He filled his lungs proudly. 'The date has been fixed,' he announced. He looked at the two men. 'Seven days from today. Are you ready?'

Castor nodded slowly. 'We are ready,' he said.

'It must be at eight in the morning,' Mattin said. 'It must be done on time, with precision.'

'Tell the colonel that it will be so,' Castor said. 'Tell him that Castor Arocena and his son are ready.'

There was a sneering laugh from the farmhouse door.

'So it begins,' Mati said, her lips curled, 'so the fatherless families have started once more.'

'Sssh, woman,' Castor said, reddening. 'Mattin, are you sure you will not enter? You are most welcome in my house.'

Mattin mumbled something and tried to make his way back to his car, but Mati had stepped forward.

'No, you are not welcome,' she hissed. 'You fools, playing with your lives, pretending you are soldiers! Soldiers!' Mati tossed her head. 'Soldiers who do what?' She laughed with venom. 'Soldiers who use their great guns to guard the drugs that every night cross the mountains!'

'Shut up, woman!'

'Why should I?' Mati shouted. 'Is the great soldier Castor Arocena afraid of the words I use? Drugs! Drugs!' she screamed. 'Drugs is what the soldiers of Euskadi fight for!'

'I am sorry . . .' Castor said to Mattin.

'Sorry? You weak fool!' Mati's face was rigid as she turned it to Mattin. 'Go and tell your Colonel Sainz Perez that this is what the soon-to-be-born think of him and his famous Euskadi.' With that she tilted back her head and spat full into Mattin's red-bearded face. Mattin recoiled, blinked, wiped himself with his arm, and then, looking strangely at Castor, began walking backwards to his car.

Blood washed in front of Castor's eyes. He stepped forward and, for the first time in his life, he struck his wife.

Mati reeled backwards two steps, then sat heavily down.

'Oh you men of Euskadi,' she cried, 'now you have found your level!' With a shaky hand she turned the unmarked side of her face. 'Come on, Castor Arocena, finish the job. Come on! After all, you and your son are ready!'

Castor stood there, trembling. He watched as Mattin turned his car and drove back down the steep track. He felt Teodoro's hand on his arm and turned his suddenly pale face towards his son.

'She insulted my country,' Castor whispered helplessly, 'she insulted my country.'

CHAPTER SEVENTEEN

Patrick squeezed between two buses full of American tourists; at the stark, black statue of Goya he paused and squinted into the sun which had just come around the Doric plinth of the Museo del Prado. He saw the sweeping stone steps rising in two graceful arcs and the hawkers and guides on them selling guided tours and wares. He looked at his watch and then crossed the Calle Felipe where the trees still held most of their leaves and the October morning sun bathed the elegant row of houses running down to the Ritz.

The crowds for the Prado had not yet built up. At the top of the first flight where the steps joined with those of the other side in a balconied terrace, Patrick looked around him. No one appeared to have any interest. He stood on the terrace, his hands on the stone ledge, looking over flowerbeds to Goya and to the trees and buildings opposite. There was a flash at eye level, over Goya and through the trees, which might have been caused by a mirror catching the sun, or might just have been a guest in the Ritz opening his window.

Patrick made his way up the remaining steps. He purchased a ticket for four hundred pesetas and joined a line of people who were being slowly cleared through a metal sensor. Patrick walked through it, handed in his ticket and entered the Museo del Prado.

The entrance hall was a lofted and domed rotunda where diffused daylight fell in a dozen colours on the stone floor. Patrick stood at its centre, blinking in the dimmer light, looking around him at the half-dozen doorways. There was movement in the shadows and as he turned Patrick saw a figure leave a recess and approach. It was that of a tallish, angular man, dressed in black with a black ribbon tying his hair at neck length. As he approached, Patrick could see hooded, blue eyes and a red mouth that pursed when closed.

'*Bienvenido*, welcome to one of the great museums of the world,' the man said. His voice was sing-song. 'It is a small indulgence to also use it as *mi oficina*, my office, but' – the eyebrows arched – 'who could ever afford such a reliable security system on one's own?' With a laugh he touched Patrick's arm briefly. 'Is this your first visit, *Señor?*'

Patrick nodded.

'What a treat you have in store,' the black-clothed man said, closing his eyes. 'You are standing, *cariño*, at the doorway of a treasure chest in which you could spend many satisfying weeks and still gain only a partial impression of what it is that made Spain a great nation.' The man's hands took flight: they were white and fine, butterflies in a summer garden. 'Take what you see behind you,' he said, pointing to a bronze statue. 'Carved and cast in the seventeenth century by Pompeo Leoni.' He joined his pointed fingertips under his nose in a gesture of appreciation. 'What lines,' he said, breathing deeply, 'what beauty! What it must be to create a thing of such beauty!' He turned his face to Patrick. 'We see beauty,' he said, 'some of us every day, some of us only once or twice in a lifetime. To see it and to understand it is accomplishment enough, but to do both those things and then to pass on one's experience to another generation, to another age, is surely one of the rare privileges bestowed by nature on a man.'

Patrick nodded and stared. His guide had turned and was leading them towards a doorway at the other side of the rotunda. Patrick suddenly wondered if he had been mistaken for somebody else. '*Perdóname*,' he said, 'but are you . . . ?'

'Of course I am, my dear, of course I am. What did you expect Anguila to look like? Some sort of derelict who dealt his trade from a pedestrian subway? Or a street merchant like Luga, or someone who also sells dirty postcards, or lottery tickets, or cigarettes, or flesh by the half hour on the Capitán Haya? I am a fortunate man, Señor . . . Cano?' The blue eyes twinkled. 'I know of no other man in my position who can adorn his workplace with one of the greatest art collections in the world.

Wherever you have been before, you must now revise your standards regarding how our business is run. There is a market here,' Anguila smiled and his two hands pointed down to the floor, 'there is production over there.' He gestured generally towards the door. 'I am the vital link between the two – I am the –' Anguila searched for the word – '*el mayor distribuidor*, the main distributor,' he said, 'bringing both sides together and smoothing the ruffles as they arise.' His right hand shaped itself and smoothed the air. 'Shall we?'

Smiling with pleasure Anguila led them towards the other side of the rotunda. He stood back to allow Patrick to go before, ushering him through with a slight press of the hand to the small of the back.

'This section is devoted to the Flemish masters,' Anguila said. He walked into the first of a number of interconnecting rooms and went down a wall until they stopped before a wooden panel. 'This, Señor Cano' – Anguila pronounced both vowels of Patrick's name fully as if he were unfamiliar with them – 'this is one of the most important works by Van der Weyden. It is the deposition of Christ from the cross.' Anguila savoured the painting. 'How lifelike the skin,' he murmured, 'how real the wounds, the blood. From whom did you get your cocaine?'

Patrick's heart whammed. 'That is my business,' he said.

'Not in Madrid, it isn't, my dear,' Anguila said, 'not in Madrid.' His face pointed at Patrick like a setter. 'Do you believe me when I say that if I want to I can have you flushed away in tiny pieces into the sewerage system of Madrid where the only trace of Curro Cano, if that is who you are, will be a flavour of slime, slippy underfoot?' Anguila smiled, his hooded eyes predatory.

'Why did you ask me here?' Patrick asked.

'Curiosity,' Anguila replied. They had entered another room and Patrick's guide stood before a large oil, one hand on his hip. 'Do you like Bruegel?' he asked pleasantly. 'He also had an amazing curiosity, Bruegel, don't you think? I believe that is what distinguishes men, intellectual curiosity, the will to ask quesions and probe, don't you?' They had stopped before a Madonna and Child. 'You see, *cariño*, this is my town,' Anguila said. 'I know what goes on here, what is moving, what is coming in, who is behind with their payments, who has just died, the volume and value of last month's business, the forecast for next, who's who, what's what, how, where and when.' Anguila's tone remained engagingly casual. He had led them into a third room and was sighing deeply before a teeming, three-part panel. 'El Bosco's *Garden of Delights*,' he said. 'It shows how man is ultimately a slave to his vices.' He stepped around a seated security guard. 'You see, my dear, everything is a vice unless it is regulated by the central exchequer.' He laughed. 'Governments are greedy, they drive businessmen underground by their demands.' Anguila turned to Patrick, one hip cocked: 'I am first and last a businessman,' he said. 'Business is what allows me the luxury of pleasures such as these. In Madrid, where drugs are concerned, I am the central exchequer.' His hands fluttered and they made their way back through the rooms of Flemish masters. 'So when someone comes without warning,' he said, 'I have to know *everything* about that person.'

'Is that why you first sent Luga?' Patrick asked.

Anguila shook his head patiently. 'I encourage initiative at the lower levels,' he said. 'But that particular attempt was without any style. It did, however, show you in a new light.'

They were retracing their steps over the rotunda.

'Take your *neive*,' Anguila said.

They walked by a tour group.

'Since you clearly brought the supply with you into Madrid, it follows,' Anguila said, 'that you will run out. But in case you don't know, let me tell you something about that cocaine itself.' They had entered another gallery and Anguila stopped inside its door. 'The product,' he said, 'exceptionally high-grade, comes from an excellent laboratory in the town of Puerto Asis, the port on the River Guames near Colombia's southern border with Ecuador. The cocaine in question was manufactured within the last twelve months.' Anguila gave his high laugh. 'If you want I can even tell you the name of the cook,' he said. 'Where did you get it, Señor Cano?'

'I got it through a contact I made in the Far East,' Patrick replied.

Anguila looked at him with interest. 'That answer,' he said slowly, 'is probably a lie. You see, all Puerto Asis cocaine goes directly into the United States market. And from what we can gather you have not been in the United States in the past year.'

'Don't think you know it all,' Patrick said.

'I never make that mistake,' Anguila said. He smiled. 'But you see, Señor Cano, you really are interesting. I know all about the wonderful *neive* you have brought into our city, and I know all about who you aren't. The remaining problem is who you are, and when that is answered, of what use can you be to me?'

Patrick's pulse raced.

'We know, for example,' Anguila said, 'that you travel on a Spanish passport, don't carry a gun, have allegedly been away at sea and can look after yourself perfectly well in a dark alleyway.' He touched Patrick's sleeve. 'We also know that you have no record with any police force and that you probably do not work for an American agency.'

Slowly, Patrick smiled. 'You took my fingerprint, didn't you?' he said. 'The woman with the calendar?'

'You are also perceptive,' Anguila said, 'but you see we can never be careful enough. They are trying the whole time, believe me, to get closer to us than our very skin.' He turned abruptly and looked piercingly into Patrick's eyes. 'Is that your objective, Señor Cano? To enter under my skin?'

'I'm interested in making money,' said Patrick quietly, holding the stare.

Anguila turned. 'El Greco's nobleman,' he said. 'An ageless portrait, painted by a Greek genius who fled to Madrid to escape the plague of Venice. Are you like El Greco, Señor Cano? Are you escaping from somewhere, or someone?'

'Up to now I've made my money the hard way,' Patrick said. 'I traded *caballo*.'

'Source?'

Patrick shrugged. 'Chiang Mai.'

'Source there?'

'Jantong Lee.'

'Quality?'

'707 was the variety I personally liked.'

'But you stopped.'

'I stopped because I saw what AIDS was going to do to the market – and I was right. The price of street heroin is now half that of cocaine. This is the European gateway, the trampoline, for cocaine.' Patrick smiled thinly. 'I decided to come home.'

'I have heard,' Anguila said, stepping lightly to one side to allow through a tour group, 'that your drug usage is extremely moderate.'

Patrick inclined his head.

'That can mean one of two things,' Anguila continued. 'It can mean that you are an undercover, an hypothesis which we may have already dealt with, or it can mean that you are a *camello* of unusual intelligence and ability.'

'You're straight?' Patrick asked him.

For a moment Anguila's eyes popped, then he hid his smile behind the back of his white hand. 'Your choice of words,' he murmured, his eyebrows flicking. 'I am sorry, yes, to answer you, or should I say no, I do not allow myself to indulge. I keep my life for pleasures.' Anguila sighed. 'Most people imagine' –he clasped both his hands – 'thank God that they do, but they imagine that to dose yourself and then to sit for the next nine hours, immobile, staring at the tip of your shoe, is a pleasure. We both know that drugs are a degradation; but so is alcohol, tobacco, late nights and fatty foods. I like to keep myself in shape. I like my body. Therefore I exercise it, I am good to it, I rise early and am always in bed before midnight. I take some good wine with a meal, eat only the meat of fish, never smoke a cigarette and never sample the stock which my business is run on. In that way my mind and my body are in complementary unison – and I can savour pleasure broken down into its very atoms.' As he had spoken, so Anguila had guided Patrick by the arm, across the central gallery, leaving El Greco's nobleman, his hand on his breast, behind. They entered a smaller, dimly lighted room. They stopped: the three-dimensional effect of the huge painting was electric.

'*Las Meninas*,' Anguila murmured, his grip still on Patrick's arm. 'Velázquez at his greatest, the ultimate achievement of depth and light, the pinnacle.'

The room was quite full with people, the only light coming from the spots which illuminated *Las Meninas*. Patrick felt his upper arm and bicep being stroked. 'Just look,' Anguila was saying, 'that's Velázquez himself at work, that's him on the left, looking out at us from around the back of that big canvas that you feel you can touch.'

Anguila smelled sweet.

'The king and queen have just entered the room,' said Anguila, 'just like you and me.'

Patrick could feel his body being pressed. A group of Japanese tourists entered.

'The great painter,' Anguila said, 'the Infanta whom he is painting, all her entourage, they all look up at the same moment, suspended for ever in a single instant of time.' He sighed and pressed. 'I have rooms not far from the Buen Retiro,' he said softly.

'Forget it,' Patrick growled.

Anguila stepped back, releasing his hold. Outside in the brighter gallery he dusted his sleeves and looked at Patrick in the defiant manner of someone who is no stranger to life's rebuffs.

'I am sorry,' he said, 'it would have been very pleasant – for both of us.' He smiled sadly. 'However, I expect that even the dawn must await the sun.'

They retraced their steps towards the rotunda.

'Señor Cano?' Anguila's tone had become businesslike. 'In my organisation we are always looking for people who are useful. I am prepared to gamble that you fall into this category. I will give you three choices.' Anguila pursed his lips. 'Leave Madrid within twenty-four hours and don't ever show up here again; stay in Madrid without cooperating with me and be prepared to be a dead man within twenty-five hours; or work for me.'

Patrick stopped. 'What does work for me mean?' he asked, his mouth dry.

'I have a job I want done,' Anguila said, a smile tugging at his mouth, 'a . . . transportation job. Call it a test, a preparation for possibly greater things. You will earn $5,000 straight off.' He appraised Patrick afresh. 'You're ideal for it,' he said.

'To where?' Patrick asked.

'*Irlanda*,' Anguila said.

Patrick blinked. '*Irlanda?*' he said as all the images of Château Diane, Alan Ridgeway and Joe Vendetti suddenly exploded.

'First to *Irlanda, Señor*,' Anguila said, 'and then to New York.'

Patrick tried to regulate his breath. 'When do you want my answer?' he asked.

'This minute, Señor Cano,' Anguila smiled, 'this very minute.'

Patrick swallowed. 'I'll do the job,' he said.

'Well then, that's it,' Anguila beamed. 'That is our problem solved.' His hands whirled around his head. 'The effect of cumulative beauty on man's capacity to be sensible never fails to astonish me,' he said. He opened his thin hand and when Patrick took it, Anguila covered it with his own.

'I never give up, you know,' he said brightly, 'never.'

Then with his head tilted and his eyes to the fore, the *padrino* of Madrid's narcotics trade strode swinging from the Prado's rotunda.

CHAPTER EIGHTEEN

A wind blew off the loch straight up the mountain. Wind caused John Ridgeway a roaring, painful sensation, so he always switched his hearing-aid off. Now he could feel the wind on his face and could make out the variety of colours on the mountain which in over seventy years had never failed to excite him.

His was a solitary world. For over twenty years he had lived alone; the onset of deafness had driven him further within himself, to a solitary place where he had found contentment. Alan's death – such a waste, he thought – and the funeral and Georgie's fussing had all disturbed a routine built up in this final stage of his life. Reluctantly he had gone to Penrith for a week. Young people were odd: when he returned, Patrick had gone off and another friend of theirs was there, a big smiling chap. John Ridgeway had been irritated. What was Georgie trying to turn the house into? And when the new chap spoke, John could scarcely understand a word he said. He had been glad, secretly, when they went to London.

John walked on the asphalt road, which curled at this point underneath the bluff which hid the cottage. He felt a certain guilt: his mourning over Alan had been perfunctory – he had gone through the motions, but deep down, where you lived grief, there had been nothing. The truth which he acknowledged was that in his solitary world there was little room now for anyone else. Georgie? She was slightly different, she was in there, but again he acknowledged that this was only because she reminded him of her mother. Even when he thought of her mother, which he did about once an hour, every hour, every day, the sadness which her memory evoked was no longer genuine sadness, more a call to duty.

John Ridgeway breasted the hill and frowned. He saw the big car parked outside the cottage. As he approached, a man got out, smallish, well-dressed in city clothes, shining shoes, a dark overcoat. John hoped that there wasn't going to be any more bad news.

'Mr Ridgeway?'

John read the lips, then fumbled with his hearing-aid.

'Mr Ridgeway, glad to meet you.' The man was smiling, his small head cocked to one side. 'My name is Smith, I'm from a recruitment agency in London.'

'You'll have to speak up,' John Ridgeway said.

'I've got an address and a telephone number here for Mr Patrick Drake,' Mr Smith said, 'so since I was in the area I thought I would come and see him.'

John looked at the round face, still smiling. The man seemed pleasant enough. But what was it Georgie had said?

'He's a lucky young man, Mr Drake is,' Mr Smith was saying, 'he put his name down with us for a position, and I'm here to tell him something that he won't believe.'

John wasn't really catching it all, but what with all the smiling, the news for Patrick had to be good. At least it wasn't more bad news.

'Come in,' John said, fumbling for his key.

The kitchen was cosy after the wind outside.

'I've come to tell Mr Drake that he's being offered the chance at something that most people only ever dream of.' Mr Smith was beaming.

'I'm afraid he's not here.'

'Oh dear.' Mr Smith's face seemed to collapse in disappointment.

'No, he's gone, they've gone, nearly a week,' John said. 'You see, we had a family tragedy . . .'

'I am sorry.' Mr Smith's face was wrinkled in concern now.

'Yes, my son was killed in an accident.' John saw the genuine interest across from him. 'I can't remember your name, but would you care for tea?'

The shadows were gathering an hour later as Mr Smith put on his overcoat and made his way to the door. John stood there until the man had driven off. He had been glad of the chat. A considerate man, interested, not rushing off like so many other people nowadays. John took the cups to the kitchen. Funny-looking little man. Reminded him of something, what was it? Genuinely interested in Alan – and Patrick too, of course, the reason he had come. John felt a shudder of disquiet. Georgie had been a bit silly. He hadn't really listened to her, going on about not telling anyone anything. Tell what? Tell whom? Patrick was in Spain, the big chap had said something about it to Georgie, one of the few things he had said which John had understood. Should he not have told that to the man who had just left? Had he told him?

John shook his head. All this business irritated him. He blamed Georgie. He frowned. Should he telephone her? He shook his head again. People nowadays just picked up the telephone and never considered the expense.

It came to John four hours later, just as he was getting into bed. The man who had called earlier, whatever his name was – the way he had cocked his head, he reminded John Ridgeway of a small, fat blackbird.

Washington DC

In the back booth of a darkened bar within a stone's throw of Capitol Hill sat a couple. She was a recently appointed assistant computer operator in the personnel section of Washington's Metropolitan Police. From his dress and manner he was a successful young politician or lawyer on his way up. He signalled the waitress for two more whiskies, then turned his attention back to the woman.

'This is a great help to me personally,' he said frankly. 'I appreciate it.'

'There's no problem,' smiled the woman, who was in her late thirties and wondered if this evening would entail going back to his apartment in the Watergate complex, the way the last evening, their first assignment, had. 'No problem,' she repeated and brought her hair forward and over her right shoulder in a way which he had earlier complimented her on.

'Just give it to me again,' he requested.

'They've been searching for him high and low,' the woman

said quietly, 'all over this country and beyond. There have been high-level communications with the police in all the main European countries and most of the South American ones. They've been in touch with Canada, Australia, places like Hong Kong and Singapore.' She shrugged. 'He's disappeared,' she said.

The waitress brought the two drinks.

'Cheers,' said the man.

His companion smiled and raised her glass.

'And you say,' he said, 'that the last thing he told anyone was that he was going to stay with his sister in San Diego?'

'That's right, but of course he doesn't have a sister in San Diego. He has one in Seattle, all right, and needless to say, she's been checked out.'

'The cop he told about going to San Diego,' the man persisted, 'the last person he spoke to – is he a buddy?'

'It would seem so.'

The man nodded to himself for a few moments. 'That's the guy I'd like to focus on a bit more closely,' he said at last. 'Nothing too detailed, just some personal facts, where he lives, his phone number, family details.' He looked at her and smiled warmly. 'Am I asking for too much?'

'Not at all,' she said, smiling playfully, and reached for her bag. 'Say but the word.' She took out a sheet of computer paper. 'His name is Hughie Cruzero,' she said. 'Here are his stats.' She handed the paper across.

The man blinked, looked at what she had given him, then allowed a broad smile to split his boyish face. 'You're amazing,' he said.

He scanned the print-out quickly, then folded it into an inside pocket. 'I really appreciate this,' he said, draining his glass. 'This is perfect.' He looked at his watch, raised his hand and squiggled the air for the bill. 'I would suggest dinner,' he said as the bill was put in front of him, 'but unfortunately tonight happens to be the one night this month when I've got an unbreakable commitment.'

She made herself smile that she understood.

'Just give me five minutes,' he said, getting up, putting on his coat and placing a twenty on the plate. He leaned across and kissed her cheek lightly. 'I'll be in touch.'

She watched as he left the bar. You blew it, she told herself, you stupid bitch, you blew it. Two scotches and you fired all your ammunition. Shit, she thought, that piece of paper was all he wanted; I could have played it out until two o'clock tomorrow morning and he would still be there, smiling, waiting, being nice to me.

'Can I get you anything else?' asked the waitress.

'I'll have another of these,' she replied, 'except this time, make it a double.'

From the booth she could still see him, standing on the kerb, waiting for a cab. All I wanted was an hour, she thought sadly, like the last time, with the lights turned down low, and him with his fit body and that baby face with the blue eyes and the soft, fair hair parted in the centre.

CHAPTER NINETEEN

Dublin. Rain. Persistent rain. The rain seemed to have slowed traffic to crawling pace and caused drivers to ignore prudence; cars were jammed solid across intersections as traffic lights went inconsequentially from red to green and back to red through amber. The driver of the bus drummed his fingers on the wheel; then with a hiss of power-brakes they were off downhill, past a red-bricked church and plastic bus-shelters packed with huddled people.

Patrick looked out at a traffic warden, her white mackintosh streaming with water, ushering a group of children over the road. The flight from Amsterdam had been on time, 11.15, and he had walked through customs without a glance from anyone.

Patrick fished in his waistcoat and came out with the address: the Emerald Hotel. He looked at his watch and out again at the water washing in rivulets down the window. On a hundred different audits, he had learned, within a day at most, to identify the well-run, profitable organisation from its opposite. The way in which Anguila worked put him head of the class in the former category.

Following their meeting in the Prado Patrick had arrived back at his hotel and found an envelope waiting: it contained 1,000 US dollars in cash, four one-way, executive-class airline tickets in the name of Curro Cano, the address in Dublin and a telephone number in Madrid.

The voice, when Patrick rang the number, had been male and unfamiliar, the instructions crisp, precise.

'What happens if I get caught?' asked Patrick eventually.

But the line had gone dead.

Patrick turned up the collar of his new raincoat as he walked from the bus terminal, across a wide street, past a classically shaped, green-domed building where renovations were in progress and over a new bridge beneath which the River Liffey raced at speed. He was soaked by the time he reached the Emerald Hotel, a dark building on a narrow street where a small, bald porter in the hall was vacuuming a carpet at least as old as himself.

Patrick pre-paid twenty Irish pounds, took a key, mounted a winding staircase and found the room at the end of a corridor whose floor surface rose and fell unevenly underfoot. The room smelled stale; there was a Victorian wardrobe, a white wash-hand basin in the corner and a grey lace curtain which partly hid the outline of a fire-escape. The bed was another piece of Victoriana: high off the floor, brass head-rail, a bulging, pink eiderdown. Patrick put his briefcase under the bed and locked the door from the corridor side. As instructed he took a taxi to St Stephen's Green, checked into the Shelbourne using a false name and went shopping.

The rain had eased when he reached Grafton Street; lunch-hour had brought people out in their hundreds and Patrick walked past women selling bunches of flowers from old prams and men with a selection of the day's papers spread out for sale on the ground. He walked with the sureness of someone who had been before, but that too was a shrouded mystery, a series of overlapping memories, some of which were half-remembered dreams, others half-forgotten realities. He sniffed. A smell wafted into a long forgotten cerebral crypt, a particularly strong smell of ground coffee which the proprietors of a coffee-house blasted out through a special ventilator.

Patrick stood: he was small, she was tall, he was holding her hand, she was smiling, he was tired, he was hungry, he wanted to be carried, and then he smelled the smell.

'Lovely smell.'

'That's coffee, Patrick.'

Then the coffee smell was gone and there was a perfume smell, a warm smell, a warm touch, a happy feeling and he was falling asleep. But the smell was still there and in his mind it was linked to happiness. Happiness. Was that what he really sought, happiness? There was no point in analysis, just an inexorable forward movement of which he was now part.

Patrick went into a department store. In the glass section, following his instructions, he selected a heavy, glass tumbler with intricate lines carved on its side and base.

'Twelve of these, please. But I wish to export them, tax-free. – I'm flying out tomorrow. And I'd like them gift-wrapped, please.' A woman wrote out a sales docket, took his money, stamped the docket and handed him a copy.

'How will I know which is mine?' he asked.

'Hand in your copy docket at the airport.'

'Thank you.'

'Goodbye now, love.'

Patrick bought a newspaper in the street, read it in a small café where he ate an omelette, and was back lying on the bed in the Emerald Hotel ten minutes before two o'clock.

The night before, from a payphone off Alcalá, he had called Georgie.

'I'm making progress,' he said, his eyes keeping watch around him. 'I'm going on a trip.'

'A trip? Where?'

'To Dublin,' he whispered. 'Remember the wine from Château Diane? Ireland, that's where it went.'

'Patrick, we agreed you should stay in Madrid.'

'Put Joe on.'

At that moment, from the corner of his eye Patrick saw the familiar figure of the hunchback rounding the corner from Alcalá.

'Call you tomorrow,' he had said and hung up.

Now he looked at his watch. He would call Georgie later on.

There was a knock.

Patrick swung off the bed, straightened the eiderdown, adjusted his tie and opened the door.

'A gentleman to see you.'

The porter stood back and another man, also bearded and carrying a briefcase came in. He had small eyes, his cheeks under them a dark red. He wore his suit as if it did not fit him; he ran one finger inside and around his collar.

'Mr Cano?'

Patrick nodded. He smelled drink.

'Could you identify yourself to me, please?'

Patrick handed over his passport.

'Do you speak English, Mr Cano? *Habla Ingles?*'

'Yes, I do,' Patrick replied.

'Oh, that's all right,' said his visitor, grinning, 'you've just heard the only two words of Spanish I know.' He sat into an armchair, the only one in the room. 'My name is Bernard,' he said. 'It isn't really Bernard, but you know what I mean.'

Patrick nodded and sat on the edge of the bed.

Bernard had put his briefcase between his feet on the floor.

'Not a bad day,' he said.

'It's raining,' Patrick said.

'Well, it is raining, but it wouldn't wet you,' Bernard said. 'It's what we over here call a soft day.' He chortled good-humouredly and clasped his hands together over his midriff. 'Did you have a good flight, Mr Cano? I suppose that's not your name either, but in this business . . .' Bernard laughed pleasantly again.

'The flight was fine, thank you,' Patrick said, an edge in his voice. 'And Cano is my name.'

'Of course, of course, don't think I meant to offend,' Bernard chortled, 'sure I wouldn't believe me own mother if she told me she was dead and she lying stiff as a board for a fortnight.' Bernard shook his head. 'Isn't it desperate what decent people have to do for a living these days?' he said.

'You have some merchandise for me,' Patrick said.

'I have indeed, Mr Cano, I have indeed,' Bernard said, bending between his feet and opening his briefcase. Patrick stared as not a package, but a half-bottle of Irish whiskey was taken out.

'Do you have any glasses here?' Bernard asked.

A single glass sat in a chrome wall-fitting beside the basin. Patrick handed it to Bernard who filled it two-thirds with whiskey, then handed it back to Patrick. The cap of the bottle doubled as a measure and Bernard filled it to brimming, then raised it to his lips.

'Cheers, Mr Cano,' he said, 'pleased to meet you.'

Patrick drank some Irish and watched as his visitor tossed his back in one.

'Aah,' Bernard said, 'thanks be to God for life's little

pleasures.' He refilled and looked over to Patrick. 'I don't know about you, Mr Cano, but the longer I go in this business the more me nerves gets the better of me.'

Patrick said nothing.

'Are you long working for these people, Mr Cano?' Bernard asked.

'Long enough,' Patrick replied.

Bernard shook his head. 'They're very good,' he said, 'very good. You get your goods and your money on the button. Now if that was an Irish outfit they'd be cowboys every yard of the way, trying to cut in, cut out, fuck the thing up for the decent people, but your men down there, they're ... they're gentlemen,' Bernard said.

'I'll tell them,' Patrick said, as an image of the weaselly Luga ran across his mind.

'Take the man who did your job the last few times, for instance,' Bernard said, 'a grand kid, Tomás, he'll go places.'

'You've met Tomás?' Patrick asked.

Bernard was suddenly on alert. 'Have I said a name I shouldn't have?' he asked.

Patrick shook his head sombrely; Bernard galloped on. 'The problem with the market in Ireland, the domestic market,' he said, giving himself another shot into the measure, 'is that it's too *small*.' He emphasised the diminutive like someone at a sales conference. 'You've got a couple of families cutting each other's throats for the same few shillings – and then there's a cash-flow problem as well.' Bernard shook his head sadly. 'The people here haven't got the money, Mr Cano. Ireland never got over the recession – the '29 recession.' He chuckled. 'Something will have to be done.'

Patrick sat, his eyes cold.

'The only way to make money in Ireland,' Bernard said garrulously, 'is to make your money outside of Ireland, if you know what I mean.' He laughed politely. 'People in Ireland have begun to realise that there's a big world out there, thousands, millions of times bigger than Ireland. Companies realise that they've got to get out there and sell.' Bernard nodded his head wisely. 'If you don't have the international connections, you're bolloxed, if you'll excuse me.'

Patrick saw another measure of whiskey leave the bottle. 'You seem to have managed to do that successfully, Bernard,' he said.

'Had to,' Bernard said, spreading his hands, 'had to, Mr Cano. Everyone has to find their place in the market and then go like shit whilst they can. Mind you,' he said, 'your man down there in Madrid, the Otter, is that what you call him . . . ?'

'Anguila, it means eel.'

'I knew it was one of those animals, well the Eel, he must make an absolute bloody fortune.'

Patrick said nothing.

'Take what I have here for you now,' Bernard rushed on. He tapped his briefcase. 'Five pounds of 90 per cent snow. That's 250,000 quid in any man's money,' he said. 'And I'm handling one of these every month. Here, give me that.' He reached for and replenished Patrick's glass.

'I suppose you know how it gets here?' Patrick said quietly.

Bernard sucked smoke, drank whiskey and looked gravely at Patrick. 'I only discovered that the other day,' he said.

Patrick nodded. 'Mullingar,' he said with a smile, allowing Bernard to feel some warmth.

'International Hydraulics.' Bernard laughed, happy as a puppy. He emptied the bottle.

'International Hydraulics.' Patrick was back with Alan in the courtyard of Château Diane.

'Normally,' Bernard was saying, 'one of their managers comes up to Dublin and hands the goods over to yours truly. Last week I got a call from another gippo down there; seems my man had gone off somewhere for himself, and this fellow was too busy to come to Dublin so he asks me to go to Mullingar. Down I went, met him in a pub and he hands over. Apologises for dragging me down the country but explains he has accountants in and they're driving him up the bleeding walls. Then out of the blue he starts to talk to me about wine.'

'Wine.' Uncannily, Patrick could feel the heat of Château Diane's inferno on his face.

Bernard shook his head slowly from side to side. 'I have to hand it to you, but you fellows are pure geniuses.'

Patrick closed his eyes.

'I mean, it's beautiful,' Bernard said. 'Bring in snow from someplace in Europe dissolved in wine. Distil it off in Mullingar and recrystallise the cocaine. Re-export the cocaine to the States, welded inside hydraulic arms.' Bernard shook his head. 'Hydraulic arms,' he said. 'I couldn't believe it.'

Patrick stared at the bearded, now tipsy man, about to entrust him with a quarter of a million pounds' worth of merchandise. He looked at his watch.

Bernard nodded and put his empty bottle into his briefcase. 'I like a chat,' he said, 'I like meeting people from other parts of the business, comparing notes with them, you know what I mean?' Bernard's finger travelled inside his collar. 'I don't get to talk to too many over here,' he said.

Patrick watched as Bernard rummaged around, then came out with a square package wrapped in gift paper.

'Well here you are, Mr Cano,' Bernard said, 'two kilos net, five pounds of joy, plus a dozen Waterford glasses for whoever the lucky person is. God only knows how many hooters this'll be snorted up, but sure God help the poor whores, I hope they enjoy it.'

'Thank you,' Patrick took the package; it was heavy. It was professionally wrapped and taped all around. On one side a docket showing the price and the tax savings was stuck in place. It looked familiar. Patrick took out the sales fiche which he had got earlier that morning and compared it to the one on the box: they were identical, down to the serial number in the top, right-hand corner.

'As a matter of interest, how was that done?' he asked.

'Trade secret, Mr Cano, trade secret,' said Bernard, beaming with pleasure. He got to his feet and belched. 'Just be sure to collect the other one at the airport before you go out and stick it in a rubbish bin.' He swayed very slightly, laughed and caught Patrick's arm. 'Only for Jesus's sake, don't put the wrong one in the bin,' he chortled as he walked to the door. 'The Otter would have your balls for his breakfast.'

Patrick closed the door quietly behind Bernard, sat on the bed and began to laugh. The package routine was almost foolproof; even if he were caught, Patrick would be able to claim that he had only collected the goods minutes before he had boarded the plane. He laughed until tears ran down his face, then he walked to the window and with difficulty opened the bottom sash. The cold air blew the dirty curtains back. Patrick rinsed out the glass, filled it with water and had half drunk it when he heard running feet and then fists crashing on the floor.

'Open up, for Christ's sake!'

Patrick slipped the package under the eiderdown and opened the door. Bernard fell into the bedroom.

'Quick, Mr Cano! The door!'

Bernard was dragging the heavy bed towards the door, his eyes standing out. Patrick put his weight to it and as they wedged the brass bed-end under the door's handle, he could hear further feet in the corridor. He looked in alarm at Bernard who was fighting to get his breath.

'Dunphy,' Bernard gasped, 'Dunphy with at least six heavies. They must have been tipped off by someone.'

'Who's Dunphy?' Patrick asked, his whole system screaming. There were voices at the door.

'Someone who wants your snow,' Bernard said, his eyes wild. 'Where is it?'

Patrick dived for the package. 'Come on,' he said. He stuffed the package into the briefcase, tore back the curtains and bent through the window on to the fire escape. He reached back and pulled Bernard out after him. As he did so he heard four or five dull thuds and saw the wood near the door-lock splinter.

Their feet clanged on the fire escape.

'To think I was in partnership with that bastard!' Bernard shouted.

The fire escape ended six feet above a narrow lane. Patrick could see a man standing, looking up at them, his feet wide apart, his hands ready. Without pausing, Patrick leaped. The two of them crashed to the ground, the man beneath. Patrick rose first, transferred his briefcase to his left hand and then hit the man under his chin as he rose slowly. The man went up, back and down. Bernard stood there, his chest heaving. 'Too good for him,' he said and launched a kick at the ribs of the unconscious figure. There was the pinging sound of a ricochet. 'Jesus!' Bernard cried and dashed up the lane as they both heard shoes on the fire escape. The lane led them to a quiet street at the back of the Emerald Hotel.

'I've a car,' Bernard wheezed, his legs pumping.

'Where?'

'There!'

Patrick followed Bernard's nod as they ran: a stark, multi-storeyed car park stood dead ahead of them. Patrick looked back and saw two men closing. He and Bernard leaped from the footpath, almost under a double-decker bus that lurched beside them. They dashed for a small door inset in the wall of the car park. The door was metal, the stairs inside concrete. Bernard hauled himself upwards on the cold, steel handrail.

'Which level?' Patrick asked.

'Third,' Bernard puffed.

Side by side they ascended; Bernard had wrenched his collar open and was now having difficulty in finding oxygen. As they reached the third floor Patrick could hear the echoing slam of the door to the street below. On the level concrete of the car bay Bernard fumbled for keys and dog-trotted to a red Toyota. The engine roared as Patrick got in, then they lurched at an acute angle out of their space and down a sharply bending ramp. From the corner of his eye Patrick saw the first of the two men enter the third level and ready a gun from his hip. In the false light of the low-ceilinged car park the flame from the gun-muzzle was visible for an instant before they hurtled down and out of sight. Bernard's bulk appeared to be jammed between the seat-back and the steering-wheel; he sat forward, his hands on top of the steering wheel, his face near the windscreen.

'That bastard Dunphy!' Bernard said. He looked at Patrick. 'Dunphy and I sat beside each other at school, you know!'

'Look out!'

Bernard had failed to anticipate the on-going turn of the plunging ramp and the Toyota struck the wall, hard, lurched to the other side and struck it as well. Patrick felt sharp pain at the point of his shoulder. Bernard swung the car to the middle again and mouthing curses he rounded the final bend where two things presented themselves: the red and white arm of a barrier beside a computerised exit box, and three men blocking the way at the far side of it. Patrick put both his hands on the dashboard and glanced over: Bernard's two eyes were shut tight; his knuckles white on the wheel, he stood on the accelerator, smashed the exit barrier from its hinges and hit the ascending ramp to the street at fifty. Patrick was aware of bodies leaping to safety and shouts. The car park's alarm system went off. Then they were in the street, high railings to their left, green traffic lights ahead, shops, buses parked two abreast, fruit vendors, children, a blue-uniformed policeman who looked at them doubtfully, a horse-drawn coal-dray.

'Do you think they got a look at you?' Bernard gasped as they swung left, into a wider street.

Patrick glanced behind. 'I don't think so,' he said.

'Thanks be to God for that,' Bernard said. He was awash with perspiration and had begun to shake. 'I'll have to give up these fags,' he said.

They turned right, hummed across the bridge which Patrick had earlier crossed on foot, then made a left, down a cobblestoned quayside where blue and yellow cargo boats sat moored. 'I'm going to get as far from here as I can,' Bernard said, 'then I'm going to let you out and keep going myself.' He looked in the mirror. 'The curse of Jesus on Dunphy!' he hissed.

'Are they on us?' Patrick asked.

Bernard nodded grimly. 'I'd say so,' he replied.

They were approaching a gasometer and as Patrick looked back he could see a white car at the beginning of the quays following at high speed. Patrick clutched the briefcase as Bernard made a severely sharp right; the Toyota's wheels spun for purchase on the cobblestones. They crossed two intersections and made another, sharp left, just as the white car rounded the turn from the quays.

The road narrowed for an old bridge and they took it without pause, travelling airborne on the other side for a good fifteen feet before the Toyota crash-landed, its chassis scraping along the asphalt with a hideous shriek. An old man with a cap was making his way from a bookmaker's shop on one side of the road to a public house on the other. Bernard leaned on the horn, swerved, clipped the man behind, and kept going.

'Silly old eegit!' Bernard swore.

Patrick looked back to see a crowd gathering around the fallen figure, making passage for the white car difficult for just a few crucial moments. Bernard did not waste his opportunity; his face two inches from the windscreen, he urged the Toyota even faster and took a left-hand incline and two succeeding sets of traffic-lights at around eighty.

'You'll have three seconds, are you ready?' he cried.

'I'm ready,' said Patrick.

'Have the door open,' Bernard said.

The sea was to their left as they hurtled along, a wide flat expanse of wet sand with two red and white chimneys which seemed to rise up out of nothing. Without warning Bernard turned off the sea road, almost too ambitiously, for the Toyota went into a sickening swerve which would have ended in certain disaster had another car been coming against them. The road widened into a crescent of red-bricked, two-storey houses with small gardens in front of each. Bernard seemed to aim for the wall of one, bounced the car up on the high kerb and lurched to a halt. Patrick leaped. As his feet touched the ground the Toyota screamed forward again, nearly knocking him.

'Cheers, Mr Cano!' were Bernard's parting words.

Patrick put his left hand on the garden wall and vaulted in and over, towards the protection of a large hydrangea. In mid-air he heard the engine of the pursuing car and ducked low just as it appeared.

His heart pounding, Patrick heard the white car pass. He kept low. The engine noise receded and then was lost completely. Patrick stayed where he was, gradually getting his breath back to normal. He became aware of the birdsong in the surrounding gardens and the scents from the shrubbery in which he knelt. Slowly he felt another presence; he turned his head and saw a pair of brown eyes not a yard from his own. Balling his fists, Patrick drew back. A very small boy with a cowboy hat was staring at him. Patrick swallowed and stood up, brushing himself down.

'Are you a goodie or a baddie?' the child asked, open-mouthed.

'I'm a very bad goodie,' replied Patrick, leaving by the small metal gate and walking briskly back to the sea road, the briefcase with the £250,000 worth of *neive* firmly in his hand.

Patrick looked down on the ordered houses and gardens of Long Island. He drained the glass of brandy and winced as the pain in the point of his shoulder flashed. The flight had taken over nine hours, beginning with the hop from Dublin to Shannon where he had cleared US immigration.

Patrick's hand went to the handle of the briefcase on the empty seat next to him. He gripped it and looked out again as they began to lose height. In Dublin he had claimed his package in a section of the duty free: his briefcase with the identical-looking packet had gone through the scanner without a comment from the bored security official; through the duty free Patrick stripped the innocent box of its identifying wrappers and left it behind a lavatory seat.

The stewardess on the flight from Shannon had flirted with him, beginning with the safety demonstration and then at every following opportunity. She had black hair and long, American legs. As he considered the ordeal ahead and hit a trough of panic Patrick briefly considered cornering her in the galley, confessing his infatuation and then giving her an infatuated gift of twelve Waterford glasses. He would get her number. She would live in Manhattan. He would retrieve the glasses later that night. He shook his head to clear it.

He had managed to doze for an hour. When he awoke there was a long US customs form on the seat beside his briefcase, awaiting completion. The flight was only a third full and Patrick walked its length, back to the toilets in tourist, scanning all the other faces on board, but none was familiar.

There was a squeal as they touched down. They taxied endlessly. Kennedy's vastness, the vastness of the structure that he was now attempting to thwart, was dizzying. The plane door opened, directly behind Patrick's seat, and New York evening air rushed in. Everywhere has its own air, he thought, like its own beer.

At the door his stewardess was in position, her mouth slightly parted.

Patrick smiled warmly to her. Another stewardess led them into the hollow-sounding tunnel and towards the terminal. The sounds were of engines and generators and battery-operated luggage floats wheeling into position. Patrick's legs felt weak above the knees, exactly the same way they always went after three rounds with a hard hitter. One part of him was lucid and calm, another was voting to panic and sending instructions to his legs, to his numb fist holding a guaranteed, ten-year jail sentence and to his throbbing shoulder. He tried to concentrate on the girl striding out ahead of them. She too had long, American legs, was slim, wore a white scarf around her neck and walked well and purposefully down a glass-sided corridor, her hair bouncing as she walked, her bottom doing all the right things inside its silk dress.

The procession went down steps and came to a halt in a brightly lighted baggage-claim area. Patrick fingered the customs form which he had completed and felt sweat run from his palm on to the handle of the briefcase which was dragging him down to the floor and into the bowels of the earth. In front of him was an unmoving, silver baggage carousel, behind him, half a dozen customs benches where men in khaki-coloured shirts and black ties waited, undoubtedly subjecting the just-arrived passengers to a preliminary visual examination.

The customs profile. Joe Vendetti had touched on it. They can't go through all the bags so they look at the people. What do they look for? Hirsutes with guitars are obviously near the top of the list. Nigerians. Fat English girls are becoming popular. Passengers who delay; passengers who examine the customs officers, not aware that the customs officers are examining them; passengers looking for the officer with the kind face, or the attractive lady officer (none in this building), or the tired, or bored-looking or inefficient-looking officer. Customs specialise in recruiting officers who look bored and inefficient but who are bastards at heart. This was a crucial time, the time spent waiting for the baggage. Patrick was under observation. He had to have a bag. No one walked off a nine-hour flight without a suitcase, certainly not if it meant that the only piece of luggage you then carried was a briefcase containing a quarter of a million dollars' worth of 90 per cent cocaine.

With a jump, the carousel came to life. Bags began appearing through a wall-flap. In horror Patrick saw his suitcase bobbing along first, leading the others merrily into the United States. Patrick had a choice: he could let it go around without claiming it, which would mean that he would not be the first out. But then if that was observed, how would that fit the profile? Not well. But to be the first was a nightmare. Why had his bag come out first? That surely could not be coincidence. Dizzy, he saw his suitcase approach. Patrick grabbed it.

It was ten paces to the nearest bench. He could have chosen any as they were all empty but he chose the nearest, dumped the suitcase and briefcase up in front of the man and handed him the form. As the man took it Patrick forced himself to look at his watch.

'Any items of alcohol?'
Patrick blinked. 'Please?'
'Any items of alcohol?'
'No, nothing.'

The man's face was only a foot away but it was formless, a pink blob.

'What is the purpose of your visit to the United States?'
'Vacation.'

The pink blob was studying the form; in order to read, the man tilted his head back so that the form was near his mouth. Was he going to eat it?

A pen appeared. The man signed the form and nodded. Patrick nodded. He took back the form, caught the suitcase and briefcase and began to walk. He felt most unsteady. It was a ruse to get him out of the hall. If not, why were they all staring? The eyes of the hall were on him as he swayed for the door, a palsy case who had spent the last thirty years learning how to walk. In a daze the door came nearer. Another customs man sat on a stool, took the proffered form, looked at it and nodded.

'Have a nice evening.'
'Thank you. You too.'

His eyes straight ahead, Patrick walked into the arrivals hall.

He walked slowly down the hall, drained, wanting only sleep. He saw telephones, opposite the information desk. There appeared to be few people around, but Patrick walked to a free booth, as he had been instructed, placed his briefcase on the ground and picked up a telephone. He stood there holding the dead receiver, his vision in that position restricted to the walls of the booth and his feet. Shoes appeared in the booth beside him, a man's shoes, and dark trousers with a crease. Patrick saw a hand appear for a moment as a briefcase the same as his own was placed on the ground. He could hear his neighbour pick up the phone and put it down again. Then the hand reappeared; this time it had to stretch as it reached over for Patrick's briefcase and Patrick saw gold links tying a white shirt-cuff over a hairy wrist. Then the briefcase was gone, as were the shoes, leaving the almost identical briefcase near Patrick's feet. Patrick turned in time to see the blue-overcoated back of a man leaving the building.

Patrick picked up the other case – it was lighter – and his

suitcase, and made his way slowly outside. It was becoming cold, more so than it had been in Madrid, or Amsterdam or Dublin. He reached inside his jacket and withdrew the fourth ticket. He looked at the date, checked it with his watch and then climbed on the airport shuttle which would take him to the Iberia terminal.

It was not until he was airborne, four hours later, that he bothered to look inside the new briefcase which smelled deliciously of new leather. It contained three envelopes, stacks of computer manuals and graph paper, and a small calculator.

The Spanish hostess had shorter legs. Patrick put on a black eye-guard. He felt nothing until a glass of tinned Spanish orange juice was placed before him.

Sitting up he slid the window blind which revealed the dramatic sky streakings of a new European day.

CHAPTER TWENTY

Coals glowed red in the narrow grate; it was Saturday noon; outside, the occasional boat or barge could be seen moving on the Thames. 'He must be back in Madrid by now,' said Georgie.

Joe nodded. 'He'll call tonight,' he said.

Georgie sat cross-legged, surrounded by papers.

'I'm impressed,' Joe said. 'Where did you get all this stuff?'

Georgie smiled. 'We librarians stick together,' she said. 'I have a friend who works in the American Embassy in Grosvenor Square, library section.'

Joe nodded and looked at the mound of information. 'So what does it say?' he asked.

' "Marshall George Kahan",' Georgie read, ' "born 1937 near Denver, Colorado of immigrant Lithuanian parents".' Georgie looked through the papers on her knee. 'He was educated in local schools, left in 1955, saw active service in Korea in '56, discharged in '57. In March 1961, he was appointed as an assistant planning officer to the newly formed Alliance for Progress, a Latin-American development programme initiated by President Kennedy. Between '61 and '62 he was responsible for economic development plans for regions of Argentina. Listen to this,' she said, 'in 1962 they say he "returned to Washington". Returned. That means he lived down there.'

They read for nearly half an hour.

'It's a pretty straightforward career,' Joe said at last. 'Copybook progress, upward momentum. How the hell are we going to find out any more? How do we find out if at any stage in his career Kahan was linked to Marcellino?'

'The information about his time in Latin America isn't

specific enough,' Georgie said. 'We need more than generalities in order to zone in.'

'That information must be available in Washington,' Joe said. He thought for a moment. 'I've got an idea,' he said.

'Are you going to let me in on it?' Georgie asked.

'I've got a good friend in Washington,' Joe said, 'he's a detective I can trust. I'm going to call him up and ask him to do some leg work on Kahan for me.'

'Isn't that risky?' Georgie said. 'Your friend might report you.'

'Hughie Cruzero? No way,' Joe said. 'Hughie and me, we've been foot soldiers together for six years, we've loaned each other money, we've got drunk together, we've covered for each other, I even used to date Jeannie, the girl Hughie married.'

'Still, isn't phoning him risky?' Georgie asked. 'They might try and trace back the call.'

Joe shook his blond head. 'I'll call him at home,' he said. 'The worst Hughie will do is tell me to get lost.'

The fire caught Georgie's eyes and held them.

'I hope you're right,' she said.

It was 6.30 p.m. Georgie put down the bag of shopping and searched for her key to the hall door. In the street behind her the kerbs were tight with parked cars. Georgie climbed the three flights of stairs to the top floor, saw the light under the door and knocked.

'Let me take that,' Joe said.

Georgie sat down; she could see sheets of paper and a notebook by the telephone.

'I just spoke with Hughie,' Joe said.

'Oh?' Georgie said.

'Sure,' Joe replied. 'There's no problem. Hughie's a good guy – he's going to try and dig up as much as he can on Kahan right away.'

Georgie shook her head and looked at Joe. 'I wish it was all over,' she said quietly, 'and we could get back to living our lives again. Isn't it extraordinary? – a month ago exactly Patrick and I were sitting here watching television. I had just made him a plate of pasta – he was going to fight the inter-office final the next day and I was stuffing carbohydrates into him. Now a month later . . .'

Joe came and sat beside her. 'Things happen fast,' he said. 'I remember when our mother died. We lived in San Francisco. It was a Sunday evening, we were all just sitting around, my mother was sewing. The next thing, she put her hand up to her head and she said, "Oh, my God". Nothing more. She fell back in her chair stone dead. The next Sunday we were sitting there again, but in the week that had gone by mother had died, gone into a coffin, been brought to a graveyard, interred, filled in and left on her own forever.'

They sat for some moments in silence.

'You and your brother Frank were very close, weren't you?' Georgie said.

'I idolised him,' Joe said simply. 'He was a combination of father and elder brother. He taught me to sail in the Bay. How to look after myself in a fight, how to handle people. My father was a little man who worked funny hours in a bakery and came home covered in flour. But Frank was where all the good times happened.'

Slowly Georgie shook her head. 'I'm sorry if I say this,' she said tightly, 'but I don't want to mourn any more.' She made a small fist of her hand. 'If anything happens to Patrick, I don't think, after Alan and everything, I don't honestly think that I could . . .' She looked away to hide her tears.

Joe took her hands gently in his. 'Look,' he said, 'this thing is getting on top of you, Georgie. I have a proposal. There is a very cosy little wine bar down on the corner of this block. What do you say if you and I go down there right now and have ourselves a bottle of their best wine?'

Georgie smiled. 'I'd like to,' she said, 'but . . .'

'No but, come on.'

'I would, Joe, but I'd really rather stay here in case Patrick calls.'

Joe nodded. 'Of course you're right,' he said. 'In that case, another but no less important proposal: I will go to the cosy little wine bar on the corner, purchase a bottle of their best wine and bring it back here.'

'That sounds a splendid idea,' Georgie said.

She carried the tray into the kitchen; she looked out the window as the big American left the house and walked down the street, past the rows of parked cars, their roofs glinting in the street lights. He walked with his hands in his pockets, his shoulders slightly hunched.

Georgie felt a warm glow as she watched him. He was gentle, generous. She felt safe when he was there. He approached the street corner and she closed her eyes. The night before she had awoken in the small hours, her stomach full of unmoving fear. She had drawn the quilt over her head and pleaded with sleep to come. He was in the next room, four feet away. What would he have thought if she had done the one thing which at that moment she wanted? Had crept in beside him? Had allowed him to shield her from her cold fear? Suddenly she felt nauseated with herself. On her eyelids she could still feel the dawn of the morning on which Patrick had left.

'No goodbyes,' he had said, standing over her.

'No goodbyes,' she said, her eyes a chrysalis.

Now she wanted to remember him as he had been on the last night, supple, beautiful.

Her hands shaking, Georgie lighted a cigarette.

CHAPTER TWENTY-ONE

Extract from wire service

AMNESTY INTERNATIONAL have called for an enquiry into the circumstances surrounding the death in Swiss police custody of a Spanish national.

The man, named by Swiss police as Geraldo Olaso, a suspected member of a Basque terrorist organisation, was detained by police in Zurich after a tip-off. Police say that as they were attempting to question Mr Olaso there was an exchange of gunfire during which he died.

Swiss police yesterday refused to speculate on why Mr Olaso was in Switzerland.

CHAPTER TWENTY-TWO

The telephone rang and rang, inexplicably. One moment he was holding on, waiting for it to be answered, another he was staring at a telephone but for some reason could not pick it up. Then he did what he always did when he wanted to escape: he ran, way above houses, away from the ringing telephone, into mist where there was only himself, as high as he could go, feeling the rushing thrill of himself at the mercy of the mountain. There had been a time when trees had faces and spoke to him as he passed them by, but here there were no trees, just boulders, blanks of rock, pock-marks in one gigantic face whose voice was sawing wind.

Patrick ran. The face had become a head, strangely bloodied and blinking in the rain. Terrified, Patrick saw that it was a girl's head. The fat girl. Consuela's head. Slowly Consuela's head turned. The mouth opened and closed and the teeth made a clacking sound.

'Clack, clack-clack, clack-clack.'
'No!' Patrick screamed. 'No!'
'Clack-clack.'
'No!'

Patrick sat up, his whole body drenched. He was lying in his clothes. It took seconds to adjust to the parameters of the hotel bedroom. His heart still raced from the dream.

'Clack-clack.'

It was dark, the sign from the neon flashing its repeated message. Patrick looked at his watch. Three. He swung his feet from the bed and faced the door.

'Clack-clack.'

Patrick turned to where the noise was coming from, to the

window, and stared. He rushed over. Twenty feet away, out on the scaffolding, sat Tomás. Tomás's face looked strange in the mixture of flashing light and darkness. Because of how the scaffolding was built, falling short of the window, Tomás sat on an outer strut, unable to get any closer. But he had managed to grab a hanging rope and was beating it against the glass.

'Clack-clack.'

Patrick put the heels of his two hands under the middle portion of the sash and pushed. Nothing happened. He tried again, then looked out and shrugged. Tomás was gesticulating frantically. Patrick tried to make out the words. Tomás was punching with his fist.

'*¡Rómpelo!*' Tomás was saying. 'Break it!'

Patrick made a renewed effort but the window remained solidly closed. Outside Tomás was going wild. He was pointing. Patrick frowned. He looked out again. Tomás was pointing *behind*. Patrick turned, bewildered. Tomás was pleading, his hands outstretched.

'*¡Rómpelo!*'

In his stockinged feet Patrick went to the bedroom door. He put his ear to it. Then he dropped and with his face to the carpet, squinted out. The vista of carpet on the other side was broken by the shape of shoes.

In one movement Patrick jumped to his feet, grabbed a chair and crashed it through the window. As if a switch had been thrown, the heat and noise of Madrid engulfed him.

'*¡Salta!*' Tomás cried. 'Jump! Get out!'

Patrick stabbed with the chair at the jagged glass still in the windowframe. Now he could hear voices at the door.

'*¡Salta!*'

Patrick looked at his boots beside the bed, thought of the cocaine lodged behind the skirting board, grabbed for the rope which Tomás had floated in and jumped. He swung out over the street, in an arc, away from the building. Painfully he crashed into scaffolding, felt Tomás's hands, felt steel beneath his stockinged feet. Then there was a violent, warm air rush, like that preceding a subway train, but much stronger, and an ear-damaging blast.

'*¡Dios!*' Tomás cried.

The steel framework to which they clung lurched out crazily, away from the building, and for a moment seemed as if it would topple across the street. At the penultimate instant it swayed back in, crashing them against itself. Almost in slow motion a great ball of masonry, furniture and glass was cascading from what had been the bedroom window into the street below.

'Come on!' Patrick shouted.

He began to swing downwards, his feet finding planks or steel struts at each level, leading the way down on the steel frame. Behind him Tomás followed like a monkey. Above them the neon flashed through a pall of dust.

They reached the street, almost at the point where the building made a corner with the Gran Vía.

'I'm three blocks away,' Tomás cried.

The Golf was in a dark alley, a lane off a narrow street off the Gran Vía. The car's roof was down and they leaped in without recourse to the doors; Tomás took three attempts to fit the ignition key. He kept up a constant jabber, then they were tearing down the street, its twin kerbs barely wide enough for one car, heading south, on the back streets, doubling back whenever their route took them near one of the main *calles*.

'They'll kill us both now!' Tomás sobbed, shaking his head and peering through his tears to see their hurtling way.

'Look where you're going!' Patrick shouted, the second time in forty-eight hours that he found himself an unwilling passenger.

'My poor parents,' Tomás kept saying.

Patrick checked behind but their dash through the side streets of Madrid appeared unattended. Eventually they came to a modern, up-market housing estate.

'A friend of my father's has a house here,' Tomás gulped. 'He's away on business.'

Tomás bounced the Golf up over the kerb and in between gates where a short avenue curved right and shrubbery hid them from the road. Tomás killed the engine and sat there, his head in his hands, weeping. Patrick reached over and put his hand on Tomás's shoulder. 'Let's go inside,' he said.

Patrick drew the blinds of the kitchen window – a designer kitchen, full of units with doors of criss-crossed, leaded glass and recessed lights – and searched up and down until he found a bottle of Spanish brandy. There was an electric fire which he switched on and led Tomás to, sitting him down and then handing him a glass. Patrick poured one for himself and then sat silently as gradually Tomás's spasms grew less.

'Why did you come to the Nevada tonight?' Patrick asked at last. 'You saved my life. Why?'

'I thought . . . I thought you could help me,' Tomás said. He looked at Patrick and shivered. 'You see, Cano, I know who you are.'

Patrick felt chill. 'Who am I?' he asked quietly.

'*Eres un clandestino*,' Tomás said miserably. 'You're an undercover, and now that I've helped you I'm finished, and probably my family as well.'

'Why do you think I'm an undercover?' Patrick asked.

'Yesterday,' Tomás answered, 'I was in my apartment. I got a call from Shirley.' He looked at Patrick. 'I'm sorry, Cano, but the number I gave you . . .'

'It doesn't matter,' Patrick said.

'Shirley was hysterical,' Tomás said. 'She's moved back in with Luga. She had just heard him speaking with Anguila; word had come through, how I don't know, about you, Cano, it came through while you were away. Anguila was savage. He told Luga to finish you tonight, however he liked, but to finish you.' Tomás's breath came in a shuddering sigh. 'He also had learned that I was working with *neive* scored from you.' Tomás looked up pitiably. 'Anguila told Luga to finish me as well,' he blurted, and covered his face with his hands. 'These people won't stop,' he cried, 'not now. Everyone connected to me is at risk, everyone. Oh Christ,' he wept. 'Will you help me, Cano?'

Patrick stood up and walked to the window. He pulled back the blind a chink: outside, the peaceful suburb slept. Patrick levered open the window and heard the chorus of night insects.

'I can only promise that I'll try,' Patrick said, 'but first I need to learn more.'

Tomás pointed unsteadily. 'There's the phone,' he said, 'ring whoever you report to, Cano, ring them now, the US Embassy here in Madrid; tell them I want to come in now and get asylum, tell them I want police to go and stand outside my parents' house in Cadiz.'

'I need to learn what you can tell us,' Patrick said.

In silence they sat for almost five minutes, Tomás staring into the electric fire, Patrick's attention divided between him and the sounds from the garden which continued regular and undisturbed.

'In this city,' Tomás suddenly began, 'cocaine is controlled by one *compañia*, by a cartel.'

'Who are they?'

Tomás looked towards the window. 'Anguila, his friends,' he replied.

'How long have you known Anguila?'

'Too long,' Tomás replied quietly. 'Over two years. At the start I was just another kid scoring a little hash for myself; then I was scoring it for others; before I knew it I was . . . Anguila's friend . . . working for him.'

The kitchen clock ticked.

'Describe the work.'

'Low-key stuff. Pick-ups in places like Barcelona, then back here to Madrid.'

'Any pattern?'

'Ships from South America.' Tomás lighted himself a cigarette. 'From Cartagena, Buenos Aires, Montevideo.'

'Who does Anguila answer to?'

Tomás's eyes shifted to the fire. 'I don't know, I swear.'

Patrick sighed. 'You're starting to bore me, Tomás,' he said.

Tomás hit his chest with his hand. 'Why should I lie?' he cried. 'I'm telling you everything I know!'

'Then tell me what is the link-up between Anguila and the Basques,' Patrick said.

'Basques?' Tomás's eyes were wide.

Patrick stood up. 'I'm wasting my time,' he said.

'Sit down, sit down, please,' said Tomás wearily.

Patrick sat silently and watched. Three minutes elapsed.

Tomás began again: 'Twice in the last month I've done a job,' he said. '*Neive* from Barcelona – from the docks there – to a house outside San Sebastián. The first time I just left the snow and came home, but the last time, I don't know, maybe I was early, but there were people there, and dope, *Dios*, Cano, the dope was all over the place, a fucking treasure, and guns, automatic weapons, lots of them. I can probably tell you how to get to the house. That's good, isn't it? Does that help you? That's all I know about the Basques.'

'There's a network up there,' Patrick said. 'Cocaine being distributed all over northern Europe. How do I get to the people involved?'

'I don't know . . .'

Patrick bent and caught Tomás from behind, at his shirt collar. 'I don't want to hear you say "I don't know" again,' he whispered fiercely. 'Now who were the people you saw in San Sebastián?'

'I . . .' Tomás choked, 'Anguila was there.'

'Who else?'

'I . . .'

'Go on.'

'There was a . . .'

'Go on.'

'I don't . . .'

'Who else, or I'll drive you back and dump you on the Gran Vía!' Patrick shouted.

'There was a woman,' Tomás gasped. 'I think she must have been La Esmeralda.'

Patrick let him go. 'Who?'

'La Esmeralda,' Tomás said, 'Marcellino's famous woman.' He looked up, suddenly terrified.

'It's all right,' Patrick said, 'I know all about Marcellino.' He sat, his face an inch from Tomás's. 'But tell me about La Esmeralda.'

Tomás buried his head. 'She's Marcellino's woman,' Tomás whispered. 'She's here in Spain, why I don't know, what I mean is,' he gulped, 'she's connected somehow to the Basques, Marcellino is a Basque, he has sent her.'

'It's Marcellino I want, Tomás,' said Patrick softly. 'Not Anguila, nor Luga, nor some poor kid with a time bomb in her belly. I want Marcellino and I want him very badly. The key to how his cocaine gets into the United States is in the Pyrenees. How do I get that key?'

Tomás's hands were shaking. 'On my mother's head . . .' he sobbed.

'*How?*'

There was no answer. Patrick got up and walked to the back door. 'It's been nice knowing you,' he said, turning the handle.

'Wait!'

Tomás slopped his father's friend's brandy into his glass. A minute passed. Patrick remained at the partly opened door.

'Three days ago,' said Tomás in a whisper, 'before they found out I'd been selling your cocaine, I got a call to meet one of Anguila's lieutenants, a little guy called Joel. He asked me for the registration number of my car and for my passport.'

Patrick frowned.

'I couldn't figure it,' Tomás said. 'They had been using me for two years – why the sudden caution? I got my answer the day before yesterday. Joel said they were looking for someone to drive an important job: it meant crossing into France and they wanted a driver and a car who would show up whiter than white on police computers at the border.' Tomás looked red-eyed at Patrick. 'I told him no way. It's murder up there. Border areas are patrolled night and day, special equipment, choppers, you name it. Cars are systematically searched for arms and drugs. The price of cocaine in France is twice that in Spain.'

'What did Joel say to your refusal?' Patrick asked.

'He laughed. He said to relax, the job didn't entail *neive*; he said all that was involved was a drive, a rendezvous, and a drive home.' Tomás shook his head. 'Now I was really suspicious,' he said. 'All the cocaine is down here, in Spain. The cartel specialises in exporting over the Pyrenees not in importing. What was the payload? Joel didn't know or wouldn't say. He said the money was good – two grand. Two grand, I said, just for driving fresh air? He laughed. Who was the person? I asked. Joel was enjoying himself – he's an asshole, he knew something I didn't so he was having fun. Then he made a shape, so, with his hands.' Tomás outlined female curves. 'A woman, I said. Then the coin dropped. La Esmeralda! It's La Esmeralda, isn't it? I asked. Joel wouldn't say. You'll be told, he said. I agreed. Very well, I said, I'll do it, but I need to know the rendezvous. Don't worry, he said, it's the seafront, near the Casino Municipal in Biarritz.'

'So what are they bringing in?' Patrick asked. 'What is so important that La Esmeralda herself has to personally go over the border?'

'I asked myself that question over and over,' Tomás said. 'I wondered, was it another drug – heroin maybe? What is it they want a completely clean car and driver for?' Tomás's face was inches from Patrick's. 'Money, Cano,' he whispered, 'it's got to be money.'

'When is this pick-up?' Patrick asked softly.

'It's tomorrow,' Tomás replied. 'Tomorrow in Biarritz. La Esmeralda will be there. If you want to find the Basques, then, Cano, that is where you go. Find La Esmeralda and you have found them.' Tomás let out a long, shuddering sigh. 'Now I've told you everything and my life isn't worth a shit.' He looked up miserably. 'I'm begging you, on my knees: pick up the phone and get me and my family protection from these vultures.'

Slowly Patrick stood. Instead of going to the phone he went to the window and opened it further.

'Tomás,' he said, returning to the seated youth. 'I want to explain something to you.'

CHAPTER TWENTY-THREE

The Golf edged forward in the line of cars. There was drizzle, a gentle mist tumbling down the sharply rising mountains either side. The Golf's windscreen-wiper jerked on intermittently and cleared the water. Ahead, grey-uniformed Spanish police in booths fed car registrations into computers as two Guardia Civil, armed and impassive, stood to one side. In the commercial section to the left up to fifty trucks stood waiting to enter an examination shed and for their papers to be cleared whilst another line stretched a kilometre back towards San Sebastián. On the other side, a lesser line could be seen, backing up the autoroute to Biarritz.

'Just imagine,' Tomás said. 'We have fifty kilos of 90 per cent snow in the back. Just think how nervous we would be.'

Tomás had recovered some of his old bounce: it had taken most of the night to persuade him, but eventually he had agreed to make the trip. The Golf was within five cars of a booth. Approximately one car in three was being searched.

'We're due to make a major drop outside Biarritz,' Tomás was saying, 'two million dollars' worth of snow, worth twice that in France. If we're caught neither of us will see the outside of a prison until we're old men.'

'You're making me nervous,' Patrick said.

'It's all a state of mind,' Tomás said. 'You did a Dublin–New York run for Anguila; that took guts – you know.'

The wipers cleared the water again and they could see the sallow features of the Spanish customs agent in his glass-fronted box. Tomás handed in his passport, the officer looked at it and glanced at Patrick. A uniformed customs official in a gleaming grey mackintosh wiped the Golf's rear window and peered into the back seat. They were waved through.

'So easy,' Tomás said as they drove twenty yards and joined another queue, this time on the French side. 'It's all to do with chemistry. Smuggling is about reaching a state of mind where you have convinced yourself that you are clean – that you're carrying nothing. You achieve that balance up here' – Tomás tapped his head – 'and everything else just follows naturally. You become relaxed, you stop emitting those electrodes that customs officials pick up as second nature. These guys you see here' – Tomás pointed to the French police ahead of them – 'they're like bats. They've grown a whole supplementary apparatus to deal with their environment.'

The French police were searching every other car. The Golf entered the booth and was waved through.

'It's not the person they look at,' Tomás said as they hit the autoroute, 'it's the persona. They don't just see, they absorb. Man used these techniques in the jungle when he was still partly beast – they've learned to resurrect these techniques today.'

Patrick looked at Tomás as he drove the car up the road: Tomás appeared to be on a high; he drove the car as fast as it would go, constantly checking his rear mirror.

'Sometimes,' Tomás said, 'they have spot patrols which stop cars, particularly here in France, up to three or four kilometres from the border. It's never happened to me – yet.'

'Why should it worry you?' Patrick asked.

Tomás grinned. 'Put your hand under your seat, Cano,' he said.

Patrick bent forward and reached.

'Strapped to the seat mounting, where it joins the floor,' Tomás instructed.

Patrick felt the contours of a small package.

'Have a look,' Tomás said.

Patrick prised it loose; Tomás's grinning face was still partly turned to him. Patrick opened one corner, felt cellophane and worked his finger in. 'You bastard,' he gasped as he smacked his lips to the bitter taste. 'You just drove through two sets of customs cool as a breeze with me sitting on a ten-year jail sentence.'

'It's those electrodes, man!' Tomás laughed as they breasted a hill. 'Those goddam electrodes!'

They began to descend. The rain had stopped and gradually the sound of the ocean filled their ears. It was a total noise, all-enveloping like the traffic in Madrid. The bay of Biarritz suddenly appeared, majestic and sweeping. They passed rocks jutting out into the sea, a statue of the Virgin on the outermost, and then swung back in until Tomás found a free kerb space. It was shortly after 10.20 a.m. Tomás reached down for the *neive* and pocketed it. They got out and walked to the cliff wall. Tomás wore a pair of army-surplus, green binoculars around his neck. 'Down there,' he said, 'right down there, was where the rendezvous was meant to be.'

Tomás handed the glasses to Patrick. The Grande Plage of Biarritz swept inwards beneath, empty but for a couple of morning strollers. Behind the beach was a concrete promenade, its surface blotched with puddles, a car park with one car and, further back, the boarded, winter face of the Casino Municipal.

'I won't be long,' Tomás said. 'My contact is within ten minutes' walk, but he'll haggle like a whore.' He tossed his keys to Patrick. 'Take the keys,' he said to Patrick, 'just in case.'

'No just in case,' Patrick said. 'I need you here.'

Patrick watched as Tomás walked away across the Place St Eugénie. Then he sat on the cliff wall and swung the lenses on to the beach below. The sand curved in and then out and upwards like the sweep of a woman's neck. Patrick thought of Georgie. The golden sand was her hair, the sweeping headland her throat.

The quarter hours came and went, marked by the bells of a nearby church which drowned out even the noise of the sea. There was no sign of Tomás. The bells hurled out 11.15; Patrick checked the time against his own watch. Where was he?

Where the top of the beach met the water, the Hotel du Palais jutted outwards. In summer its elegant terrace would be colourful and alive with people; now the point was deserted. Patrick adjusted the binoculars. He blinked and narrowed his eyes. From the deep shadow, from the protective lee of the promontory, a figure had stepped out. It was a woman. As Patrick locked on her she walked two steps towards the shore, bent for a stone, then skimmed it out to sea, her body angled as she threw. Patrick caught his breath. She took another step, bent for another stone, skidded it out again on the grey flatness of water. Now she walked back into shadow.

Patrick took down the binoculars and rubbed his eyes. With mounting panic he checked the empty square for Tomás. He put the glasses back up, just in time to see a white car, an Alfa-Sud, pulling up at the very far end of the promenade, beside the side-gates of the Hotel du Palais. As Patrick watched, the car's headlights flashed, once. He switched his vision to the woman. She had seen the signal and now walked up the beach, on to the promenade. She walked unhurriedly, but purposefully, well. She was tall, her hips swung. Patrick looked wildly around for Tomás. He swung the binoculars back to the beach and saw the woman unlocking the door of the other car which, up to three minutes ago, had been the sole occupier of the car park. She lifted out a coat, slammed the car door shut and made her way to the white car whose engine was running. Patrick gritted his teeth in frustration. Tomás would know if this was La Esmeralda, but Tomás was with some *narcotráfico*, haggling over the price of cocaine. The rendezvous that Patrick was witnessing on the beach below him was probably a woman meeting her lover and setting off for a few hours of innocent peace. Patrick stared. The door of the Alfa-Sud had been pushed out open for her; her hips swung; she stooped to get in. Patrick had his first view of the car driver's face. A powerful charge went to Patrick's very core. Leaping from the wall he ran for the Golf.

Patrick swung downhill, along the seafront and around the corner of the Casino Municipal. He was sure beyond any doubt that the driver of the white Alfa-Sud was the foreman from Château Diane.

Punching the Golf into first Patrick roared uphill. At the top the road ran straight. Two hundred yards ahead the white Alfa was just rounding a bend.

They left Biarritz in heavy rain, passing small hotels with palm trees in their gardens; a pitch-and-putt course; wet and deserted seaside restaurants. At Blanc-Pignon the road took them right, along the banks of the estuary of the Nive, then over it and northwards again. The road was straight, wet and empty.

The white car suddenly swung left. This road was also straight but plunged downwards, narrowly, to the coast. There were houses either side: the rain was sheeting but through it Patrick could see the white car, much nearer to him, stopped just fifty yards ahead. Patrick swung the Golf into the gateway of a house and killed the engine. He leaped out, and using the house gates for protection, peered around. The Alfa-Sud was still parked there, its tail-lights glowing in the rain, smoke wisping from its exhaust. Patrick heard gears being engaged, then the Alfa continued on down the hill.

Patrick locked the Golf, sprinted up a tarmacadam driveway and over smooth lawns dotted with standard roses. He scrambled through a thick shrubbery belt, water bucketing on to him from shining leaves.

At the far side he was suddenly in a field, an uncultivated bluff running out to a cliff. Patrick ran, then dropped and wriggled to the edge on his elbows and knees. He could see nothing except the sea; the Alfa, if it was there, was below him. Then there was a new engine sound, high-bore. Patrick was nearly at the lip. The new car's sound was killed. Patrick still could not see below him. He walked his elbows outwards, then abruptly fell to his left as the surface beneath him collapsed. He cried out as earth and stones tumbled down to the pebble beach. He snatched back, grabbed firmer ground and hauled himself up.

The rain had pasted Patrick's hair and was pouring into his eyes and over his face, but now he could see the scene below. A Mercedes 450SE with French plates and the Alfa-Sud stood side by side, the Mercedes looking out to sea, but the Alfa pointing uphill, the way it had come.

Patrick stared. The foreman had left the Alfa. The same head, elongated like a pole, a head on the top of a stick, the drooping, ginger moustache. Patrick stared. He could see the roof of the Mercedes, almost beneath him, a wide expanse of shining, blue metal, the Alfa-Sud beside it and the foreman walking around the back of the Mercedes, to the driver's door. Patrick could not see the Mercedes driver's face, just his hands, long and thin, now handing a brown briefcase out of the window. The foreman was wearing gloves; he took the briefcase, nodded and walked back to the Alfa where he handed the briefcase to the woman who had taken the wheel. Immediately the Alfa's engine came to life. Patrick strained to see her face. Her window was closed again and the Alfa's wipers, on fast, were spinning the rain off, but still Patrick could only see an outline, no detail, a face blurred by rain and deflected light. Patrick's attention switched to immediately below him: the foreman had come around the back of the Mercedes and was unbuttoning his jacket. Whether the driver of the large car saw what was happening or not, the engine of the Mercedes suddenly roared. The foreman was at the rear wing side nearest to Patrick. He was reaching. Patrick craned out, perilously close to the cliff-edge. Thirty feet below him the Mercedes's white reversing lights had come on, bright in the grey day. The foreman leaped around to the passenger door, his legs straddled wide apart, his hands held out before him. There was a screech of rubber as the big car's tyres fought for purchase against the hill, then flames seemed to lick from the foreman's hands. There were dull, thumping sounds. The car was flying backwards, in an arc. The foreman stood his ground, his outstretched arms rigid, the squirts of flame still coming. Glass shattered. The Mercedes had rammed unchecked into the bonnet of the Alfa. The foreman aimed again. The driver of the Mercedes had white hair and brought his hands up to protect his head. The heavier car was now powering itself and the Alfa back down the incline in a mad grinding of noise, the Mercedes reversing, its hazard lights for some reason flashing and the Alfa in forward gear, straining impotently uphill against the greater weight. Like two creatures in a death battle they gradually slipped back until the Alfa, the victim, was pressed hard against the sea wall, and the Mercedes, the full-blooded predator, kept blindly on, engine screaming, lights flashing, wheels spinning, intent on finishing the unfinishable.

The foreman was walking to the wall. At the ruptured Mercedes's window he pointed in his weapon and loosed off three deliberate rounds into the interior. Each time he fired Patrick could see the gun in his hand buck a little.

The big car's wheels ceased to spin. The door of the Alfa was with difficulty being opened, and now, despite the rain, Patrick could see the driver as she emerged, briefcase in hand, looking in concern at the wreck of the smaller car. She was tall with long, black hair. Patrick watched as she went to the foreman who was returning his gun to its position at the small of his back. She pointed to the Mercedes. All at once, at the same instant, she and the foreman turned their attention back up the road, out of Patrick's field of vision. Their actions changed tempo. The foreman sprinted around to the driver's door of the Mercedes, flung it open and, reaching inside without ceremony, dragged out the slumped figure. The woman jumped in. The Mercedes sprang away from its union with the useless Alfa. Glass tinkled to the ground. The foreman scrambled into the passenger's seat. With a roar they disappeared.

A jogger in rain gear rounded the bluff of cliff, stared at the scene, at the wrecked car and the figure lying face up on the road, its upper body punctuated by crimson-flowering splotches. The jogger backed off a few paces and then retraced his steps uphill at a different speed.

Patrick knew he should move. He knew he had to follow the Mercedes, to get away and complete the reason for his being there, but movement itself seemed beyond him. He could neither move his head, nor blink his eyes, nor breathe, nor bring his hand to wipe the water from his face. Both his eyes were unseeing, locked forever on the face of the man below, whose unviable, wet body would soon be as wet as Patrick's own.

Slowly Patrick rose. It took a major effort to make himself run for the shrubbery and the Golf, to unlock his eyes from the surprised, dead face of John Abelson.

Patrick picked up the blue Mercedes two kilometres south-east. He felt at once totally confused and lucid. With Abelson gone, so some of the motive for persisting on in this crazy world had gone with him. Yet Patrick now felt compelled by some inner force. He would follow the foreman and La Esmeralda. They would lead him to where the cocaine came over each night. And maybe to where it went. Or maybe none of these things. Maybe he would end up stopping a bullet. He felt cold, unemotional. He wanted to laugh and cry. His hands hurt, they held the steering wheel so tightly.

He got caught behind a truck. Cursing he eventually passed it, but the Mercedes had disappeared.

Patrick was on the valley bed now, hurtling along as fast as the Golf would go. To the right was a river making froth over red rocks. Beyond the water a mountain thatched in firs ran up vertically and where it followed the bends and contours of the river, the tar-black mouths of tunnels could be seen, and a train, weaving in and out of them like a playground model. The road swung left. There was an intersection: straight on for St-Jean-Pied-de-Port, right, a lesser road, but blocked by railway barriers, down for the approaching train. Patrick stood on the brakes. The lone Mercedes stood there patiently.

Patrick flipped down the Golf's sun-visor and parked behind, his engine running. He could see the woman trying to examine him in her rear mirror, and the foreman do the same using the mirror on the car door. A small truck pulled in behind Patrick, its rear piled high with vegetables. Then the toy-town train rattled out of the mountain and past the red and white barriers hinged upwards.

The Mercedes was three hundred yards ahead as they entered the main square of St-Etienne-de-Baigorry; the larger car turned right, over a tiny bridge beside a church.

The road climbed. Within two minutes Patrick's ears were popping and the village he had just come through suddenly appeared below him, a tiny grouping of roofs, two spires and the river in their fold of Pyrenean valley. The road zig-zagged up and every thirty seconds or so Patrick could see the late sun flash on the Mercedes before it again disappeared in its ascent.

There were no other cars – the road was barely wide enough for two to fit abreast. There was no barrier on the valley side, just a sheer drop which became sheerer as each further upward bend was taken. To the right was raw rock, its seams standing out like blue arteries, rock gouged out of the mountain so that the road could be wrapped around its face. Some of the turns bent back on themselves so very sharply that Patrick had to nose the car out into the void before making the turn back into the mountain.

Patrick was now approaching yet another hairpin, uphill and right. He appeared to be driving straight out and over the cliff. He changed down, swung the Golf's steering wheel all the way right and then came to a sickening, involuntary halt. The Mercedes was thrown across his path, its nose for the abyss. Patrick slammed into reverse. Then he froze as he saw the gun-muzzle levelled two-handed at his ear, separated only by three millimetres of window-glass. Patrick saw the foreman take one hand off the gun and reach for the door. Cold air whipped in.

'*¡Fuera!*' the foreman said in guttural Spanish. 'Out!' The gun was quivering. 'Out!'

Patrick stepped out.

He saw the woman; she had been standing behind the Mercedes and now stepped from its shadow. She had ink-black hair and the wind whipped at it. Patrick found himself staring. Her face had the assurance of great beauty and her eyes glinted green in the changing evening light.

'Hurry!' the pole-headed foreman shouted to the woman and she came to the Golf and threw her coat and the briefcase into its back seat. Patrick felt apprehension sweep him as the foreman's gun bit the back of his neck.

'Hurry!' the foreman repeated. 'Before another car comes!'

The woman opened the driver's door of the Mercedes, leaned in and flicked the engine to life. In a fluid movement, she engaged its automatic gears in low, jumped backwards and kicked the door shut. The big blue car inched forwards in slow motion, stood on its head for the briefest moment, then disappeared.

'Drive!'

Patrick got in, the foreman beside him. The woman sat in the back. As they drove on uphill the foreman's eyes were riveted on Patrick's face.

'I think I know him,' the foreman said in a strange voice.

'*¿Él?*' The woman looked at Patrick curiously. Patrick felt light-headed.

'I've seen him somewhere before,' the foreman said to her, 'I'm sure of it. I have a very good memory for faces.' He poked the gun into Patrick's right ear. 'Where have I seen you before, pretty boy?'

Patrick grabbed the wheel as they rounded another bend. 'How do I know?' he said. They swerved violently for the edge as the gun caught him deep in the ear with a blinding shaft of pain. At the last minute he corrected their disastrous lurch.

'For Christ's sake!' La Esmeralda cried at the foreman. 'You fool! Are you trying to kill us?'

'I've seen this one's face before,' the foreman hissed. 'I tell you, I don't make mistakes.'

'What does it matter as long as he gets us across?' La Esmeralda asked. 'We could not have gone in a car without papers.'

The foreman transferred the barrel of the gun to Patrick's throat. 'I'm sure this is the same car as we thought we saw behind us in Biarritz,' he said, 'I'm sure.'

'Leave it, Dani,' La Esmeralda said, 'let him drive.'

'This is more than a coincidence,' the foreman persisted. 'First the car, now him.' His lips came back over his gums. 'I tell you . . .'

'Leave it!'

The authority in La Esmeralda's voice silenced the foreman for the moment. They rounded a left-handed hairpin where water cascaded down the cliff and under the road.

'This is a mistake,' the foreman began anew. 'I took too long to finish that bastard off back in Biarritz. If I had been quicker we would still have had my car and this would not be necessary.'

'If, if,' La Esmeralda said. 'Forget "if".'

'I have a bad feeling about this,' the foreman said. He gestured towards Patrick. 'I hate coincidences.' He saw Patrick's eyes wandering to his pole-head. 'You keep your eyes on the road and your ears closed, pretty boy.'

They had passed under a tree, rounded another bend and were now mounting hillside where the ground either side of them was more level. Patrick saw buildings outlined against the sky and flags flapping on poles.

'Just drive over as calmly as if you were taking your family home after a day out,' the foreman said softly. Slowly he brought his gun hand over and inside his jacket so that it still pointed at Patrick. 'Your life means nothing to me, pretty boy.'

Patrick swallowed. 'You're going to kill me anyway,' he said. 'Why should I bother?'

The foreman's face stiffened. 'Don't try me!' he hissed.

'Do it.' The woman was addressing Patrick. 'You have my word that you will not be harmed.'

Patrick looked in the mirror. Her eyes were large and steady and in a sudden shaft of reflected sunlight, brilliantly green. He looked ahead: a single car stood between them and a *gendarme*. Patrick chanced a look over: the foreman was staring at him in astonishment. He whirled to La Esmeralda, then back to Patrick.

'Now I know him . . .' he began.

'*Monsieur.*'

The *gendarme* saluted Patrick. He looked at the Golf's Spanish plates.

'*Vous venez d'ou?* Where are you coming from?'

'Biarritz,' Patrick replied.

'*Et vous rentrez?* Are you on your way home?'

Patrick nodded. '*Oui.*'

The *gendarme* strolled around the car, looked at the foreman, smiled at La Esmeralda and looked in through the back windows. At the rear of the car he dropped to his knees and peered underneath.

'*Identité,*' the *gendarme* said, dusting himself down and returning to the driver's window.

Patrick handed over his Curro Cano identity. He felt strangely detached, unconcerned, unsure about who he actually was.

'*Merci.*' The *gendarme* snapped off another salute and waved them through.

The French post was at the top of the hill. They were now in no-man's-land, a section of less than fifty yards, downhill to another hut and a barrier which marked the entrance to Spain. The foreman was turning to La Esmeralda. 'I tell you I have seen him . . .'

'Shut up!' the woman said.

Patrick could see the gun-muzzle press against the jacket. A nerve was pulling at the corner of the foreman's left eye. The Spanish barrier rose to let the car in front through, then fell.

'Drive normally.' La Esmeralda's voice was calm and in control. Patrick could hear the broken breathing of the man beside him. A grey-uniformed, pencil-moustached Spanish policeman stepped out to the Golf.

'*Señor. Algo que declarar?* Anything to declare?'

'*No tengo nada que declarar,*' Patrick replied.

The cop nodded. He looked into the car, nodded again, then his hand went to the barrier. It rose.

'*¡Pascal! Un momento!*'

The cry was from the hut. In horror Patrick saw another policeman hurrying out, putting on his cap. He was holding a sub-machine-gun down by his side.

'*¡Para ese coche!* Hold that car!'

The first policeman turned. The barrier was fully raised and he made to re-lower it. There were two muffled explosions as the foreman's shells caught him high in the chest and slammed him on the handle of his barrier. Then Patrick felt agony as the gun was again rammed into the cavity of his right ear.

'*¡Arranca!*' screamed the foreman. 'Drive, you bastard!'

Patrick flung the Golf down the sharp hill. In the mirror, past the head of La Esmeralda, he could see the other cop steady himself and bring up his gun. They were hurtling into a hairpin, dead for a truck which was crawling up the hill towards them. Behind them the Uzi spoke. The hairpin, if they made it, would bring them under a fold of mountain and temporarily out of sight. Patrick swung out into the approaching truck's path in an effort to reduce the angle of the uncoming bend. Then he heard the Uzi cough again. There was a cry from the back seat and Patrick could see slugs beat into the front of the truck. Patrick lurched them left, scraping the length of Tomás's Golf against the truck fender, righted, then took the corner, almost overturning. They were in the lee of the hill and hurtling downwards, the road to the valley laid out before them, a gracefully folded ribbon winding symmetrically down the mountain.

They were well out of the range of any gunfire, but the need to escape was uppermost. There was a metallic noise to Patrick's right as the foreman's pistol hit the handbrake. Patrick looked in alarm, then cried out as the man's whole upper body slumped heavily across until it was wedging Patrick against the door.

'Christ!' he cried, and tried to push the weight back. 'Get up!'

'He can't hear you,' La Esmeralda gasped, 'he can't hear anyone.'

Frantically Patrick tried to shove the foreman away with his right elbow, tried to free the steering wheel in order to keep a straight course. He felt something wet and hot. The dead man's head was at Patrick's neck, the eyes in his pole-head puzzled. Blood oozed on to Patrick's neck.

'Take him off!' Patrick shouted. 'I can't drive! Take him off or we're going to crash!'

He heard La Esmeralda cry out as she levered the foreman to the other side of his seat. 'We must get out of this car,' she said, her voice in pain.

Patrick looked at her in the mirror. 'Were you hit?' He passed two cars and swerved into another hairpin.

'*Sí*,' she replied. 'Across the legs.'

They were rapidly losing height: a group of houses appeared ahead and they roared straight through.

'They are waiting for me at the other side of Elizondo,' the woman said, 'but now it is too dangerous. It would put everyone in danger. I must get away.'

The road had flattened out and they crossed a river.

'After the next bridge,' La Esmeralda said, 'there's a track which goes right. Take it.'

Patrick could see her wince. She had made no attempt to take the gun from the foreman's rigid hand.

The race of water flashed as they crossed the river again and then lurched off the road, right, five hundred yards from another group of houses. Patrick drove like a madman, his only desire to get away from the incriminating car, his eyes locked on the bumpy path as the Golf bounced along, its chassis often scraping rock, its wheels spinning, catching and propelling them forward. They sped along a face of mountain; below, the hamlet they had by-passed was now visible. Patrick thought he could see blue, flashing lights. The track had begun to descend. Several times the foreman, reacting to the camber of the mountain, fell heavily across and the woman had to haul him back. Then, without warning, they were among houses, in a walled, curving lane, paved underfoot.

Patrick ploughed into a gateway and jumped out. He looked wildly around. He was trembling all over. His knees swayed and threatened not to take the weight of his body. He steadied himself against the Golf as his whole system tried to collapse. His thinking self had deserted: the animal fighting for survival remained, exhausted, beaten, but still fighting. He could hear traffic. He began to lurch towards it, away from the Golf and the corpse and the woman and all the madness he had just come through. He stumbled like someone who had been steamrollered. He approached the bend of the lane. Panting, he looked back for a last, awful look. He stared. La Esmeralda was hobbling after him, the precious briefcase in her free hand.

Patrick stood rooted. She said nothing, just kept coming, but her eyes never left his face. He stood there, she approached. She had to hop as one leg could take no weight. The effort exhausted her. Her marvellous face was lined with sweat and distress. Blood dripped behind her on to the smooth paving slabs.

Finish it, Patrick. This time finish it.

Patrick ran back. She caught his shoulder.

'*Gracias*,' she gasped.

'Give me the briefcase,' Patrick said.

La Esmeralda shook her head. Using Patrick for support she forced herself forward and together they limped towards the sound of the traffic.

CHAPTER TWENTY-FOUR

Castor was weary. The car was a ten-year-old Simca and every effort at overtaking was a struggle; earlier it had rained and trucks sent up shooting curtains of spray which dangerously obliterated vision at the moment of overtaking. Castor's weariness was caused by an accumulation of worry about the cause, apprehension about his mission, constant concentration in poor light on explosives and the strain of an unhappy wife.

Mati had had her baby, eight days late, in the same bed in which Castor himself had been born. A midwife came up from Aldudes and Castor had stood there at four in the morning, holding the storm-lamp, watching as Mati's contractions came with greater regularity. He winced as she winced. He saw her grit her teeth and grip the brass bed-head.

'The head!' the portly midwife said with glee. 'I can see the head!'

Castor held the torch and stared.

'Castor!' Mati's breath was coming in very short gasps.

'I am here, beside you.'

'A very big effort, now,' the midwife said.

The muscles in Mati's abdomen locked in spasm and with a low, gurgling intensity she pushed.

'*Ona da*,' the woman from Aldudes comforted, '*ona da*.'

'*Castor!*'

'I am here.'

The midwife had taken the lamp and Castor now dabbed Mati's face. Castor could see the head of the child another fraction forwards on its journey.

'Castor.'

'*Bai.*'

'Castor, I want . . . you . . . to . . . promise me.' Mati was panting, her metabolism haywire. 'I . . . want . . .'

'Now, another big one,' urged the midwife.

Speechlessly Mati arched her small body and pushed mightily, the veins and arteries in her neck and breasts swollen with the pressure. The midwife was trying to get a hold of the head. 'Next time,' she said.

'Castor!'

'I will promise you,' Castor said, 'I will promise you.'

'That you won't drive . . . that . . . bomb?'

Castor looked away and made a covert sign of the cross. 'I promise,' he whispered.

But Mati's hand gripped his shoulder fiercely. 'On . . . the . . . head . . . of . . . your . . . child?'

Castor looked at her hopelessly. Mati lay there, fighting for her next breath. Castor's eyes swam; he wanted to choke.

'Now!' The sturdy woman from Aldudes was back in control. 'Now, Mati! For the life of you! Now!'

Mati braced and pushed. Her whole body underwent a change to uniform scarlet and a noise like a steel drill hammered out between her clenched teeth. She kept it up, one enormous, gigantic effort, her eyes bulging, her body rigid in its final, desperate expulsion. Then the midwife was suddenly holding a head and a hand and pulling, and the ruddy child was delivered, attached with his white-grey, sinewy cord, and his mother's juices lapped out on the rubber sheets.

'*Mutil!*' cried the midwife, laughing. 'Another big boy for the farm of Arocena!'

'*Mutil!*' Castor cried in excitement. He watched as his wife reached for her son. 'A son!' Castor laughed, but Mati's eyes were on the wet child at her breast.

Mati had stayed in bed for three days; understandable for a woman past her middle thirties, yet unlike her all the same. When she left the bed, she went back to her usual tasks, wordlessly. With the child she was isolated, contented, bonded; with Teodoro she was sharp; with Castor she was cold. At night he slept facing her back. He rose before her and endured the day again, until at nightfall she withdrew to her infant and her room. Her joy with the child was like that of the dappled cow with its calf: unshared. It was as if, with the arrival of the new son, a new Mati had arrived, someone to whom Castor Arocena was a stranger.

The situation left Castor drained. He could cope with almost any form of hardship – had coped – but against the alienation of affection he had no answer. He knew the truth: that at the moment of supreme importance for any woman he had made his choice: Euskadi. It was only in that word, that concept, that for Castor the idea of love had any real meaning: everything else was a varying grade of farm enterprise. One part of Castor wanted to run into the bedroom, throw himself on his knees and make the promise which he had avoided, but the other, vital part held the upper hand. Just as the birth of their son had caused a sea-change in Mati, so Castor understood that only a catharsis of the same magnitude would enable him to escape the grip of the force that drove him.

The three pressure-cookers, two lidded, with their complement of steel filings stood tamped and ready. To the open cooker Castor added saltpetre, a collar of commercial explosives, a blasting cap and a small radio receiver, which he had spent the morning testing. Then it was time to gingerly load the three heavy cookers into the old Simca and go to the kitchen for the meal which would have to sustain them through the night.

Castor kept checking his pocket-watch. Military precision. And loyalty. Castor was aware of the recent split within the cause, a split brought about by a refusal of those like Xalbador and Caro to obey Sainz Perez's orders on the pretext that drug running was beneath the dignity of Basques. Castor shook his head. He knew the value of military discipline as well as military precision. Castor would not be found wanting.

Mati served out the thick ham, the bread heavy with the grease of the pan and the succulent eggs of the mountain hens in a wordless way which made them both forget that she had up to recently been quite talkative. The two men ate in silence. The infant began to cry from its cot in the warmest corner of the kitchen and Mati went to it, clucking with her tongue, lifted it, kissing it, soothing it so that it fell silent and asleep on the round of her shoulder.

Time rushed. Teodoro stood in the yard, near the back step,

Castor at the door, the Simca's keys in his hand. Mati's back was to him, at the sink.

'*Agur*,' Castor said, 'goodbye. We will return tomorrow at noon.'

There was no response from the kitchen. Outside a wind had got up and was blowing dust indoors. Castor shrugged, felt his heart dive, turned to close the door, then at the last moment, went back in, closing Teodoro outside.

'Will you not bid your husband goodbye?' he asked, approaching the bent back. He stood directly behind Mati who stood motionless, her hands plunged into water. 'Will you not bid me goodbye?'

Trembling, Castor reached and touched her with his fingertips. Mati's entire body tensed and stiffened as if she were a species of threatened, exotic plant. Castor breathed in deeply, then took his hand away. 'Very well,' he said, 'it is your decision.' Firmly, his man's anger again to the fore, he strode from the house banging the door, and with Teodoro beside him, drove the car from the yard and down the mountain.

And again Castor knew the truth: that his final words had been to wound, had been to mask the reality which her dignity rejected and against which she had gambled everything, even a last opportunity to say goodbye. He kept checking in the mirror as if some miracle might transport the mother of his sons faster than the car and bring her waving and running up behind them.

But it took over half an hour to reach Aldudes on foot and they were now through it in the car winding their way in the sudden darkness towards the border.

Teodoro narrowed his eyes against the rain. It was after 6.30 in the morning, but no shaft of dawn yet relieved the clinging night. In San Sebastián the deadly cookers had been transferred from the Simca to the back of a builder's van. Thick batons of wood braced them in place, then, covered with tarpaulin, the load had been disguised with ladders, barrels and planks. Teodoro took the wheel and Castor led the way in the Simca. Now Teodoro kept his eyes on the tail-lights of his father's car. They had just passed through the town of Guernica. Teodoro thought of his phone call from Aldudes the day before. Paulina had been as he knew she would be: mourning in dignity, calm, determined.

'Geraldo was sent to his death,' she had said. 'Because he dared to disagree.'

'In two days' time when our work is over, I want to be with you,' Teodoro said.

'My heart is with you today,' Paulina said. '*Maite zaitut*. I love you.'

'And I you, Paulina,' Teodoro had said.

His heart had soared. He would come back and plan a proper life for himself and Paulina, somewhere away from the Pyrenees, perhaps. His father would be furious but Teodoro did not care.

The rain eased as the Simca led them through a sleeping Bermeo and then along the twisting coastline where they skirted Cabo Machichaco and wove down the corkscrew road which in daylight would present spectacular views of San Pelay and the sea.

All at once Castor waved him to a stop. Castor jumped out of the Simca and ran back.

'Good,' Castor said. Grey light had replaced night and Teodoro could see a forestry cutting, leading uphill on the far side of the road. 'We are within two kilometres,' Castor said. He checked his pocket-watch. 'Not yet seven,' he said, 'good.' He pointed to the woods. 'I leave the car here and go to the top of that hill, through the forest. From there my signal will travel straight as an arrow to the truck.' He looked at his watch. 'You have thirty minutes. Now go!'

Teodoro engaged the clutch and prepared to leave, but then his father's and his eyes met as simultaneously they both heard the noise. In horror Castor looked to the road. The back, right-hand tyre of the truck was crumpling to its wheel-rim in a steady hiss.

Castor looked at Teodoro in disbelief, then back at the reality at his feet. 'T-t-the spare wheel, quick!' he cried. 'Where is it?'

Frantically Teodoro leaped from the truck and threw himself under its chassis. Castor sprang up on the back and began to tear at the mountain of builder's equipment. Teodoro rolled out, ran around to the passenger door and opened it.

'Here!' Teodoro shouted.

He wheeled the spare to the punctured side, knocked the hubcap from the dead wheel and applied a brace to the first of the five nuts.

'The time, the time,' Castor kept repeating. He was on his knees and was positioning a rudimentary lifting-jack on smooth road under a sold section of chassis.

There was a squeak of metal as another of the nuts yielded.

'She's on a slope,' Teodoro said. 'The weight of the load is all on the back, she'll be hard to jack.'

'Stop talking!' Castor cried.

'All loose!' Teodoro said.

Castor grabbed the brace from Teodoro and inserted its handle end into the jack where it served as a lever. Then he began to pump. He pumped mightily and as he did so, with agonising slowness, the pressure could be seen to come off the flattened tyre. There was the sound of metal groaning as the weight was lifted, fractions at a time, from the springs of the truck. Teodoro stood, licking his lips, squatting, his hands ready to strip the loosened nuts and whip away the useless wheel. Castor pumped. The truck was nearly to its normal height. Then without warning the jack gave way and the whole vehicle fell backwards with a deafening crash.

The two men froze in horror, their eyes on the covered pressure-cookers. Then Castor began to catch fistfuls of his own hair. 'We are going to fail!' he wailed. 'There are only twenty minutes remaining. We have failed!'

'Here!' Teodoro had grabbed the jack again and rammed it in under the chassis. 'This time I will try and hold her!' he cried. 'Now, pump!'

Castor stared at his son, then grasping the lever he pumped the lifting-jack for all he was worth. Teodoro positioned himself with his back to the tail of the truck and braced his legs against the road. Again, almost imperceptibly, the jack lifted the weight above it, a millimetre at a time. As the truck rose, so Teodoro braced the more; the more the truck rose, the more its weight went back with the hill and the greater the pressure on Teodoro. Now Castor's fingers were scrambling the loosened wheel-nuts free; with a scrape he dragged off the wheel and threw it to one side. He looked in dismay at Teodoro: the youth's face was contorted in a supreme effort of strength as he fought against the massive gravity of the truck. Castor caught the spare between his two hands, squatted and tried to fit it to the naked hub. He rammed the wheel to the protruding bolts; he rammed and then cried out. The hub was a good inch too low for its new wheel.

'It's too low!' Castor screamed.

Teodoro was almost at the end of his great reserves of power. 'Let . . . out . . . air!' he said in agony.

Castor's fingers fumbled with the tyre-valve. After what seemed a lifetime there was a hissing sound.

'I can't hold it!' shouted Teodoro.

'Hold it! Whatever you do, hold it!' Castor was on his knees again, positioning the wheel. The smallest possible gap now prevented the wheel from being married to the hub. 'Lift!' Castor cried.

With all the intent at his disposal, Teodoro willed his body in one supreme effort. Bracing with every last muscle, pushing with all he had, he lifted the enormous weight behind him.

Then he collapsed.

Castor's fingers were spinning the nuts into place. 'Get up,' he hissed, 'get up. There are fifteen minutes, no more.'

Teodoro lay on the road, looking up at the brightening sky, overwhelmed by a fantastic urge to curl up and go to sleep. He felt the peace of completion of a great physical task; his body was telling him that it saw no reason why he should move.

'Get up!'

Teodoro got to his feet. Castor had thrown the punctured wheel and lifting equipment into the truck and was gesticulating, pointing to his watch. 'Fourteen minutes!' he cried as Teodoro climbed into the driver's seat. 'Hurry! Get in there. Leave it and run, do you understand?'

Teodoro nodded wearily and started the engine. He eased the truck down the hill and saw Castor reaching into the Simca, then running up the cutting for the hill-top.

The downhill road twisted and turned around the mountain and Teodoro could catch glimpses of the sea. He pressed the truck as much as caution would allow, lurching dangerously as he took the sharp bends, feeling the weight behind take him to the wrong side after each successive turn. Eventually he was on flat ground. A sign indicating nuclear activity appeared on his left. Teodoro pressed on.

The road at this point plunged in another downward phase, through trees, and suddenly there was a fork, left carrying on for Arminza and the sea, right for the Lemoniz reactor. Teodoro swung right. Excavated earth had been smoothed upwards on both sides so that the road was collected inwards to a neck, at the top of which stood a gatepost and a small hut. Teodoro gripped the wheel. He could see the guard in the hut; he was wearing a cap and he turned at the sound of the truck. Teodoro sucked in air and flashed his lights. He kept driving for the closed gates. Magically the gates opened and Teodoro drove through, waving at the seated guard and beeping his horn. Teodoro looked at his watch: the hands stood between ten and five minutes to eight o'clock. He looked in the rear mirror: the guard-hut was still visible. He put his foot to the floor and tore along the narrow asphalt road, smoother and cleaner than the public road he had left, the grass on both sides neatly mown and every ten yards beds of roses, each cut in a different shape. He had imagined that the bend his father had referred to would come quickly, but he was still within sight of the entry point and ahead seemed to be endlessly straight. He urged the truck faster. At last the road began to turn. Teodoro looked in the mirror. He could no longer see the guard hut. He did not dare look at his watch. He jerked the truck to a halt, leaped from it and hurled the ignition key, as he had been told, as far as he could. Then he turned around the bonnet of the vehicle, running flat out for the incline and stopped as if he had run smack into a concrete wall. Shielded by shrubbery a uniformed man with a Doberman on a leash and a Uzi in the crook of his arm was pointing the gun-muzzle dead at Teodoro's chest.

'Halt or you'll never run another yard!'

Teodoro was transfixed.

'Put your hands above your head!'

Teodoro stared at the man, then at the truck. He looked at the watch on his wrist: eight o'clock lacked four minutes.

'Above your head!'

Slowly Teodoro complied.

'Now, very slowly, lean across the bonnet of the truck.' The man advanced a pace, the dog snarled. 'Lean across the truck!'

Teodoro stood there, unmoving. Whilst every instinct he possessed screamed at him to explain why they should get away from the spot, he calmly realised, almost outside himself looking in, that he could not do so. The alternating faces of Castor and Paulina kept blotting out the face of the man in front of him.

Teodoro saw the man's ugly mouth and the dog's mouth, two of a kind.

'Do you understand what this is, farmboy? This is a gun. Now lean across the truck!'

The man was saying something but no noise came from his mouth. The only sound which Teodoro heard was the song of birds whose dawn chorus he so often heard over Aldudes and which was now in full swing, here at Lemoniz near the sea.

The man let out a reef on the dog leash and the animal lunged forward, saliva flecking from its mouth.

'Lean over the truck!'

Teodoro knew he should not be there, that he should run, that the consequences of inaction were terminal. Suddenly he felt gloriously amused by the fact that the armed man with his dog was unaware of what was in the truck, or why Teodoro was there. Teodoro leaned not over the truck, but against it. He leaned back on the fender of the small truck as the snarling dog moved another foot closer and its owner shouted angrily. Teodoro felt secure in his position as one in a chain, a chain that had started long before history had come to be written, one which his grandfather and his father and his new brother and Paulina and Geraldo and Caro were all part of, a chain which, no matter what happened in any one irrelevant second, would go on and on, certain of its ultimate success, secure in its integral justice.

The dog nipped Teodoro's knee, then was leashed back. Its keeper had stopped shouting and was looking at Teodoro's handsome, smiling face in bewilderment.

Everything has its life, Teodoro thought. A butterfly, a lamb bred for the slaughter. Even the child who is taken whilst still at its mother's breast may have had a life in the terms of the weeks that it lived, fuller than a man who dragged on until he was ninety. A good death, the priest in Aldudes had said, was as important as a good life. A good life, a good death, a vague promise of sweetness and eternity. A timeless void. Time. And Paulina, what of her life?

There was a noise.

CHAPTER TWENTY-FIVE

The bus had been almost past them as they emerged between the two rows of houses. Patrick leaped, his hand out. They limped for thirty yards and hobbled on, to an audience of staring faces. Sideways, Patrick edged them towards the back and slid La Esmeralda before him into a window seat, her face creased with pain, her leather briefcase on her lap. Small blotches of blood marked the passage behind them down the aisle.

The bus flashed through Elizondo and along the open road for no more than a kilometre. Patrick saw the unmistakable shape of a Guardia Civil hat. The bus's pneumatic doors flew open. La Esmeralda had put her briefcase on the floor and kicked it beneath the seat in front of her.

'¡*Hola!*'

At least a dozen officers, nearly all with sub-machine-guns stood in front of and beside the bus; three green jeeps blocked the road and funnelled traffic in both directions.

'¡*Hola!*' responded the bus driver to an officer who had come to the first step. He was dressed in green uniform, shining boots laced to mid-calf, the shining tricorn on his head.

'*Es una emergencia*,' the officer was saying, 'an emergency. Terrorists have shot dead a customs guard on the Puerto de Izpeguy.'

'*Madre de Dios*,' the bus driver said, 'Holy Mother of God, where will it all end?'

Patrick closed his eyes. If he opened them he could see the fresh bloodstains on the bus floor, brimming like lakes.

'They are in the area,' the Guardia said, 'three of them, driving a white Volkswagen Golf, the type with the soft top.' His eyes swept the passengers. 'Have you stopped to take anyone on board in the last three kilometres?'

The bus driver shook his head. 'No,' he said with great deliberation. 'No, not since Amaya.' None of the passengers in the bus moved a muscle. 'And from what you're telling me,' the driver continued, 'I think I will keep going until I reach Pamplona.'

'It might be wise,' the Guardia Civil responded. He came to the top step; through the barely opened slits of his eyes Patrick saw him advance two steps down the aisle, but the man's face was on the people, not the floor. Abruptly he turned back. 'It might be wise,' he repeated. 'These people are dangerous – they will kill if they are cornered.' He nodded to confirm his own words, then he saluted smartly. '*Gracias, buenos dias.*'

'*De nada*,' said the bus driver as he pulled slowly through the roadblock and hissed his doors closed. Only once in the mirror did his eyes meet Patrick's.

There were no further roadblocks, but intense military activity was evident.

'They are everywhere,' La Esmeralda whispered as another line of jeeps and troop-convoys passed them going north. 'I cannot get off, they are everywhere.'

Twice in the next hour they passed armoured carriers with helmeted and goggled drivers, head and shoulders protruding out of each steel box on wheels, the snouts of big-bore guns tethered in place. It was dark when the bus reached Pamplona. The driver disembarked them in the shadows of trees and a high wall.

He murmured something as Patrick helped La Esmeralda down the steps.

Patrick nodded. 'What did he say?' he asked her as she leaned against the wall for her breath.

'He said "good luck",' she said, 'in Basque.'

Her legs had stopped bleeding but had stiffened painfully during the journey.

'You should go to a hospital,' Patrick said.

'No!' The grip on his arm was fierce. 'No hospital! There is a safe apartment not far from here.' She cried out as she tried to put weight on her feet. 'Take me there.'

Half-carrying, half-dragging her, they made their way along

the wall, a few yards at a time. Out of nowhere a squad car from the *policia nacional* came around the corner and La Esmeralda flattened against the wall, her arms around Patrick's neck, pulling him in, the sacred briefcase between them.

They left the road and began to make their weaving way through narrow, dark lanes. A few passers-by stared.

'Get on my back,' ordered Patrick.

He bent and allowed her to climb on him, so that her arms clung around his neck and the briefcase swung under his chin. She was a dead weight, her legs hanging uselessly down, but they could travel faster.

They entered an old square, houses on three of its sides, the fourth open and showing the lights of the river valley. La Esmeralda directed Patrick to a corner house and, getting off him, she entered it and dragged herself up the stairs to the very top. There was a rough door. She knocked at it, waited, then knocked again. She grimaced in pain and bent double. 'Kick it in,' she said.

The *apartamento* consisted of one room, a toilet and a clean kitchen. Patrick left her lying on a bed and walked for fifteen minutes before he found a late-night pharmacy where he bought disinfectant, painkillers, bandages and gauze. In a small grocer's he bought packet soup and milk.

The wounds to her legs were serious; Patrick gently sponged her as she lay face-down on the bed.

'*Gracias*,' she cried softly as her tears of pain ran on to the pillow.

Her left leg was torn near the calf-muscle, a deep, raw flesh wound marking the passage of the bullet. Patrick sponged the caked blood away with disinfectant and warm water and then bandaged around with gauze. The other leg was worse: when wiped clean, the bluish black mouth of a wound, swollen all around, stiff and hot, could be seen nine inches below the back of the knee.

'You'll have to go to a hospital or get a doctor,' Patrick said. 'There's a bullet in there.'

'No hospital, no doctor,' she said, her teeth gritted.

He gave her four painkillers; still clothed she slipped under the bedcovers.

As the night wore on, her body began to tremble and jump as

the fever caught her. Patrick soaked a rough towel in a basin and bathed her head and neck, and then helped her peel off her clinging wet dress and underclothes, and took the soaked sheet on which she had lain and hung it over a chair-back near the window. Her body shook uncontrollably. Patrick drew back the sheets on the other bed and pulled the thick-knit over his head. She allowed him to put it on her, to help her lie down again and to take another handful of tablets.

'You are kind,' she gasped, 'you are kind. What is your name?'

Patrick thought quickly. 'Patrick,' he replied.

Suddenly she became distraught. 'Where is the bag?'

'Here,' Patrick said. Her hand was circling and grasping air. He put her fingers around the leather handle.

'*Gracias*, Señor Patrick.' She tried to smile.

'Relax. No one is going to take it whilst I am here.'

'Are you a Basque?'

He had to lean forward to catch the words. 'No,' he answered.

'I can trust you, Señor Patrick,' she said. 'You are kind.' Her eyes were closed. 'This bag,' she said, 'should have been handed over today at Elizondo. The freedom of many people depend on it.'

'Their freedom?'

La Esmeralda had begun to slip into sleep, but snapped awake. 'You must make contact for me, telephone for me, tell them I am safe,' she said.

Patrick watched as she slid under. He arranged blankets on the first bed and kicked off his boots. John Abelson's face kept appearing in his mind's eye, its skin taut and washed by water. Beside him La Esmeralda's breathing had evened off. Quietly Patrick swung his legs off the bed; lifting her unfeeling fingers from the briefcase handle he brought it to the kitchen. It was a soft leather case with a flap and a brass catch. Patrick took a pointed knife from a drawer and began to probe the lock. He could not work out what was inside. What was John Abelson handing over to people who ran the cocaine monopoly of Spain? What had he been killed for? The lock clicked. Patrick peered and frowned. There were plain, brown envelopes, arranged neatly in two fat rows. Patrick listened for the regular breathing around the corner, then dumped the contents out on the table:

all the envelopes were identical and all were sealed. Patrick took the knife, picked an envelope at random and slit it along its bottom seam. Between thirty and forty tiny brown envelopes fell on to the table. Bemused, Patrick tore one open. He blinked at the flash. Fascinated he tipped the brilliant stone into the palm of his hand. Its shape was rounded, but cut with dozens of angles. He picked it up. The diamond was almost the size of his thumbnail; it was blue-white, almost colourless. He held it to the light: it was flawless, an example of perfection.

Patrick opened ten more envelopes. The mound of diamonds on the table glinted and winked like fairytale treasure. Patrick counted what remained: there were thirty. And nine further, larger envelopes.

Repackaging everything, Patrick returned the briefcase to La Esmeralda's side and went to bed.

If Patrick looked right he could see the massive city walls of Pamplona and further on, through a stand of trees, the valley of the River Agra. If he reached out his hand he could touch red, corrugated roof-tiles, a layer of roof in the six-storey building, below the dormer window in which he stood and which overlooked a sprawling, walled medieval convent. The convent had a large garden where two nuns hoed brassicas. There was a courtyard in deep, morning shadow, overlooked by a long window where a line of young and old nuns, black robes and white starch, bent over washing and ironing. Bells rang the hour of ten. On a tiny, sunlit balcony below a woman plucked the dead heads from geraniums and tossed them into the street. The air, the expanse of warm, ochre roof-tiles, the busy nuns; Patrick filled his lungs and closed his eyes.

There was a sharp cough. He turned. La Esmeralda lay on one of the two beds, her black hair spread out around her head. She looked drowsy. Patrick made her warm tea and served it to her from a bowl. He could see one of her legs, puffed up like a tyre.

'This is where you call, Señor Patrick,' she said and recited a number. 'Memorise it. It is Elizondo. You should say: "La Esmeralda is safe – but she wants to know what she should do with the message." Exactly that.'

'Very well.'

'On no account say where you are calling from – their line may be tapped.' She kicked the sheets off her leg, shook her head and pulled the sheets over it again. 'I used to be considered a good-looking woman,' she said and tried to smile.

'You are a good-looking woman.'

'Hah!' She indicated her legs. 'With this? Don't mock.'

'I am not mocking,' Patrick said. 'Repeat the number once more.'

Patrick walked out from the maze of side-streets across a dusty square with trees and benches, out on to a modern thoroughfare. His excitement was palpable: the opportunities represented by the diamonds justified everything. If only he could now get more information, Joe Vendetti's wildest dreams would be achieved.

At every other corner there were groupings, either of Guardia Civil, or police, or troops in trucks. A large-scale mobilisation was taking place. There was a roadblock on a bridge and police were noting the numbers of each car. In the mall of a shopping centre, beside a branch of the Banco de Vasconia, he found a telephone booth. He walked past it and surveyed the crowds for fifteen minutes before making the call. A woman answered. Patrick could discover nothing from her reaction as he spoke his message.

'*¿Entiende lo que he dicho?*' he asked. 'Do you understand what I have said?'

'*Sí.*'

'What is your reply?'

'Is La Esmeralda safe?' the woman asked.

'She is safe but wounded,' Patrick replied. 'She cannot walk.'

'Where is she?'

'I cannot say.'

There was a pause and Patrick could hear a discussion taking place.

'Are you still there?' he asked.

'Tomorrow night,' the woman resumed, 'you must come to the village of Elizondo. Parked directly outside *la panadería*, the baker's shop, will be a small van. Drive right at *la panadería* and continue towards the hamlet of Bealzun. Someone will meet you and take La Esmeralda's message. *Comprende?*'

'*Comprendo, gracias,*' Patrick said and hung up. He was barely able to conceal his jubilation for the next call.

'Georgie?'

'Patrick! Are you all right?'

'Of course I'm all right.'

'Thank God! When you didn't ring I thought . . .'

'Is Joe there?'

'No, he's not.'

'Georgie, listen!' Patrick looked around him. 'Tell Joe that I've discovered more than we could possibly have hoped for.' There was a click. 'Georgie, are you still there?'

'Yes, I'm here. It's this line, it's been funny lately, but Patrick, what have you found?'

'Georgie, not only have I found out how things operate, but I'm with a woman who I think is Marcellino's wife.'

'His wife?'

'I can't explain. She's . . . she's ill. And she's got a collection of diamonds with her that must be worth millions.'

'What are you going to do?' asked Georgie, uneasily.

Patrick thumbed coins into the payphone. 'I'm coming home,' he said, 'tomorrow, and I'm bringing the diamonds home with me.' He could imagine Georgie's face.

'Patrick, is that wise?'

'Georgie, in one move I can stop Basque terrorism being funded for ten years and knock a huge hole in Marcellino's reserves.'

'Patrick . . .'

'Just listen,' Patrick said. 'If I'm stopped coming in with these gems I could find myself in jail without much chance of explaining how I got them. You know Mervyn Lang?'

'Your solicitor?'

'Yes. I want you to ring Mervyn straight away and explain to him what's happening. Tell him I need his help on my way in. I'll ring you in two hours to hear what he's said, OK?'

'All right,' said Georgie as the line went dead.

In a small shop Patrick bought coffee, bread and eggs.

'Why all the activity?' he asked the owner who had been sitting reading a newspaper.

'*El terrorismo*,' the man shrugged, as an armoured personnel-carrier rattled past. 'They're rounding up every known suspect.' He shook his fingertips as if trying to cool them. 'In the last two days,' he said, 'they've really gone too far.'

'Have you got a newspaper?' Patrick asked.

'Take mine,' the shopkeeper said, folding it, 'I'm finished with it. Anyway, I've read it all a thousand times before.' He gave a grudging laugh. 'Ten thousand times before. *Buenos dias.*'

The stone-flagged entrance to the house was warm with the morning sun. A dog lay outstretched on it and opened one eye as Patrick's shadow crossed him. In the bed La Esmeralda was sitting up, her hair tied back, her face expectant when she saw him. She still wore his thick-knit.

'Did you get through?'

Patrick nodded as he put down the bag of groceries. 'Yes.'

'And?'

'I am to call back tomorrow,' he said.

'That is all?'

'That is all.' He smiled at her. 'How is the leg?'

La Esmeralda turned the corners of her mouth downwards. 'I feel nothing.' She looked at Patrick. 'What is happening out there?'

'A lot of troop movement, police, Guardia Civil,' he answered. 'They are stopping cars and rounding up terrorist suspects.'

La Esmeralda sighed. She saw the paper. 'What does the *Diario* say, Señor Patrick?'

'It talks of an *emergencia*,' Patrick said quietly, 'a mobilisation on both sides of the border. "Within the last forty-eight hours",' he read, ' "twelve Spanish police have been slaughtered, five tourists and one terrorist have been blown to bits and the nuclear reactor at Lemoniz has been threatened, all by a faction which call themselves Government of 27 April." ' Patrick paused, then continued: ' "It is time, once and for all, to bring these atrocities to an end." ' He put the paper down.

'It is starting,' the woman said. Her eyes closed, she lay immobile, her profile drawn and grey but beautiful in the sunlight streaming in the window. 'It is starting.'

Patrick sat on the adjoining bed. 'What is starting?' he asked quietly.

Her eyes remained closed. Patrick leaned across and placed his hand on her forehead; she had begun to sweat again.

'I know what is in the briefcase,' he said.

'I know you know, Señor Patrick,' La Esmeralda said. 'I checked it.'

'There is a fortune in there,' Patrick said, 'more than most men could ever imagine.'

'It represents the life's work of a man who has achieved more than most men will ever dream,' La Esmeralda said.

Patrick said, 'Marcellino?'

La Esmeralda did not move.

'I have heard his name whispered like a legend,' Patrick said, 'but until now I did not know if he really existed.'

La Esmeralda sighed. 'Who are you?' she asked. 'You are unusual, you do not fit.'

'You are the second person in ten days to tell me that,' Patrick said.

She lay back wearily. 'I suppose you are a police agent, Señor Patrick, or an *Americano*?'

'No, I am not,' Patrick said. 'I've been doing drugs in Biarritz.'

'Not in Madrid?'

'Never in Madrid.'

'You know Anguila?'

'Anguila? I do not know any Anguila.'

'I do not believe you, Señor Patrick,' La Esmeralda sighed. She lay, looking up at the ceiling. 'However, your motives, whatever they may be, have been transcended by your actions.' She looked at him. 'First you have helped me when you need not have, and then at risk to yourself you have brought me here. You have nursed and cared for me.' The incredible eyes flashed. 'Are you someone on the outside, Patrick, running like me? Probably. Are you someone who has fallen foul of Anguila and who now must run for his life?' She smiled. 'I won't give you away, Patrick. I won't betray you.'

Patrick could not help admiring her courage. 'Tell me about Marcellino,' he said. 'Is he what they say? *El mayor narcotráfico del mundo*, the biggest drugs operator in the world?'

'He is a genius,' she said, 'a real man beside whom all other men are *camorones*, shrimps.' Her face was shining as she spoke. 'He has built what few men have ever built, not for himself but for Euskadi.'

'What is Euskadi to Marcellino?' Patrick asked.

'He was in Guernica,' La Esmeralda said simply. 'He saw what was done to his people.'

'But now he is a drugs lord,' Patrick said.

'What does it matter what he is?' La Esmeralda asked. 'A crime in one country is a way of life in another. People's lives are formed by conditioning and by their expectations. Does it matter if you smoke tobacco or marijuana or opium or if you snort cocaine? We all employ some form of self-destruction to blot out the reality of the hopelessness of the human condition. Why? What is the answer? There is no answer.' La Esmeralda looked straight at Patrick, almost through him. Slowly she reached out and caught his hand. 'The only true measure of a man's integrity, Patrick, is his response to the call of his own destiny.'

'What is your destiny?' Patrick asked, feeling the kneading motion of her thumb on his palm.

'To serve Marcellino,' she replied.

'What is his destiny, then?'

'To free his people.' The reply was simple. A wave of pain crossed her face.

Patrick stood up and went to the window. 'This is hopeless,' he said. 'You are in pain. That bullet has got to come out.'

La Esmeralda shook her head. 'Someone with a bullet wound has to be reported to the police,' she said. 'I cannot risk that until I deliver.'

'You are not going to be able to deliver anything,' Patrick said. He handed her more tablets and a glass of water. 'The Basques will have to come here and collect.'

'The risk is too great,' La Esmeralda said. 'With the present mobilisation they are confined to the mountains. They risked coming down to Elizondo yesterday, but for them to journey to Pamplona endangers not only themselves but the diamonds as well. You saw yourself what is happening outside.' She looked at him. 'Will you help me, Patrick?'

Patrick looked to the window to hide his face. 'If I can,' he said.

La Esmeralda slipped into a sleep which, as the afternoon wore on and the shadows lengthened, grew more fitful.

Patrick crept from the apartment and found a telephone box three streets away. He dialled Georgie's number and waited in puzzlement as it rang out, unanswered.

He returned to the apartment, shuttered the windows and sat

and watched as La Esmeralda kicked and turned, her face a river. He tried not to look at her leg whose toes were now acquiring the darker tinge of the calf above them. He looked at her face: it was mesmerising – no photograph or magazine cover or painting could quite communicate the mixture of beauty and sensuality which was her face. Even now in fever, her eyes closed, she was infinitely desirable, endlessly watchable. Patrick reached out and dabbed her face with a cloth; La Esmeralda kicked off the bedclothes and began to mutter. Patrick drew the clothes back up as she chattered, incomprehensively. Her hair glistened with sweat.

'Where is Cherry?' The question was asked with such clarity that Patrick was sure that she had come awake and was addressing him. 'Cherry – where is Cherry?'

Patrick placed the towel on her brow. 'Who is Cherry?' he asked.

But the fever had not broken; rather it was in full tumult. Several more times in the next twenty minutes La Esmeralda repeated her question, but if her voice was clear, her mind was somewhere far away.

Patrick continued to bathe her until at last her breathing became more regular and she slept.

Night-time sounds replaced those of the day: crickets, the absence of birdsong, the hum of the walled city settling down for its night. Twice more Patrick phoned London but in vain.

Propped in the bed La Esmeralda took a mouthful of the soup which Patrick had prepared. Only the light from the kitchen showed their profiles, hers stooping to drink, his watching. They sat in silence; outside, Pamplona slept.

She handed him the cup and shook her head before he could tell her to finish it. 'I have no appetite,' she said.

Patrick stood. He said, 'It is time those bandages were changed.'

She sat whilst he drew the bedclothes back and spread the sheet from his own bed beneath her legs. Gingerly he peeled off the bandages, first from one leg, then the other. The crusted blood tore from the flesh in scabs and the wounds began to weep red. The left leg looked sore but healthy; the right was puffy, dark and ominous. Patrick cleaned her as best he could, then redressed the wounds with fresh gauze and bandage. Never once did she let him know her pain.

'You are very brave,' he said as she lay back. 'I have some idea of what you must be going through.'

She closed her eyes and shook her head in derision. 'If I succeed in what I am meant to do,' she said, 'it will have been a privilege to have led my life and to have accomplished something.' She collected her hair together in her hands and in a few swift movements wound it in a plait.

'Where have you lived your life?' Patrick asked.

'Mostly in Argentina,' La Esmeralda smiled, 'until I met Marcellino.' She looked at Patrick as if she had just noticed him. 'I loved it then in Argentina,' she said distantly.

'Tell me about it.'

Her eyes sparkled on their own account in the dimness. 'It was a time of youth and freedom,' she said. 'The youth we have nearly forgotten. Looking back, the food was always good in Buenos Aires, the days fine and hot and long but always with a little breeze blowing off the Rio de la Plata. There were parties almost every night and long, lazy weekends out in the Campos des Sierras. It was a time of great love.'

'Is that where you met Cherry?'

Her breathing stopped. 'Where did you hear that name?' she asked.

'From you,' Patrick said. 'When you were in fever.'

La Esmeralda came up on her elbows. 'What did I say?'

'You spoke of Cherry, the whole time it was Cherry; you were looking for him.'

She sank back. 'Cherry,' she said and nodded. 'After all these years I still think of him.' She turned her head. 'When the mind is in fever it goes back,' she said.

'Was he your secret lover?' Patrick asked.

'Not secret. He came as Marcellino's friend – Marcellino, you see . . .' Her head went from side to side. 'It was such a long time ago.'

'You wanted Cherry, but you loved Marcellino,' Patrick said.

'Yes.'

'Why?'

La Esmeralda smiled in the darkness. 'I loved those times,' she said. 'Cherry was an amazing lover, every time he came near me I had a chemical reaction that I couldn't control. He had this *apartamento* on the Avenida Corrientes.' She leaned back and smiled as she recalled. 'Any time I wasn't with Marcellino I was there in the *apartamento* with Cherry.' She smiled. 'Then he went back.'

'Went back?'

'In '62,' La Esmeralda replied. 'He went back to the States. I never saw him again.'

'Why was he called Cherry? Was that his name?'

'I don't know,' she replied. 'I think Cherry may have been where he came from.'

Patrick showed no reaction.

'You see,' La Esmeralda said softly, 'what Marcellino saw in Guernica as a child meant that in almost every other way he became a man, do you understand?'

'I think so,' Patrick said.

'He is unselfish, he understands my needs, you understand?'

'I understand.'

'Cherry was my lover – the best I have ever known – but Marcellino is the only man I have ever loved.' La Esmeralda laughed lightly. 'It is complicated,' she said.

There was silence between them for some moments. 'I have this dream,' La Esmeralda said. 'It is of the day that Marcellino will come back to Euskadi. Because he has promised himself for so long, that day will only happen when the people of Euskadi are free. But on that day that part of Marcellino which has been missing from his body – and his soul – it will be restored. That is my dream.'

Patrick could see the rise and fall of her chest. 'Where is Cherry today?' he asked casually.

'In the States,' she said simply.

'Where? Washington?'

'Yes, Washington,' she replied. 'But now no more questions.'

Patrick went to the small kitchen. He should have felt elated with the information he had just learned, but instead he felt oddly empty. He returned with water and tablets.

'I don't want them,' La Esmeralda said. 'They take away the pain but they make my head spin.'

'You must sleep,' Patrick said.

'I never sleep well alone,' she said quietly.

Patrick put out the light and lay on his bed. He felt exhausted from the need to remember everything which had been said. He lay there, listening to her erratic breathing, smelling her smells, trying not to think.

'Patrick?'

'Yes?'

'What will you do tomorrow?'

'I will call the number. If your friends in Elizondo cannot come for the diamonds, then I will deliver them.' He closed his eyes.

'Patrick?'

In the darkness he turned towards her voice.

'Thank you,' she said simply.

He felt her move.

'Patrick?'

'Yes?'

'I am lonely,' she said in a small voice. 'I am frightened.'

Patrick reached and found her hand as it travelled towards him.

'Pull your bed nearer,' she whispered.

He rose and shoved the two beds together, then lay again, his eyes open, his hand held. The only light was some tiny pinpoints which were able to find their way through the shutters. He kept thinking of Georgie.

'When I was a child, Patrick,' La Esmeralda said, 'we lived in a very small village, a railway junction called Veronica.'

Patrick felt his hand placed in the warmth, next to her.

'In the summer,' she went on, 'it was often so warm that it was difficult to go to sleep. My mother would put out the kerosene lamp, but still I could not sleep. I used to play a game.'

Patrick could feel her warmth, right down his length.

'I would close my eyes very tight,' La Esmeralda said, 'and then try to make out the flashing images, the flying sparks which my closed eyes could see in the dark. I would go to sleep making up stories for myself about these magic pictures.'

Patrick tingled as her fingers ran through his hair.

'My favourite story was about ten thousand little Indians. I closed my eyes and they used to dance.' La Esmeralda laughed. 'Even now when I do it I can see them. You should try.'

'I am trying,' Patrick said, his eyes wide open, 'but I can see nothing.'

He heard her raise herself and then felt a wisp of her hair brush his face as she leaned over him.

'Then let me help you dream,' she murmured and brought her warm mouth down on his.

Patrick closed his eyes. Ten thousand little Indians danced.

La Esmeralda awoke as Patrick stood in the doorway, the light behind him.

'You are going to call them?'

'Yes. I will return and tell you what they say.'

She was drifting back into a feverish sleep as he closed the door. Outside, the tops of trees could be seen beneath the city walls and, further out, the plain, an expanse of whites and yellows and deep rich browns where recently ploughs had broken earth.

He allowed the cobbled lanes to lead him. They wound forever downwards, a mixture of modern shopfronts and glass woven into façades of the sixteenth century. He looked in the shop windows, at the balconies above him and the slim path of blue sky overhead: everywhere he looked he saw her face. She had planted something in him, a yearning, that even now was moving.

Patrick shook his head and tried to clear it. He walked to a little square, more an opening where two lanes met than a square, and sat on an old, stone horsetrough. He was going to steal the diamonds and this made him feel a traitor, a cheat: it would destroy everything she lived for. But what did he owe her? A moment of pleasure? Patrick closed his eyes. She had made love to him in a way that was entirely new. She had exploded his desire in waves of euphoria. At the penultimate moment he had experienced the incredible sensation that she was someone else, a beautiful Spanish woman from far back in his memory, someone who had wrapped him inside her coat, had allowed him to share her smells, had held him warm and close and protected him. This was the creature he had been part of; whose world he was about to destroy. The ultimate desecration. There was a creaking of machinery behind him and the first reverberating chimes of the angelus began to rumble out over Pamplona. They were still ringing when Patrick entered the phonebooth on the Cortés de Navarra. As he dialled he could see the red berets of the special Basque police directing traffic in the distance, and armed, blue-hatted Policia Nacional grouped at the corners of buildings three blocks away. The phone answered on the second ring.

'Hello?'

'Is that you, Joe?'

'Patrick, this is Mervyn Lang.'

'Mervyn? What are you . . . ?'

'Don't say anything, Patrick, above all don't say where you are.'

Patrick felt suddenly giddy. 'Mervyn?'

'Patrick, please listen,' said Lang in his precise, serious voice. 'The line we are speaking on is being listened to, do you understand?'

'Yes,' said Patrick faintly.

'Patrick, you're going to have to brace yourself for some really nasty news.'

Patrick felt his knees give.

'I heard from Georgie last night,' Lang was saying, 'and I think I have an idea of your position.'

'What's the bad news?' asked Patrick quickly. He could hear the solicitor in London take a deep breath.

'Patrick, whoever you're involved with, they've taken her, taken Georgie, and the American.'

Patrick pressed his forehead against the steel of the phone box. 'Taken her?' he said.

'Yes,' answered Lang, sighing again. 'They know that you have their diamonds and they heard you telling Georgie last night.'

'How do you know?' Patrick asked in a shaking voice.

'Because someone has called me,' Lang replied. 'Don't ask me who. The message was loud and clear. Either you deliver the diamonds – and they say you know to where – or Georgie . . . well, they say . . .'

'Go on.'

'I hate to tell you this,' Lang said, 'but I'm afraid I believe her life may be in danger.'

Somehow Patrick managed to stay silent although he was aware that his teeth had almost punctured his tongue.

'There are several options . . .' Lang was saying.

'Mervyn,' said Patrick, 'just tell them I'll do it.' Then he lurched out of the box and was sick on the footpath.

He walked slowly back across the centre of Pamplona, through roundabouts with bright beds of azalias, and over the quiet Cuidadela, thick with feeding pigeons. Georgie gone. Patrick swayed. Georgie taken. He knew he should go home. He tried to clear his mind. He tried not to think about Georgie gone.

Across a dusty square with benches an old man passed Patrick. His head was covered by a flopping Basque beret and the yellow stub of a cigarette was fitted between his lips; as they passed each other the old man's eyes, old shells, locked on Patrick, and the butt quivered as his mouth muttered something. Patrick walked two strides and stopped. He looked back. The old man was at the far side of the square, still going his way, unturning. But whatever he had said had included the words *apartamento* and *policia*.

Patrick began to run. He cut right, down an alley, avoiding the direct route back to La Esmeralda. He pumped along in deep shadow, trying as best he could to muffle the sound of his feet against the stone. As he ran he was conscious of eyes: eyes of dogs, of cats, in one window of goldfish in a bowl, of birds in a cage, the dead eyes in a pig's head on a butcher's tray, the near-dead eyes of a hundred old men and women, gimlet eyes, fastening on him from behind an inch of shutter as he ran flat out and past them.

He ran for three long blocks, then began a curving, left-hand approach which would bring him into the top of a street at the very far end of their square. He turned the final corner and stopped, fighting for his breath. With total prescience he knew what he was going to find. He edged along, houses to his right, and without surprise saw the blue and white colours of police cars, the green trucks, the blue hats, the black tricorns and the guns two hundred yards away. Patrick went as close as he dared. The windows and doors on either side of him were tightly shuttered and locked. In one house, just as he went by, a baby cried from the ground-floor room. Patrick leaned against someone's door and tried to focus. Every reserve and pocket of energy had been drained from him. He blinked as the sun moved over a roof and hit him.

A commotion was taking place at the door of their building: first the dog came trotting out, then armed soldiers who took up defensive positions, and finally two further police, their pistols in white hip-holsters, their arms cradling the sitting figure of La Esmeralda.

Nothing more.

Patrick watched mute as they put her into the back of a car. He remained part of the pavement as the blue revolving strobe-lights came alive, and as the armed men, walking briskly backwards, jumped into their truck, and the convoy pulled away.

Patrick waited ten minutes and then walked into the square and leaned on its wall looking out on the Agra. He waited. After twenty minutes, two men, one in a suit, emerged from the door of the building; he carried a briefcase. It was a cheap, shining, black affair, box-shaped with chrome locks.

Patrick waited another hour. No one came or went. Shutters began to open, there was the sound of voices, a woman with a pram came to sit and look out on the valley, the dog resumed his place on the step.

Patrick took the stairs two at a time. He knew that every moment inside increased his risk. His adrenalin surging, he splintered the door inwards, causing the gleaming new police padlock to fly into the room.

It took thirty seconds to verify the evidence of his eyes: the brown briefcase had not come out with La Esmeralda, but neither was it there.

Patrick stopped at the bed. Her smell was almost tangibly sweet. He turned. The window which had allowed in the early sun was now closed and shuttered. Patrick opened it inwards and then flung the shutters out: the upper air of Pamplona hit his face and the vista of spires and roofs sprung up as if to say they had always been there.

Patrick cast left and right, his instincts guiding him. His fingers grasped the wooden windowframe and he stared down. Deep shadow had enveloped one part of the convent garden, but the other end was still bright, and in it, at her brassicas, a nun hoed. A wooden wheelbarrow stood beside her, and on the pile of weeds which it contained stood the briefcase.

Sunlight hit Patrick's eyes. He closed them tight as if he could not believe what he was seeing. Ten thousand Indians danced. He ran for the stairs.

CHAPTER TWENTY-SIX

Using the water in the toilet cistern to sluice the razor, Patrick stretched the skin beside his right ear and began to scrape the beard from his face. He squinted into the small vanity mirror; he had purchased it together with the razor, an aerosol of shaving cream, a pair of scissors, a needle and thread and a raincoat.

He pulled the blade downwards, surprised at how easily the soft face hair lifted off, leaving the skin beneath smooth and fresh. He shaved very slowly, careful to avoid a telltale path of patched cuts; when he finished he wiped himself off with toilet paper, took the scissors and went to work on his hair.

The toilet was in the basement of the Estación de Autobuses on Pamplona's Conde Oliveto. It was five minutes' walk from the post office in which he had just spent fifteen minutes and over two minutes by bus from the convent garden, the high wall of which he had scaled via a tree and surprised the gardening nun, a very old woman with a lined face very like one of her cabbages.

'*Perdóname*,' Patrick had said pleasantly, 'but I think this is mine.'

The nun looked up at him; for an instant Patrick thought she was going to scream, but all that happened was that her head came forward in a nod.

'*Gracias*,' Patrick said and turned, with the briefcase.

'*De nada*,' the old woman muttered.

In the distance they could both hear the siren from a police car. As Patrick walked to the wall he heard her say something else. He turned. Her face was down to the earth, but she had said, '*Goro Euskadi*! Long live Euskadi!'

Patrick chopped the last uneven spike of his hair and examined himself. He looked like someone who cut his own hair. He ran his palm over his smooth chin. He wished he had bought some aftershave.

Removing his pullover and T-shirt he went to work with the needle and thread. Turning the T-shirt inside out he folded its end upwards on itself, creating a pocket all around about ten inches deep. Now he bent and removed the diamond envelopes from the briefcase which sat on the lidded toilet. He placed them upright, one at a time in the fold of the T-shirt, then looped the thread in and out, first with stitches far apart, then more tightly, until eventually the T-shirt looked like a clumsy corset. He turned it right-side-out, put it on, then the pullover. He put on the raincoat, stuffed everything into the briefcase, flushed the toilet, left the cubicle and by a supreme effort of will contained the urge to bolt back in again: two Guardia Civil stood in the washroom, one smoking, one washing his hands. Patrick made himself put the briefcase on the floor and filled a basin. The policemen looked at him briefly. They were discussing their duty roster.

'They say five hundred extra troops are being switched from Catalonia,' one said.

'Not a minute too soon,' his companion remarked.

Patrick walked slowly up the red-tiled steps into the daylight, grateful for the fresh air which felt momentarily strange against his face. In the terminus the departure lounge for Elizondo was already half-full. Patrick made his way towards it, walked the long way around, dumped the briefcase in a hand-wheeled garbage cart and boarded the bus which would bring him back to the Pyrenees.

Dusk had not yet gathered as they pulled out. They left the sparse, industrial suburbs of Pamplona and immediately began to climb the foothills, small, climbing fields bordered often with stone walls, home to milking cows and horses, all with neck bells, and small sheep with long fleeces and gracefully curving horns.

Straight away there was a roadblock. On a stretch of road between mountain bends, three jeepfuls of Guardia Civil were stopping traffic in both directions and scrutinising the occupants of each vehicle. Two officers, looking like men playing Napoleon at a fancy dress, climbed into the bus and strode down the aisle, gravely assessing each face. Patrick looked up at them briefly, then returned his attention to the *Diario de Navarra*. As the bus pulled slowly away uphill Patrick read the main story, about the pot-boiler which the Basque country had become, described variously as 'tinder-ready', 'a rapidly burning fuse', or 'a crate of explosives ready to blow'.

The bus climbed higher in the approaching dark, breasting hills which caught the evening sun at the expense of the valleys below. They detoured into sleepy villages where houses had low eaves and pigs grazed in paddocks lined by hydrangeas. The bus doors hissed open, admitting passengers, messages and the smell of dung. It was a mirror-image of the bus which he had taken two days ago with La Esmeralda; if he looked hard he imagined he could see the dull, red stains of her blood, traced in a line from the pneumatically operated doors.

The further they went, the more he thought of Georgie gone. The interior lights had come on so that now his own reflection was the first thing he could see in the bus window. The vehicle's wheels took on a rhythm. Georgie gone. They had begun to descend, through rows of winding hedges, visible if he pressed his face to the glass. Georgie taken. Georgie gone. Georgie taken. Georgie gone. They passed churches and graveyards. It was night as they crossed the floor of the valley of Baztan and the bridge of the River Ibur. At nine they reached Elizondo.

From the window of the café Patrick could see almost all of the main street. Shops in Elizondo were still open for business, including a *panadería*, opposite the café and about thirty metres north; except for a truck and a motorcycle the kerb was empty. There was constant troop movement through the town, all heading northwards: at one stage a long line of trucks, armoured Land Rovers and high-wheeled, steel-plated transports suitable for mountain terrain streamed past. Guardia Civil shot up and down in both directions. A squad car of the Policia Nacional stopped outside the café and a policeman holding a map came inside and asked the owner for directions.

'*Mucho movimiento*,' Patrick said to the landlord when the man came to wipe off his tabletop. The man's eyes flicked over Patrick, then he nodded faintly and continued with his work in silence.

One by one the shops extinguished their lights and locked up for the night. In some cases lights came on upstairs, over the shopfronts; in others their owners pocketed their keys and ambled down the street. The baker was one of these, a short man in a striped dustcoat, hardly the terrorist type, a man going home to his wife and bed, knowing he would have to be up early to bake for the village.

There had been no sign of soldiers or police for over twenty minutes. At the café bar a group of leather-faced men in black berets drank small glasses of liquor and chided each other in Basque. Patrick finished his third coffee. He was at once on edge and calm to the point of detachment, often the same as he felt before he fought: in control, but conscious of the necessity of keeping the body on charge alert. He shifted and felt the shape of the package around his chest. He checked across the street for the hundredth time; far above and behind the unchanged scene he could see distant lights in the mountains, twinkling.

There was an engine noise in the street. A bus, maybe the same one which had earlier brought him, returning south to Pamplona. It was parked at the far kerb, concealing *la panadería* from view. The bus doors hissed and then it pulled away in a cloud of dust and exhaust. Patrick blinked. It was as if a magician had caused stage to be filled with smoke; as it cleared the lonely outline of a tiny van could be seen standing outside the baker's shop.

Patrick left the café and walked northwards, keeping to the same side. After five minutes he had nearly cleared the town. He crossed the road and walked back, keeping tight to the shadows. A car approached and its lights swept him – Patrick tried not to turn his face away. He passed an electrical shop, a butcher's and then a row of houses. A launderette was still doing business; he had not noticed it as it was in the gable of a building hidden from the café. The door of the launderette opened and a young woman came out, almost colliding with Patrick. She had dark hair, big eyes, a white angular face; something hung on a chain around her neck. Patrick murmured his excuses and stepped around her. More lights caught them, this time from a truck as it rounded the bend of the village and steamed on its way northwards.

There was a narrow alleyway, left; the baker's was next, so Patrick assumed that this was the alleyway he had been told to take. The van sat innocently, partly illuminated by a pool of yellow street light. Opposite, in the café, the men still sat at the bar. Patrick put his hand to the van door. Behind him there was a siren noise. Not daring to look, Patrick opened the door and got in. Now he looked in the direction of the noise: it was at the other end of the village. He thought he could see a police car's lights, illuminating the pavement and the legs of the girl from the launderette who had stopped walking.

Patrick tried to concentrate. Keys hung from the dashboard. He turned them. Lights came on in the dashboard but there was an absence of any noise. He turned the key several times: the lights went on and off. Ahead he could see uniforms, less than a hundred yards away. He turned the key, wrenching it. There was nothing. He stared around him, looking for an alternative starting switch. He flicked the key again, swearing savagely. Then he felt something which must have been there from the start – a mild vibrating of his seat. Flicking on his sidelights Patrick let out the clutch on the battery-powered van and swung into the alleyway.

The drive up the walled, rising lane was eerily silent. The van made no sound: a slight tingling sensation in the seat and steering-wheel were the only indication that an engine was at work. After less than a hundred metres the village fell away and Patrick was climbing a hillside on a path surfaced with rough stone. The vehicle's wheels slushed through heavy cow dungs as they wound higher into a deeper night. Above there were stars, but either side and below there was only plunging darkness and the glow of Elizondo.

Patrick concentrated on maintaining an even speed, afraid to push on the incline and strain the battery. He willed them higher, his eyes fastened on the pitted track ahead, searching the margins of light for whoever he was meant to meet.

He was on an incline which shot straight up into the mountain's darkness. All at once there was a flash, then a light moving up and down, dead ahead. Patrick slowed. He could now see two or three people, men, standing in his path, one of them signalling him down with the torch. Patrick pulled up and slid the window open.

'¡*Hola*!' he said, his mouth dust.
'¡*Hola*!'

One of the men stepped towards the van. From Patrick's position two things then happened together: there was a deafening report and the approaching man collapsed at the knees.

'¡*Mierda!*'

The scream was from one of the remaining figures as a second shot thunderclapped and then a third. Patrick stared uncomprehendingly as the two men fell skew-ways. Then the van's door was wrenched open and the small vehicle shook as someone crashed into the passenger seat.

'¡*Adelante!* Go on!'

Patrick's mechanism for response had deserted him.

'¡*Adelante!*' His passenger slapped the steering wheel with force.

Patrick stood on the pedal and they jumped ahead. He turned and tried to speak but found he could not.

'¡*Canalla!*' his passenger said and spat. 'Filthy drugs peddlers! Quick! The shots will have been heard!'

Patrick glanced and saw his passenger sitting forward, his hands on the dash, peering out; he was an enormous, young-faced man with thick black curly hair and forearms like ten-pound salmon. 'Filthy scum!' he repeated.

Patrick was concentrating so hard that at first he did not notice the stabbing lights behind. They were below him now, but clearly visible, twin lights close together, a jeep's lights and the noise of a roaring engine. The road had become steeper and the van hesitated on a corner before recapturing its momentum. Patrick saw a sloping wall of red earth, rock outcroppings and bushes of scrub and thistle as they swept up and around another bend.

His passenger was staring ahead.

'Careful!'

Patrick followed his gaze and suddenly saw the reason for the caution. A deep, black trench was cut into the road ahead, horizontally – a drainage trench, it appeared, from the large pipe sections which lay along the roadside. As they came closer they could see two boards laid flat across the cutting. Patrick felt a pain in his gut as suddenly the lights of the following jeep dazzled full beam on the mirror.

'Cross it!' the huge man shouted. 'Cross it quick!'

Patrick inched the van forward, praying that he had lined up right.

'Drive!'

It was impossible to see down. There was a sensation of swaying and then of a void. The engine of the pursuing jeep was deafening. Patrick went for it; the van purred over the chasm and lurched off the other side.

'Wait!'

His passenger had readied the door open; now he caught the frame and pulled himself out. There were shouts behind. Patrick turned. The scene was partly illuminated by the headlights of the jeep and by a searchlight mounted on its roof. The enormous passenger bent to grab one of the heavy planks; he lifted it skywards and tossed it like a caber, down into the valley.

'*¡Alto!*'

There was the rattle of a gun-breach. Wildly, Patrick looked around for a way of escape.

'Come on!' The big man was running beside the van, physically pulling it with him up the mountain. The van crept forward pitifully.

'*¡Alto y entregense!* Halt and give yourselves up!' The order echoed through a megaphone.

Patrick depressed the van's accelerator as far as it would go. Then he saw the running man drag at his waistband, turn, and loose off half a dozen rounds in the direction of the trench. There was an explosion as the searchlight fizzled and went out. A bend loomed ahead. The small vehicle was trying to graduate from a crawl. The big man put both his hands to it. Feet could be heard running behind, shouting voices and then gunfire. The tinny shell of the van pinged to the impact of bullets. The bend was made. Giving the van a final push, the big man opened the door and crashed into his seat.

'*¡Mierda!*' he said. 'Can't this thing go any faster?'

'It can't!' Patrick cried. 'Not on a hill like this!'

They continued to climb. Gradually they regained darkness and silence. The big man's breath came more regularly. Patrick felt a hand on his shoulder.

'*Eskerrik asko*,' he said. 'Thank you.' He checked behind. 'Have you brought a message from La Esmeralda?'

Patrick nodded and patted his chest. 'Yes.'

'Don't worry,' the big man said, 'you are with friends.' As he spoke he thumbed a fresh load into the chambers of his pistol.

The road had levelled off in high mountains, a widened track rather than a road, its surface often shining rock or slippages of shingle from the cliffs above. The valley side fell away sharply but in the darkness one could only imagine the precipice which lay beneath. No lights or sounds or signs of human habitation broke the surrounding night. The only sound was of their breathing and of the van's wheels as occasionally it crunched over stone. Gradually the headlights became perceptibly weaker and momentum began to decrease.

'Listen!'

It was Patrick who heard it first. They stopped and slid open the windows. The clatter-clatter sound of a helicopter was echoing in the night and growing louder.

The big man raised a finger. '*Milicia*,' he said. 'A Sikorsky. Hurry! – and kill your lights!'

They bumped along but at much reduced speed, sometimes climbing, sometimes on level ground. The van's heart, its battery, was dying, exhausted by its load and the murderous uphill task. Although the night was clear there was no moon and more than once Patrick had to lurch left to avoid the lip of the ravine. The helicopter's noise rose and died, climbed and fell.

'They're searching,' the big man said. 'We have less than a kilometre to go.'

Suddenly the van slumped sideways to a stop. Patrick attempted to reverse but the left front wheel had gone into a culvert. Patrick's companion levered himself out and with one hand picked the front of the vehicle up and out of the drain. Then he stood like a huge beast, motionless, scenting the night. Patrick heard the chopper's engine, heavy duty, then, regretting the day he had been born, he saw the downward light beam, prodding through the trees, turning the night beneath it into day.

'Over the next hill!' The big man's weight rocked them again and they crawled forward, but now only slightly faster than running pace. The track wound under a hill bluff. There was a terrifying roar and then they were abruptly caught, only for a second but squarely caught in a blinding white beam of light.

'Keep going!'

Mercifully the gradient was in their favour and the van picked up speed and fairly hurtled into the next bend. Patrick's foot was part of the floor and as they turned the van banked and he nearly lost her. The Sikorsky was turning steeply and its light operator was angling his beam, probing, following the line of the track. The bend hid them for an instant but suddenly it was daylight everywhere and thunder overhead. The big man leaned out of the opened door and began to fire repeatedly at the dogged light.

'Keep going!' he kept shouting. 'Keep going!'

Then the chopper began to return fire.

The track was a straight, level run, mountain to the left, plunging valley to the right. The Sikorsky had again banked, out beyond them, and was coming with a run, its searchlight transfixing the van like a fly on a pane of glass. The big man sat, his door jammed open with his foot, the gun in his hand pumping at the light in the sky. Patrick heard the click of an empty chamber. Then without warning the van was caught, lifted as if by a puff of wind, turned right around and slammed in against the cliff face. Patrick felt a sickening thud and a jagged pain somewhere near his belt. He put out his hands and felt broken glass. In horror he became aware that the impact had crushed the steering wheel and dashboard in on top of him and that he was unable to move.

'I'm caught!' he cried.

He felt fear and giddiness at once. He was completely pinioned, trapped. They were in a bright pool of light. Through the clattering din above them someone was shouting through a megaphone. The passenger door was jammed tight to the rock; Patrick watched speechlessly as his enormous companion punched out the windscreen on his side and then began to fire his gun again. The helicopter, a massively dark shape behind its blinding light, surged up and away, back out over the valley.

'I'm caught! I'm fucking caught!' Patrick shouted. He tried to use his arms; everything below his waistline was wet and sticky, but surprisingly there was no pain. Something in his mind flipped.

'I can't feel anything!' he screamed.

He watched in mute awe as the chopper banked and readied for its final swoop. With all the strength at his disposal Patrick tried to lever himself up but his efforts were fruitless. He watched as the big man with the boy's face yet again filled the empty chambers of his gun. The Sikorsky's engine changed tempo. It pivoted on its nose and began its homing kill.

'Jesus, help me to get out!' Patrick cried. 'Help me!'

The Sikorsky's guns began to speak.

Then there was another sound and another light.

The sound was a thump, muffled but loud enough to be heard above the helicopter's engines and guns. The light was a streaking, red-hot tail of flame. There was an explosion which stopped the big, iron whirlybird dead in its tracks and lighted up the valley above Elizondo like the sun at noon. In the van the two men gaped. The Sikorsky's engines screamed as it fought to stay aloft, then slowly its searchlight began to turn upwards as lost its rotational axis and went over on its airborne back.

'*Se aluia!*' hissed the big man, with venom.

The chopper began to drop, first in slow motion, then faster, roaring as it fell into the void. There were a series of smaller explosions and then, far below them, the fireworks of a hundred million sparks as the stricken Sikorsky hit high-tension power lines, bounced off them and in a massive ball of orange flame, rolled into its grave that was the valley.

'The SAM,' the big man grinned. 'We got them with the SAM.'

Patrick was barely conscious. He was lightheaded from shock and from the letting of his life's blood below his waist. He saw shadows, heads and shoulders, heard other, urgent voices and saw his companion crawl out of the van by the window. Hands grasped Patrick's upper body.

Men spoke quietly to each other in a strange tongue. His coat was cut across the shoulders by a razor-edged knife. He felt his pullover being removed, then the precious T-shirt. Two large figures came to the front of the small van, reached inside to grasp the one-time dashboard and hauled. Patrick could feel pressure being relieved. The men pulled again, inching the steel frame outwards, their movements guided by someone who stood by Patrick's naked shoulder and kept up a constant stream of meaningless but reassuring words.

He was lifted out. They held him. A man shook his head. Another man swore and spat into the valley. The two big men who had freed him went one each end of the van caught it up and tossed it over the precipice.

He was lying on something looking up at stars. He had no idea how old he was, or where he was, or who he was. He was moving along but he didn't know if the movement was forward or back.

But there was no pain. Just a black sky. And brilliantly bright stars. Some of which were turning green.

PART FIVE
The Snow Bees

CHAPTER TWENTY-SEVEN

In the beginning there was birdsong. The repeated song of a warbling bird, somewhere near, the centre of all meaning, the beginning.

Everything was white. The walls, the ceiling, the bedclothes. His hands, if he could raise them high enough to look at them.

When the pain came it came in a great rolling peal of noise, heard before it was felt. It came every day. And every night. He thought he was losing to it until he somehow realised that as each day ended the gaps between the rolling pain had minutely lengthened. Terror visited every two hours instead of one. Instead of three capsules he was given two.

He had no memory, just images. Time had become irrelevant — unless it was the gap between bouts of agonising pain.

There were two sets of images. The first ones were of his former life. Sea, sand, his beautiful mother, infinite happiness now strangely recaptured in the strange half-life which his existence had become. He had lain then, staring up, asking to be picked. He lay now, the white ceiling his field of vision, and was lifted and turned effortlessly. In the meaningless time which he knew must be the present, a happiness like the gas from a cannister sealed thirty years ago had returned.

The second images were of violence, explosions at night, movement through darkness, rough hands and gentle. There had been a vaulted crypt which he first thought was a morgue, a tent of stone with the white-chalked forms of running animals inscribed magically on its sides. There was a ballooning, oddly shaped emblem, made from metal, almost like a swastika, dangling near his eyes, the smell of a woman, sweet, and the pain of a needle, sharp. There was more movement, daylight, darkness, hushed voices, the smells of antiseptic, pain, the feel of clean linen under his head but nowhere else, feelings of detachment, sweat, and the fear of incomprehension.

The stand at the left side of the bed with its clear, plastic bag of liquid and the tube running from it to the needle embedded in the vein in his arm had always been there. He had been born with the catheter which ran from beneath the bedclothes to somewhere underneath the bed.

Each day he tried to reconcile the faces who smiled down at him, but the next day they were meaningless and new and he had to start all over again.

Life, apart from the pain, was pleasantly uncomplicated. He lay there. He did nothing. No eating or bodily functions. No talking or deciding, no duty to be done. His mind floated like featherdown.

The happiness, although present, irritated him deliciously. Why was he so happy? Days, weeks perhaps, were spent on this theorem. As his body was turned and nursed and new veins were sought and he was washed and spoken to, kindly, his mind grappled with two irreconcilable propositions. The first was that he was happy because everything that was being done for him was being done by his mother. The second was that his mother had stepped on a charter flight in Manchester years ago and with two hundred other people had died when the plane ploughed into a mountain in Tenerife.

Pain alternating with happiness. His mind had no fixed abode. Until one night, as he lay suspended in his new world of darkness and light, the monster had come out of the cave and had begun to tear with its teeth at his bowels and there was a pain whose voice would not be denied, a screaming which echoed back into the cave and brought running feet and concerned, chattering voices.

CHAPTER TWENTY-EIGHT

Washington D.C.

Mike Izaguirre sat at his desk, glumly. Despite himself, every day for at least fifteen minutes his thoughts returned to the same subject. He had done everything. Everything. The conclusion which he tried to force himself to accept, as a reasonable man, depressed him inordinately. Izaguirre sighed. He had used all the means at his disposal to verify even one small fact which might make this hypothesis acceptable. He had contacted Interpol; the FBI and the CIA; the DEA. He had been in touch with police departments in every state of the union. The simple absence of any other theory was now, inexorably, forcing him to accept something which by instinct he was loath to: Joe Vendetti had disappeared and he was never going to learn why or how. He shook his head in frustration. If someone had called up to tell him that Joe Vendetti was orbiting Venus in a Russian probe, he would have been happier than he was now.

He shook his head again, then began to tackle the mound of unattended paperwork in front of him.

CHAPTER TWENTY-NINE

He heard the birdsong as if for the first time. The girl who held him upright, her arm firmly around his shoulders, had a pale, angular face and very large, dark eyes. She held him with her left arm while with her right she spooned a minute portion of something smooth and milky into his mouth. Whatever it was could not have been rough but it tore his throat savagely.

'*Bueno.*' The girl smiled her encouragement. 'Good.'

He tried another spoonful, then shook his head weakly and lay back. For the first time he noticed the copper clover-leaf at her bare neck. He lay back, exhausted, and watched her. She was familiar although he knew he had never seen her before.

'That was good,' she said again, 'very good. Another few spoonfuls and in a few days we can do without this altogether.'

He followed her glance to the stand at the bedside with its inverted, transparent pack. He watched, without surprise, as now she came to the bed and gently drew the sheets down to his knees. 'So how is it today?' she asked. 'I think it is better,' she said, not waiting for an answer, not expecting one.

He lay inert, unashamed as she removed his bandages, washed him gently, turning him easily, towelling him dry. He noticed something yellowish and stick-like on his chest. He blinked as he realised that it was his wrist. He felt warm comfort as she replaced the sheets over his bare chest and then, with a small plastic brush, stroked the hair of his head.

Patrick awoke feeling ravenous.

'You must eat very slowly,' she said. '*El doctor* has warned. Your throat, here,' she ran her hand down her long neck, 'it has shrunk from not being used. You must go very slowly.'

He ate the contents of the bowl, unmindful of its lacerating pain. Then he lay back and stared in horror at his stomach; the part he could see that was not bandaged was leaping around and hissing. The girl had put her small hand flat on it.

'That is also expected,' she said gently. 'Try not to be afraid. It will pass.'

She stayed with him as his stomach recovered from its shock.

'Is this a hospital?' Patrick asked.

The girl smiled. 'No,' she replied.

His mind, up to now a pleasant, unconcerned blank, suddenly re-activated, humming with demands.

'Where am I?' Patrick asked.

'In the house of a friend, near the village of Isla on the coast of Cantabria,' the girl said. She produced a cloth and used it to wipe the sweat which had gathered on his forehead.

'What is your name?' Patrick asked.

'Paulina.'

'Paulina.' Patrick tried to smile. 'Paulina. You are both beautiful and kind.'

Her lips parted showing sparkling, even teeth. '*Gracias*,' she replied.

The fingers of his right hand probed, beneath the sheets, his chest, his rib-cage. In a burst of panic he sat upright, pulling the sheet down, and stared at his emaciated torso.

'Jesus Christ!' he shouted. 'I'm a skeleton!' The sudden movement caused the needle from the feeding drip to spring from his arm. Paulina caught him by both shoulders and, without difficulty, pressed him back on to the pillows.

'*Calma*,' she murmured, 'easy.'

'How long have I been here?' Patrick gasped.

Paulina sat on the bed, refitted the needle, taped it in place and then turned to him, smiling. 'Quite a long time,' she answered, 'but better than eternity in a grave which you very nearly had.'

'How long?'

'Over three weeks,' the girl replied gently, her head nodding.

'Three weeks.' Patrick needed time to try and absorb what she had said. 'Three weeks. So this is . . .'

'*La ultima semana de Noviembre*,' she replied, 'the last week in November.'

'And who are you? I mean, why are you nursing me?'

'You very nearly died, Señor Patrick.'

Patrick stared at her. 'Yes, but if this is not a hospital, why am I here? What is happening?' he asked, sounding stupid.

'Do you not remember?' she asked, always smiling. 'Tell me what you last remember.'

Patrick stared at her again. He remembered being in Scotland. All at once he felt dread. He was out of a job. Georgie. Georgie. Taken. Again he sat up, bewildered.

'I remember . . .'

'*Calma, calma.*'

'Am I . . . all right?' Dimly he was aware that all along they had been speaking Spanish.

'Yes, believe me, you are. It will take time. But beneath it all you are still strong. Your memory, it too will come.'

'But I remember nothing.'

'You will.'

'Help me.'

Paulina sat. She caught both Patrick's hands in hers, firmly, her confidence flowing into him. 'Do you remember La Esmeralda?' she said.

Then Patrick began to remember.

The days became ordered, the nights easier to put by. The room was sparse and square. It had one window which overlooked a small, badly kept garden, which in turn was overlooked on its other side by windows which were always shuttered. The days were warm, the nights could be cold. Daylight came at just after seven each morning, stayed less than ten hours, then abruptly left. Sounds: voices, clucking hens, the occasional drone of a tractor, a ginnet who screeched dawn and dusk. Smells: sanitised bandages which held his guts in, antiseptic, the dull, musty smell of the bags and vessels into which his body fluids drained, sick smells, and beyond them, if he concentrated, floor wax, cooking, kerosene, maybe garlic.

And the people. Paulina, for whom no task was too repulsive. A woman who cooked and who Paulina referred to as *señora*. And once, when they thought he was asleep, a familiar, enormous figure with black curly hair and a child's face at the bedroom door.

'Who knows I am here?' Patrick asked Paulina.

'No one,' she said with a small smile.

'No one? Who . . . ? Why . . . ?'

'You are a lucky man, Señor Patrick,' Paulina said quietly. 'Here you can hide, can recover.'

'Hide?' Patrick's mouth felt dry.

'There are others who seek you,' Paulina whispered. 'From as far away as Madrid.'

'I must call Georgie,' Patrick said, half to himself. Then reality crushed him as he realised that Georgie was not there and that even if he tried to call Mervyn Lang he would probably be giving his location away.

'You wish to call someone?' Paulina asked.

'No,' Patrick said, exhausted. 'Until I am well again I cannot call anyone.'

One afternoon a doctor came. Young, fair-haired, ill at ease. Paulina stood over him as he peeled off the bandages and examined the crimson-mouthed wounds.

'How is the pain?' he asked.

'Every day I try to win another minute,' Patrick said.

The doctor shook his head. '*El estómago*,' he sighed as if the stomach was the one part of the anatomy which he had always regretted having to deal with. 'Heart transplant is easy compared to *el estómago*.' He shone a light down Patrick's throat. 'It still has to stretch,' he said, making claws of his hands and pulling them outwards. 'How is the food?' he asked Paulina.

'Better,' she said.

The doctor looked at the feeder, then down at Patrick's body. 'Very well. From tomorrow discontinue the artificial feeding, but only as long as he continues to eat.' He opened his bag and gave Paulina bottles filled with tablets.

'What about this?' Patrick asked, pointing to the tube from his side.

'In a couple of weeks,' the doctor said, 'when everything inside you is knitted and free, then it is a small job to reverse that.'

'It is a nuisance,' Patrick said. 'It is uncomfortable.'

'Uncomfortable! A nuisance!' the doctor laughed. He turned to Paulina. 'Have you told him what a nuisance he was, eh?'

But Paulina's eyes silenced him. As the young doctor left the room Patrick saw a big profile standing, waiting outside the door, and recognised his companion of the trip in the van up the mountain from Elizondo.

Patrick began to absorb information as the days wore on. His memory had reached a point where he was sure there were no gaps. Physically he was outrageously weak, barely able to move in the bed, needing the help of Paulina to swing his legs over the side and sit for a minute. Gradually pains were replaced by sores and aches. He could not lie without a cushion beneath his backside; the stitches in his belly began to itch; every time he ate a runny meal the wind-pains in his intestines cramped him up in agony, so badly that he cried out.

Most of the time, Patrick and Paulina occupied the house alone. The *señora* came in each day, including Sundays; the enormous youth with the child's face, whose name Patrick learned was Caro, came and went, every couple of days.

The doctor was from Santander, Paulina said. He had performed the operation on Patrick, with another doctor, a great friend of the cause, in a hospital near Santander at the dead of night, so that not even the regular hospital staff knew it had taken place.

Paulina got Patrick walking. At first they must have looked a ridiculous sight, the thin girl supporting the emaciated man with the rubber legs. But she hauled him up and down the room, and when one day he shakily stood, she applauded him like a little boy who had done something clever, and like a little boy he had beamed.

Depression swept him in black, ugly waves. He looked at his ruined body and tried to come to terms with the sequence of events which had brought him to where he was. He thought of Georgie, somewhere still alive – nothing else was thinkable. He thought of Pamplona and La Esmeralda, and her calling out for Cherry. Cherry: was Cherry Kahan? In Washington, betraying trust, responsible for everything, including Alan Ridgeway's death? How could this be proven?

Patrick drew his hands unsteadily through his hair. He was confused. Somehow, he could not explain why, the proof was here in Isla.

Patrick felt fear. He felt the cold of a north London cemetery.

A Catholic priest; a freezing altar-boy holding the holy water; and Patrick Drake. No one else. After a life of not quite sixty years, no one. Not a single, solitary representative of the good times, the old days, the laughter, the honest ambition, the days in Clifden, the horrifying decline, or the last, futile, mind-splitting struggle. What would Mama have thought had she lived? *No one.* Patrick felt terror. Drake and Son would both die in the same way: friendless and unmourned. Patrick began to weep.

There was a sound he could not at first identify. Patrick put on a faded robe and shuffled towards it. He reached the door of the kitchen and stopped. Paulina was sitting on a stool, her back to him. Patrick could discern her sobs above the excited, staccato tones of the newsreader's voice on the radio.

He tried to creep away, but Paulina heard him. Her face was unrecognisable from the one that had tended him an hour before.

'It is over,' she sobbed, not caring how he saw her. 'For us it is over.'

Patrick turned down the jabbering radio. He knelt beside Paulina. 'Caro?'

Paulina shook her head. 'Caro is safe,' she replied. 'He sent word an hour ago. He was in the mountains.' Her eyes and nose were red. 'You should be in bed,' she sniffed.

'It is now my turn to help you,' Patrick said.

His arm around her thin shoulders, he led her to a more comfortable chair and lighted the kerosene stove. He took a kettle, filled it with water and brought it to a gas ring. He came and sat beside her. Her face came up to look at him; in the weeks before it had been a bright, alive face, full of giving; now in distress, it was small, expressionless, dead.

'We have lost everything,' she whispered.

'Tell me,' Patrick said. 'Who were they?'

'First there was Geraldo,' she sobbed, 'and then . . . and then there was Teodoro.' She choked on the last name, closing her eyes and clenching her fists until their knuckles stood out. 'Now Xalbador,' she resumed in a whisper. 'He was in Bilbao, trying to negotiate some of your diamonds for cash. Sainz Perez's men betrayed him to the *franguinistas*. He is . . . dead.' Her tears flowed uncontrollably.

Patrick poured rough wine into glasses, added sugar and topped the mixture up with the boiling water. Paulina took the glass between her hands and stared into the bluish flame of the stove.

'Teodoro,' she said distantly. 'We were to have such a great life together.'

As the evening shadows began to creep and the little kitchen drew further in around the stove, Paulina's halting voice was at first the only sound.

Patrick forgot his own pain and listened. Every sentence she spoke was another layer of healing on the grief which she had concealed from him for all the weeks she had nursed him. She spoke and he listened.

It was the first time that Patrick had spent more than a minute or so in the kitchen and the first time he had been there at that time of night. There was another sound, coming from beyond the kitchen window, and he blocked off part of his listening ability to deal with it. At last he recognised it. In the twilight hour a great swarm of honey bees were settling down for their night in Isla.

As Patrick helped Paulina, so his own strength grew. One night at the end of the second week in December the doctor returned with another man, an anaesthetist. Patrick was allowed no further food and the two men set about transforming the kitchen into a rudimentary operating theatre.

'Things are too dangerous in the towns,' Paulina explained. 'They are watching everyone.'

The next morning the young doctor performed a brief operation, removing Patrick's stitches and relieving him of the colostomy installed five weeks earlier. When Patrick awoke the two men were gone.

The house in which they were staying was hidden from the road by folds of hillside and separated from Isla by less than a kilometre of undulating, green land. It was a land of mists; at the tops of little hills sometimes the mists cleared enough to give a glimpse of the sea at the horizon.

Patrick willed himself to recover. He drove himself without respite. He tried to think of it as training; preparation for what would be the most important fight of his life. They began walking out of doors, Paulina ready to steady him if he faltered.

'What happened to La Esmeralda?' Patrick asked.

'They saved her leg in the hospital. Then the best lawyers in Madrid arranged her bail.' Paulina turned down her mouth. 'But La Esmeralda is Marcellino in Spain and Marcellino will always side with Sainz Perez against us.'

They walked across the internal yard created by the cottage and its outhouses, past green, wooden doors, their paint flecked and peeling. One of them was ajar and through it Patrick could see an old tractor and a bicycle, leaning against a stone wall. They walked out to the road and towards the outline of a church.

'Does Xalbador's death mean the end of the cause?' Patrick asked.

'Probably for the moment,' Paulina agreed. 'But for us, *ruptura*, total independence, will always be something we will fight for. We are a people apart.' She shrugged. 'Now we are down. Our loved ones have either died or are in prisons, the diamonds are taken. But time is ours, because time never ends.'

They neared the church; it was the first occasion that Patrick had come so far. He saw its peeling edifice, the clock which had stopped at six o'clock God knows when, the grass growing from its belfry. And then as he focused upwards he saw the swarming bees, tens of thousands of them, massing into crevices the whole length and height of the church's structure.

'Look at the bees,' he said. 'I could hear them from the cottage.'

'*Las abejas*,' Paulina smiled. 'They are many. They have been here for as long as anyone can remember. It is good that they make use of such a fine church here in Isla.'

Patrick's gaze went from the faded, but structurally intact church to the cemetery which surrounded it. The headstones were old but the graves well tended.

'This was the church of an old priest,' Paulina said, 'a rebel priest named Padre Sangroniz. For Padre Sangroniz, Euskadi came before everything, even his God.'

They entered through a creaking gate. Beneath the high-flying bees, Patrick walked amongst the headstones, lists of names, faded with the years.

'They are all in their teens or early twenties,' he said, 'and they all died in 1937.'

'To us they are still our young men,' Paulina said. 'They are there waiting for friends like Geraldo and Teodoro to join them.'

Patrick's eyes took in the rows of neat graves. 'Why is this a cemetery from that time?' he asked. 'Why are there no graves of this year and last?'

'Padre Sangroniz had been the priest in Guernica,' Paulina said. 'He and Marcellino, then a child, escaped with their lives during the bombardment of 27 April. After the German war Marcellino was sent to South America, but Padre Sangroniz came here and soon this place, this church with its cellars, became a meeting place for all those who wished to dream of a free Euskadi.'

'He sounds like quite a man,' Patrick said.

'There was a scandal,' said Paulina. 'The local bishop came here on the instructions of Rome and ordered Padre Sangroniz to sign a promise. He refused. As a result he was defrocked and excommunicated. Gradually Padre Sangroniz's supporters drifted away. Now only the bees remain.'

'I remember my mother telling me about this place,' Patrick said, getting to his feet. 'I'm sure it must be here. They used to come on picnics from Noja, riding in a donkey and trap. I never thought I would come here.'

'Is your mother still alive?' Paulina asked.

'No,' answered Patrick, 'she died many years ago.' He held the churchyard gate for Paulina. 'When did Padre Sangroniz die?' he asked.

Paulina smiled. 'He's not dead,' she replied. 'He still lives in that little house over there.'

It was the next day. Patrick was making his way back to the cottage where he knew the *señora* would have lunch prepared. As he passed the church he could hear the bees. He stopped to listen, their sound comforting on his ears. He looked across the church wall to the small house. It was beyond the cemetery, seen over headstones and the wall, a small whitewashed house, no more than two rooms. As Patrick looked he saw the door open. He stopped. A woman emerged; she was sturdy, in her fifties, wearing a blue, paisley apron, her hair tied in a bun. She placed a low armchair in the sunlight and then stood aside. A very old man emerged. He was bent so severely, both in the back and in the legs, that at first sight he resembled a huge black crab, lurching forward with the help of a walking-stick in each hand. A black crab, because he was clothed entirely in clerical black, with the exception of his peaked cap which was white. Patrick watched as he steadied himself into the chair. Suddenly the old head turned, but to the old man's eyes Patrick could not have been more than a blur.

CHAPTER THIRTY

On the eleventh floor of the building at the junction of Fourteenth and I Streets, Marshall Kahan leaned back in his chair. Around the walls were plaques and scrolls, maps, paintings, class photographs, a photograph of Mrs Kahan and their three girls, a calendar, a blackboard, a noticeboard and a large TV, wall mounted.

Two people sat before the DEA Administrator: one was the Deputy Administrator for Operations, a small, compact man with neat, light brown hair; the other was a bespectacled black woman in her mid-forties, a specialist in transportation.

Kahan slapped his desk-top with his hand. 'So, down to business,' he said. 'What are the short strokes?'

The Operations Chief cleared his throat. 'In an operation like this,' he said, 'clearly the main procedures to be followed are swiftness and secrecy.' He looked around the room uncomfortably. 'We start from the standpoint that, at this time, no one knows what we are about to do.'

Kahan nodded. 'All right,' he said.

The operations man took a deep breath. 'This is Friday,' he said. 'On Tuesday morning next, we airlift half the contents of the San Francisco, Los Angeles and San Diego evidence vaults back here to Washington. We already have signed orders from a Federal District Judge allowing us to destroy the whole lot on arrival.'

Kahan nodded his approval. 'That's good,' he said. 'Our new procedures in McLean, will allow us to do in three days what it would take them a month to destroy on the coast.'

The operations man shifted uneasily in his chair. 'I just hope they can cope with this kind of volume,' he said.

'We have to move it anyway,' Kahan said. 'After the recent busts their vaults out there are full.'

The Operations Chief shook his head from side to side. 'Not so full that this sort of volume has to be transported at once,' he said.

'The decision has been taken,' Kahan said icily. 'Now, give me a number.'

The operations man looked down at a pad. 'Rounded out, just short of ten tons,' he sighed.

Kahan's eyes were bright. 'That's a lot of cocaine,' he said softly.

'It certainly is, sir,' the transportation specialist said. 'With a street value of a hundred dollars a gram, it's worth a billion dollars in any man's money.'

Kahan turned to the woman. 'Run the logistics past me,' he said.

'We have hired armoured trucks which will be driven and armed by west coast agents,' she said crisply. 'No one knows that more than one vault is being cleared. We have arranged for the goods to be assembled at a small airfield near San Diego that few people have ever heard of. It's called Brown. A 146 British Aerospace freighter, piloted by our own crew, will pick the goods up at Brown, then fly them home, via Fort Worth. Here in National, security trucks will meet the plane on the apron, load directly and drive under armed escort to McLean.'

'Very good,' said Marshall Kahan slowly. 'It sounds like you've got it all buttoned down.' He smiled at her. 'As usual.' He got to his feet, and turned to the Operations Chief whose eyes were on the floor. 'Is that it, or is there anything else I should know?' Kahan asked harshly.

The Operations Chief appeared to be on the point of speaking, but then changed his mind.

'Let me know if you've got any reason whatsoever to change any part of these plans,' Kahan said, ushering them to the door.

The man and woman filed from the room. Kahan pressed a button on his communications console. 'Hold my calls,' he instructed.

He turned to his left; in the back corner of the room, a door in the oak panelling which had been open three inches throughout the meeting now swung inwards and Special Agent Waters emerged, a pad in his hand.

'Did you get it all?' Kahan asked.

Waters nodded. He handed Kahan a sheet of paper from a legal pad. Then the private line on Kahan's desk rang and he picked it up.

'Kahan,' he said.

The voice which he heard on the other end had haunted him now for over half his life. Kahan felt his breathing shorten as he took the paper from Waters and recited its contents into the phone.

'And what about my diamonds?' the caller asked in a voice which was almost a whisper.

Kahan spread his free hand helplessly. 'We are no further,' he said. He wiped sweat from himself. 'But we will get them, they will come to us, I am sure that I am right.'

'I am coming up to see for myself,' said the caller as the line was disconnected.

Marshall Kahan slowly replaced the receiver. His gaze was unfocused: it swept the blurred face of the blond-haired agent, the comfortable room, the American flag proudly in its place. At a wall of photographs Kahan's eyes came to rest. They picked out one in particular. It showed a group of smiling young men and women.

The caption read: 'Cherry Knolls Highschool, Denver. Class of 1955.'

CHAPTER THIRTY-ONE

It was past midnight. Earlier that day, without the knowledge of Paulina, Patrick had given himself a test: outside Isla, within view of the sea, he had run, flat out, for one kilometre. Although his lungs had burned savagely and his legs had screamed for rest, nothing else had happened, nothing inside him had popped out of place as he had feared and he had jogged slowly homewards, with new confidence now in each springing stride.

He lay in bed and listened. He was ready. He knew what had to be done. Flicking back the bedcovers he went to his bedroom door and eased it open. The corridor was dark. He stepped into the narrow hallway. In the kitchen, fifteen yards away, he could see Felipe, sitting at the table, chatting quietly to Paulina. Unbreathing, Patrick listened and watched. He could not make out the content of their speech, but he was sure that apart from himself and these two, there was no one else in the cottage.

He returned noiselessly to his room and went to the window. It was an old window with wooden sashes; the bottom part was open. Bending, Patrick ran it up halfway, then slipped through and out into the clear Isla night.

In the unfamiliar darkness he walked briskly down the hill and then upwards again until the towering edifice of the church could be seen, a shape black in the black night, just visible. There were no sounds: the bees, like the people of Isla, slept. Patrick felt for the low, iron gate and winced as it creaked open. He crossed through the churchyard and then the cemetery, the high headstones rearing on either side. At the boundary wall he climbed a bank of earth. He was no more than twenty yards from the front door where days earlier he had seen the old priest being helped into the sunlight.

Without waiting to think about it, Patrick put his two hands on the top of the wall and vaulted over.

The door was secured by a simple latch, unlocked. Patrick could smell a kerosene stove, the same as the one which heated his bedroom. He listened but could hear nothing. He pushed a second door. He stared.

He was looking into the living-room of the cottage, which also served as a bedroom and a kitchen. The bed in one corner was narrow, made up, unoccupied. There was a sink opposite it, and a cooker and a small dresser with plates and cups. The kerosene stove was in the centre of the room and before it, sunk and unmoving in a low chair, was the oldest person Patrick had ever seen.

From a distance three days ago, Padre Sangroniz had obviously seemed very old; now the close-up showed just how old. His face skin and head could have been a hollowed, Halloween turnip. The eyes, long ago cataracted over, had withdrawn into the back of their sockets, distant pools in caves of flesh. The top of the head was a patchwork of black spots and white tufts of bristle. This whole papier-mâché head sat on a withered neck stalk, complete with Adam's apple, which plunged through the circle of a yellowing clerical collar. He sat, motionless, bent, a walking stick on either side of his legs, his chin almost touching his knees which were clasped by surprisingly large, black-spotted hands, their white-capped knuckles gleaming like porcelain caps.

'Who is it?' he asked in Basque. He turned his sightless head. His voice was clear and strong.

'I am a friend of La Esmeralda's,' Patrick replied in Spanish. 'My name is Patrick.'

'Ah,' the old priest said, '*un Americano del Sur?*'

'*Sí*,' Patrick said, '*sí, Padre.*'

'What do you want with me?' the priest asked. 'The hour is late, is it not?'

'Yes it is late, *Padre*,' Patrick agreed. 'But I must move by night. The *Franguinistas* are everywhere. I have heard so much about Marcellino's *padre* that I had to come and meet you, to see the famous Padre Sangroniz with my own eyes.'

Patrick swallowed and watched the ancient man weighing him up in his blind world. Then Padre Sangroniz smiled.

'Well, you see me,' he said. 'I am so old that I thank God every day for borrowing for himself the sight of my eyes, for sparing me the pain of having to look at this feeble shell of a man.' Padre Sangroniz banged his knuckles to his chest. 'So feeble!' he cried. 'So treacherous!' He tapped his head. 'Up here I think the thoughts of my youth, every day. I forget nothing. I still retain the smells, the visions, the voices. I remember my own mother! Look at me! You sound like a young man. Can you imagine that someone like me ever had a mother?'

'She must have been a marvellous woman,' said Patrick.

'We lived in Aulestia,' Padre Sangroniz said. 'Now I can remember not only my mother, but her mother before her, a very old woman who had lived in Guernica and married my grandfather when she was nearly forty. So, you see, I can remember the voice and face of an old woman from whom I am directly descended, who was born not when this century, but when the last century was merely a few, fresh years old.' The old man's head shook from left to right in frustration. 'I could go on and on,' he said, 'if this wretched body would allow. I no longer want to eat, I can no longer smell, I yearn for tobacco but I have not smoked for twenty years. I will never feel the sun of another summer. But up here all the summers are there always, and all the memories.'

'I am sure you will enjoy the coming summer,' Patrick said.

Padre Sangroniz shook his head. 'I don't want to,' he said simply. 'I have run my time. I have forced myself to live to see what I thought would happen in these last few weeks. A free Euskadi.' The priest bent even lower. 'But it has not happened. Like the Jews in the Old Testament, the wait must go on. But without me. Soon, very soon, my flame will be extinguished and the young like you can take over the vigil.'

'These past weeks have given Marcellino much pain,' Patrick said, his mouth dry. 'He had hoped by now to be home in a free Euskadi.'

'Marcellino is young,' Padre Sangroniz said. 'Young and strong. He will recoup his resolve and fight on. His strength is that he is not here, he is out of their reaches, they cannot harm him, yet he can provide Euskadi with the means to fight on. That is a great strength.'

'He may feel that to start all over again is too much,' Patrick said. 'He may forget Euskadi.'

Padre Sangroniz turned his undiscerning eyes on Patrick. 'Marcellino?' he said. The old priest gave a contemptuous cough. He picked up the walking-stick at his right hand and poked it generally into the air behind him. 'Did they give up?' he asked. 'Did they forget, any of them?'

Patrick followed the stick and noticed for the first time the row of pictures on the dim, back wall of the room. Slowly he got up to study them. There were five. The first was a painting in the traditional style of a priestly man with an imposed halo.

'Excuse my ignorance, *Padre*,' Patrick said, 'but you will have to help me. I am here at the beginning of the line.'

'The first great Basque who made his name outside his homeland,' Padre Sangroniz replied, 'Ignatius Loyola, the founder of the Jesuit order.'

Patrick moved to the next painting, of a man against the background of ships and the sea. Padre Sangroniz sat slumped. Patrick thought he had fallen asleep.

'Next is de Elcano,' Padre Sangroniz said suddenly, 'the great sea captain, and after him, of course, is Simon Bolivar.'

Beside the founder of Bolivia were two photographs, one faded and old, the other clear. Both were framed.

'Who is next?' Patrick asked.

'Next you have de Lesseps,' the priest replied, 'the designer and builder of the Suez Canal, one of the great wonders of the world.'

Patrick stopped before the final picture. It differed from the others in that it was not posed, but a photograph taken unexpectedly, its subjects surprised. It showed two men in white tuxedos with a dramatically beautiful woman, all standing at the open door of an old coupé. The scene was at night, the three faces turned to the camera at the instant the flash went off.

'And my little boy from Guernica,' the priest chuckled from his chair.

Patrick stared. He recognised La Esmeralda, between the two men. Of the men one looked somehow familiar: he was young, open-faced and had an even, engaging smile. But it was the other man who really dominated. In the background, it was to him that the doorman looked. This man looked out from the photograph with a totally natural authority, emphasised by the bulk of his physique, twice that in width of the younger man.

'For years I begged a photograph,' the old priest was saying, 'but never would he let one be taken. It was La Esmeralda who brought me this, years ago. It is from their time in Buenos Aires.' He cackled. 'See how handsome he has grown.'

Padre Sangroniz's voice drifted off as without warning he began to sleep. Patrick reached for the picture. The frame was a cheap black affair; without difficulty he prised open the back and slid the old photograph out.

Then, with the old man's whistling snores in his ears, he crept out.

It was still deep night as Patrick eased open the outhouse door and wheeled the bicycle outside. He checked the shopping bag of food which he had tied to the crossbar and walked away down the other side of the hill, eastwards, away from the church and from Isla.

It was the last leg of a journey which he had started many ages ago. When he was clear of houses he swung his leg over the bicycle and pedalled, along the line of the eastbound coast.

After an hour he had put over ten kilometres between himself and Isla. He regretted not having been able to thank Paulina for her kindness which had saved his life, and he regretted his deception of Padre Sangroniz. Would anyone notice the photograph gone from its place on the wall? Would anyone tell the old man?

The road dipped and rose; sometimes he came to a hill which meant his dismounting. Animals, some with neck-bells, grazed either side.

Patrick rode eastwards, picking his unlighted way without difficulty in the clear night. As the hours passed and the gentle rhythm of his legs was broken by rests and refreshment from the bag, he could see the subtly changing texture of the sky ahead, slowly changing colours, gradually driving the stars from the sky.

Patrick's greatest regret of all was having to leave before the dawn – he would have liked, one last time, to return to the churchyard and sit under the song of the bees.

An hour later Patrick came to a wide road where bleary-eyed, blue-overalled men waited for transport to take them to the steel furnaces on the outskirts of Bilbao.

Parking his bicycle, Patrick joined them, just as a bus rounded the bend of the road.

CHAPTER THIRTY-TWO

The room measured ten feet by twelve. It was windowless and stank of sweat and urine. A single spotlight picked out a man bound hand and foot to an upright chair. His hair, a ragged mass, hung forward on his chest. Naked to the waist, his torso revealed a patchwork of deep bruises. He appeared to be asleep.

The door to this cubicle opened and three men came in, one young, blond; one grey, red-faced; the third a man of great width and girth. To him the blond man turned inquiringly.

'*Intentalo otra vez*,' he rasped. 'Try once more.'

The blond man went to the chair. He caught the head and jerked it upwards so that the light revealed the face: two eyes uniformly swollen to a point beyond opening; a nose swelled up grotesquely, its bone shattered; a straggling moustache over cracked lips.

'Can you hear me?' the blond man asked.

There was a low moan.

'Good,' the questioner said. 'Now listen well. We are running out of time.' As he spoke, the questioner jerked the head. 'We must find Drake, we must find the diamonds,' he said. 'Only a fraction of them were recovered. We must find him. Now, where is he?'

The reply was a long groan, spoken from the belly. 'I . . . don't . . . know.'

The questioner pulled back his head so that the man looked directly at the ceiling.

'*Where is he?*'

There was no reply.

The other grey-haired man stepped forward. He forced open

the mouth and rammed in a small block of wood between the back teeth. He then reached down for a pail and, whilst the younger man held the head rigidly in position, began carefully to pour water down the opened throat. The seated man automatically tried to swallow. After three seconds he began to choke. Relentlessly the pouring continued. The prisoner began to drown.

'¡Pregúntale otra vez! Ask him again!'

The head was released and the seated man went forward, water vomiting from his lungs.

'Where is Drake?'

The man gasped for his life's breath.

'*Where is he?*'

Slowly the head shook from side to side. The men stepped forward, grasped his head and the whole procedure was repeated. This time they thought they had lost him. The man to whom the others deferred stepped forward quickly and, with a knife resembling a cut-throat razor, sliced the binding ropes. The body slumped face first to the ground; the younger man pumped the back until the lungs worked again.

'Tell us where Drake arranged to go. Tell us and you will come to no further harm.'

The prone man's response was an erratic whisper. The younger man dropped down so that his ear was at the mouth. 'Tell us!'

In the small room, the reply was strangely clear. 'Go . . . fuck . . . yourself.'

There was a snarl, so menacing that the blond man jumped in alarm to his feet. The prostrate body was grabbed from the floor with great power and slammed into the chair.

'If you will not speak,' spat the huge man, forcing back the head, 'then, you shit from a dog, you will never speak again.'

In a fluid motion he inserted the knife tip at the corner of the mouth and in one clean stroke removed the hairy upper lip.

As Marcellino strode from the room, sunlight for a moment illuminated the cubicle, twinkling in briefly on its way to set behind Washington's Capitol.

CHAPTER THIRTY-THREE

Nothing had changed in the small street off the Paseo de la Castellana. The same cafés; the same people; Patrick felt he was playing himself in a remake of his life. In the bright, safe-deposit company the same woman compared Patrick's signature to the one on the card. She had hair held in place by something out of a can. Her eyes swam behind spectacles which were attached to her by a sparkling neck-rope.

'There are over four weeks to pay,' she said with apprehension.

'*Bueno*, that's all right,' Patrick said. 'The money's in the box.'

The woman delivered the small box suspiciously to the counter. Patrick opened it, then in a single moment of panic, upturned its contents out. There was an envelope and his own passport which he had put there on the first day he had arrived in Madrid a lifetime ago, but nothing else.

'The package!' he cried in dismay. 'Where's the package?'

'*Señor?*'

Patrick closed his eyes. 'There should also be a package,' he said with control. 'A brown package, about this size.' He made a shape. 'I mailed it from Pamplona over four weeks ago.'

'*¡Lo mandó por correo!*' the woman said. 'Mailed it!' She went to a wall safe. 'Anything that is mailed must be put in here.' She swung the safe's door open. 'You see, we cannot open the deposit boxes without the owner's permission. Now, what is the name again?' She peered at the card, returned to the safe and began rummaging. 'Drake,' Patrick could hear her saying, 'Drake.' He felt sick. Then suddenly she was turning with a parcel in her hands, and it was on the counter, and he could see the label he had addressed to himself. The relief which swept him was so great that he leaned over and planted a kiss on her cheek.

'*Milgracias*,' he said, 'thank you a thousand times.'

'*Hay más que tagar*,' said the woman, momentarily confused. 'There is extra to pay.'

'How much?' Patrick asked.

'*Tres mil quinientas*,' she said, then smiled again as he slit the envelope from the deposit box and peeled off the money.

In the toilet of a nearby café he prised open the parcel and shook out the tiny bundles into his hand. He opened several of them and the diamonds, even in the dim light, winked and sparkled.

From the envelope he took out the photograph of Marshall Kahan which Joe Vendetti had given him in Inverary. He held it, side by side, with the old snapshot from Padre Sangroniz's wall. There could be no doubt. Although age had filled and thickened the face, thinned and changed the colour of the hair, the basic face was the same, the man was the same: Marshall Kahan had known Marcellino and La Esmeralda in Buenos Aires.

There was a telephone box on the corner: Patrick fed it coins and dialled.

'Mr Lang's office.'

There was a long pause, then Mervyn Lang's voice came on, almost a whisper. 'Patrick?'

'Yes, Mervyn, it's me.'

'I knew it. I knew as long as they kept phoning me that you must still be alive.'

Patrick clenched his hand until it was white. 'What about Georgie?'

Lang sighed. 'Nothing more. You may not know this but her father has informed the police about her disappearance. There was a lot of publicity, her photo in the papers, on TV and so on. It's died down now.'

'And you . . . ?'

'I never told the police anything, Patrick. I decided that her best chance lay with you.' There was a pause. 'Don't tell me where you are, but have you still got the wretched diamonds?'

'I've got most of them,' Patrick said.

'The calls I get are all long-distance,' Lang said. 'I think they may be from the States.'

Patrick thought of the photographs in his pocket. 'I'm not surprised,' he said.

'What will you do?' Lang asked.

'I'm catching a flight,' Patrick said. 'To Washington.'

'How can I help?' Lang asked.

'By telephoning someone there,' Patrick said. He thumbed in more coins and spoke to Mervyn Lang for five more minutes. Then he walked back to the Paseo de la Castellana and into the Iberia office on the corner of Calle de José where he booked himself to Washington one-way, departing that afternoon at three o'clock.

The Iberia girl put Patrick's ticket and receipt on the counter with a smile. '*Gracias*,' Patrick smiled at her.

'*Gracias, Señor*,' she smiled. 'I hope that you enjoyed your stay in España.'

CHAPTER THIRTY-FOUR

A light westerly blew over the face of the small airfield. Beyond the perimeter fence a panorama of shimmering scrub stretched as far as the eyes could see, westwards towards the Pacific Ocean and southwards towards Tijuana and the Baja Calif Norte.

In a shack beside the Brown Field building, Captain Mike Helman scanned the weather actuals and forecasts for the Dallas, Texas area, the rest-leg of his 2,600-mile flight to Washington DC. A pilot who had seen action in both Korea and Vietnam before joining the DEA, Helman, now past his middle fifties, was a slightly stooping six-feet-two with thinning hair and a greying, spiked moustache. He was in shirtsleeves and wiped the perspiration from his forehead.

'That your Quiet Trader out there?'

Helman turned. The other pilot using Brown Field's self-briefing was looking out at the squat plane with the overhead wings on which four turbo fan engines were slung. A forklift trundled to the plane's loading bay with a pallet. There were two armoured trucks standing on the shimmering runway and a couple of guards in blue helmets lounging beside them.

Mike Helman smiled. 'Yep,' he said. 'That's her. You could sneak her up your path and into your garage, if it was big enough, and your old lady still wouldn't know what time you got in at.'

The other pilot laughed and picked up his jacket. 'Have a nice day, wherever you're going,' he said.

Out on the apron a man in an open-necked blue shirt walked to the first armoured truck, said something to the driver, then turned and gave the OK sign to the driver of the second. Both trucks started up and drove out through a gate in the airfield fence. The man in the blue shirt then helped two ground staff to secure the plane's cargo doors, before he walked back across the tarmac to the shack.

'We're all set, Mike,' he said. 'Jesus, it's hot out there.'

Mike Helman turned. 'What's the final payload, Jack?' he asked.

'Twenty thousand one hundred and sixty pounds,' answered Jack Perillo, Helman's co-pilot. 'All well stowed and fixed.' He looked at an ancient telex machine that was chattering out weather reports. 'What have we got?' he asked.

'Pretty nice day to Dallas,' Helman replied. 'No cloud worth talking about and a five-knot wind up our ass. We should do it in under three hours.'

Helman picked up his jacket, an almost threadbare US Airforce combat jacket, and the two men left the shack and approached their plane. Perillo was forty, dark and heavy-set; he came to Helman's shoulder.

The plane's cockpit was baking. Helman activated a small fan then levered himself into the left-hand seat. Flies buzzed on the window. Outside, Jack Perillo completed his visual check, climbed in, slammed the cockpit door to shut and buckled his seat harness.

Helman's hand turned the radio control frequency. 'Ground, this is November Seven Oscar Lima,' he spoke. 'Start up clearance.'

One by one the Textron Avco engines came to life.

'Checklist,' Mike Helman said to Jack Perillo.

The co-pilot rattled off the checklist.

'Oscar Lima request taxi,' spoke Helman.

'November Seven Oscar Lima,' said ground control, 'you're cleared to taxi via Charlie and Delta to hold short of runway 26 right.'

'Roger, ground,' said Helman and eased the 146 off the spot. 'Taxiing check,' he said. He powered the big freighter from left to right, around the back of the tiny control tower.

'Oscar Lima change to the tower on 11.6,' said the man at ground frequency.

Mike Helman taxied the plane along the slip road towards the end of the runway, received clearance from the tower, turned and lined up. He scanned his instrument panel one last time.

'November Seven Oscar Lima, take a right turn-out over Poggi and then you're west underneath Victor Three One Seven.'

'Roger,' answered Mike Helman. 'Oscar Lima cleared to take 'Oscar Lima cleared to take off.'

Helman pushed the throttle forward first slowly, then more sharply, causing the plane's engines to rise in a modulated whine as she gathered forward momentum.

'Eighty . . . one hundred . . . V–1 . . . rotate . . .' intoned Jack Perillo, reading off the speeds.

'Positive climb,' said Helman as the ground fell away. 'Gear up. Instrument cross-check.'

'Gear up,' said Perillo, 'speed 150 knots, runway heading, climbing.'

'November Seven Oscar Lima turning right over Poggi,' Helman said.

The radio crackled. 'November Seven Oscar Lima,' came the voice of an air-traffic controller in San Diego. 'Squawk ident on 3264.'

'Roger, San Diego,' Perillo said, 'identity coming down.' He pressed a button on the aircraft's transponder.

'Flaps up,' said Mike Helman.

'Flaps up,' said Jack Perillo.

'November Seven Oscar Lima,' said San Diego, 'identified on radar.'

Mike Helman engaged the plane's auto-pilot, leaned back and lighted a cigarette. They were flying at 5,500 feet. Below them the relentless sun flashed on pinpointed, invisible objects in the California desert.

'Did you notice that little Mexican piece last night?' Perillo asked.

'In the hotel?' Helman smiled and shook his head. 'How could I not? There was a mark on the carpet where you'd been pawing it.'

'She was a horny little broad,' Perillo said. He sucked air. 'I couldn't sleep all night – she was on my mind.'

Mike Helman swallowed smoke and closed his eyes briefly as the plane droned along, making a speed of 400 miles an hour.

In the three years in which, on and off, they had worked

together, Helman had never seen Jack Perillo do anything other than talk. Mike Helman's idea of a good night out was a meal with a bottle of wine and then early bed with his attractive third wife. Today he was tired. He had accumulated an extra week's leave; he would take it in two weeks' time, fishing off the old ship's tender he kept in Florida.

'Any idea of the value of what we're carrying?' asked Jack Perillo, cutting across Helman's image of a boat and the faint smell of creosote. 'I was working it out: if it's all cocaine for destruction which I'd bet my ass it is, then you're talking about a billion bucks back there.'

'I don't give a shit if it's frozen angel-piss,' responded Helman. 'I just do what I'm told.'

There was a crackle. 'November Seven Oscar Lima.' It was the controller in San Diego. 'Unidentified traffic at six o'clock, two miles, height unknown.'

Helman frowned and looked out of the side window of the cockpit but was unable to see anything except deep blue morning. 'Anything your side?'

Jack Perillo shook his head. 'Negative,' he said.

'Negative contact, San Diego,' said Helman.

The two pilots settled back.

'Just imagine living down there,' Perillo said, after a minute. 'What would you do every day, for Christ's sake? What the fuck goes on in a place like this?'

'November Seven Oscar Lima.'

Mike Helman made a gesture of impatience as San Diego came on once more.

'Unidentified traffic overtaking you. Still negative contact?'

Again the two men carried out a visual check of the skies around them. Mike Helman looked at Jack Perillo and shrugged. 'Negative . . .'

At that moment there was a spine-jarring crash which sent each man's coordinates wild and which caused the heavy freighter to plunge 500 feet. Jack Perillo looked frantically out of his side of the cockpit and upwards. He could see the two elongated landing bars of a huge helicopter.

'Jesus!' Perillo shouted. 'There's some sort of a chopper up there!'

Mike Helman had steadied the aircraft.

'She's closing again!' Perillo shouted. 'Christ . . . !'

Helman thought that the top of the Quiet Trader would buckle in, such was the force of the second impact delivered by the helicopter as it came down on them with full force. Helman grabbed the plane's joystick and pushed it downwards, hard. His stomach lurched as they plunged for the brown earth.

'November Seven Oscar Lima, do you read?'

'San Diego, November Seven Oscar Lima!' Helman shouted. 'We're being attacked by an unidentified helicopter! We are attempting to take evasive action.' In horror he looked left and saw that the helicopter was now flying beside him, trying to nudge them right, over the Mexican border directly underneath.

'November Seven Oscar Lima,' said San Diego Control, 'confirm attacked?'

The chopper gained fifty feet and then hit the Quiet Trader fair and square with a massive crunch just behind the pilot position.

'Confirm attacked,' San Diego intoned.

'Christ!' Helman shouted. 'They're taking us down!'

The 146 had descended to nearly 1,500 feet. Helman tried to power them left, but once again the helicopter hit them uncompromisingly.

'If they hit a wing, we've had it!' Perillo cried, his face grey.

'I guess we now know the value of what we're carrying behind!' Mike Helman said, his teeth clenched, his hands gripping the joystick and throttle.

'November Seven Oscar Lima, there are two more unidentified aircraft about to merge with you,' said San Diego. 'Please confirm situation.'

Mike Helman stared. To his left, at eleven o'clock, another helicopter had appeared, its lights blazing in the bright afternoon. The scene reminded Helman of Vietnam. The new chopper appeared to steady, hovering, then there were two distinct and separate explosions of flame and two winding tracers, as the second helicopter discharged its cannons. Instinctively Helman put the Quiet Trader into a nosedive and swung it sharp right. At 500 feet he levelled off and banked left.

'Jesus H. Christ, have a look at that,' he said.

The offending helicopter was thrashing its way earthbound, smoke streaming from its fuselage. Above the scene hovered two compact-looking Sikorsky Black Hawks. They began to tack northwards, soon becoming lost to view.

'Who the hell were they?' Jack Perillo asked.

'Coastguard,' replied Helman. His hand shook as he brought his lighter to a cigarette.

'November Seven Oscar Lima, confirm situation.'

'Some son of a bitch tried to zap us,' Mike Helman said, 'but he's been sent to the scrap heap. We're returning to 5,500 and continuing to Dallas.'

'November Seven Oscar Lima,' said San Diego, 'confirm situation stable.'

'November Seven Oscar Lima,' Mike Helman sighed. 'Situation stable.'

The yellow cab swung around the Lincoln Memorial and then shot out over the Potomac. Below him Patrick could see small white caps where the northerly wind was stiffening the grey water. Ahead there were trees, masking the outline of Virginia.

The cab swung through the gates of Arlington Cemetery and into the car park. Patrick paid him off, then looking at a map he began to walk westwards, up a gently inclining path. Either side were thousands of military graves, each marked with a simple white headstone, all of them laid out in a great symmetry.

Patrick walked uphill. The wind from the north which was ruffling the Potomac (the river now behind him, over the Parkway and between him and Washington) had now started to carry fluffs of snow, scraps of it, spinning through the leafless trees, gusting over the undulating green hills of the huge graveyard. There were few other people about – a woman with a pram, caught in the sudden squall, sheltering in the lee of a thick tree, a single jogger, up and to the right, some other joggers climbing from the left, a couple linked together, their heads down, battling uphill.

The snow thickened into Patrick's face making him turn and walk backwards. He was surprised that he could no longer see the car park because of the snow. He looked at his map; according to it if he looked downhill and right he should be able to see the Pentagon.

Patrick turned and saw that he had come to a sign which read 'Eternal Flame'. There were steps, then the ground levelled out for the stone amphitheatre. The couple whom Patrick had noticed earlier now huddled together, staring at the methane flame as it curled smokelessly up into the snow. They were people in their forties, Patrick could now see, not a young couple as he had imagined, but a pair who could still remember Camelot and the legend of the sixties.

Patrick gazed for a moment at the flame, then walked right, downhill. His caller at the hotel had been quite specific: the diamonds should be handed over at the Robert Kennedy grave at three o'clock. Patrick looked at his watch. There were three minutes to go.

The green of Arlington was turning white, fusing the white headstones and the earth. Patrick came to a small hollow, just green earth, now dusted white, roped off with plain white rope, and a small white cross. Patrick felt the contrast: the public nature of the stone amphitheatre uphill, the sense of privacy down here. The meeting here would be alone. Then he heard the car.

Patrick had imagined that, like him, Kahan would come on foot. This was the impression which Kahan had given on the telephone. But now he saw that the narrow roads were wide enough to take a car, and through the snow, he saw the limousine with the obscured glass, its sidelights on, slowly winding up to him.

There were long, cobblestoned steps, now almost snow-covered, leading down to the roadway. Patrick stood at the top of them, his hands deep in the pockets of his coat, and watched the car below him as it drew up. Patrick's coat collar was upturned: he had not brought anything to cover his head, so that now his hair was covered like the branches of a bush, soft snow clinging to each black strand. The snow, as always, deadened the sound of everything. There had been no sound in the great cemetery before the snow, and now, even the silence seemed to be sealed within a vacuum as the car tyres made only the softest, crunching sound on the pathway. They were in a dome, a vacuum, here at Bobbie's grave, the only sound that of rubber rolling over snow.

The limousine came to a halt. Its windows were, with the exception of the windscreen, black. Patrick could see a boomerang-shaped antenna on the trunk. The back door of the car opened.

Patrick took a step towards it. He stopped. He saw not the face of Marshall Kahan, but a youthful, open face, blond hair . . .

'Mr Drake?' The man's voice carried strangely in the silence. Patrick walked towards the car.

'Mr Drake, have you brought what you promised?'

Patrick nodded, patted his coat and kept walking. The man in the car was getting out. The angle of the opened door concealed his lower half from Patrick. He was doing something with his hands. He stepped out around the door. He was not wearing an overcoat. His arms came up. To shake his hand? Patrick stopped, stared. The man was pointing a gun at his chest, held in both his hands. There were explosions. Patrick felt a thump. He fell.

Both the blond man's hands shot to his face as the gun spun out of his grasp and he fell in the gathering snow. The hand which had pushed Patrick downwards continued to hold him there. From his supine position, his face wet with snow, Patrick could see the male member of the couple who had been at JFK's grave steady his revolver; then he saw his hands jump as he loosed off three more rounds into the sprawled body.

The limousine was clawing wildly as its driver began to swerve back downhill in reverse. The long car dragged its dead passenger along with it for twenty yards, then freed itself, its front wheels spinning over the body which went under the chassis, the rear door slamming closed as the car's angle changed. The driver was unable to hold it and they spun off the path, still in reverse, swinging in a wide arc. The car crashed through chains at the roadside, became momentarily airborne as the gradient plunged, then careered crazily among the white headstones, knocking them like skittles, the car's wheels scarring the virgin snow.

Patrick could see downhill. He stared as the limousine stopped, then lurched forward on to the roadway again, gathering speed. A man was standing in its path. Ten yards away from him was a small shape, black in the snow, which Patrick dully realised was a pram. The man held a weapon at his hip and as the limousine made its fruitless way downwards, the man began to spray it. The long car slewed left, off the pathway again, and shuddered to a steaming halt.

Patrick got shakily to his feet. The snow gave everything an unreal air: blood on the snow, raspberry dye on ice-cream; halfway down the hill, a puppet body; car tracks among scattered headstones; the limousine and the lonely pram.

Then all at once, the private, snowy scene was full of people, some in track-suits, all with guns in their hands.

'He's all right, Captain.'

Patrick realised the comment was about himself. Mike Izaguirre, his dark, crinkled hair snow-dusted, was holding him by the arm.

'You did a great job,' he murmured. Then he turned Patrick gently towards a long, black Cadillac, which appeared to have materialised out of nowhere. 'Let's take a ride,' said Mike Izaguirre.

The back of the Cadillac comprised two facing, comfortable leather seats. Patrick sat beside Mike Izaguirre. Opposite them sat a burly man in a three-piece suit, whose eyes constantly probed Patrick's face, but with whom there had been no attempt at introduction. Beside this man sat a younger man, also three-piece-suited, who sat on the edge of his seat, holding a notebook.

The burly man raised his left hand and made a slight, beckoning motion with his fingers.

'We have positive identification on the two deceased, Mr Director,' the younger man began. 'They are Marshall Kahan and a DEA special agent named Waters.'

'Holy Christ,' said the man whom the agent had called director. They were approaching the roundabout before the Arlington Memorial Bridge. 'We put a red alert on anything to do with DEA after you called me,' he said to Mike Izaguirre. 'Do you realise that these Colombians tried to take down a plane carrying a billion dollars' worth of dope this morning, somewhere near the Mexican border with Arizona?' The director shook his head. 'That bastard Kahan reported to me, he was my responsibility,' he said grimly.

'Any reasons?' asked Izaguirre.

The director looked briefly at Patrick, then nodded. 'We've had four people in Buenos Aires Police Headquarters since you called,' he said. 'Three hours ago they came up with prints from an unsolved murder case way back in '62. They're Marshall Kahan's.'

They swept across the Potomac. Patrick tried to summon his reserves to ask the only question which was of any relevance to him, a question more basic than the reason for creation or the end of the world. Then the director turned to him.

'Mr Drake,' he said quietly. 'Clearly, ever since Mr Lang relayed your message to Captain Izaguirre here, the Washington police and the FBI have been working closely together. We threw a tap on all lines going into the DEA building, and were able to intercept calls going to Marshall Kahan which traced to a room in the Washington Hilton, just across the road from the Colombian Embassy in Le Roy Place. The hotel have the guest in this room listed as a Señor Zumeta from Bogotá, but from listening to Kahan's conversation with this person, our guess is that he is the one known as Marcellino and that he was in Washington to co-ordinate the cocaine heist I've just mentioned.'

Patrick looked at the director, then at Izaguirre.

'Patrick,' Mike Izaguirre said gently, 'we've found Joe Vendetti.' The policeman closed his eyes briefly. 'He's alive. Just. Our surmise is that both he and Georgie Ridgeway were abducted here to Washington, probably by Kahan on Marcellino's instructions.'

'Our concern,' the director said, 'is not to alert this Zumeta or Marcellino to the fact that we're on to him. We believe that he still control over Miss Ridgeway's movements.'

'And where is Marcellino now?' Patrick managed to say.

The director's fingers beckoned at the agent once more.

'At noon today, sir,' the agent responded, 'a limousine from the Colombian Embassy picked up Señor Zumeta or Marcellino, together with an unidentified lady companion and drove them both to the Embassy of Equador on 16th Street. They are still there.'

'Lady?' said Patrick.

'Hispanic female, fifty years, long black hair, dark glasses,' the agent retorted.

'La Esmeralda,' Patrick said, as everyone in the car looked at him.

They had stopped at the traffic lights at the end of Constitution Avenue. There was a purring noise and the telephone at the director's elbow began to flash. The others watched as he grabbed it.

'I see, I see,' he said rapidly. 'Well detain it, for Chrissake!' The director's jaw was rigid. 'OK, I'm coming out, but don't let them go.' He threw the phone back and leaned forward to the driver. 'Dulles International!' he shouted. 'And fast!'

The limousine screeched through the lights; the driver placed a strobe on the roof and they tore back across the Potomac via the Theodore Roosevelt Bridge.

'That was our field man on 16th Street,' the director said. 'They've just got their electronic equipment into place at the Embassy of Equador. Marcellino isn't in the building. We've also just established that a private Gulfstream has filed a flight-plan for Mexico out of Dulles. It's about to take off and think we Marcellino is on it.'

'Can you stop him?' Izaguirre asked.

'We're sure as hell going to try,' the director replied. He began speaking urgently into the phone as the car swung on to Route 66.

'Is Georgie with him?' Patrick asked.

The director looked at Patrick. 'That's not clear,' he replied, grimly.

The Cadillac sped westwards. It was dark and the lights of communities could be seen shining either side of the highway. Ahead, the glow from Dulles International began lighting the sky. The car swung into an approach road. They saw the flashing lights of police cars at roadblocks. The barriers were dragged aside to let the big car through. They passed through two more roadblocks, then drew up in front of Dulles International which was shining like an orbiting space station in the clear Virginia night. Half a dozen men, some in flack jackets, all armed, stood on the kerb. The director and Mike Izaguirre jumped out.

'We've got the plane, sir,' said an agent, 'but we've just established that there's only a crew of three on board, all Hispanic. We're holding them, but for the moment they won't talk.'

'All right,' the director said.

'The suspect is definitely in the area,' the agent said. 'A car drew up to the private aviation area which is separate to this building. There is some confusion as to the number of people in it: one report says that there was just a driver and a woman; another that there was a second woman in the rear seat.'

'Where's the car now?'

The men turned to look at Patrick who had joined them on the kerb. The director nodded to the agent.

'The driver sensed something was wrong,' the agent said. 'He continued on at speed for this building, and, our guess is, entered it with the one or two women, as the case may be.'

'Could they have left the airport complex?' the director asked.

'Impossible, sir,' the agent said, shaking his head. 'Everything has been sealed for over thirty minutes.'

'And inside?' the director snapped.

'The entire airport is closed, sir,' the agent responded. 'No air traffic can come in – flights have been diverted to Washington National. All outward flights have been delayed. All approach roads have been sealed and no one is being allowed to leave the vicinity.'

'Describe this building to me,' the director said.

'There are two levels, sir,' the agent answered. 'Departures at this level, and arrivals below. We have thoroughly searched this level and are certain they aren't here. They've got to be downstairs.'

The director took one step towards the building, then stopped as Patrick made to follow him. 'Mr Drake, you must stay here,' he said.

Slowly Patrick shook his head. 'No way,' he said.

The FBI chief and the Washington cop exchanged glances. Patrick saw Mike Izaguirre nod.

'All right, but put on this jacket,' the director ordered.

They walked briskly into the bright building, one huge side completed in sheeted glass. The building's height disguised its length, which was considerable, and diffused the noise of the several hundred people on its floor. Uniformed policemen stood, controlling access to the escalators which went to the lower level. Patrick could see FBI agents behind the check-in desks, scrutinising faces. They took a down escalator. At the director's entrance a further group of young, dark-suited men stepped forward.

'Sir, we've done an extensive check,' said one. 'The only area that's left is the baggage area at the end of this building.'

'OK, let's take it,' the director said.

They ran in lock step, ten men, past dozens of staring,

cordoned-off travellers, down the hall to a door to where another two agents stood, both armed with sub-machine-guns. A plain, white door with no handle faced them. Beside them, a baggage carousel with suitcases went round and round.

'They've got to be in here, sir,' said the senior agent.

'Give me a gun,' the director said.

He turned to an agent who was holding an Iver Johnson .30 carbine. 'Cover us,' he ordered.

Then without warning the door slowly opened, inwards. Half a dozen FBI men went into combat crouches, their weapons at arm's length, pointed. Patrick stared. From the blackness that was the door mouth something was slowly emerging, something white. There was a total silence in the hall. With the slowness of a face emerging from the depths of a pond, Georgie's deathly white face came towards them.

'Georgie!'

Patrick took two steps, then felt himself held.

'Nobody move!' said the director.

If Georgie's eyes were open, they were unfocused. Her face was slack. Patrick could see that she was not walking but being half carried, pushed forward, and at her throat, something long glinted. Then Patrick saw Marcellino. The contrast in the leather of his skin and Georgie's could not have been greater. Whilst her face swam against the blackness of the room behind them, Marcellino's face seemed part of it. He cradled her to his massive chest like a doll, the steel of the knife pressed upwards into her gullet.

'Everybody back off!' the director shouted.

Slowly, an oasis of space grew around the doorway. In the awful silence, Marcellino began to make his way with his captive towards the outer door. Patrick could hear the breath rattling through the Basque's nostrils like that of a bull in the final stages of a battle. Georgie was within five yards of Patrick. Suddenly, as if whatever drug she had been fed was wearing off, her eyes opened. Patrick shook off the hand next to him and leaped into their path.

'Marcellino!'

The huge man stopped and Georgie's chin went upwards as the knife was pressed more.

'*¡Quiétate de ahí!*' the Basque hissed. 'Get out of my way!'

'You want your diamonds?' Patrick cried. He reached to his pocket. 'The diamonds to save your Euskadi?'

Patrick saw Marcellino's eyes, mad, and Georgie's, terrified.

'Here then is the salvation of Euskadi!' Patrick cried and flung a package on to the ground.

It was as if a fountain of light had exploded, for all at once the floor they stood on was awash with sparkling, rolling gems. Georgie slipped as momentarily Marcellino's grasp loosened. A single rifle shot rang out.

Before Patrick's gaze, a hole, a third eye, appeared between Marcellino's eyebrows. He staggered backwards, his arms jerking up and down, his mouth opening and closing. He appeared to say something. Both his eyes, either side of the new hole, blazed for an instant like lighted phosphorous. Then their lights went out and he sank down on the carpet of twinkling stones.

He knelt beside her on the ground, his arms around her. Slowly the airport's noise resumed. The baggage carousels went round. He held her and stroked her, oblivious of the bedlam which had erupted around them.

'It's all over now,' he whispered over and over.

'Mr Drake.'

Patrick became aware of the director beside him.

'Mr Drake, I'm sorry to persist at this time, but we are under great pressure to re-open the airport. We feel that the woman known as La Esmeralda may still be here.'

Half a dozen men in suits stood around the director. They looked coldly at Patrick. 'I'd like you to help us find her,' the director said. 'She may adopt a disguise and try to leave by scheduled flight.'

'As a matter of interest,' asked Patrick, lightheaded, 'what has she done that you can detain her for?'

The director allowed the ghost of a smile to cross his features. 'Nothing,' he said, then patted the breast of his jacket. 'But by virtue of a very fortuitous extradition request from the Spanish police we can see to it that she goes nowhere in a hurry.'

Patrick kissed Georgie and whispered to her. Then he got to his feet and joined the squad of FBI agents as they made their way to the upper level. Patrick looked up to a central board which listed departure times. Red lights flashed beside flights for

Havana and Rio de Janeiro. At the check-in points along the hall, lines had begun to re-form, lines of people and suitcases.

'This way,' the agent said.

Patrick followed as the man approached a check-in desk, then showing his credentials, stepped around the desk, beckoning Patrick to follow.

'It's easier to see faces from this side,' the agent said.

They walked the full length of the hall, scrutinising the faces which looked blankly back at them. Patrick shook his head. 'She's not here,' he said.

'OK,' the agent said, 'come on!'

The FBI badge got them straight through two security checks and a passport control. Passengers were seated in a central area awaiting their call to the mobile lounges which in Dulles bring them to the planes.

'Take your time,' the agent said, 'look at every face.'

Patrick did as he was told. He shook his head.

'What gates are ready for South America?' the agent asked an official.

The man looked at a sheet of paper and gave the FBI man two numbers. The agent led the way, running. Patrick could see some of the other agents whom he had seen earlier, working through the passengers.

They came to a desk with a flashing light and a sign which read 'Rio de Janeiro'. The agent showed his identity; he and Patrick entered. After thirty seconds Patrick shook his head.

The next lounge flashed 'Havana'.

'This flight is about to close, sir,' an airline official said to the agent.

'OK, OK,' the agent said, 'this won't take long.'

The lounge had seats all around its perimeter and a double row, back to back, up the middle. Patrick saw a number of Spanish-looking men, some with shirts and ties, some with casual T-shirts, a group of bright-eyed schoolchildren, a holiday couple, a blonde woman with a child, two dark-haired girls in their early twenties – sisters most likely, an elderly, obviously American couple, the man wearing a fishing-hat. At the end of the central aisle Patrick saw black hair, a floral-patterned dress, its wearer looking out through the lounge portholes at the Virginia night. The agent nodded and reached to unclip his gun.

His heart racing, Patrick walked down the aisle, then turned around and looked. A pair of eyes met his. They were brown. Their owner no more than eighteen. She looked at Patrick curiously, then looked away. Patrick felt sick. He looked back up the lounge to the agent who was waiting apprehensively by the door.

'Sir, please, we must load.' The airline official had come into the lounge from his desk. 'We're already two hours behind schedule.' The agent nodded and turned. Patrick took a step after him, then stopped like a man made of rock. He stopped, staring downwards. It was the legs. He was level with the blonde woman with the child. She sat on one of the perimeter seats, the child on the seat beside her, her face turned in towards the child as she laughed and spoke to it. But on the backs of the legs turned towards Patrick there were scars. Patrick dragged his eyes upwards. Her figure was full, firm. He saw the mane of blonde hair, seemingly so natural. He could not move. The woman had stopped talking to the child. Slowly she turned her face.

'Sir, please!'

Patrick lurched up the aisle and joined the agent outside the lounge.

'No luck,' the agent was saying. 'Perhaps she'll turn up in Washington.'

There was a pneumatic sound and both men turned to see the Havana-bound lounge slip from view as it began its journey out to the waiting plane.

'Perhaps she will,' Patrick said.

They walked slowly out through the assembly area. Another agent ran up to them, his face inquiring. The agent shook his head. 'She's not here,' he said.

They made their way back through passport control and security, out to the busy hall. Other agents continued to scrutinise the faces of arriving passengers. Downstairs the director and Mike Izaguirre stood a little removed from Marcellino's body. Georgie was beside them. An FBI agent was taking photographs. Patrick put his arm around Georgie and she leaned her head against his shoulder.

The director nodded grimly. He said to Patrick, 'We found this on him. Mean anything to you?'

Patrick fingered the yellowing, clipped newspaper cuttings, and the copybook pages, written in the childlike hand.

Who says that we forget?

'Mean anything to you, Mr Drake?'

'Quite a lot,' answered Patrick slowly, 'quite a lot.'

There is no forgetting. It is market day in Guernica.

'We have some talking to do,' the director said. 'There are more than a few questions to be answered.'

Patrick nodded, the bones in his cheek working. 'I'll answer your questions,' he said. Then he smiled, looked down at Georgie's head and kissed it. 'But not here.'

The director frowned. 'If not here, where?' he asked.

'In Scotland,' Patrick said. He nodded pleasantly to the staring men, then up at the big board where a light was flashing a flight for London. 'I'm sure you know where to contact me,' he said, turning. 'But now we're going home.'

AFTERWORD

This has been based on a true story told to the author.

The different survivors continue to live their lives, some changed, some not by the events described.

Mike Izaguirre still works for the Washington Metropolitan Police Department.

Joe Vendetti left the police; he has not been seen for some years, although one report says that he lives as a recluse in San Francisco, sailing alone every day on the Bay.

In London, Abelson Dunwoody merged with a big US firm; Sammy Mitchell retired but still works as a consultant in Bournemouth.

In the Pyrenees, Mattin still drinks *izarra* and dreams about his freedom.

Above Aldudes, Castor and Mati are rearing their new son, now a strapping boy who will soon go to school in the valley; a photograph of Teodoro hangs in pride of place over the mantelpiece, but Euskadi and Basque freedom are never discussed in the Arocena household.

Caro and Paulina stayed in Isla and got married; she nurses at a hospital in Santander and he works in a factory in Bilbao.

In Barcelona there have been rumours of a new drugs ring in the city, run by a gay who previously operated in Madrid, but who left following the break-up of the cartel there.

The last report on Tomás was that he completed his law degree and went home to Cadiz to work for his father.

Shirley went back to the United States and underwent extensive treatment for drug addiction at the Betty Ford Center in Rancho Mirage, California. She is now happily married and lives with her husband, a doctor, in San Francisco.

Bernard is halfway through a five-year sentence for drugs trafficking in Mountjoy Jail, Dublin. His name, of course, is not Bernard . . .

Following the widespread investigation resulting from events in Washington, there was a temporary halt in the volume of Colombian cocaine entering the United States. The diamonds are still in Federal hands, pending the eventual closure of the case, but despite an examination of bank accounts in the United States attributable to Marcellino Adarraga and the questioning of diamond dealers in Antwerp, it is not yet clear if all the gems have been accounted for.

Patrick married Georgie and, when her father died, they moved to live permanently in Scotland. They appear to be comfortable. Patrick tried to write a book. Today he is still trying. Georgie worries about him: he runs in the mountains behind the cottage but seems to have no wish to leave Scotland again. She notices that he has become increasingly detached and withdrawn, and although she badly wants to have a child, he says he is not ready.

And in Washington DC, reports have been received from DEA offices in Peru: they talk of a new figure in the cocaine trade, a woman, who conducts business from a fortified jungle mansion, whose wealth is spoken of as great, and who is surrounded by a group of men whose origins are mainly Spanish Basque. No firm descriptions of her exist, although one report describes her as beautiful with hair of ink and eyes of changeling green.

P.C.
St-Etienne-de-Baigorry, 1988